CW01619960

The Last Terrorist

© Antoinette Moses 2021

The right of Antoinette Moses to be identified as the Author of this work has been asserted by Antoinette Moses in accordance with the Copyright, Designs and Patents Act 1988

All rights reserved

First published in Great Britain in 2021 by Black Crane Press

Black Crane
PRESS

blackcranepress.co.uk

No part of this book may be reproduced or transmitted in any form or by any means, electronic or mechanical, including photocopying or recording without the permission of the author.

This book is a work of fiction, and except in the case of historical or geographical fact, any resemblance to names, place and characters, living or dead, is purely coincidental.

Paperback ISBN 978-1-8382977-3-2
.ePub ISBN 978-1-8382977-4-9

Cover design and layout by spiffingcovers.com

For

The families and friends of those who were killed or injured by the 17 November Terrorist Group

November 17 was a real terrorist group that operated in Greece from 1975 to 2002. The members of the group and their actions have been described factually in this novel to the best of my ability. The story in this book, however, is fiction as is the creation of the last member of the group.

Except for the fictional village at Chiona, my favourite beach, the places in the novel do exist as do the streets, shops, hotels, cafés and restaurants

NOTHING IS FINISHED.
IT ALL CONTINUES.

Athens graffiti.

PROLOGUE

March 2018. Crete.

The fume machine came to life with a low hum, creating an electronic harmony with the whine and purr of the air conditioning and refrigeration units. Lefteris Zembatakis flexed his sweating fingers inside the nitrile gloves he was wearing over his latex ones. He'd been right to wear them, he couldn't risk his hands slipping or for the smallest drop to penetrate the latex. One false move and he was going to die.

'Breathe,' he told himself: 'breathe.'

He could still back out, couldn't he? He laughed even as he asked himself the question. Who was he kidding? There was no turning back, he was in too deep.

All he had to do was decant ten drops of dimethylmercury into a tiny bottle and place it into the silver cylinder they'd sent him and into the padded bag. Then deliver it and receive the money which would pay off his family's debts. Then it would be over. Just a few more minutes and a short drive to the sea road near the airport for the handover.

'Breathe,' he told himself again. 'Everything's going to be fine.'

An hour later, the sound of an EasyJet Airbus taking off from Heraklion airport drowned the splash as Lefteris's unconscious body was kicked off the jetty and into the sea.

CHAPTER 1

July 2018. Paris

The early morning sun gilded the rue Mazarine and sent rainbow patterns across the windows of its still-shadowed galleries and shops. In an hour, the street would be bustling with people and traffic, but for now it was empty apart from a solitary black and white cat that was making its way down the road towards the fishmongers in Maubert market, unaware this was a Sunday morning.

In an apartment two storeys above a small gallery, Patrice Girard rolled slowly and quietly out of bed so as not to wake his wife, Didi. Didi, despite being seventy-six, two years younger than he was, had almost certainly read and listened to music until two that morning, and would sleep another two or three hours. She was still an owl, but he'd become a lark. He liked it that way; he enjoyed his early mornings; time to read and write, and then enjoy the daily circular walk down through the Buci market to pick up bread for their shared breakfast.

He had a quick shower and went into their second bedroom which now served as his dressing room. Although it was clear that it would be another hot day, he dressed formally as usual in a pale blue, button-down shirt, a dark tie and a fawn linen suit. His famous silver and enamel cufflinks, however, revealed another side of him, being in the form of a hammer and sickle. He always wore them, much to the annoyance of his late mother. They'd been given to him over forty years ago by Didi, to show her shared passion for the Soviets. Not that she'd mellowed a great deal in old age; unlike him, she still favoured the far left. She and her friends still talked about putting the world to rights and how the young needed to be more active. Personally, he felt that these days what one needed was moderation.

That was what was worrying him. No, worry was too mild a word. He was frightened. He should never have responded the way he did, making it clear that he opposed another terrorist action. But he'd been right; this wasn't the time for extreme action, those days had passed, at least here in France and in Britain, too.

Patrice walked into his book-lined study and shut the door. What he was considering was a betrayal, the worst betrayal he had ever considered, the betrayal of one of his oldest friends. Yet did he have a choice?

He took a battered and much-read book off the shelf. When had Alex given this to him? It must have been in '68. And yes, here was the inscription. He read it with a wry smile: "To my comrade Patrice, in solidarity, Alexandros Yotopoulos, 1968." There was a single quotation. 'Terror is the people's justice. It is the weapon of the poor".

'Ah, Saint-Just,' Patrice muttered to himself. Such a brilliant man, one of the heroes of the French Revolution whose legal code was still the basis of the French judicial system. But now he was better known as the Angel of Death, the creator of the Terror. Of course, that had led to the guillotine for both him and Robespierre. A hero for the young, perhaps, Patrice thought, but not for those who had seen how terror caused suffering and rarely effected change.

The book itself, *Judicial Strategies*, which Alex had given him, had been written by a mutual acquaintance, though Patrice wondered sometimes whether Alexandros had had a closer relationship with its author, Jacques Vergès.

That made sense. Vergès proposed what he called rupture defence. Instead of defending his client – and how do you defend the Khmer Rouge or other murderers? – he told his clients to attack the court itself. 'You have to put on a show,' he'd told Patrice once over lunch. 'Justice is a game; you have to play it.'

And that's exactly what Alexandros had done when his terrorist group, 17 November, was finally brought to court. 'I reject the charges, of course. I am here because this is what the Americans and their collaborators in the government, who hate everything Greek, want.' Patrice had smiled, wryly, at the rhetoric when he read it. He hadn't gone to the trial, which was a circus with an inevitable dark ending. Yotopoulos, himself, received the harshest sentence: seventeen life sentences plus twenty-five years imprisonment, which for a man of fifty-nine, as he had been in 2003, was a true life sentence. The only way he would come out of prison would be to a hospital on his deathbed.

Patrice opened a drawer and took out a faded black and white photograph. It had been taken by one of the swarm of photojournalists who had hung around the Sorbonne, hoping for a prize-winning picture of demonstrating students. And workers, and others, too. Even Vergès had managed to get himself photographed with blood dripping down his face.

The meeting had been in that old Jussieu building and had been promoted as the coming together of the May 29 Movement. How they liked dates, these revolutionaries.

'Why May 29?' he'd asked Alexandros some years

later.

'Because it was on May 29 in 1968 that we were on the verge of revolution. A million people had marched in the streets. If our leaders had had the courage, we could have taken over the Élysée Palace that day and brought down the government. But they held back. And in Greece they allowed the fascists to take control. The people need to be shown we have no fear. We will do anything to bring about the revolution.'

Patrice walked over to the window and looked out. Where had that conversation taken place? Down the road at the Café Buci, he thought. Where he still went for his morning café crème. Revolutions begin in our cafés. Even unsuccessful ones.

His eye was caught by a blue Provençale vase in the window of the gallery opposite, Didi would like that; it was her birthday soon. There was something about it that might remind her of some of the jars she'd excavated when she was still working as an archaeologist. Although would that be a sad memory? So hard to know. Didi was certainly happier in Provence in the old house he'd bought for his mother where they now lived each summer. It had been such a pleasure to be able to buy his mother a comfortable home and see her happy in the last years of her life after his father's death. She quickly made friends in the neighbourhood and enjoyed getting the bus into Nice to go shopping or walk along by the sea.

'Such a wonderful son,' she said to him one evening when he'd taken her to have drinks on the terrace of the Grand Hotel at Cap-Ferrat. 'How he spoils his old mother!' Didi had smiled and nodded, but neither of them had let his mother know that the money for both the drinks and her house had largely come from the Kremlin. A solid conservative, she would not have enjoyed living there if she'd known that.

Patrice opened the window and looked down into the quiet street. It was going to be hot this year, it was hot already, but they had better air conditioning in Colomars, perhaps they should go there earlier. Next week perhaps; heat was hard to deal with as you got older. Yes, he'd suggest that to Didi over breakfast, unless she was planning a trip to Greece to see her old friend there. There was nothing to keep him in Paris, and if he needed to meet Henry, he could do so just as easily in Nice. If he decided to meet Henry. It all depended on his meeting later today. It might be safer to leave Paris now.

He turned back to the photograph. There were almost forty young Greeks in the hall that day, but many left the Movement when they realised just how radical Alexandros was. But as for the 'grandfathers of 17N', as the Greek papers called those who first founded the terrorist group, there had been three of them. Only two were still alive, and one of those was in prison. But the group hadn't only been Greek; there had been others from Italy and Germany. They'd also gone home and set up their own revolutionary cells: the Red Brigade, the Baader-Meinhof. All of them dead now except Horst Mahler, who'd turned away from left wing politics and reverted to the fascism his father had espoused.

He fingered his cufflink. How often it came down to fathers. His own, a fascist, had been a brutal man who terrorised his own family. He expected Dimitris Yotopoulos had been the same.

Nobody had a good word to say for Alexandros's father, the man who'd worked briefly for Trotsky, who'd described him as, what was it? Yes, an autocratic and egocentric individual. Patrice had always thought that you could say the same about Alexandros. But he, unlike his father, was rigidly true to his beliefs and faithful to his friends. Dimitris had betrayed everyone. Twice sometimes. Not surprising his son had never forgiven him, not surprising that his son had become a revolutionary. Betrayal was something he could never forgive.

Which was why he and Alexandros had remained friends, despite their political differences. And terrorism hadn't prevented his passion for good wine, and Brigitte Bardot. He'd never betrayed Alexandros, even after they'd argued about what 17 November was doing, and how innocent people were being injured and killed including the families of those the terrorists had targeted because of their association with the military or the CIA. They'd argued and disagreed. But never betrayal. Now?

It was the mention of using extreme measures that so disturbed him. What did it mean? Who might be killed? He'd been right to act, but he shouldn't have mentioned Henry's name. It had slipped out during the conversation and after too much brandy. Had he betrayed the old historian, too? But he'd been right to tell Henry; Henry could pass on the information and prevent the bloodshed. Perhaps he should have told Henry their name. He'd do it today, he had to act.

Patrice took out a lighter from the drawer, and lit a corner of the photograph, letting the ashes fall into an old glass ashtray on his desk. When was the last time he'd had a cigarette since that warning from his doctor? He could certainly use one today. Perhaps one? Though Didi would know; she always did.

If anything happened to him, he didn't want anything that associated him with 17 November to be found in case it implicated Didi. For once in his life, he was glad they had never had children. But then Didi had always been afraid for him and worried that if she had children they could be targeted. He'd agreed, but now he regretted it; it would be good to have grandchildren in their lives.

He finished burning the photograph and brushed

away the ash that had fallen on his desk with his handkerchief. There were no papers or diary entries that mentioned Alexandros, only the book which he doubted anyone would find. And the burned photograph.

He walked over to the bookcase and took out another well-thumbed paperback. *Adieux*, Simone de Beauvoir's farewell to Sartre. Perhaps someone one day would take this out and find it. His old friend Henry Cox, perhaps. He would understand the reference. Patrice opened the book and wrote down the name of the photographer and the date it was taken: 'May 29, all of us together,' he wrote. Then he replaced the book on the shelf.

He knew he was preparing for his own death. He hoped he could postpone it a few years more. In the meantime, he'd enjoy a coffee. And perhaps a cigarette.

Patrice left the apartment and began to walk southwards towards the Boulevard Saint-Germain when he heard a car race down the road and stop beside him. He turned his head and saw a small grey Citroen with a driver. It wasn't a car he knew, but he certainly knew the driver.

He stepped forward, cautiously and stopped as he saw the small gun aimed directly at his head. Not the first time he'd had a gun pulled on him, but this wasn't a threat. He wanted to run, but his feet wouldn't move.

'No,' he pleaded. 'Not yet.'

The volleys echoed from shop to shop across the road and a small flock of pigeons, fighting over some dropped sushi, rose into the air, flapping their wings

'Didi!' Patrice called out as he fell. 'Forgive me!'

Neighbours rushed to their windows, woken by the sound of gunfire, and a small white delivery van raced down towards the market, almost hitting the bollards as it slammed on its brakes to avoid hitting the slumped body of the lawyer. The driver got out and telephoned the police, but by the time they arrived the small grey Citroen had already disappeared into the morning traffic, along the Quais and out of the city.

CHAPTER 2

July 2018 Crete

DI Pam Gregory sat back in the comfortable director's chair and smiled at the two men sitting at the table beside her. 'This was the best supper ever,' she said. 'Thank you so much, Henry, you've been so kind.' In the last few days, she had grown increasingly fond of the elderly historian. Both of you,' she added, smiling at Mike Petersen, a former DI with London's Metropolitan Police Force, who also now lived in the small Cretan village of Chiona,

Her leg was supported on another chair, a reminder of how the killer of the archaeologist, Stephanie Michaels, had shot her ten days ago, before ending his own life. Beside her was a large plate with bite-sized pieces of honey pastries which she was making herself eat slowly. She shifted slightly, and a shaft of pain raced down her leg to her ankle. She'd been incredibly lucky; the bullet had passed straight through her, avoiding both bone and muscle, but she knew these things didn't heal overnight. The shooting was something she didn't want to think about, along with the passionate evening she'd spent the same night with a certain Greek police officer, who was now safely in Athens. She didn't think Henry knew about Stavros. Possibly only Mike had guessed;

she'd rung him first when she realised who Stephanie's killer was. She still blamed herself for not being in Chiona when Jen, Stephanie's daughter, was abducted, for not realising sooner who had killed Stephanie.

'You and Mike spoil me,' she told them. It was true, she thought. She'd never been in a situation with friends looking after her like this, though her colleagues back in Cambridge had often brought treats from nearby cafes. But so had she; they took it in turns. Here, recovering in Stephanie's house, now recently bequeathed to Mike, she had to rely on other people, and she knew that had changed her.

She'd talked about her marriage for one thing, which she had never done before, ashamed of the abuse. And tonight Henry had prepared a dinner for her to celebrate the ten years since her divorce.

'I've been thinking about what I should do next,' she told them.

'Next is an interesting word,' Henry replied. 'It was originally about kinship, whom you were near to. Proximity, like the Italian, *prossimo* or the French *prochain*. Though the French also have *suivant*, meaning following. Which makes me think of life like a long cord with knots which you follow, knot after knot.'

'Is this about philosophy or what you think I ought to be doing?' Pam asked. Henry Cox lived in a world of his own, a world crammed with words, and quite often Pam found herself understanding only half of them. Though it didn't irritate her now she'd got to know him. It had nothing to do with wanting to show off, but the result of a long, rather lonely, life with mostly books for company. Funny how she'd thought he was a pompous liar when she first met him; she'd got that totally wrong, it was just his way of talking. And the stories had all been true.

She'd learned so much about Greece. She'd

discovered there had been a civil war after the end of World War 2, there had been a right-wing Junta in the sixties, and then a massive student demonstration against the Junta in 1973, when many students had been killed and injured. One of them, Andreas, who'd been shot, had ended up seeking refuge in the flat of Stephanie Michaels, but had been arrested later and killed. It was this that had led inadvertently to Stephanie's own death.

'One thing that puzzled me, when I read Stephanie's notebooks,' she'd told Henry the previous day, 'was how Andreas behaved towards her when she was protecting him. He didn't respect her at all.'

'You're seeing it from your own point of view, Pam, and Stephanie's. Not from that of Andreas. She just wanted to think of him as some kind of hero from a movie, but never bothered at the time, or later, to think about who he was and his motives for being at the Polytechnic that night. He was one of the organisers, he wasn't just a student who happened to be there. And if you read any of their communiqués, which aren't so removed from those of the 17 November Terrorist group I'm writing about, you'll see that some of them were fanatically communist. They wanted to tear down every part of the old order and destroy capitalism. When they waved Mao's little red book – oh, you won't remember this – that wasn't a symbol, that was their goal. To create that form of communist regime here in Greece. That's what Stephanie never saw. She wasn't interested in ideas or politics, she used to say she was apolitical. But in Greece you don't have that luxury.'

'Yes,' replied Pam. 'I'm beginning to see that. How the legacy of the civil war here lingered on...'

'It still does...'

'Yes. And how families could be penalised for decades, and it was all down in those dreadful folders. Like the one on Manolis's family which showed that

Stephanie didn't betray Andreas. If only he'd read his folder before he killed her.'

'Indeed. And to go back to Stephanie and Andreas, Andreas was almost certainly a committed communist; for him Stephanie was middle-class and enjoying fake poverty in Athens with a nice home in England to go back to if she needed it. If she disliked him, and she did, it was certainly mutual.'

'But she'd saved his life.'

Henry shook his head. 'This must have been hard for him to accept, when so many Athens doors were closed that night. But it wouldn't have changed his beliefs. She was on the wrong side of the barricades, whatever she might have thought. But with Steph, it was always about her.'

Pam nodded in agreement. She'd learned a lot about the archaeologist during her investigation. And since, she'd gained two new friends.

'Solipsistic to the end,' Henry added.

'Solip...?'

'It's an extreme form of egotism. Means looking at your world only from your own point of view as if you're the only one who exists. It's one of my own flaws, too. I do tend to live inside a very small world of my own. A rather frightening one at the moment. I'm so sorry,' Henry smiled at them and nibbled the edge of a sweet pastry. 'I shouldn't be burdening you both with this.'

'No, please,' replied Mike. 'If there's anything we can do.'

Henry shook his head. 'Probably my imagination, but I do find myself rather alarmed. I always thought that I'd welcome death, but feeling it nudging on the horizon, I realise that I don't want to die right now. I want to finish this book and write some stories after that. Next as it were. Following.' He gave a small self-conscious laugh.

'Are you ill?' Pam asked him, concerned.

'No. Never been healthier. Had a check-up just last month, and it seems I have the heart of a forty-year-old. That's what walking and swimming do for one. Recommend it.'

'Ah, swimming. You've no idea how frustrating it is to be so close to a perfect sea and not able to swim. Have to wait for the dressing to come off. But if not your health?'

'Just a niggle. Something I've uncovered; don't know why I mentioned it. Writing about terrorists, I suppose. It does make you look over your shoulder. It's something a friend told me in Paris, which as you know was where I went after Cambridge and before coming back here for Stephanie's funeral. Anyway, I should find out more very soon.'

'I was very suspicious of you at the time,' Pam laughed. 'Put you high on my suspect list.' She paused. This wasn't where she expected the evening's conversation to be going. 'Are you saying that you think you're in danger from a terrorist?'

'I'm sure I'm not,' he replied, though saying it didn't remove the fear. Should he burden these young police officers? No, sharing his concerns would be selfish. 'Nothing for you to worry about,' he told them. 'Now, let's converse about you, Pam. Are you going back to Cambridge?'

'It's my home, my work. Where else would I go?' replied Pam who had been asking herself this question for the past few days, knowing there was a good chance her unit, the East Anglian Special Operations Unit, or EASOU as it was better known, which she'd headed now for just over a year, was likely to be cut. 'And I have a new place to stay,' she added. 'Did you know Jen has asked me to live in her house while she stays in London with her father?'

'I didn't. What a splendid idea.'

'Of course, you'll always be welcome,' Pam added. 'It does have two bedrooms, doesn't it? I've never been upstairs.'

She knew that Stephanie often had Henry to stay. During the investigation into Stephanie's death, she'd discovered that Henry had spent the night there, unknown to Jen.

'By the way,' she added, remembering a detail that had bothered her, 'how did you get one of the new keys when you let yourself in? Jen changed the locks after her cat was killed.'

'She sent her mother a spare key and Stephanie gave it to me to copy.

'I hope she didn't give out too many; Stephanie seemed to have given copies of the previous key to everyone and their dog.'

Henry smiled. 'Just me, I think. If you're going to stay there, I should get a copy made for you, too.'

'Thank you. That would save me having to ask Jen.'

'Consider it done. And, to answer your other question, it does, indeed, have two bedrooms. Stephanie always made it my other little home when I was doing research at the Cambridge University Library. And it enabled me to spend time with Jen. I am still so grateful to you for saving my darling goddaughter,' his voice trembled slightly. 'She means so much to me. She could have been killed.'

'If Pam hadn't acted, she would have been,' said Mike, remembering that moment when he entered the barn and found Manolis holding Stephanie's daughter at gunpoint.

'Jen is lovely,' Pam agreed. She recalled the conversation they'd had after Stephanie's funeral when Jen told her that she actually didn't want to go back to her Cambridge home now.

'It's Caroline, my stepmother,' she told Pam. 'We're worried about her. Dad's been talking to her since we got here, but she's not at all well. And she also wants to be closer to her grandchildren. So I've said I'll stay with them for a few months while they find a house near Bristol, and then help with their move. It will give me something to do that's absolutely nothing to do with Mum or Crete. I just want to put all this behind me.'

'That's sensible,' said Pam. 'But do get help if you need it.'

'You, too,' said Jen. 'You're the one who got shot.'

'I have to see some welfare person anyway,' said Pam. 'They won't let me back on duty until I've had half a dozen sessions with someone from the Department. Actually, I think I've rather upset HR because I haven't filled in the serious incident form yet. Apparently, they're going to discuss my case and call me again this afternoon. They offered to come round, but I told them I was in Greece, which completely floored them. They couldn't work out how I could be on duty and in a different country, so I told them to talk with my boss before they bothered me again. Bloody forms! I'm grappling with something called a FIN27 form and trying to work out how to put down the accommodation I got from Mr Leotakis plus the free ride in his private jet getting to Crete. The kind of questions that ask why did he make that offer, and what were the background circumstances. And would it have hurt his feelings if I'd refused. Decided to put down that it came via the Prime Minister and the Home Office and let them deal with that.'

'Sounds like a university,' groaned Jen. 'It's all about box ticking these days. Not sure half the time why I stick it. Except I love the subject and the students. The paperwork gets worse every year.' She smiled at Pam. 'Anyhow, it's about my staying at my Dad's that I wanted to talk to you,' she continued. 'I need someone to keep an eye on my house in Cambridge. To be honest I don't want to be there for the moment, too many memories. Mum and Skimble,' she added, naming her tabby who'd also been stabbed by Manolis simply because he was afraid of cats. 'I hope you don't mind my asking you,' she continued, 'but you did say you lived in a tiny flat...'

'A kennel, my colleagues call it,' Pam laughed.

'Well. Would you be willing to live in my house for the next six months or so? No rent or anything, just the bills and they aren't huge. Dad designed it to be very economical.'

Pam thought of the exquisite blue and white house with its massive windows leading on to a safe and private courtyard.

'Are you sure?' she asked. 'You could get a huge rent for it.'

'Yup. I don't want to be bothered with that. I just want to know it's safe, and there's someone who will water the plants if they look limp.'

'I can do that,' Pam, replied. 'It's probably as far as my gardening skills go.'

Everyone seemed to be offering her homes; it was all a bit much to take in. Her life seemed to be changing so quickly and in a way she didn't yet understand.

CHAPTER 3

I'm sitting having dinner on a Greek island with a historian and a half Cretan half Barbadian former cop, with an MA in criminology, and yet I'm perfectly comfortable. How is that possible? Pam asked herself. She ate another piece of honey cake and tried not to think about the calories.

'Before you arrived this evening, Henry was telling me about Greece after the Junta.' Mike was saying. 'A strange period the Greeks call the *metapolitefsi*, which just means regime or political change.'

Another word I'll never be able to pronounce or remember, Pam thought. 'Is that what your book's about?' she asked Henry. He sat back and nodded.

'In a way. When there's a major shift of power, people have hope. In 1974, after years of a right-wing Junta under the Colonels, those who'd campaigned and fought for change had so many hopes and expectations. Understandable. People had died standing up to the Colonels, people had been tortured. Like dear Popi.'

Pam thought briefly about Stephanie's friend, Popi. She must be blaming herself, she thought, just as both she and Mike were.

'Is this a competition to see which of you can blame yourself most?' Henry had asked them at supper in the fish restaurant the previous evening. 'You're beating yourself up, Pam, when you couldn't have been back in time. Mike, you can't forgive yourself for trusting Manolis and not driving Jen back to the villa, and, above all, dear Popi blames herself for bringing Manolis to stay with Leotakis.'

'Though I have to say Popi was more of a pragmatist than many others,' Henry was replying now, back in his own world. 'That's when I met her, attending the trials, first the trials of the former Junta leaders, then those who'd implemented their worst acts, the secret police, the torturers.

'Some were jailed, but while the Colonels did receive death sentences, these were commuted to life imprisonment by Karamanlis. That was what those on the far left would never forgive. You have no idea what it was like then,' he added. 'Karamanlis had to walk a tightrope in those early days. It wasn't a smooth transition. There were bomb attacks in the cinemas, people feared the army would stage a right-wing coup; there were endless demonstrations. Both left and right were fighting their corner.'

'That's so interesting,' said Mike. 'When Aunt Sofia talks about the period, it's as if the Colonels' regime ended in 1974, and then as if by magic, everything was all right again.'

'Except it wasn't,' said Henry. 'History has a habit of smoothing uncomfortable peripheries. There were massive changes, that's true. The Communist party was legalised, despite the Yanks' protests, but for some they weren't extreme enough; there was a lot of jostling for the soul of the far left.'

He broke off. 'I imagine this is all new to you,' he said to Pam.

'Yes, totally,' she agreed. 'I'm beginning to feel that studying history is a bit like being a detective,' she said. 'Don't you think so, Mike?'

'I'd never thought of that before,' he replied, 'I don't think I was as good a detective as you are, but you're right.'

'Sounds like the perfect subject for an academic paper,' murmured Henry.

'There speaks the professor,' said Mike.

'Who never was,' replied Henry.

'But could have been,' said Pam.

Henry nodded. He had been offered a professorship after his last book but had decided that he preferred the freedom of his life in Crete. He always had, ever since Laurent, a young French archaeologist had brought him here. Henry had been thirty years old then, feeling alive for the first time. He had a job to do, the possibility of an important role to play in the future, and the company of the man he loved. The days were hard. In court all day listening to the trials and making notes and trying to improve his Greek half the night. But the remainder of the nights belonged to Laurent.

'This is important work, Henry,' Laurent used to tell him and Monty Woodhouse, the man who had offered him the job had said the same when he first approached him.

'The Greeks need allies at the moment. Moreover, there is a significant danger that our friends across the Pond might support the military. We don't want that. As you know, the Americans supported the Junta and we went along with that, but this new regime offers the potential of a lasting European peace which would serve us much better. We need ears on the ground.'

It seemed so much more important than staying on in Cambridge to finish his PhD, which he'd been working on intermittently for several years. Who needed another thesis on the lost chances of peace in the 1930s? His entire school career had echoed to the praise of the heroes of the War. He'd wanted to be like them, but there had been no war for his own generation, no place for a new hero.

But behind the scenes? Working for the Secret Service like a character in those novels by Le Carré, who Monty told him had been one of their own? This was the role he'd been born to play. And there he was, making the notes that Monty could use for his updated history.

'Can't be there myself all the time,' he'd told Henry. 'Have an election to fight and constituents to keep happy. You observe and let me know what's going on.'

And so he had. And he'd been here in Crete ever since, for over forty years.

'I don't think I would have been a good lecturer…' he began but stopped as his phone rang. He glanced down at the number. 'I need to take this,' he said.

'Didi?' he said to the caller. 'Patrice...?' and continued in French, asking a string of questions which Pam couldn't understand.

There were words she could recognise from her school studies. 'Assassiné' followed shortly by 'où' and 'quand'. She tried to piece together the words: 'killed', leading to 'where' and 'when', two of the key questions always asked at the beginning of an investigation. Pam felt cold. They had been talking; it had been words, history, ideas. Now somebody was dead.

Henry's hand shook as he put down the phone and picked up his small brandy glass.

'Do you want to tell us?' Mike said, 'or would you prefer us to leave you in peace?'

'Don't go,' said Henry. 'Please, don't go. I think I need you to help me.'

'Anything we can do…' replied Pam instantly and then regretted the words almost as quickly. As a British police officer on sick leave, the one thing she couldn't do was begin an investigation of her own. If there had been a murder in France, it was up to their forces to solve it.

'I don't know how much French you both have...' he began.

'Fairly fluent' and 'pretty much non-existent,' said Mike and Pam simultaneously.

'I'll explain then,' said Henry.

'That was Didi. Deirdre. She's the wife of Patrice Girard, a very old friend of mine, the friend I was talking about. Patrice was killed today.' He found himself repeating the words she had used. 'He was shot. The police say it was a very professional job. They asked her who would want to assassinate him.'

'Did she have any answers?' asked Pam.

'Too many,' replied Henry. 'Patrice had been a lawyer before he retired and worked for many people who some felt did not deserve representation.'

'Such as?' asked Mike.

'Agents for countries which used to be controlled by the Kremlin. The far right hate him.' Henry paused and wiped his glasses with a large white handkerchief. 'But that's not the right question.'

'No,' said Pam thoughtfully. 'That wouldn't be my first question.'

'Which would be?' asked Mike. He'd worked only briefly with Pam at the end of an investigation, he'd never seen her at the start of one.

'Why now?' said Pam. 'That's the question I'd ask. You have a man who is retired and ... old?'

'Seventy-eight,' Henry supplied.

'So, what is it that's triggered his killing? It's what I kept asking about Stephanie. People kill for a reason, not because they hated someone in the past.'

'Yes, that is the right question,' agreed Henry. He poured himself some more brandy. 'I'm very afraid it's because of what I asked him to do. I think I might have been the trigger.'

'Why? What did you ask him?'

'I asked him to tell me the name of the missing original member of the 17 November terrorist group. He knew, he's always known, but this time he finally agreed to tell me.'

'17 November?' asked Pam.

'The Marxist terrorist group, Revolutionary Organisation 17 November, or 17N as they're often called.'

'Why didn't he tell you previously?'

'He was faithful to the cause. Old bonds. A very old friendship. But he told me this person was planning a major attack somewhere, one that might endanger many innocent people. He told me... when was it? It was the day before I came back for Stephanie's funeral, on the Sunday, so Saturday 16th. He was deeply worried. I'd never seen him like that.'

Three days after I interviewed Henry in Stephanie's garden, thought Pam. When I still thought he might be a suspect in *her* murder.

'He said this time was different. He thought the killing had to stop. He thought he would give me their name but needed to think about it.'

'You've no idea who the person is? The terrorist?'

'I've many ideas, Pam, but no evidence, and you know how difficult that makes things. It goes back to the sixties when they were all young idealists together setting up their organisation.'

'Organisation?'

'I'm assuming knowledge you don't have. This is a group which formed during the seventies, the period I was telling you about. It was founded by a man called Alexandros Yotopoulos, who is now in prison in Piraeus for the rest of his life.'

Henry took his phone out of his pocket and clicked on the picture app.

'This is Yotopoulos.'

Pam looked at the photograph. The man was looking across a room at someone with a wry smile on his face. He had white hair, bushy at the back, but thinning on top, and he wore a grey button-down shirt and green tweed jacket. His eyes were clear and a greyish blue. Pam could imagine him and Henry being friends.

'He looks like an academic. I can imagine him wandering around Cambridge on his way to a seminar.'

'He was an academic. He studied economics in Paris in the sixties and later taught mathematics in Athens under the name of Michael Economou. He founded the 17 November Terrorist Group.'

Henry poured himself another brandy and sat down. He'd come to know so much about Yotopoulos over the past few years and it felt odd, that they'd never actually met or even corresponded.

'I've been thinking about this for so long and was sure that in a few days I'd know the answer, and now I may never know.'

'Know what?'

'Who was Yotopoulos' original accomplice, the one who may have shot their first victim and then given the first of their endless communiqués to Sartre.'

Pam looked blank; they'd wandered into the fields of her ignorance again. But this time Henry didn't explain, he was too upset.

'If you go to Paris and examine Patrice's papers, won't that make you a target?' Mike asked Henry.

Pam bit her lip. If Patrice had talked to the accomplice, which seemed likely if his death was the result of that, then Henry could already be a target.

'There are no papers to examine. The police emptied his study and took his computer and all his files.'

'Sounds as though they are taking this very seriously,' said Pam.

'They think it may be a political assassination, and

of course that means the Elysée Palace are interested. The police will have military intelligence looking over their shoulder.'

'They'll hate that,' said Pam. 'I had the Prime Minister wanting to be involved in Stephanie's investigation.'

'Did you?' asked Henry, interested. 'Why?'

'Because Mr Leotakis was a friend of hers.'

'Of course.'

'It's dangerous, isn't it?' she said, thinking how Leotakis could make things happen at the click of his fingers.

'What is?' asked Mike.

'If I picked up the phone now and asked Nikos to help me as a favour, I'd bet you he'd have access to the French intelligence services and you'd be able to get what you want.'

'But you won't...' said Henry, horrified by the suggestion.

'Absolutely not. The only thing I've allowed myself to receive from Nikos is the flight he's offered for my friends Zofia and Grace to come here and stay. And I only accepted that because it was the day after I'd been shot, and I was full of morphine. It's so seductive all that money. But somehow, I feel that at the end of the day there would be a bill. It could be something small: just asking me to look something up on the police files. It could be something larger. With Stephanie's investigation, I didn't have a choice, and anyhow he was doing it because he loved her, not for me. I don't want favours.'

'That's very wise,' said Henry.

'Nikos isn't like most billionaires, though, is he?' said Mike

'I don't know, I've never met one before. I don't think I've even met a millionaire. Oh yes, there was a racehorse owner whose son got into trouble. But I merely interviewed him, I couldn't say I got to know him.'

'No. Can't say I've met any others either,' said Henry. 'I've never mixed in those circles. Archaeologists, fishermen, writers, academics… not much money there.'

'It was strange,' said Pam thinking back. 'Everything changed when Leotakis started to help in the case. Suddenly anything was possible. You need to be somewhere, there's a private jet and a hotel waiting for you at the other end. Or a helicopter. Most of us just scratch away at life trying to get somewhere or do something. When things are that easy, it makes everything happen faster. In this case, that saved Jen's life, but sometimes you don't want to rush things.'

'You can destroy worlds with money,' said Henry cheerfully, biting into a pastry and spraying flakes of pastry around him. 'Look what Leotakis did with this village and, before you tell me that the new houses and the new village are lovely, I know that. But I had a home I'd lived in for almost fifty years and I didn't want to be thrown out. But thanks to Leotakis, our village was demolished to make way for the dig, and this new village put up instead. The finds, of course, are wonderful, and I know that finding the palace has enabled them to understand so much more about Minoan life. But going back to Leotakis, that kind of power frightens me, when it meets an obstacle, it simply blasts through it.'

'Did I tell you both I met a journalist in London who's writing a book about Nikos?' Pam told them. 'He works for *The Guardian*. Told me about Nikos's days as a pirate in the Caribbean which were extraordinary.'

'I've heard rumours about gun running and all that, yes. Central America in the Fifties,' he replied. 'A lawless time, rather like Russia in the Nineties – vast amounts of money stolen, and fortunes made and lost. Happily, not my field.'

'You don't think Leotakis was involved with 17 November?' asked Mike.

'Not directly, no.'

'At one time he was being paid by Moscow,' said Pam. 'I got that from his biographer. Hard to believe when you see him in his country house in Dorset or his estate here.'

'The Russians enjoy grand houses, too,' replied Henry. 'What people say does not, necessarily, correlate with their actions.'

'So how can you get access to Patrice's papers?' asked Mike.

'I don't know. I have to go to see Didi first to offer my condolences, but also to see whether Patrice left anything behind. First, I think I'll go to London. I've already sent a very rough outline of my concerns to someone there.'

'In Vauxhall?' suggested Pam. She knew that Henry had worked for MI6, because an agent had told her to keep away from him in her previous investigation. She imagined Mike had guessed the same.

'And you say this because?' asked Henry.

'Because a very rude man called Christopher, something rang me up.'

'Christopher Grey. Did you meet him?'

'No. He just threatened my career if I investigated you.'

'Did he? How very odd. And I've been waiting to hear from him.'

There was something off here, thought Henry, but this wasn't the moment to voice it. He sighed. He was going to miss Patrice. Yet another friend's death.

Pam was about to get up and hug him, but as she began to move her leg, there was a lightning bolt of pain, and she gave a small cry. Both men turned to her anxiously.

'Nothing serious,' said Pam. 'Just the blood flow. But I do think I'd better go to bed. Thank you for my supper,' she added. 'And I'm so sorry about your friend.'

'I'll see you home,' said Mike.

'You don't have to,' Pam replied. 'It's almost next door. I'll be quite safe. I've got my stick.'

'I'm not taking no for an answer,' said Mike. 'You could still slip on the cobbles.' He turned to Henry. 'If you want to talk, I'll come back.'

'Yes. I rather think I do want to talk this evening,' said Henry. 'That would be kind.'

'And I need my sleep. Zofia and Grace arrive tomorrow afternoon and I don't want them telling me how tired I look.'

'Compared with how you looked when I first saw you online, you look positively radiant,' said Mike.

'It's why you have to stay here,' smiled Henry. 'It's good for you.'

Pam smiled back at him and thanked him once again for the supper. He was right, she did love it here in Crete. So, what was she going to do about her job? And if she did leave the police force, what else could she do?

CHAPTER 4

'A nation regenerates itself only upon heaps of corpses.'
Mirabeau

CHAPTER 5

Henry woke up at five and forced himself out of bed to get some water. He swallowed three aspirins to stop the hammering in his head, then fell back into his bed.

'No fool like an old fool,' he chided himself, as he pounded his pillow to make it more comfortable. He wondered who it was who first wrote the aphorism down, he should look it up. It had been stupid; he was going to need a clear head over the next few days. An hour later, his headache had faded to a vague pain behind his eyes, but he knew he wouldn't sleep again. A swim would help. He put on the trunks lying on the chair, picked up a towel from the line, and walked slowly down to the beach.

It was one of those perfect mornings, still early, the sky a blend of rose and lemon, but blink, and it would turn blue, and then a deeper blue every minute. The sea was calm and glacier-clear, yet warm. He took a deep breath and swam powerfully out towards the rising sun that was already changing the colour of the water and the land behind him.

It had been an emotional evening, triggered by the death of Patrice. He and Mike had talked first about their mutual friend, Popi, and how they were worried about her.

'She's not speaking to anyone at the moment and

has stopped all her therapy work,' Henry told Mike.

'Popi saved my life when I first came out here,' Mike replied. 'Along with Stephanie.'

'Popi saved Stephanie's life after Laurent died,' Henry added. 'She had a miscarriage after he drowned.'

And he's back there again as he has been so often in recent days since Stephanie died.

'I never really knew what happened,' said Mike.

Henry poured himself another glass of brandy. 'I've written about it a few times. I think I hoped that if I wrote it enough times, I'd write it out of me. That hasn't happened,' he added wryly. 'Laurent was this beautiful young archaeologist.' Henry stood up and went back inside, returning with a photograph.

Mike studied it.

Thick dark hair, crinkled you might describe it, like his smile. He looked to be in his twenties, in a faded blue T-shirt and a battered sun hat and was looking up at the photographer as if any moment he was going to start laughing. He looked like someone you would want to spend time with to have as a friend. Or a lover.

'I'm not gay and I fancy him,' he said, smiling.

'It wasn't just how beautiful he was,' said Henry sadly. 'He was so kind, brilliant too. His area of expertise was in Minoan pottery tools, in particular how they made the very large urns and bowls. He taught me about that, invited me down here – I was living in Athens back then – and we rented a little apartment in Sitia.'

Henry sighed. 'He taught me about pottery, and I taught him about Greek politics. This was in 1975, you have to remember, only a year since the fall of the Junta. I was helping old Monty Woodhouse revise his history of modern Greece. It was a volatile time. Karamanlis had only been back one year...'

He broke off and topped up his glass. Mike, as usual, was sipping water.

'You know nobody these days gives proper credit to Karamanlis.'

'I hardly know who he was. He was Prime Minister, wasn't he? But then, I don't even know the Prime Minister in England at that time. It was before I was born.'

'Wilson, followed by Callaghan in 1976.'

'There you go, then'

Henry nodded though he was not really sure what the expression meant. There you go where?

'You should read Monty's book. I've probably got a spare copy somewhere here.' He gestured vaguely indoors towards the massive bookcase that ran the entire length of the house. It had been Mike who'd designed it and shown him how he could build his new house around this feature. Most of it was filled with books and the rest with files of Henry's research. A lifetime of work on show, thought Mike. And what did he have to show for half a life? Nothing at all.

'Until Karamanlis came back from exile in France, Greece had swung left and right under a particular personality at the helm of government, rather than a party. It was Karamanlis, with a lot of help from the French President, Giscard d'Estaing, that pushed Greece into the European Union, even though it didn't really qualify for membership. And that saved the country from further divisive civil war.'

Henry leaned back in his chair remembering the days after the fall of the Junta.

'Laurent and I were actually here in Chiona the day Karamanlis came back. I'll never forget it. We were drinking wine on the veranda, just as we are now. The house belonged to a French couple, friends of Laurent: Patrice and Didi. She was an archaeologist; he was a lawyer. Nice people; still good friends. And then suddenly there was this old woman, the mother of Vassilis, the fisherman, though I didn't know her back then, rowing across the bay and screaming: "Karamanlis is back!" And he was. And just like that, everyone came out of their houses with their Easter candles lit and started to walk up the slope to the chapel to give thanks. Though, of course, the Church had helped keep the Junta in power, as became very clear with the trials that followed. But that didn't diminish the power of that moment. It was extraordinary. Very moving.'

'Was that when you first met Stephanie?' asked Mike trying to piece together the former lives of his friends, rather than the background politics.

'Yes. I'd met her in Athens and invited her to stay with us in Crete that summer. She was so lovely back then, so full of life. But I was hardly here, I was in court following the trials, first of the Junta and then of the torturers and the secret police. But you don't want to hear about all that.'

'Another time,' Mike suggested. 'You were talking about Laurent.'

'He fell in love with Stephanie, and they moved to Palaikastro, to a little place just down from the church. I always hoped he'd come back to me. Foolish, I know. After he died, in Athens, in that terrible rainstorm and the flood – this was of course in the winter when we were all living there in our different flats – I went round to see Stephanie. I hated her for taking Laurent away from me, but she was the only person, apart from myself, who loved Laurent, so the only person I could talk to. Always was. It remained a bond between us.'

Henry shook his head. 'I can't tell you how terrible it was. She was lying in the bed … she hadn't moved for I don't know how long. She'd had a miscarriage.'

Mike could hardly hear him. He was thinking of another death, the death of the woman he loved and her unborn child. He found he was tensed up, clenching his knuckles.

'Stephanie was scared she couldn't have a child after that,' Henry was saying. 'Which was why she was so happy when Jen was born, but later...' He paused and sipped his wine. 'Later, it was as if she blamed Jen for not being Laurent's child. Jen never knew, but I think that was at the heart of the problems between them.'

'And now that her mother's dead, Jen never will know,' Mike said.' She must never know.'

Then they'd talked away the night, about anything else apart from their own lives. Boats. Legends.

'It was here in this very bay that Jason had sailed only to find that Crete was guarded by the bronze man, Talos,' Henry told Mike.

'Really? I hadn't heard that.'

'It's a fairly new piece of research. Talos himself may have been worshipped by the Cretans in the form of the bull.'

'Which makes it rather exciting that they found the golden bull in this very bay, doesn't it?'

'Yes,' said Henry, carefully. 'Except that the bull may have symbolised death. It could have been a place of sacrifice.'

They couldn't help it. It always came back to death, like the ominous chord in the opera *Carmen*. We must turn and face our fears, Henry thought. He was beginning to sound like Popi. He wished he could talk to her now, tell her about Patrice and ask her advice. Except. Except...

Except she'd tell me to write the book without mentioning the final terrorist, Henry thought, as he swam out to sea. Which I would have done if Patrice hadn't confided in me, if he hadn't told me about a new plot which could kill any number of innocent people. But it's not down to me, argued Henry in his head, now swimming back in an efficient crawl. It's down to Christopher, and all of them in their riverside tower. If England *was* the target, and Patrice hadn't been sure of that. But he didn't think it was Greece.

The one question that nobody had voiced yesterday evening, but he guessed that both Pam and Mike had thought it, was whether Patrice had mentioned Henry's name to the terrorist. What was so frightening was the fact that by asking questions he'd stirred up a nest of hornets or at least one particularly vicious one, and he might be the next person they were targeting. No, he thought, I am. He couldn't deny any more that there had been someone following him when he last drove back from Sitia, a car that came much too close to him and then stopped and turned round. They'd made their point. Here, he was vulnerable.

'Nothing I can do,' he muttered as he shook the water off him. 'Zero security and no protection.'

But he could leave. He needed to go and talk with Didi to find out if Patrice had said anything. He'd talk at the funeral, which would probably be in a week. The next Saturday, Didi had said, if the authorities gave her permission. There was no reason for him to go to Paris before then, especially since the police had all of Patrice's papers. He'd do better to have a meeting with Christopher.

But would Christopher help? Henry had a bad feeling about the man which had only been heightened by what Pam had said. Why would Christopher threaten her and warn her not to investigate him? It made no sense. And he still hadn't replied to Henry's report.

There was one man who might help. Long retired, but who might still be in touch with former colleagues. Oliver, his oldest friend. He'd sent him a copy of the report he'd sent to Christopher and had immediately got a card back thanking him. At least Oliver was still alive; he'd checked before posting the report. 'Because when we're in our seventies, that's what we do,' he said to himself as he showered and dressed. 'We check each morning that we're still alive and then we check our friends.' His acquaintances were slipping away one by one, as well as the friends. And the latter were dying even faster.

Who were his other friends now? Popi and her husband Alexander, of course, though Alexander was himself in hospital.

In the meantime, there was something at the back of his mind that could be a helpful lead. He opened his laptop and waited for the machine to come to life; he really did need to update it. The screen was black which was unusual, but then it exploded into stars of words and went black again.

'No, damn it,' Henry muttered. 'Don't tell me I've got a virus.'

He unplugged the computer, waited, and plugged it in again. Now it was completely black. His book, his research, his emails and his photographs. His whole life had just disappeared. He stared at the black screen in horror. Everything had gone.

Pam was towel-drying her hair when Henry knocked on the door

'What's the matter?' she asked, seeing his anxious face.

'I believe I've got a virus. My computer appears to be dead,' he said bitterly.

'Oh God, how awful!' Pam thought about how she'd feel if this happened to her. 'It's not just the Wi-Fi down, is it?' she asked. She clicked on her tablet and got an immediate connection.

'No. This is fine,' she said. 'Do you want me to wake up Mike?' she asked.

'Do you know if he's any good with computers?'

'I don't,' she said. 'You'll have to ask him.'

'Ask him what?' said Mike coming out of his room. He was surprised Henry was standing seeing how much brandy he'd knocked back the previous evening. It was the mornings that made him so glad he no longer drank.

'Henry's laptop's been attacked,' Pam told him.

'Do you think you clicked on something yesterday?' asked Mike. 'Maybe last night?'

'That's just it. I haven't gone online for a couple of days. Just made notes in Word. And I've been using my phone for emails.'

'Is your phone working?' he asked.

Henry reached into his pocket and pulled it out. He clicked on the icon and his emails were all there. 'Testing,' he wrote and sent the email to himself. In a moment it arrived.

'Yes. it's fine. But I'm worried that it may not be just a virus. It's closed everything down.'

'I think you need a specialist,' said Mike, 'someone who can save your hard drive. If you've backed up, you might be able to download some software that will find the virus, but it sounds as though it's not that simple.'

'Thanks anyway,' said Henry. 'I rather think I just needed to share my woes. Sitting alone staring at a black screen is a gloomy occupation. It'll be fine. I'm going to fly to London today, and I'll seek out a computer man who can help me.'

'I think I know one,' she told him. 'But he's in Cambridge.'

'That would be even better. Would you mind if I stayed in Stephanie's house?'

'It's your house, too, I'm only going to be squatting in it for a bit.'

She smiled at Henry. 'Why don't you sit down and have some coffee and I'll ring him later. It's only just six in England. His name's Stuart by the way, Stuart Weir, and he's ex-GCHQ. If there's been an attack, I'm sure he'll be able to see it.'

'Do you think it's connected with your research into 17 November?' Mike asked.

'I don't know,' replied Henry. 'But experience has shown me that coincidences are rare.'

'I don't believe in coincidences either,' agreed Pam. 'But what about back up? Have you lost everything?'

'Thank goodness no,' said Henry. 'I'm somewhat fanatical when it comes to backing up. Belt and braces and suspenders as well.'

He held up a small flat box. 'I've got the whole hard drive copied onto here, but I don't want to open it until I know it's safe. Meanwhile, the new book is on various memory sticks along with all my notes, the ones that I typed, that is. A great deal of my work is still written longhand into my notebooks.' He handed Pam a small memory stick.

'Do you know that this holds hundreds of thousands more memory than my original Epson computer? It's astonishing, isn't it? And wonderful when it works. Oh,' he added. 'I also sent everything to Stephanie. Do you know where her computer is?'

'I do,' said Pam, 'it's on my desk back in Cambridge, inside an evidence bag. I very much doubt whether anyone's touched it. I'll be sending it and everything else of Stephanie's to Jen when I get back. Would you like me to download your files on to a stick and keep it for you?'

'That would be very kind. Now, don't let me invade your breakfast. I feel quite reassured. I'll come back in a while after you've had time to telephone your specialist.'

'You can join us for breakfast, Henry. It's no problem. We always like your company.'

'That's very kind, but I need to have a few words with Maddalena about my post. I also want to ask her to let me know if there is anyone asking about me.'

'We'll keep an eye on your house,' said Mike. 'And those notebooks. Would you like me to take them while you're away, just in case?'

Pam wondered whether they were all being alarmist. After all, it might simply be a virus attacking Henry's computer, and it might have been a political assassination of his friend. There was no evidence to link them. Was it enough to call it a coincidence, or were they leaning into conspiracy territory? She wasn't sure, but she recognised the niggle of worry in the back of her head. Over the years, that niggle had proved to be a reliable indicator that things weren't right. She just prayed that Henry would be safe. She'd had enough danger here already, she wanted to put those memories behind her.

'Do you think he's right about this 17 November terrorist?' she asked Mike after Henry had left.

'Don't know,' replied Mike, 'but I can ask around. My cousin's friend is a police officer in Sitia.'

'Which cousin is that?' Half of Sitia seemed to be related to Mike's Aunt Sofia.

'Spiros. Actually,' he added. 'I think it's time you visited Sitia.'

'That would be nice. I drove through a bit of it, but I don't think I saw the real town, just a few streets and some very ordinary buildings. Then it was winding round by the sea and all I remember is the purple thyme everywhere, the scent coming through the window.'

'Yes, it's a lovely road to walk in the winter when it's cooler. And if you like swimming from the rocks, there's a little bay just after the port. But Sitia isn't an old town like Chania,' Mike replied. 'It isn't picturesque; not like Santorini or any of the Cycladic islands, not that I've visited many of them. That's the thing of having family here; you don't go anywhere else. I did some island hopping when I was younger.'

Pam tried to imagine a past which included that

kind of freedom and failed.

'The thing about Sitia, well to me, is its people and I'm not just saying that because of Aunt Sofia ... they're survivors. Maybe all Cretans are, they've had to put up with enough, they've had to contend with so many invasions and rulers. Ask Henry.'

'I think that would let me in for something of a lecture,' Pam laughed.

'Oh yes. He wouldn't just tell you about the Hellenistic period, he'd divide it up between the Dorians, the Mycenaeans and every other ancient Greek lot, and that would take a few hours before you'd even got to the Romans and the Venetians. There's a lot of history. Sitia was a famous Minoan port, in fact there's probably lots of archaeology under the city. There would have been lots of Venetian buildings here at one time, but the only one we have left is the ruined castle on the hill. We'll walk up there when your leg is better.'

'Lovely.'

'I think I told you when we first Skyped about the Sitia earthquakes.'

'Not sure I was really listening. Except for the bits about Stephanie.'

'Don't know why I decided to tell you all that stuff.'

'I do. It's because I had to know that Crete was about history. And you were right though, I didn't know it then.'

'Except that what you actually needed was a different history...a bit more recent. Listening to Henry, I always feel that history is all around us.' She paused and smiled at him. 'So, if Sitia hasn't got an old town, and it isn't picturesque, so why are we going there?'

'Because it's special....' Mike stopped. Was he boring her, did he need to explain? He decided he did. 'It's like...well...I was sitting with Monique ... she has the house behind Maddelena's ... and she asked me if

I knew why she'd bought a house here. And I replied: sun, sea, archaeology, and she said yes, all that, but she and Daniel had travelled all over Crete and visited lots of Cycladic islands, but Sitia was unique. It wasn't something easy to put into words, but it was because of the beating heart of the place.'

Mike smiled. 'That sounded better in French. Monique said there was a kind of fidelity about the place and its people. Once you found it, and really found it, you had to come back. She and Dan wouldn't want to be anywhere else. And she's right. There's an honesty about Sitia, nothing flash or touristy, but it's real. It was built for its own inhabitants, and not for the tourists. I love sitting by the port. The houses are all different heights and sizes, jostling together like spectators crammed against each other looking down as if they don't want to miss what's going on below. And in the still of the early morning their reflections shimmer like gold in the sea and you forget they're rather ugly concrete boxes.'

Later that evening, sitting by that port, eating the famous Mitsakakis *loukoumades*, small honey doughnut balls, which, as Mike said, were the best in the world, Pam looked out at the white and blue boats floating above their own shadows in the still water.. Their table was one of many cafes and restaurants which circled the port with only a line of sturdy palm trees between them and the sea.

No, Pam thought, watching friends and families chatting together, and children running around, laughing, and shouting, this wasn't a place for clubbing or to grab a photograph and get back on a tourist bus, but it was wonderful. This was a place to stay. It was a place where you felt you'd come home.

'Are you okay, Pam?' Mike asked her.

She smiled and nodded. 'It's just I never thought I'd deserve to come to a place like this.'

'You deserve everything. And you belong here.'
Pam looked at him thoughtfully and nodded.
'You know something, I rather think I do.'

CHAPTER 6

'You look radiant,' said Grace, smiling at Pam. 'Despite being shot at.'

'I expect it's all the sleep,' replied Pam. 'I've slept more over the past two weeks than all the previous two months.'

Zofia smiled and shook her head slightly. It felt a tad surreal. Here she was with her wife, Grace, sitting in the white-painted courtyard of the house of a woman whose autopsy she'd carried out hardly more than two weeks ago, and Pam, her friend Pam, who never went anywhere, and never stopped working, was lounging on a sofa in this picture-perfect Greek village as if she'd been doing this all her life. And although she was still recovering from the bullet wound, she looked wonderful. More than that, she was wearing a dress. Zofia had known her for over thirteen years and she had never once seen her in a dress.

'Right, hen,' she said emphasising the Glasgow accent she'd long smoothed out, 'Gonna tell me what ha ye done with ma old frien Pam? Whaur has she gone?'

Pam laughed. 'She's still here. Just having a holiday.'

Zofia was about to say something else about the fact that Pam didn't take holidays when she caught Grace's eye and stopped herself.

'Is that water as glorious as it looks?' asked Grace.

'Better, said Pam. 'Go and have a swim, the two of you, and make me jealous. I can't until the doctor gives me permission.'

'Quite right,' said Zofia. 'Bullet wounds can easily get infected, and from what you've said, the air in that old barn, where he took Jen, could have had all kinds of bacteria.'

'I'm allowed to take off the dressing to shower now. You can look at it yourself. No swelling, no redness, no infection.'

'All good,' said Zofia, who had been on an A&E ward during her training and before she decided to specialise in pathology. 'But if that's because you want me to give you permission to swim, you're asking the wrong doctor. I only treat cadavers these days. They do what I say.'

'Worth a try. Now go before I start behaving like an invalid and making demands.'

'Well?' Zofia asked Grace a short while later. They were swimming in the calm clear pale green water of the small bay, watching the occasional fish beneath them.

Grace trod water and looked back at the village. There were around a dozen small stone white houses on a gentle slope in the lee of the strange flat-topped hill which rose from the edge of the water like a miniature table mountain. Behind the small village, a smudge of hills lead to distant mountains.

'It's beautiful.'

'Utterly. It's perfect. Every bit of it, that's the problem.'

'Why?' asked Grace.

'Because it's like the fantasy of a Greek island village, the little white houses, the decorative pebbled streets. It doesn't feel real. And Pam seems to be living in that fantasy. I know it was recently rebuilt after the last village was pulled down for the excavations of that palace, but there's only two Greek families living here all year. It's just holiday homes plus these two new friends of Pam's, Henry and Mike.'

'Isn't that true of lots of small Greek resorts? They're summer places.'

'Exactly. Fine for a holiday. But Pam is behaving as though this is her new home. She has a job to go back to.'

'You think she doesn't know that? Is that what's worrying you?'

'Doesn't it worry you?'

'No, not really. I don't think we should rush in and condemn Pam till she's had a chance to tell us what she feels. And what she wants to do.'

'It's so strange and quick. And, yes, it could be a reaction to being shot. You do expect any number of PTSD reactions from that. But I feel that this started before then.'

'You last saw her after you'd done Stephanie's post-mortem, when was that?'

'Thursday the fourteenth,' said Zofia, flipping over on to her back, and doing enough small movements with her arms to keep herself afloat. Pam had been right; the water was perfect, cool, but not cold, and perfectly clear. She was tempted to allow Pam to swim. It wouldn't do her any harm if the wounds were no longer bleeding. She'd been lucky, she thought, there were all kinds of tendons and muscles in the leg, apart from bones that could have been hit and damaged. Pam was already able to put her weight on the leg with some support; it was unlikely to cause her long-term damage.

'That's just over two weeks ago,' continued Grace. 'Pam can hardly change personality in two weeks.'

'That's just the problem,' argued Zofia. 'She has. She's not talking about work, and she's never talked about anything else, she's changed how she looks, she's sleeping – and she was a chronic insomniac – and she's got new friends.'

'That's all good, isn't it? She needed that jolt; she's been in a rut and it's been gradually destroying her. You know we've been saying that for years.'

'I know. But why now?' She looked down where a small fish was darting between a swaying plant. 'You know what bothers me most?'

'The fantasy or the new friends?'

'Both, I think. They're connected.'

'It's because she's talking to them rather that us? And about Richard?'

'We rescued her from that bastard…'

'Which is precisely why she could never open up to us. We were too close.' Grace paused. 'Are we jealous of them?' she asked carefully.

Zofia splashed water at her partner. 'Don't try and analyse me,' she laughed. 'This is about Pam.'

Is it? wondered Grace moving away across the bay towards the distant stones, which must be the site of the ancient palace. They'd go there another day and examine it. Pam said that she'd ring the archaeologist to show them round. That was another thing. Yes, Zofia was right, Pam had instantly become at home in this village, and in a way she'd never been at home anywhere. Grace needed to talk with her. If being here had allowed all that pent-up emotion to finally come out, she needed some help. Plus, she was bound to be in a vulnerable state after being shot, it wasn't something you could shrug off. The James Bonds were fictions.

'Be gentle with her,' she said a little later, kissing her wife, as they took a shower in the empty cottage Mike had found for them. Mike, himself, had (tactfully?) gone to Sitia for the day to watch the World Cup. She wanted to meet him, though she wasn't at all sure she liked what she'd heard. He was a former cop who was now a builder? But why was he living here? It didn't make a lot of sense. Perhaps Zofia was right to be wary.

Pam joined them in their borrowed cottage an hour later, and was sipping an alcohol-free *mojito*, while she and Zofia had theirs with rum. Zofia had discovered pots of mint in the garden which, it seemed, Mike had cultivated because this had been his home before Stephanie died, although there was no trace of his personality if you discounted the pots of nurtured herbs.

'So, when do you think you'll get back to work?' Zofia asked casually.

'Not sure I want to go back there,' replied Pam. 'To be honest I'm not sure what I want.'

'Well, you certainly need time off,' replied her friend. 'You must be owed a lot of holiday time.'

'A good few weeks,' agreed Pam. 'But that's not it.' She smiled at them. 'I've been wanting to talk with you about it and get your opinion. Since I've been here, I've been thinking maybe I need a change.'

'What kind of change?' asked Grace carefully

'A different job, a different life. Maybe a different country. That's the problem. I don't know. Obviously, I can't stay here. Even Mike feels that. It's only Henry who is never going to leave, but he lives in his books, so where he inhabits is secondary. And I don't think Greek's a very easy language to learn, though I suppose I could.'

'But you're brilliant at your job. You've built up that unit and you know you love it.'

'Do I? Are you sure?'

'But...' began Zofia.

'You're right to give yourself time,' replied Grace. 'And you're right to ask us. We want you to be happy above everything else.'

'You make me sound as though I don't know what I'm doing,' snapped Pam. 'It's not as if there aren't other things I could do. I do have a brain, you know.'

'We do know,' said Zofia. 'Which is why you're such an effective cop. I don't understand. Just a couple of weeks ago you were going on about how happy you were to have saved that kid who was being used to smuggle dope. It's what you've always wanted to do. And now you're going all Shirley fucking Valentine.'

'How dare you! You're talking to me as if I don't have a choice. I can't believe you could... This is... I thought you'd want me to branch out.'

'We do,' said Grace quickly. 'But we don't want you to rush into anything.'

'We? We? Have you been talking about me then? Oh dear, what's happened to our Pam and how do we get her back?'

'Of course not. But you have to admit that this place isn't real life. It's not somewhere you could stay indefinitely.'

'I've just said that, so what's your problem? Is it that I've now got other friends who look after me and who aren't you?' She slammed her glass on to the table. 'God! You're just jealous I've got new friends. And that I've changed, and it wasn't down to you.'

'Rubbish,' said Zofia'

'Pam,' began Grace. 'Listen...'

'No, I don't want to listen. I'm not having you come here and criticise this place. It's special, very special. Mike wanted to kill himself when he came here, and it healed him, and it's changed me. Do you know I've started to talk about Richard? And I never talk about him.'

'You told us.'

'And Mike and Henry gave me a celebratory dinner last night to mark the ten years since my divorce.'

'Well, that makes all the difference,' said Zofia acidly.

'I think I'd better go,' said Pam. She felt tears coming and gritted her teeth to stop them. 'I've been so looking forward to having you here and now you've ruined it.'

'Zofia, why don't you go to that bakery and get us some pastries for breakfast?'

'Actually, I think I'll go for a walk,' said Zofia and stomped out.

Grace poured Pam a glass of water and sat down beside her.

'Is this a therapy session?' asked Pam. She blew her nose; she was not going to cry.

'No, I can't be your therapist, I'm your friend. But I can talk to you as a friend, can't I?'

Pam sighed. 'I do feel all messed up. I've been happier and sadder and everything all at once since I've been here.'

'That's good.'

'Is it?'

'Pam, you've been bottling up your emotions for decades. You've never allowed yourself to let go.'

'I know. When I got here, I met this amazing woman called Popi, she's a therapist like you. Popi Filotaki, she was Stephanie's best friend.'

'You've met Popi Filotaki?'

'Yes.' Pam saw the excitement in Grace's face and smiled. 'Is she famous?'

'She's possibly the most famous therapist in the world when it comes to treating torture victims. I've read a lot of her articles; she's an extraordinary woman.'

'I know. It's a pity you can't meet Henry, he's known her for decades and knows all about her. But he's had to fly to London today, a close friend was shot and killed yesterday.'

'Shot? This isn't a case that going to involve you?'

'No, not at all. It happened in Paris, and you may think I'm going doolally, but I do know I can't interfere in a French criminal investigation. Especially a political one, which this seems to be. But I am worried about Henry.'

Grace let that pass for the moment. 'Tell me about Popi,' she said.

'Well... she's in a wheelchair a lot these days, though I think she can get around without it for short distances, and though she doesn't really work anymore, she feels powerful. I don't know how to describe it, but she exudes both energy and calmness simultaneously. That sounds odd, I know, but there's something sphinx-like about her as if she had this wisdom...' Pam broke off. 'Actually, you have a bit of that, too, but Popi is amazing. Which was why it was so awful when she broke down.'

'What?'

'You see, it was one of her lost souls, as Henry calls them, that she always has around her, who killed Stephanie. She brought him to the Leotakis house, and he almost killed Jen. Mike and I are still both blaming ourselves for not realising it was Manolis, but it really disturbed Popi.'

'Manolis being the young man who killed Stephanie and then himself?'

'He thought Stephanie had betrayed his family after the Polytechnic massacre in 1973. But she hadn't, she'd tried to save his great uncle, but the police found him and killed him. It was the janitor who betrayed him.' Pam stopped and sipped her drink. 'You see, Grace, to get to the heart of the case I had to start learning about the history of this country and I've never done anything like that before. And the more I read about it, the more interested I got. And still am. Which is why I spend a lot of time with Henry. His new book is all about that time; he's writing about the terrorist group that emerged after the fall of the Junta.'

'You're right. I've never known you interested in

history.'

'And Popi is part of that. She lives the history in a way that I can't think of anyone doing back home. Perhaps it's because we take our freedom for granted and they've had to fight for it.'

'Why are you worried about Henry?'

'I suppose because he's worried. He thinks there's a member of the 17 November group who wasn't caught. I was reading about them this morning. They were a terrorist group here who were responsible for a huge number of bombings and killings. They didn't get caught until 2002. But there could be one last member, Henry said. Patrice was going to tell Henry his name, but then he got shot. And Henry thinks that's the reason.'

'Is that what the French police think?'

'I've no idea; it only happened yesterday. I expect they're keeping all options open. And I'm certainly not getting involved. But I am worried Henry might be lifting up a stone that's covering a scorpion.'

'Historians don't often get killed because of their research,' Grace said mildly. 'Scorpions? Do they have scorpions on Crete?' She'd have to stop walking about barefoot.

'Just on the hillside, according to Stavros, and their sting isn't usually fatal. They're not the big black ones you get in the tropics.'

'Stavros?'

'Ah, yes. I let that slip out, didn't I? He's a Greek policeman I met. Well, we sort of fell for each other. But then Jen got abducted and we had a row... I'm trying to work it through. We're still talking. Actually...' She laughed, suddenly. 'Actually, I was thinking of inviting him over this weekend, he told me he had some time off. Would you like to meet him?'

CHAPTER 7

As long as there are classes, as long as there are rich and poor people, there must be violent acts to counter this prevailing state.

These are not the words of the Revolutionary Left, but of Plato some 2,500 years ago. Their truth remains. Only a revolution can save the people!

CHAPTER 8

I should never have invited them here, said Pam to herself, as she made herself coffee. Mike had gone across to Henry's house to pick up some more notebooks and she had the house to herself. She imagined for a moment what it was going to be like back in Cambridge where she would have a whole house all to herself all the time.

The idea pleased her. For the six months she was house-sitting Jen's home, she could enjoy having somewhere people could come and visit. It had taken her twenty-odd years to get there, but at least she didn't have the burden of a mortgage like Roberta and Josh, she reminded herself, thinking of how all her sergeants had that additional pressure on their lives. She was in a position now where she could afford to buy a small place with a mortgage, especially if she went for promotion to Chief Inspector.

She needed to talk with Grace and Zofia, but not now. Her friends' visit wasn't the joyous one she'd anticipated, and she'd been irritated that Zofia had stopped criticising her as soon as she'd heard that Pam had found a new man. As if she'd needed Stavros to make her realise she needed to change. When actually was it, she wondered, that she had begun to think differently about everything? That Friday morning, perhaps, the day before she came out here? When one of her sergeants had come out with a volley of misogynistic racist abuse and that creeping sense when she reported him that nothing was going to be done and he'd get away with it? Yes. And it was interesting that nobody had mentioned Dave Butcher, probably for that very reason. They were sweeping him under the carpet.

That had been the trigger, she thought. Somehow, she'd turned away from the job, and almost immediately she'd begun to see things differently. Like the history of Leotakis which would have irritated her in the past because it wasn't relevant to the case, but which she'd found fascinating. As was meeting the billionaire who had been utterly charming and made her feel special. As had Stavros. Though differently. And now Mike and Henry. As if I was a person, not a police officer.

'And when did I last feel like that? Did I ever feel like that?' she murmured.

Relations between her and her two friends had been smoothed over since the first afternoon, very much helped by Mike who had turned himself into the perfect tour guide and had won over Zofia by revealing a mutual passion for the Kaiser Chiefs. Soon all of them were predicting a riot with Zofia and Mike dancing together, and Pam and Grace singing along and laughing. Yes, he'd broken the ice, but the crystals that had formed it were still there, below the surface; it wouldn't take much for them to freeze together again.

Pam decided not to talk about whether or not she should go back to work, although she repeatedly went through the arguments on her own. If she was back in Cambridge, she'd have discussed it with her sergeants Josh and Roberta; it was strange not talking to them every day after working together for so long. Josh, her former work partner, had rung a few times, but said little except that he was moving to Norfolk. It would be easier to do the Inspector exams once he was there, as it wouldn't be easy to transfer while he was doing them. Pam felt that mentally he'd already gone, and just told him again that she would write any report supporting him that he needed. He would do well; he deserved to do well.

The rest of the team hadn't been in touch since their calls of sympathy after the shooting. They'd be busy, crime doesn't go on holiday and County Lines were an ongoing problem. A Hydra-headed beast, she thought, using one of Henry's metaphors: cut off one head and another grows.

She sipped the coffee, cut some bread for breakfast, and took a jar of the local honey out of the cupboard. The jar was sticky, and she went over to the sink to wash it, licking her fingers before she washed them. Crete: honey and sea and everything. Outside, as the day warmed, the cicadas started their constant *ts ts ts* sound that was also part of life here. Yes, all this had changed her. And the poems, she'd discovered, as if Crete and the poems had come together at the same right moment.

No. It was definitely not that she'd fallen in love; somehow, she'd have to make Zofia and Grace realise that, but not right now. Her doctor was coming this morning to change her dressing, and she'd talk to them later. She didn't have to rush.

She smiled at Mike as he came back and watched him stow Henry's notebooks among Stephanie's own, so they didn't stand out. He was taking Henry's worries seriously. Perhaps she should, too, though she couldn't see quite what she could do right now. Later, she thought. Later.

Doctor Yiannis Stamatopoulos was a slim young man from northern Greece; he had a warm smile and long delicate fingers. Just like a pianist, as her father used to say, not that he knew any pianists any more than she did. But she still found herself using the phrase. There were fragments of her father embedded within her.

He arrived at ten and told her she was a perfect patient. The pink skin around the scar was puckered, especially around the exit wound, but there was no inflammation.

'Excellent,' he said. 'I think we can now move to a simpler dressing you can do yourself,' he told her. 'And then just a plaster.'

'Can I swim?' she asked him.

'The water here is clean, and it will be good to help strengthen your leg muscles,' he said. 'You've been wanting to swim, I'm sure.'

'It's been so tempting,' she agreed. 'Especially in the mornings when it's so calm.'

'The best time of day,' he agreed. 'In which case, I'm not going to put a dressing on. You can go for a swim, and then you should wash with this diluted antiseptic, and then you can put this dressing on.'

'That's marvellous,' she said. 'Thank you. By the way,' she added. 'Don't I owe you some money for all of this?'

The doctor laughed. 'You're the fourth person trying to pay me for your treatment,' he said. 'The first was your Embassy, saying that all hospital and medical costs would be covered, then Henry asked whether he could help. But, as it happens, I am already on the occasional staff of Mr Leotakis who said that nothing is too good for you. I think most of the village here would agree. In helping find the person who killed Stefania, you have bought a lot of love. And that is real,' he added, as she waved her arms to push it away. 'You cannot escape Cretan love. Like hate, it is fixed for ever.'

Pam bit her lip. 'I'll have to learn how to accept it then,' she said.

Mike knocked on her door after the doctor left.

'All good?' he asked. 'All very good,' she said, 'I'm

allowed to swim, and I can go in straight away.'

'I'll come with you,' he suggested.

'That would be nice. I'll ring Grace and Zofia and tell them they can join us.'

Twenty minutes later, they were all swimming across the bay. Mike was watching Pam to make sure she was all right and Zofia and Grace watched Mike doing this, while at the same time not letting Pam notice his concern. They smiled at each other, confirming their opinion that he was okay.

'According to Dr Stamatopoulos, I have to learn how to accept Cretan love,' Pam told them after they'd showered and made themselves drinks.

'I told you so,' said Mike. 'Every time I go shopping, they ask if I'm buying things for you and then they don't let me pay. I could lie,' he added. 'It would reduce my bills!'

Pam laughed.

'It won't last of course,' he added. 'The love will, but the free stuff won't. We're a pragmatic race.'

'Do you think of yourself as Cretan?' asked Zofia.

'I suppose I do. English and Cretan.'

'What about your Barbadian side?' asked Grace.

'Yeah. That's tricky. I mean I'm aware of it more back home because every time you step outside as a young black guy, you have to be cautious. Here in Chiona and Sitia, I'm just another of Aunt Sofia's massive family, and that's all I am. It's the only place I've ever felt totally safe. As for Barbados... I was seven when my dad died, and my mother never kept in touch with his family, so I never got to meet them. Never been there.'

Pam's phone rang and interrupted whatever it was that Grace was about to say. It was Roberta, the woman she felt was the closest thing she had to a friend at work, though they'd never socialised much out of the office.

'Is this a good time to talk, Pam?' she asked.

Pam noticed the Pam, rather than the boss, which meant it was a personal call, not an office one.

'Yes, it's fine. Zofia and Grace are here, they're waving hello.'

'Can I Skype you this evening?' Roberta asked. 'I'm calling from the café and a few of us want to talk to you.'

Pam felt herself go cold again, just as she had when Henry had heard of Patrice's death. But this was almost certainly the bad news she'd been expecting ever since her boss, Superintendent Murton, had suggested that management wanted to dismantle her unit. She'd been so proud when she got appointed to run EASOU, the East Anglian Special Operations Unit, but she knew that there had been the danger of it being closed down in the next lot of budget cuts. Murton had promised they'd postpone that if she'd had a successful outcome on the Stephanie Michaels case, and it could hardly have been more successful: tied up within a week of the killing and needing no expensive trial. Had he already gone back on his word?

'Yes, I can be in,' said Pam. 'There's no football tonight.' Until this week, the World Cup had passed her by, but watching England beat Colombia on penalties on Tuesday evening with Mike and her friends had all four of them fired up.

'I'll make it early,' said Roberta. 'Say five thirty our time.'

'That's fine,' said Pam converting it to seven thirty Greek time. They could eat afterwards. She was beginning to get used to the Greek habit of big late lunches and smaller late suppers.

'We can go out if you like,' suggested Grace.

'Actually, I'd like you all to be here if that's okay with you,' Pam replied.

'I'll cook supper,' suggested Mike. 'Make us a

proper moussaka the way Aunt Sofia does it.'

'Great,' said Pam. 'Thank you. And I'm off the antibiotics now, so I can drink wine.'

'In moderation,' said Zofia.

'Yes, doctor. Though I can't think it will do me any harm.' She told Zofia about reading Stephanie's diary about how she'd taken in a student who'd been shot who insisted on drinking ouzo rather than sweet tea.

'Looking at her liver, she didn't drink much tea,' said Zofia, and then realised that Mike being a close friend of Stephanie's might not want to think about Stephanie's autopsy. She noticed Grace glaring at her. 'Sorry,' she added.

'I knew she was dying,' Mike said. 'She was so ill that if she'd stopped drinking it would have killed her. But she wanted to keep going and see the opening of the gallery.'

'Is that still happening?' asked Grace.

'It's the end of August,' said Pam. 'Tuesday the twenty-eighth. Prince Charles has altered his diary specially. He's flying down from Balmoral and going to stay at Sandringham, according to Nikos.'

'Nikos is it now?' teased Grace. 'It will be Charles and Camilla next.'

'For a republican like me?' laughed Pam. 'Never!'

'You're going to meet Charles, though, aren't you?' Mike turned to Zofia and Grace. 'I bet she hasn't told you, but she's been awarded the Queen's Gallantry Medal.'

'You've what?!' they shouted. 'And you never told us?'

'I haven't told anyone. I feel a bit embarrassed by it all. Mike just happened to be there when I got the news.'

'Pam!' remonstrated Zofia. 'I haven't given you a proper hug, but I'm bloody going to do it now.'

'What do you think the call's about?' Zofia asked

Grace as they had an afternoon siesta. 'Pam's really tense. It's how she is at home on bad days.'

'Yes. And it shows just how relaxed she is here. Maybe we were too quick to criticise her.'

'You didn't, hun. That was me.'

'I need a drink to take this call,' Pam told Mike a little later. 'I think it's going to be shit.'

'You could see it as a push in the direction you want to go,' he replied.

'You're assuming I know where that is.' She paused and looked at him. 'What about you? Where do you want to go?'

'No idea,' he admitted. 'Everything about that undercover work was so fucked...so I could never go back to the police. Or England. I don't feel...'

'What?'

'It doesn't matter.'

'Mike?'

'Sorry, Pam. Nothing I can really talk about. Now about this drink. I think I could manage to create something a bit special. My lemon daiquiri with just a bit of rum.'

'Cocktails already, is it?' asked Zofia coming in through the open door. Her pink hair almost matched the lilac and pink pattern of her loose cotton dress and Pam thought she had begun to relax a bit herself.

'Only with a smidgeon of rum for Pam,' Mike told her. 'But lots more rum for you ladies.'

'I could get used to this,' smiled Grace, pushing the lemon slice to the other side of the glass.

'But it's not real life, I know,' said Pam, unable to keep the anger out of her voice. 'As you told me when you arrived. Well now you're going to hear real life.'

She looked down at her computer; a minute to go. Roberta was always punctual. Pam was aware that they were all watching her as she waited for the Skype call.

A minute later she heard the familiar bouncy sound of a signal filtered through bubbles. She clicked the call receive icon and saw Roberta with Paul and Sue, two of her best DCs behind her.

'Hi gang,' she said. 'That bad, is it? Go on, tell me; they're going to dismantle EASOU.'

'It's worse than that, boss,' said Roberta. 'Paul found out today from Julia, Murton's secretary. It's happening right away. They've decided to chop EASOU completely and amalgamate us all into Cambridge CID unless we want to move. I think they'd actually like us to go. Josh has already been accepted in Norfolk. He's starting there next week, and Matt and I are thinking of moving, too, if we can find somewhere with good schools.'

'So sorry, Roberta,' Pam commiserated. 'So does that mean I'm going to run CID with Martin?' She didn't get on with DI Martin Hawkswood, who already ran the Cambridge CID, and didn't know how they were going to share the job.

'Don't know how to tell you this.' It was Paul. 'They're making Hawkswood a DCI, and they're saying you'll work for him. Julia heard Murton on the phone.'

Paul, Pam remembered, had a close relationship with Julia.

'So, basically, he wants me out. Doesn't surprise me. I had a feeling about that. He wanted me off the Stephanie Michaels case the moment it brought me here, where he couldn't control me. Is that it?'

'Just about,' said Roberta. 'Except that Hawkswood is taking over your office. I've put all your things into boxes before he starts chucking them away. Would you like me to take them to your house?'

'Actually, if you have the time, could you take them to Stephanie Michaels' house in Flower Street? There is a key in Stephanie's handbag which is in an evidence bag on my desk. Or on the desk which was mine.'

'Why that house?' asked Paul.

'Jen Michaels has asked me to house-sit it for a few months while she looks after her stepmother in London.'

'Would you like us to bring all your stuff from your old house as well?' asked Roberta. 'I mean the stairs in that little place are really difficult. I imagine you're on crutches.'

'Just a stick actually,' said Pam. 'It's healing really well. I even got to swim today.'

'Course we'll move your stuff,' said Paul. 'It's the least we can do. I can tell you that everyone is fuming. You're the best boss ever. I just can't believe what they're doing.'

'I think there might be another reason,' said Pam 'You heard about Dave?'

'His racist rant. Yes. We all made sure the word got out.'

'It was even worse than that. Really vile sexual stuff about me. I taped it when he came into my office the morning I left and played it to Murton. He said he was going to deal with it.'

'Well, he did,' said Paul. 'But not in the way any of us would have wanted. Julia overheard Murton tell Hawkswood to get your phone and remove the recording.'

'What?'

'Sorry, Pam. It's crap. Actually, I've got the letter he's about to send you on my phone. You want to hear it?'

'No but read it anyway.'

'First there's all the bits about reassignment of duties, etcetera, post the necessary dissolution of EASOU. Then it goes on to the stuff about Dave. Who's been allowed to retire on full salary, by the way.'

'Shit!'

'This is what Murton has written,' Paul continued. '*I did not have time that morning to condemn your use of a personal phone to record DS Butcher, but in retrospect I should have done so, and I am afraid that your action is being written into your record. That is the reason that I am not recommending you for DCI. After a year or two working within DCI Hawkswood's team, you may very well be eligible to apply and take a position in another region*. The bastard!' Paul added.

'Right' said Pam. 'Thanks for the warning, everyone. That makes my decisions a bit easier. Oh, by the way can you make sure that all of Stephanie's things are put in her house, too, so I can return them to Jen. I don't trust Hawkswood to do that.'

'What are you going to do?' asked Roberta.

Pam smiled bleakly. 'I've no idea. But right now, I'm going to have a cocktail with my friends and try to forget that either Murton or Hawkswood exist.'

CHAPTER 9

Bishop's in England. Current location: Flower Street, Cambridge.

Received. Details?

'Received? Who the fuck writes "received" in an email?' Stephen Mawson muttered to himself. 'What are you going to write next: "over and out?" And what else do you want me to say, you stupid prick? Henry Cox visited the Box Café and spent four pounds fifty, probably on coffee and something. What on earth is that going to serve? And what's point of all this, anyway?'

Stephen had no idea why he was following Henry Cox, codename Bishop any more than he knew why he'd had to do all that stuff on some man in Heraklion in March, codename Clay. 'And why these stupid codenames, anyway,' he said out loud. 'You're not a spook? At least I'm pretty sure you're not.'

That brought him back to the question which annoyed him most: Who the hell was his client? Moros, as he called himself, was the only client whose identity he hadn't managed to uncover within moments of being contacted. He should have refused the job. The only reason he hadn't, was the money, which was good, even by his standards.

'Fucking idiot', he said, flexing his shoulders and

getting up to make himself some more coffee.

He walked across the marble floor, softened and warmed by the addition of the two antique Qum silk rugs he'd bought at auction after his first client paid him a bonus. He gently touched the corner of one of his kitchen cupboards. It opened revealing two bottles of botanical gins and a bottle of rare cask Macallan malt whisky. There were also three packets of single origin Costa Rican coffee beans. He picked up one of the packets and poured some beans into his Sage Oracle coffee machine. At two thousand pounds it was pricier than his old machine, but the coffee was as good as any barista coffee in London, and he enjoyed playing with the touch screen. It was his favourite new toy after his Bang & Olufsen sound system which he loved as much for its sleek design as for its sound. His car, on the other hand, was low key: a black 2011 BMW 3 Series model that was reliable and didn't call attention to itself.

He remembered the first car he'd bought new. It had been a VW Golf, and the first person he'd driven in it was his father who'd passed on his own love of mathematics. He'd been an engineer, too, working for the railways, until cancer put a stop to all of that. And less than a year later, his mother had married the next-door neighbour, the one who'd always called him a moron because of his dyslexia, having picked up that fact from his own son, Harry, a greasy, vicious little prick who was in his class at school.

Funny how things turn out. Harry was now in jail, and his mother and her new husband lived in Australia to avoid the shame. All that kiddie porn the police found on Harry's computer; they never knew how it got there.

Stephen's father had never mocked him; he'd believed in him, just like his maths teacher. One day he'd show how successful he'd become. Except he couldn't because he was now Stephen Mawson, which wasn't the name he'd been at school.

Stephen sipped his coffee and thought about this Moros job. He'd initially spent a week fruitlessly trying to find out who his client was but had to put it on hold when he got busy on another job finding a mountain of undeclared paintings hidden in the Geneva Freeport. Now that had been a challenge to unlock, but it had been worth it in the end. Millions locked away which his client had really appreciated. She'd been a good fuck, too.

That job had been straightforward, but Stephen had no idea what the fuck Moros was doing. First lots of stuff in Greece, in Crete and now Henry Cox. Why him?

Stephen prided himself at being able to get through security walls; it was the reason he was paid such large fees, but with Moros he hadn't even found the wall, though that could also be the language barrier.

'Right, you bugger. I'm coming for you.' He sat down again and went through his notes. 'Well, you're almost certainly Greek, but probably not Intelligence. At least not that I can find. And whoever set up your email was fucking good.'

He'd still not managed to find the source of Moros's email. So many false leads which went round in circles going nowhere. At one point, he thought he was getting somewhere, several leads were taking him to the same hub, but this turned out to be a lighthouse: an empty space that simply emitted signals. Somebody very skilled had set this up, and yes, it could have been a national cyber unit. It was someone whose skills were as good, if not better than his own, but there had to be a link with Greece. Stephen had to be careful there, the Greek Cyber Crime Unit was one of the best in the world and he didn't want to find himself in their crosshairs. Did they know Moros? he wondered. Was Moros linked to Greek Intelligence?

Next the money route. The first part of that was easy, the money Moros paid him came from a Greek account in Athens, but again, it was a dead end. The actual named owner of that account had died ten years previously, and their address now belonged to a Greek chiropodist and his family. Fancy footwork, he thought, and wondered whether it was deliberate, did Moros have a sense of humour? The joke probably didn't translate anyway.

But the money was somewhere. Last time, he'd got as far as finding a shell company based in the Cayman Islands, and now he saw that it received its funds from an account in the British Virgin Islands.

'Would be the bloody Virgin Islands,' he shouted, hurling his coffee cup at a pristine white wall. 'Go on, Moros, really piss me off and choose a country which never reveals the names of its account holders. Make my life really hard why don't you?'

But was there more in that choice, he thought a few moments later, wiping away the coffee stain. The offshore accounts in the British Virgin Islands were loved by serious criminal gangs as well as certain countries wanting to wash large sums. Was Moros attached to one of them?

'OK. You're not my average client.' Not that his clients could be said to be average; ordinary people didn't employ hackers who demanded fifty thousand pounds upfront. Moros certainly had money, but Stephen wasn't going to find out their identity unless he targeted someone who worked in the bank. But that would take his time and money. Did he really need to know? Moros said he'd been recommended by another of Stephen's clients, which is how he had his email, but his only Greek client was the Greek billionaire Nikos Leotakis. He could ask Leotakis directly, but that might make him think that Stephen asked others about him.

Which he didn't. He kept his clients in separate boxes. For his security as much as for theirs.

'So, you're different. Stuff that. Let's put that aside and just look at the job itself.'

The first request had been in Crete. He'd been given the name Zembatakis, codename Clay, a man working in an engineering company in Heraklion and told to insert mistakes into his calculations at work. That was easy; the company had no firewalls or any cyber protection at all, and after Stephen had manipulated some figures, the man lost his job. Moros had then sent Stephen details of a Greek loan shark and asked him to place his ads in Clay's timeline. It was an inviting hook, and he took the bait. Going into Clay's bank account, Stephen found that his rent had also quadrupled. Interesting. Who was the new landlord?

Not too hard to find, even with the language problem. Zembatakis lived in a block of flats which had been bought in February by Alexandros Holdings, which just happened to be based in the British Virgin Islands and pay via the Cayman Islands. 'Got you!' he shouted. It was Moros who'd bought the flats. But why?

Alexandros Holdings did have their real estate online, and there in March they'd sold the block again. But again why? Some family feud? There had to be a reason; there was nothing special about this block. He'd driven past it on Google maps, and it looked like any other anonymous concrete block in a working-class neighbourhood. He looked at the Zembatakis account again. After March, it was suddenly a lot healthier. So why?

'Let's look at the date, Moros. Let's find out why you needed the block just then'. He keyed in March 2018 and Zembatakis. It was all in Greek, which made it harder as it had to go through an automatic translation feature. It wasn't good English, but it was understandable.

The first thing he found was a short piece in the Cretan newspaper *Nea Kriti* and a shorter piece in a paper called *Patris*. Tragedy was how it led in the latter which was a summary of the first article. Death of a promising student, tragic loss.

The body of research student, Lefteris Zempatakis, was deposited on the shore near Heraklion Airport, he read. *It was found by a local fisherman who contacted the police.*

Who was Lefteris? It was the same surname as the engineer. Ah, he read on, it was the son of the engineer. So how did this death fit in?

Stephen read on, using an online translation, and trying to make sense of it all. According to the local university where Lefteris had studied and his boss, he'd been an outstanding student and promising research scientist. Both had made statements regarding his excellent work and promise. It read as though they had assumed it to be an accident, thought Stephen. But no, the next paragraph read *pithani aftokonia*, which translated as possible suicide. The police had reported that his friends said he had been very quiet in recent weeks. There was no report, however, about his parents' money troubles and how they'd ended. But what if Moros had got Lefteris to do something and paid him in cash, using the family debts as leverage? If this was the case, it had been an incredibly complex and time-consuming exercise, and had cost Moros a huge amount of money. He'd sold the apartment block at a loss.

Of course, it might have been a suicide and nothing to do with Moros, but that didn't explain the whole money thing. He read on slowly, translating the obituary word by word. Nothing.

There had to be something he was overlooking. Where did Lefteris work? Was that important? Stephen read the statement made by his boss. Lefteris was based in a unit associated with the Heraklion Medical School, in a Laboratory of Clinical Microbiology and Microbial Pathogenesis. Stephen clicked the link. Happily, there was a version in English. Areas of research were fungal pathogenesis, parasitology, bacterial infections, and environmental microbiology.

Bacterial infections.

Stephen stared at his computer as if it, itself, was infected. No, it couldn't be. Could it? Had he helped set up another nerve agent attack?

He got up from his desk and opened the French windows and stepped onto the wide balcony overlooking the River Thames. In front and to the left was Tower Bridge and beyond it the Tower of London. They used to lock up people like him there.

Had he helped set up another fucking Salisbury? Or was it that the recent novichok incident had made him paranoid? He pounded the metal rail of the balcony until the pain made him stop. He wasn't getting involved in something like that for any amount of money.

'Fuck? Fuck! Fuck!' he yelled.

He came back indoors. Maybe he was just paranoid. There were all kinds of things in a laboratory like that which had a less than benign use, things which certain small armed forces would pay to get their hands on. But why the Cretan link, and how did it tie in with the historian Henry Cox?

He needed to know more. He had to put the bits together.

There was this Cretan bit of the puzzle, and then there were the others. It wasn't just the historian Henry Cox, Moros also wanted him to observe two British police officers who were living in the same village. The first one, Mike Petersen, had been there for a while Stephen learned, and had family in Sitia on his mother's side. Mike had got married at twenty-five in 2003 and divorced five years later. No children. He'd gone undercover in 2012, as part of the Met's now disbanded and criticised National Public Order Intelligence Unit, where he'd reported on the extreme members of an animal rights group. He'd been hospitalised in 2016, and subsequently moved to Crete.

So perhaps this Mike was simply recuperating. But if Moros wanted Stephen to attack him, that wouldn't be hard: the undercover period would be very fruitful. People there who would love to know where Mike was today. As for the policewoman, she'd gone there after leaving the Leotakis residence (so there was a Leotakis connection ... he needed to look into that.) There was a lot of recent media stuff about DI Pam Gregory, making her out to be some kind of supercop, though she was probably the kind who let others do the work while she took the credit. She was hardly using either her phone or her computer at the moment, and he couldn't see any reason to target her. Nor could he see any reason to follow Henry Cox, who appeared to be precisely what his record said he was: a mediocre historian with a private income. He'd checked that, and it was totally legitimate, not a legend placed later. Henry had also done some work for MI6; that came up, but that was nearly forty years ago, and he seemed now to be retired. As he should be. How old was he? Seventy-four?

Then so was that lawyer who had died two days ago. Stephen had been tracking Cox's calls and apart from ones to other English residents of the Cretan village where he lived, there had been just this one. The name was one he knew: Patrice Girard. He'd come across him a couple of times previously as the lawyer who had defended his clients. He'd had links in the past with the Stasi, the French external intelligence agency, the DGSE and possibly the KGB or FSB as it was today.

Maybe Cox was not the ex-agent he appeared to

be, though one thing was clear, people around him were dying. First his closest friend, the archaeologist Stephanie Michaels, and now Patrice. Was Lefteris another man connected to Cox? Had they been lovers? He'd found out from Henry's own writing that he was gay, but there had been no mention of Lefteris, although he did make three trips to Heraklion. Had it just been shame that made the young man end his life? Was being gay something a Greek didn't admit to? Was the lab he worked in merely a coincidence?

One of Henry's latest emails was one he'd sent to Girard's widow, Deirdre. It had been a seemingly sincere email telling her how much he had valued the lawyer's friendship and saying if there was ever anything he could do. But there was more there, thought Stephen, one interesting sentence:

I do understand why the police have taken all of Patrice's papers to aid them in their search for the killer, but once they are returned to you, I would be very grateful to have the opportunity to read them again as part of my research into Patrice's life and work.

Had he been writing about Patrice? That would bring a few nasties out of the woodwork. But there had been no reference to Patrice in any of Henry's other emails. In fact, he'd made it clear that the book he was writing was about Greece after 1973. More specifically, in his recent emails, he'd stated it was about the terrorist group 17 November. Which every source Stephen examined clearly stated that this was now a defunct group. All its members had been arrested. And he couldn't see any link with Patrice Girard. He hadn't acted for any of the defendants at their trial in 2003.

Where was Henry going with this and why did Moros want to know? There had to be something, otherwise Moros would not be paying him large sums to follow him. One useful lead had been an email Cox had sent to an MI6 agent called Christopher Grey.

Just checking you got it. Henry had written. There hadn't been a reply.

Henry hadn't emailed his report, so he must have posted the hard copy. But he had typed it. Stephen had made a copy of Henry's hard drive before placing a small cyber explosive into his system as Moros had asked him to do. People always thought that their word documents were as private as if they'd been written on paper. How wrong they were. Often, they saved them online, sometimes unaware they were doing so, because the system did it automatically. And once online, people like him could read them so easily. He hadn't bothered to read it before, but now he would. If he was setting up Henry's death he did, at least, want to know why. Henry Cox had written himself into danger; Stephen was beginning to have a feeling that the next thing he'd read about code name Bishop was his obituary. And who else was Moros going to target next, the English cops who lived nearby?

He had to get access to that bank account in the British Virgin Islands. Stephen took his leisure phone out of his pocket and called the number of the girl who had only this morning left his bed. He had several girlfriends but had never wanted to commit to any of them, though Tina was the one he saw most often. She was also the most intelligent, running her own small London art gallery and had the most useful friends.

'Tina,' he said when she picked up the phone. 'How would you feel about a weekend in the Caribbean?'

CHAPTER 10

It had been a highly satisfactory few days, thought Henry. He'd done what he needed to do, and everything was ordered and in place, just as he liked it. He looked at his watch, just after half past six; it was still remarkably hot, or had the English climate changed so much that these hot summer temperatures were now the norm?

It was most certainly an evening that called for a cold drink. He wondered whether there was any wine in Stephanie's house, he hadn't yet checked. Jen and Pam had both told him to make himself at home and enjoy anything that was there. Jen had already taken her clothes and a few things to her father's house but said she hadn't bothered emptying the cupboards. There was still coffee though she'd emptied the fridge. He'd already partially replenished that with milk, butter and bread acquired at the local convenience store.

Henry walked briskly down Devonshire Street, his long strides proof of his daily long walks across the mountains at home, and soon arrived at Cambridge Vinopolis, one of his favourite Cambridge shops, perfectly situated on his walk from the station to the house. In the past, he'd have bought a couple of bottles for Stephanie or Jen on his way to Flower Street. Perhaps he should indulge himself with a bottle of something special this evening. Nicolas would be able to suggest a good wine.

He'd enjoyed some excellent conversations with the shop's owner over the years, telling him about the best Cretan wines, but he wasn't in the shop this evening. Instead, a charming young man behind the counter persuaded him to try a bottle of Lucanto, from the Trebbiano grape. The bottle wasn't chilled, so Henry also bought a bottle of cold Alhambra Verde beer from Granada to enjoy while it was cooling.

Henry then turned into Mill Road, the most international of Cambridge's streets, not picturesque like so many or architecturally harmonious like Trinity Lane, but vibrant with people and life, and went into the Al-Amin Stores. Here, the owner was on hand to help him choose some spinach falafel and other bits and pieces for his supper. I do enjoy how these small places have grown in Cambridge, he reflected, as he cut through the cemetery to Norfolk Street. It was heartening to hear success stories like Mr Amin's; it all added to his good mood, and he'd needed good news ever since hearing about Patrice's death.

It was of course possible that his murder had nothing to do with Henry's own research, but the thought of it hung over him along with the nagging question: who was this last member of 17N?

Henry walked down Blossom Street and into Flower Street, the small cul-de-sac that turned into a footpath where it met the playground. He glanced behind him as he turned the corner: the backs of a couple of houses, a garage and the children's playground which was now closed. It was a quiet private space, which was excellent for its residents unless you were afraid that someone might attack you. At night, you could park outside, and nobody would notice; the houses on the other side of the playground were just that bit too far away. This was what had made it so easy for Stephanie's murderer.

This evening there was nobody here, and he let himself in with the new six-pin key that Jen had had cut after her mother's death. Pam had warned her not to give out too many of these. But she'd clearly given it to someone, since there was a note on the glass table in the sitting room addressed to him. He put on his glasses and picked it up.

Dear Mr Cox, it read. So written by someone who didn't know him.

Pam asked us to come by and put some milk and water in the fridge and a bottle of wine. She says you should make yourself at home.

It must be one of Pam's colleagues who'd got the key from the time of Stephanie's investigation. How very typical of Pam to think about him. He was so glad he'd just yesterday put her into his will. She was a delightful young woman with so much potential. He thought he might encourage her to do an Open University degree. She'd enjoy that, and he'd be able to advise her. It was a very long time since he'd had a younger friend he could help; the thought made him very happy.

He'd have the wine with his supper and save the Italian wine for tomorrow. He opened the sliding back door which blended the house and the garden. Colin really was an exceptional architect, this house he'd built for Stephanie when they'd first been married was magnificent. Built on an awkward plot, it was a triangle which led to its walled garden and maximised the light.

He brought out the beer and a glass and put the pistachios and the herb-flavoured olives he'd bought into two small white bowls. Everything here was blue or white; Colin had tried so hard to recreate Greece in Cambridge, but it had not succeeded. Stephanie had never felt at home here. He remembered her many letters, often confessing how guilty she felt that her kind husband and baby daughter weren't enough for her. She was always looking for something else

'Perhaps she found it at the end finding the Chiona treasure and planning the exhibition,' he murmured to himself. 'And with Leotakis.' There was no doubting now their mutual affection. Her death had been so shocking, and in the end, as it turned out, based as it was on false rumours, so senseless.

That was why he mustn't allow himself to write hearsay, he decided. He mustn't mention the possibility of there being a final terrorist who had escaped arrest unless and until he had firm evidence. I'm a historian, not a tabloid journalist, he told himself sternly. Perhaps he should just cut it out of the book altogether and concentrate on why it was inevitable, under the circumstances, that such an organisation would emerge. There were other perfectly satisfactory books about 17 November. There was no need for another.

He knew his publisher, Jules, would be annoyed if he decided not to put it in. They'd had a very enjoyable lunch together today in his favourite tapas bar in Dean Street, the food and wine both being as good as he remembered. The idea that Henry had something of a scoop, as Jules put it, and might therefore sell a few copies of the book, had delighted him and, for once, he had insisted on picking up the bill. Though he'd also mentioned that he'd received a strange email attacking Henry's work.

'From that Greek millionaire, Leotakis. Outrageous. What does he know about history? Threw it straight in the bin.'

'I know Leotakis doesn't like me. Remember I complained about losing my old house, but ...'

'Must be that. So... the sole or the pigeon?'

Henry knew that Jules only published him because of their friendship which went back fifty years; he'd never made money for the company. Friends like that were worth everything. He was so pleased he was able to give Jules a sizeable bequest.

Yesterday, he'd visited another old friend, his solicitor, Ian Coules, and he'd been more than helpful, getting his will written up for him while he waited.

He'd had the idea a few days now. Pam had been a surprising new friend. She'd told him that he was like the perfect uncle she'd never had, and he also thought that in a small way he had begun to replace her much-missed father, perhaps in a way like Mike, who had also lost his father. 'Well, if you can leave your house to Mike, Stefi, my old love,' he said to himself, 'I can leave mine to Pam, she'd appreciate it.' He liked the young policewoman very much and thought how good it was going to be to get to know her better over the coming years. And Jen wouldn't mind, he knew she didn't want to live in Chiona, although Mike had made it clear that her mother's house which she'd left to him, was always open to her. Besides which, his goddaughter was getting the houses he owned in Clarendon and Elm Street, which were currently administered by Emmanuel College, and were bringing in around fifty thousand pounds a year. That kind of money would bring her the freedom to leave academia when and if she wanted. It could even help finance the documentary film she'd told him she might make one of these days. It was good to think that he could make 'one of these days' come a little closer. That was the main estate, but his investments had also done well over the years.

He could use those for the rest of his bequests. He'd decided on a hundred thousand pounds each for Pam and Mike to buy them time to decide what they wanted to do next in their lives. It was the least he could give them. Then there were smaller bequests to his publisher, to others in Chiona and to the LGBT Foundation and the Terence Higgins Trust and a painting for Oliver, who certainly didn't need any money, but whom he made his executor along with Ian himself. He'd very much enjoyed the thought of how happy they'd all be.

Roderick Beaton was high up on the list. Henry had been very touched by the warm review he'd given of his last book, unlike so many. Roderick wrote so well; didn't have his own habit of over-complication and pedantry. They'd had many enjoyable dinners together over the years. Another lunch would be good. They could go to that charming restaurant in Somerset House overlooking the river, next door to King's. He took out his pen.

'A bequest for a scholarship in the name of my admired old friend to be known as the Roderick Beaton award, at £10,000 a year with a capital sum of 200,000. My library and archive to King's College London, along with a bequest of £200,000 towards the storage and display. A bequest in the name of Popi Filotaki to be administered by Mrs Filotaki, and thereafter by whoever she names for helping young people: €200,000.

Finally, he wrote a note for Christopher to be sent to him immediately on his death.

I assume you will now know what to do, he wrote. He'd decided not to visit Christopher, he wasn't sure why exactly, but the lack of response to his report worried him. As he'd said to Oliver. Sending his report to Oliver had been a wise decision and their subsequent telephone call had been most satisfying.

He'd also sent his old friend a letter with details of the funeral service he wanted along with a CD of his selected music and told him he'd made him next of kin in the absence of any family. He'd had a lot of pleasure planning the service. Music from his days in Cambridge attending evensong at King's, some Theodorakis, naturally and Tallis. He would have happily expanded it into a full concert.

'Rather like a person on Desert Island Discs, an indulgence of the old,' he told Oliver.

'You're not that old, Henry,' Oliver replied. 'You're younger than I am.'

'Yes, and I have no wish to depart yet. But it's better to be prepared,' he replied. He'd said much the same to his solicitor, Ian Coules.

'Anything I should know about?' Ian had asked. Henry shook his head. He wasn't about to tell him that he was frightened of being killed by a Greek terrorist. Ian wouldn't have believed it in any case; it was so implausible. Oliver, on the other hand, took the news very seriously.

Henry sipped the beer which was delicious and had a faint taste of oranges. The Alhambra gardens were famous for their orange trees, weren't they? He'd look it up later on his phone. He'd already contacted Pam's colleague, Stuart, who'd been very kind and met him in the café near the police station where Henry told him about his computer and gave him one of his memory sticks, his portable hard drive, and his laptop.

'It could be a virus,' he said, 'it could be something worse. Have you got any enemies out there?'

Henry had smiled as if it was a joke. But he was beginning to think that it very well might not be. He had no wish to die, indeed he felt more energised than he'd been for many years. He discussed a new book with Jules, based on his diaries during the excavation of the Minoan site. He'd been there every day watching the treasures emerge, some from beneath where his former house had stood, and he knew all the archaeologists working there.

'I was there the very moment Petros Manoussis found the golden bull. It was extraordinary, as if you'd been there the momen that they found the Jockey of

Artemision. Except that was found underwater in a shipwreck.'

'I didn't know that,' Jules said. Henry then showed him the bronze sculpture of the racing horse with its young jockey.

'It's in the Archaeological Museum in Athens,' Henry told him. 'You must go and see it.'

'I will,' Jules smiled. 'We could go together if you're in Athens.'

'That would be splendid,' agreed Henry. 'There are daily flights from Sitia. And you could come and sojourn a few nights in Crete. You haven't seen my new home yet. It has a bookcase the whole length of the house.'

'Now that I do envy,' said his friend. 'I never have enough space for my books at home.'

A very satisfactory trip in all ways, he considered. He went to the fridge and took out the bottle of New Zealand Sauvignon Blanc that had been left for him. It was perfectly chilled, and he took out a corkscrew and began to pull out the cork.

He didn't notice, and since his glasses were on the table in the garden, would not have been able to see it, but the spine of the corkscrew went down into a narrow fissure as if a needle had previously been inserted into the bottle.

A few minutes later, when he'd only drunk half a glass of the wine, he found himself becoming incredibly weary.

'Overdoing things, I suppose,' he muttered. 'All that worry about Patrice.'

He brought in the supper things and left them beside the sink and walked heavily upstairs where he undressed, put on his pyjamas and got into bed. Within moments, he was deeply asleep.

Two hours later, a small blue Ford Fiesta pulled up and parked outside the deserted children's playground.

A slim figure, dressed in black, got out, a backpack on their shoulder and, taking a key from their pocket, let themselves into Stephanie's house.

Henry slept on unaware, not even waking when the intruder entered his bedroom. No liquid was in the syringe when it was plunged into his vein, but a small bubble of air began to travel through his body.

As he felt the pain of the needle, Henry jerked upright and only half conscious, opened his eyes. He almost focused on the person in his bedroom then, still drugged from the wine, fell back, unconscious.

It's a dream he's had before. The strange island, white in its heat with a jetty leading to a derelict building he knows, without having ever been inside, has once been used for fish packing. The road beside the sea is long, but never tiring, he's always there, where he needs to be, beside the sea. Usually, the sea is too rough for swimming, the waves foaming dangerously, and besides, every time he's dreamed this dream, he knows there is an injunction against this. If he enters the water, he will never return.

But this time it's different; there is a boat moored on the jetty and it's waiting for him. He can dimly hear the voices of friends … is that Stephanie's laugh? And, yes, yes, it is Laurent in the boat.

'You came back?' he is saying.

'I've waited for you for a long time, Henry,' smiles Laurent, and it is Laurent as they first met, tanned, golden, his dark hair flopping over his eyes.

And he's there in the boat now, and the sea is as calm as it was that morning when together they swam towards the morning sun.

'Laurent,' he whispers, 'I'm home, aren't I?'

CHAPTER 11

Mike lay in bed unable to sleep. All the problems he'd been putting aside for some undetermined future date had come back. Pam was talking about resigning, and wondering what she could do with her life, which forced him to ask the same questions.

Which Henry had asked just the other day. As had Zofia and Grace, who missed nothing. When he'd told them he couldn't go back to England, Zofia had asked why. 'There are people there who want me dead,' he replied, as he always did, the reply that usually ended the questioning. But Grace hadn't let it go.

'A lot of us, even those working in mental health, as well as the police and others working in criminal justice have had people say they'd kill us,' Grace replied. 'It rarely happens. Very few of them become murderers and risk further jail terms.'

'As you say, it's a risk they take. I can think of at least one of them who'd take that risk. And if anyone published a picture of me, it would get back to him and his friends. Some of them have killed before.'

'In cold blood or as part of an operation?'

'The latter. A bomb went off in a building they thought was empty.'

'Very different from face-to-face murder.'

He'd nodded but felt that she thought he was

exaggerating the risk. Was he? And what would be the point of going back, what would he do in England? He certainly didn't want to go back to being a cop.

Mike heaved himself out of bed and looked at his phone. It was three am, a vile hour to be awake. He wondered whether Stephanie had spent sleepless hours in this house. What did she do?

She probably wrapped herself in one of her shawls and went and sat in her garden waiting for the dawn, he thought. And opened another bottle. There were times these days when he really wanted a drink, which made it all the more important he didn't start again. Maybe he should go for a night swim. Put all these thoughts aside. Something would turn up.

He walked through the house and saw that the door to the garden was open. He stiffened. 'Mike?' came a whisper.

'You can't sleep either,' he replied.

'No,' said Pam. He could see her now in the moonlight; she was lying on the wicker sofa, a shawl round her shoulders. 'My leg aches and my head aches and feels like the inside of a washing machine, everything going round and round.'

'Yeah. Just the same. Fancy a cup of tea?'

'Yes please. Proper tea.'

They sipped for a moment in silence. The sea plashed softly on the beach just beyond the house and, in the distance in one of the hillside farms, a dog howled.

'It's brought it all back to you, hasn't it? All this stuff about my job.'

Mike nodded and Pam looked at him anxiously. Nobody should ever spend so much time undercover, she thought, it's not fair on them or those they encounter. If she'd been ordered to do that, would she have had the courage to say no? She wasn't at all sure.

'It's not just about being undercover. It was my

girlfriend, Julie. There was an incident… I was in a pub with Julie and there was this group of hoorays making it hard to hear the music. It was a great local group. I asked them to be quiet and they threatened me, and I, like an idiot, threatened them back. When we left, they were waiting for me and one of them was an off-duty cop. He beat the crap out of me and I ended up in hospital. Later, I found out that he told Julie who I really was, but I didn't discover that until her inquest. One of his mates told me.'

'Oh Mike!'

'The inquest only gave the bare bones; I got the details later from a friend. Apparently, before the bastard of a constable kicked me in the spleen, I'd broken his nose. He made a point of going to visit Julie and telling her fake details of my undercover work. He made it out that I'd reported on her and slagged her off. Which wasn't true. She killed herself and our kid. She was four months pregnant.'

'Shit!'

'But that's not all. You see the name I used, well it's the way all of us chose our names. We called it the jackal hunt because that's what the guy does in the *Day of the Jackal*… we found out the names of babies and children who'd died and made legends for ourselves using those names.'

'I didn't know that. I always thought that was fiction.'

'Well, it came from fiction.' He got up and began to pace across the courtyard. 'I keep thinking if my name comes out, along with the name I used, Mike Cowley, it could start a witch-hunt. There are reporters looking into all this. There could be a mother out there still mourning for the baby Mike Cowley. I never had the right to take his name.'

Pam took a deep breath. Think what Grace would

say, she told herself. What you say now matters.

'You can't undo what happened,' she told him. 'But you can control your future and what you do with the rest of your life. You have the opportunity now to turn it around and make the world better.'

'But what if I can't get past what I did?'

'You have to. I used to think that it was my fault that Richard hurt me. And he really did hurt me. He kicked me just like that copper kicked you – same uniform boots. And he killed my son, too.'

Pam stopped. 'You don't mind my telling you this?'

'Course not.' Mike sat down on the chair and sipped his tea again. In the past he'd have reached for a drink. He tested himself: did he want one? Actually, he didn't. He'd passed that test. He thought about how Pam managed to deal with her own pain; one day he'd tell her how much he admired her.

'It was just over ten years ago,' she was saying. 'He'd have been ten now. I try not to think about that too often. He was a boy. I already knew that; I was five months pregnant. Richard was drunk. He wanted me to stop working – give in my notice, but I knew if I didn't have the job, I'd have nothing except him and the baby. I wouldn't have any support. So, for the first time, I stood up to him and refused. He went crazy. Beat me up and then when I was on the ground, he started kicking me until I passed out. Then he got scared. Called one of his buddies and they made him take me to the hospital. I lost the baby. And any future babies.'

'I'm so sorry.' He reached out and put a hand on her arm. She patted it absent-mindedly.

'Zofia got to hear of it. I'd met her a few times. When I was able to leave hospital, she smuggled me out without anyone knowing – via the morgue which is quite funny, really – and she and Grace hid me in their house until I managed to get a restraining order against

Richard. He tried to break it a few times, but by then I had a couple of my colleagues on call, and they kept him away. He'd got himself thrown out of the Force by then and moved to Northampton. He'd grown up round there. I've never seen or heard from him since, thank God.'

'I hope you never do,' Mike told her.

'I'll second that,' she half-laughed.

'So…' he began.

'So? That's one of my words. Josh, he's my sergeant… was my sergeant… once told me I begin almost every sentence with that. But, Mike, the problem is that right now I don't have a 'so', which is why I'm sitting out here. I've always known what I was doing next. Ever since school. And now…'

She let the sentence hang unfinished and he knew it was equally true for him. And now what? he wanted to ask, now what do either of us do with our lives?

'Trouble is,' he found himself saying, 'trouble is, Pam, I'm still not at all sure I deserve to go on living.'

Pam turned and smiled at him.

'I'm not going to answer that,' she said, 'but I will tell you some of the stuff that Grace told me when I felt the same. She draws a lot from Buddhist teaching and how it makes us live in the moment. I can remember what she told me back then. She said we live in a world obsessed with time, constantly looking back, and picking at the scabs of our wounds. We can't change the past and the future is something we can't control, but we can control the present. Do the best that you can every day and be kind to yourself and to others. Make your life be about the present.'

Thinking of the past interfering with the future reminded Pam about Henry. She wondered how he was. He'd been in Cambridge a few days now. She'd give him a ring in the morning. Except it already was the morning, and Stavros was arriving first thing Saturday and she didn't want to look as if she hadn't slept all week.

Stavros. Another question mark in her life. She felt exhausted by it all.

'Think I'll go and get a few hours' sleep,' she told Mike.

'Good idea,' he told her. 'I'll go for a swim and make us all breakfast later.'

'Bacon and eggs, please,' she told him.

Without anything being said, it seemed as though everyone had picked up the underlying current of the day and understood that Pam wanted some time on her own. Zofia and Grace swam in the morning and spent the rest of the day exploring Sitia, having drinks and supper in the town. Mike had some work repairing a dry-stone wall for a Dutch family who had a holiday home in Palaikastro, and in the evening, he went into town to watch the England-Sweden quarter final with family and friends. Pam spent the day reading and swimming and made herself salads from the cheeses and vegetables in the fridge. She tried ringing Henry a few times, but it seemed his phone was turned off. Probably writing or busy, she thought.

There was a distant sound of music from one of the houses and laughter. The various families were all beginning to arrive for the summer and soon Chiona wouldn't be so peaceful. It would be different living here at the height of the season.

Later in the evening, she decided to have a look at Stephanie's library. There were a lot of books about Crete she'd love to read sometime and books on archaeology that looked too academic for her. She took down a book called *Spirit of Place* by Lawrence Durrell, who she knew from the television series was the writer brother of the animal collector who'd had his childhood on Corfu.

The second line of the preface was in Latin which

almost put her off, but that was the editor, not Larry, as she couldn't help thinking of him after the television series. The book was mostly letters and bits of travel writing that seemed pleased with itself. Then, glancing at the end, she came across a letter to his aunt about coming to Greece being a sea change, a journey into the heart of the Minotaur and she found herself carried away by his description. That is what it's like, she thought; he's nailed it. You don't come through this and remain the same; it's what Zofia and Grace don't get, and what she knew nobody back home would understand at all. But every Cretan would know exactly what he meant. And why it spoke to her. She couldn't wait to talk about it with Stavros. She was longing to see him again, she realised, and decided on that happy note to go to bed.

She pulled out one of Henry's notebooks to take with her to her bedroom. She wanted to learn about this terrorist group he was writing about; she'd never heard of them before. Was there really a lone member still out there? It was probably something they'd never find out. She read a little, but soon found herself falling asleep and allowed herself a very early night.

Stavros had got the overnight ferry from Piraeus and drove up in time for breakfast. Mike had bought fresh bread from Maddalena, squeezed some oranges, and put out honey before tactfully leaving for Palaikastro again. Whatever else happened, she knew that he was going to remain a very close friend. She was glad he'd given her time on her own to spend with Stavros. They were both slightly shy having fallen for each other so quickly, and then falling out when Pam took over Jen's rescue. She didn't know which Stavros she was going to face today. Was it the man she couldn't keep her hands off or the one she wanted to slap?

It seemed as if it was the first. Stavros was in holiday mode in faded jeans and an olive-green T-shirt, that looked as though it had been dried in the sun. It was the first time she'd seen him when he wasn't on duty, and she liked his more relaxed look. She was wearing the same button-through sleeveless dress she'd worn when she first arrived in Crete, and she wondered whether he'd remember that. He did and remarked on it.

'Though you look much better now than you did then. Sun and sea suit you,' he told her.

'The doctor is very pleased with me. I'm even allowed to go swimming. I thought we might this morning unless...'

'Sounds perfect. I've had a vile week, had to drive twice to Corinth and back because an infuriating Scottish driver thinks local laws don't apply to him when he's on holiday, and refuses to pay for the damage for driving into a field of melons.'

Pam laughed. 'Which was a serious o-fence,' she replied.

'Boum boum!' laughed Stavros.

'You know Basil Brush? How?'

'What else do students watch, especially after a few puffs? When I first went to uni in Brighton, I improved my English watching Postman Pat and Grange Hill. Though to start with I couldn't understand a word the kids were saying.'

'I grew up watching Postman Pat,' she said.

'I'm trying to imagine you as a child,' he told her.

'I had plaits, which I hated.'

'I'd have pulled them.' He moved his chair closer to hers and stroked her hair.

'Only once,' she told him. 'I'd have decked you.'

'Really?'

'No,' she laughed again. 'I was far too well behaved.'

'I wish I knew you better.'

'How could you? After all we've only known each other for how long... three days?

'Even less,' he replied.

'You see. We need to get to know each other.'

'You want me to woo you?

'That would be nice.' She watched as Stavros got up from his chair and walked across the room; it was just the same as she'd felt that first evening: this was the man she'd wanted all her life. Her feelings hadn't changed. If anything, they'd intensified.

'For how long?' he asked. He turned and smiled at her. Pam looked at him. Her body tingled.

'At least until I've finished my coffee.'

Later, in each other's arms they planned the rest of the weekend. Stavros was due to catch the evening ferry on Sunday which gave them almost two days together.

'I thought we could go to the monastery at Toplou. Your friends will like that. It has some excellent icons. And the monks make wine and olive oil.'

'Yes, they'd love that. I said we'd meet them for lunch at the taverna at two.'

'Two! You're becoming positively Greek.' He kissed her shoulder and then her neck.

'Oh I am. I can even make Kolokith… you know the courgette rissoles with feta. But I still can't say it.'

'Say after me… *kolokithokeftede*s.' Never had a word sounded sexier, she thought. '*Kolokithokeftedes,*' she repeated until his kisses made speech impossible.

The rest of the morning, which wasn't spent in bed, was spent swimming and talking and by the time they met up with Grace and Zofia at the taverna, she'd begun to wonder whether she could start a new life with him in Athens. He'd tactfully not mentioned it, though she knew it didn't mean that he wasn't thinking about it.

They nibbled on a Greek salad with fresh chopped oregano sprinkled on the cheese while they waited for their fish to be cooked. Stavros and Grace shared memories of Brighton pubs since it turned out that Grace had once had a girlfriend who lived there.

Zofia gave Pam a surreptitious thumbs up when Stavros wasn't looking, and while she didn't need him to get her friends' approval, she was glad they liked him.

Pam was just about to tell Zofia about the trips she and Stavros had planned for the weekend when her phone rang.

'It's Roberta,' she said. 'I'd better take this.'

'Pam,' said Roberta, 'are you sitting down?'

'Yes,' she replied. 'Why?'

'I'm afraid I've got some very sad news. Henry's dead.'

CHAPTER 12

Pam shushed the others with a hand as she listened to her former sergeant.

'I'm ringing you now because you're likely to get a call from Hawkswood. It's about Henry... no, don't ask anything yet,' Roberta continued, as Pam began to interrupt, 'let me tell you what happened. I went round with Paul to take your stuff from your old house ...we actually did it in one trip, you don't have a lot of stuff, do you? And when we got there, it was clear someone else was there. Paul made one of his jokes about never having guns when you need them. Sorry, I'm not telling you this properly. We saw that someone was there or had been there...there was a jacket on the chair, and a plate and a glass and a beer bottle on the kitchen worktop. As if someone had just had supper.'

'Was it Henry? He said he might...'

'I went upstairs,' Roberta continued, 'I'm so sorry, Pam.' She gulped. She hadn't often been the one telling family and friends about a death, that was something Pam always did. Her boss. Soon to be her former boss. She'd never let on how hard it was. 'I am doing this really badly ...Yes, it was Henry. His wallet was still in his jacket. I found him in bed.'

'In bed?'

'He'd been dead a while, possibly a day or two. Paul

called it in, and the deputy pathologist, Peter Croyden, came straight away. Zofia's on holiday,' she added.

'I know. She's here, sitting opposite me right now.' Zofia raised her eyebrows quizzically.

'Well, Croyden said immediately that he didn't think it was a suspicious death. Heart failure, he thought. Actually, I don't know whether this helps, because Josh says you've got to know Henry a bit… I rang him to let him know.'

More than a bit, she thought. Almost like the family I've always wanted.

'I've never seen a more peaceful death.' Roberta thought back to the last death she'd seen. Not Stephanie Michaels, she'd only seen photographs of her, but a young junkie they'd found down behind the station. Ray. He'd looked drained of life in every way, and old. Way older than his age which had been fifteen. Henry had just looked as if he'd been dreaming and younger. She told that to Pam.

'He actually looked happy. He had that transparent look you get, but you could tell it wasn't a violent or painful death. I thought that would help.'

'Thank you, Roberta. It does. When's the autopsy?'

'Monday. Croyden organised it since it didn't seem that Henry had a doctor in England.'

'He didn't. His doctor is in Sitia. He had a check-up recently and said that he was fighting fit.'

'Well, things can seem like that, can't they? But it will probably be straightforward; we've signalled it as not suspicious. Looked like a natural death.'

'But I'm sure it wasn't. That's what I'm telling you.'

'Pam, there was no sign of forced entry, the front door was locked, and the place was immaculate. Henry was in his pyjamas. But if there was something, Croyden will find it. Oh, by the way, do you know who the next of kin is?

'He didn't have any family,' Pam replied. 'Only his goddaughter, Jen. I'll let her know. But...' she thought for a moment. 'He might have used the same solicitor as Stephanie. It's just the kind of thing they might have discussed. Can't remember his name right now, but ask Sue Forrester,' she continued, remembering how her constable had got on really well with Stephanie's solicitor. 'She'll know. In fact, she'd be the best person to go and ask him.'

'Sounds like a plan, boss, thank you. I'll let Martin know. Can't guarantee this will prevent him from calling you, but I'll do my best. Oh. I'm sorry for your loss.' I ought to have said that much earlier, thought Roberta. Damn, I did that badly.

'No,' said Pam, sharply. 'No. I want to talk to the DI, sorry, DCI. I know you said it was a natural death, but I do have a reason to believe it wasn't. Henry Cox thought he was in danger. It could have been murder.'

'Right,' replied Roberta, slowly. 'I'll tell him.' If only to annoy him, she thought. She'd already applied for a transfer to Leicestershire where her husband could also find work; without Pam at the helm, the EASOU team were scattering.

'Murder?' said Stavros as she clicked off and put the phone in her pocket. 'What's happened, Pam?'

'I'm sorry everyone, but I need to get back to the house. I have to make some calls. Henry's dead.'

'Pam, I'm so sorry. Are you okay?' asked Zofia.

'No,' Pam replied. 'I'm most definitely not okay. My sergeant thinks Henry died in his sleep just because he looked peaceful. I think he was murdered and because I'm not there, his death isn't being investigated properly. Zofia, you know Croyden, is he willing to accept he may be wrong? Can you ask him to have another look? Actually,' she continued, 'I think I need to go back to Cambridge. I'm sorry to cut short your holiday, but if we go back tomorrow, could you have a look at Henry?'

'For God's sake, Pam,' said Zofia. 'You're just rushing ahead here. Croyden is perfectly capable. If he wasn't, I wouldn't have left him in charge, and no, you can't ask him to take another look unless you've got clear proof of wrongdoing. It's not even as though it's your case. And also no, I can't barge in on his patient and have a look myself even if I wanted to. Which I don't.'

'You don't understand...' began Pam.

'No, I bloody don't,' shouted Zofia. Several people stopped eating and talking and turned to stare at this tall, loud, pink-haired woman.

'Look,' said Stavros getting up. 'I think we'd better continue this back at the house. I'll go and tell the restaurant we won't be having our lunch.'

'Oh God, they all know Henry well, they'll be so upset,' said Pam balancing herself with her stick.

'I'll tell them tactfully,' said Stavros getting up from his seat and going inside. Almost immediately, they heard the sound of sobbing.

'Maddalena! I have to tell Maddalena,' Pam said urgently

'Who?' asked Zofia.

'The baker. She's known Henry for decades. They're all going to be devastated. And so soon after Stephanie.'

'Let Stavros tell them,' suggested Grace.

'No,' said Pam, beginning to make her way back towards her house, Stephanie's house, the house where Henry had also spent so much time. 'I'll go and tell her first, and then I'll ring Jen. Poor Jen, so soon after her mother. Oh, and Popi,' she went on half speaking to herself and half to Zofia and Grace who were following her. 'I must tell Popi. Unless Jen wants to. Yes, maybe that's best; she'll want to speak to her godmother.'

Zofia looked at Grace anxiously. She knew that

there were all kinds of psychological reactions connected with PTSD, if Pam was still suffering from the trauma of being shot. But as far as she could remember from her studies, these involved anxiety and personal paranoia, not this kind of hysteria. But maybe it could lead to this, too. She needed to ask Grace and look it up. In the meantime, she had to calm Pam down.

'Just let her talk it out,' whispered Grace. 'Don't contradict her.'

'Easier said than done,' Zofia whispered back. 'You know she's talking absolute rubbish. It's almost as though she wants this death to be murder.'

Pam stopped at Maddalena's on her way home. She felt that a new friend like her owned it to Henry's oldest friends to let them know. And Maddalena was also a hub of information; the whole village and soon, Palaikastro and half of Sitia would know, too.

Stavros had caught up with them and was able to translate. The elderly baker began to weep, and Stavros helped her to a chair. Tears ran down her lined cheeks and she wiped them away with a corner of her apron, as she started to tell him how she'd met Henry, and how kind he'd always been to her and her husband, who had died not two years ago.

'The police in England said it was very peaceful,' said Stavros in Greek. Maddalena nodded and thanked him. 'He was smiling in his sleep.'

Stavros decided not to translate this to Pam. Like her two friends, who seemed very sensible, he couldn't understand why she wanted to think it wasn't a natural death. He sighed.

Just an hour ago he'd been so happy that he and Pam were back together again; it was years since he'd felt like this about a woman. He'd even imagined that they might have a life together, that she might be able to move to Athens, but now this. Once again, she'd turned into this manic creature, just as she had before when she suddenly realised who Stephanie's killer was. Well, it was better to know now than later.

Back at the house, Grace and Zofia busied themselves in the kitchen putting together some bread and cheese to replace their missing lunch, while Stavros called the local police whom he'd got to know on his last visit, and Pam went out into the garden and called Mike.

She heard his intake of breath. He's holding himself together, she thought; this is going to really upset him when he's so vulnerable. But at least he wouldn't think she was inventing her murder fears.

'I'll be right back,' he told her. 'I'll just ring Aunt Sofia. Then I'll be back. Oh, Pam…'

'Yes. I can't bear it either,' she said, thinking how quickly the word would now get out now. Mike's aunt knew just about everyone in Sitia, and half the town were cousins or half-cousins. And Maddalena would tell the other half. 'Will the funeral be in England?' he asked.

'I don't know. I've suggested that one of my constables go and talk to his solicitor, I'm hoping he had the same one as Stephanie.'

'I have a vague feeling he did,' he replied.

'That will help.' But it won't help Henry, she added silently to herself. I've only just got to know him, and I'll miss him so much. 'You must…

'Yes,' he said unwilling to finish the sentence or articulate how much Henry's death hurt.

Action, she told herself: ring Hawkswood. It was a phone call she didn't want to make.

'I do not understand why you are calling me,' he said sneering, 'unless you simply want to interfere. There is no case here and there won't be a case. Excuse me,' he added and then cut her off.

'You bastard,' she swore. 'You fucking bastard. You really enjoyed that.'

The day was just getting worse and worse, and next she had to do the really hard job, ring Jen. How was she going to cope, so soon after her own mother's death? Or maybe she should ring Colin, Jen's father? Yes. It would be easier for Jen to hear the news from him. Having seen just how close they were after Jen's rescue she knew he'd know how to comfort her. Like my own father would have done, she thought, too, suddenly missing him dreadfully.

Colin, it turned out, worked from home and Jen was there for the weekend. Oh yes, Pam remembered, it was Saturday. And he was very grateful Pam had rung him first.

'I'll let you know about the funeral arrangements,' Pam told him.

'Another funeral. So soon,' he sighed. 'It's so sad. We were all so fond of Henry. He supported me tremendously when I was married to Stephanie and she was being impossible, and then again when she walked out on me. I feel I've known him most of my life. But at least this wasn't a violent death. That's one thing to be thankful for.'

Pam decided it was better for both him and for Jen not to contradict him on this. Her investigations wouldn't concern either of them. They didn't need to know that Henry had been murdered. She was sure this was the case, that Henry had been right to be scared, and that it was all about this last terrorist person. And whatever anyone else said, she was going to investigate it. She listened to Colin and murmured reassuringly. He was saying that Jen would ring Popi.

'She'll be glad to talk to her,' he said. 'Popi's been very strange these last few days. She hasn't wanted to talk to Jen at all. I think she may have had a bit of a breakdown.'

Even therapists can suffer trauma, reflected Pam,

putting the phone down on the table; guilt can be incredibly harmful. She thought about Mike. She was so glad he'd be back soon.

She realised she'd been standing all this time and her leg was beginning to throb. I have to investigate this somehow, she decided, but they're not going to let me go back on duty. It's not going to be easy unless I can persuade Martin to look into it. And Zofia.

She sat down on the wicker sofa and began to cry.

Stavros came out and put his arms around her and she allowed herself to cry into his shoulder. Then she gently pushed him away and blew her nose.

'I know you think I've gone crazy,' she said, as Zofia and Grace joined them. Grace passed her a glass of water and she gulped it down. 'But Henry was convinced that his investigations had uncovered the identity of a terrorist, and one who'd kill to keep their name hidden. He'd known that because of what he'd been told by a French lawyer friend of his. Who was shot on Sunday.'

'Is that what the French police believe?' asked Stavros.

'I've no idea what they think,' replied Pam. 'But Henry said that they'd removed all his papers from his home.'

'But there's no evidence linking that murder with Henry?' continued Stavros. 'You only have Henry's own thinking on that.'

'Yes, I know,' said Pam. 'And the lawyer, his name was Patrice, did have a lot of possible enemies.'

'But his death could have been something completely different. You don't know.'

'No, I don't,' conceded Pam. 'But Henry certainly thought it was because Patrice was upset by something this terrorist said about another attack. And because of that he was to tell Henry their name. It's all about 17 November, which was the group Henry was writing about. The final terrorist who was never caught.'

'17 November?'

'Yes. Henry was writing about the seventies in Greece.'

'Pam, this is something I do know about,' said Stavros. 'This case was very important to us. You can't just leap in and accuse us of letting one of the terrorists go free because that never happened. All the terrorists associated with the 17 November Group were arrested and are now in jail. I even temporarily worked alongside one of the police officers who was involved in the arrest when I was in London. They uncovered thousands of pages of documents from the safe house which detailed everything. There are *no* missing terrorists. It's simply untrue.'

'You don't know that,' retorted Pam.

'I do, because I know there is the evidence to back up my argument. Please, Pam, be sensible. Think like a cop and not like Henry's friend. Henry had a theory and it led to him becoming afraid because of it. That's just the kind of thing that can lead to someone elderly having a heart attack, isn't it?'

He turned to Zofia who nodded. 'It sounds exactly like the kind of nagging worry that could create stress and lead to an attack,' she agreed.

'But there are drugs that can simulate heart failure, though, aren't there?' insisted Pam. 'What about insulin?'

Zofia sighed. 'Yes, Pam there are such drugs, but they all usually lead to heart attacks where the victim dies in pain. And often from choking on vomit. They don't lead to heart failure and the peaceful death that Roberta reported. That sounds to me like a release from stress and a natural death. And that's the last thing I'm going to say on the subject. I am not going to get involved.'

'Even if I can find the evidence that shows that

Henry was on the track of a terrorist.'

'A terrorist, who as Stavros has just pointed out, also doesn't exist. Pam, you have to stop this right now. If you don't, you'll start to become one of those conspiracy theorist nuts, and I really couldn't bear to see that happen to you.'

'I wouldn't enjoy it either,' said Pam, dryly.

'Then you'll let it go,' echoed Grace.

'You can be sure I won't mention it to any of you again,' she replied.

'That's good,' said Zofia, but Grace frowned at Pam. That was very specific wording.

'But I don't want to ruin your last day,' Pam continued, smiling at her. 'Stavros, my love, would you mind taking Zofia and Grace to that monastery without me? I need to be here when Mike gets back and .... well, you and he have never really got on.'

'That was before,' began Stavros. 'When I first met you both, and I thought you and he were... Anyhow,' he turned to Zofia and Grace, 'I'd be happy to spend the day with you. We can go to the Toplou Monastery, and then I'll drive you down to the beach at Vai. It's not so busy in the late afternoon, and it is worth seeing. It's like the Caribbean, a forest of palm trees.' He smiled at Pam. 'I'll take you another time.'

Pam tried to smile back. He really believed she agreed with him about 17 November, she thought sadly. He thinks I'd be willing to drop the whole thing just like that and write off Henry as some kind of conspiracy nut. He doesn't know me at all.

'But I do think I need to go back to Cambridge,' Pam added. 'I have to make sure Jen's house is okay, and also find myself a new job. Just as well as you're flying back on the Leotakis jet tomorrow. I'll let Eleni know so she can tell the pilot and get me put on the list.'

'Eleni?' queried Zofia

'She's Mr Leotakis's organiser. She makes things happen, doesn't she, Stavros?'

'She could run the country, that woman,' said Stavros. 'Formidable.'

'She even scared Superintendent Murton,' added Pam.

'Now that's something I'd have enjoyed watching,' said Zofia. 'I'm sorry,' she added. 'I'm sorry you've lost your friend. I'm sorry if we sounded heartless earlier.'

'He was like an old uncle,' said Pam. 'I shall miss him.'

She lay back and shut her eyes. She couldn't keep it up any longer. But they'd be gone soon, and she'd be back in Cambridge.

A little later, after Stavros had left with Zofia and Grace, she heard Mike's car pull up. He came into the house and hugged Pam, who started crying again.

'So, he was right,' she said, sniffing.

'Looks that way.' His eyes were also red.

'I'm going back to Cambridge tomorrow,' she told him. 'We have to find out who killed him.'

CHAPTER 13

'One does not make revolutions by halves.'
Louis St-Just

CHAPTER 14

The Royal and National Bank wasn't the oldest bank in the British Virgin Islands, nor the largest, but it made up for these shortcomings by having the grandest facade in Road Town. Stephen moved his mouse up and down the road outside and pictured himself going in. There would be checks and security, he imagined, and then, when he revealed how much money he wanted to transfer to their bank, there would be a private room. Coffee or cold drinks. Whisky. Or, being the Caribbean, would they offer rum? No. That was for tourists, not for investors with a couple of million dollars. It would be a rare Macallan or another well-aged malt.

He could go there another year, but not during the hurricane season. Tina had proved her usefulness by having done the checking he never bothered to do.

'The Caribbean?' she'd said when he phoned her, 'Lovely. Don't have a lot on right now, most of my clients are away and I don't have a new show till September. As long it's not somewhere that's about to be hit with a hurricane.'

'Hurricane?'

'Beryl.'

'Beryl! What kind of name is that?'

'So where were you thinking of going?

'The British Virgin Islands.'

'The British Virgin Islands? Forget it, sweetie-poo. It's bang in Beryl's pathway. I know because my friend Etoile is on a salsa holiday in Cuba, and she's petrified. Sorry, Stephen, but I can't say I fancy a bumpy flight followed by a dangerous helicopter shuttle, or even more frightening boat trip to a small island, which will be flooded.'

'I don't either.'

'It isn't fun. Tropical hotels are simply awful when it rains. Have you seen that old film *Rain*? People stuck in a bar ready to kill each other. Think Joan Crawford was in it or was it Ava Gardner? Can't remember much about it except lots of people shouting and the sound of rain on the roof. You can take me to the Caribbean after Christmas if you like, but when the weather's this glorious I'd rather stay at home and drink Pimm's in the garden.'

Stephen hadn't seen the film, though would now look it up so he could comment on it. Tina was, as usual, an invaluable link to the world of the rich. Her father was a minor diplomat working at various embassies around the world; Tina had been sent to boarding school in England and had then done some kind of history of art course in Florence before using some family money to open her own gallery.

'Of course,' he said. 'It was just a business trip, but not essential. I was so caught up in work I hadn't actually thought about where I was going. I'll contact him remotely. What would I do without you?'

Tina laughed. 'Pimm's in your garden sounds delicious,' he told her.

It was not a major problem; instead of doing it in person, he worked online and decided to follow the pattern of the Cretan student and his father. Whoever Moros was, they weren't stupid.

'Computer ...' he muttered, as his coffee machine

purred, 'find me an employee with money problems.' Two days and endless cups of coffee later, Stephen found Salvador Martinez.

'Oh, you little rogue,' he laughed, delightedly to himself. 'You're exactly the man I need.' It was even better than he'd hoped; Salvador didn't just have financial problems he was stealing small amounts of money from his clients' accounts.

Now it was time for the pitch:

Hello Salvador, you don't know me, but you're a thief. You've stolen this and that. But this is your lucky day. I am not the police.

An hour later, Salvador agreed that it would be in his interest to find the name and address of one of the bank's clients in return for his thefts being covered up and the money restored.

You can do that? Why you do that?

Because I need you and you now need me. Watch. Stephen commanded over the shared screen. Stephen had now taken over control of Salvador's screen to the latter's horror. I ought to be happy to see the money returned to the original account, thought Salvador, but dreaded what he'd have to do now. It was going to be something bad, something which could see him fired or even arrested. But he didn't have a choice, he had five kids and a pile of debts. He wished he'd never stolen the money in the first place; he'd never have done it if he hadn't been desperate and if his family hadn't been at risk.

Stephen neither knew nor cared about this. It was merely a way to achieve his goal. The money he used to pay off the clients' loss came from one of his own new accounts at the bank he'd set up the previous day. No record now remained in Salvador's clients' accounts of there ever having been a few hundred dollars missing.

Of course, I could move larger sums from your

clients into your account which would almost certainly be noticed, Stephen told the hapless cashier who was still hesitating.

What do you want? asked Salvador. He prayed it wasn't going to be something impossible.

Find me the current account for an organisation called Alexandros Holdings.

We have one account in that name, Salvador typed. *It has the original address of an Athenian bank and there is just under three million US dollars in this account today.*

Excellent, responded Stephen, wondering whether he might take some of it out. It could certainly prove a useful source of finance in the future. *Send me the account number and also the original address given when the account was opened.*

I can do that,' Salvador replied. *But we are talking thirty years ago, I would have to go to the archive.*

Then go to the archive, Stephen told him.

I will, replied Salvador. *But you do not want to draw attention to this, I think. I will go when I have another reason. A real reason. This happens about once a week and I can arrange it. Then I can tell you the original name and address.*

I don't have time. Be creative and find an excuse. I need to have the address today. You know what might happen if I got annoyed with you.

I'll do it,' replied Salvador.

Good, wrote Stephen. *Then all your troubles will go away*. He put more of the money Salvador had stolen back into the original accounts and replaced it with some cash of his own. That would keep the cashier focused, and, in the meantime, he was free to look into Moros's latest target, the English policewoman, Pam Gregory.

He could also ask Tina over a drink and take her to dinner.

'Do you mind dreadfully,' she said when he called her, 'but Charlie's just flown in from Cannes, she's staying at Ariadne's flat in Fulham with Squeak and Possum, and I promised to go over there for a few drinkies.'

Squeak? Was that a female? It seemed Charlie was. And Possum?

'He's really called Sebastian, but he's been Squeak ever since prep school.'

'You go,' said Stephen. 'Enjoy yourself. Another time.'

'You're so sweet.'

If she really knew, he thought, then put her out of his mind. He wanted to explore the world of Nikos Leotakis, his most important client and the man who might have recommended him to Moros.

It seemed highly unlikely that Leotakis was Moros. If Nikos wanted chemicals, he'd buy a research laboratory. The way that Moros had set up the researcher and used him was sly and relatively inexpensive. It didn't have the footprint of the billionaire and as for chemical weapons...no, that didn't tally one bit with what he knew about Leotakis. This was a man who was sincere in his environmental work and who appeared to have had a rigid code of ethics. At least now, in his eighties, he could afford one; he had not been so particular when he was young.

Stephen took a beer from the fridge and opened it. Nikos Leotakis was the only man in the world who knew that Stephen Mawson was a fiction and that he'd invented himself. He thought back to their first meeting. Four years ago, just when he'd first begun to develop his fictional identity. It had taken several months to create Stephen with his schools, (Kensington in West London, rich and anonymous), colleges (his own, Keble, Oxford) and even one or two pieces about him that looked as though they had been printed in the school magazine. It was miles away from his actual birthplace just outside Swindon, and his fictional family (now conveniently deceased) had nothing in common with his real family.

It was not merely that his mother had never bothered to understand him; she didn't belong in his new world. Since his gym training, she probably wouldn't even recognise him. Today, he was Stephen Mawson, and Stephen Mawson was charming, good looking and rich.

With Tina's guidance, Stephen had also started to buy art, specialising in the Italian Futurists. He now had oils by Umberto Boccioni and Carlo Carrà, in addition to several watercolours and prints by Gino Severini and a relatively unknown Italian artist who had specialised in set design called Luigi Veronesi whose work he liked a great deal. He wanted a large Balla oil painting, but they rarely came on to the market. That would have to wait.

He'd also invested in a gallery in New York. The building had previously offered free space to the Earthworks Arts Group, and he agreed to keep the agreement. It was a fairly new company doing art works and theatre projects on environmental themes and the loan was tax deductible. The main thing was to keep his name away from the media.

He thought he'd done that until he received an invitation from Nikos Leotakis to lunch at the Reform Club. He'd seen that Leotakis was one of the trustees of Earthworks, but assumed he wasn't actually involved.

It was quite a meeting. Nikos Leotakis had reminded him of one of those statues of Greek emperors with his strong nose and thick white hair, brushed off his face and Stephen expected any moment he'd turn down his thumb and the police would arrive. The billionaire was tanned like expensive old leather, and wore a navy blazer and grey trousers, a pale blue shirt, and a tie with a motif of interlocking trees. Stephen had agonised on what to wear for the lunch and ended up in a shop in

Jermyn Street asking their advice.

'I want to look smart, but not as if it's a job interview,' he told them. They sold him a navy jacket which fit perfectly, cream chinos and a very expensive blue shirt. He then crossed Piccadilly and went into the Royal Academy shop where he bought a Paul Klee Polyphony tie.

He arrived at the Club early to be told that Mr Leotakis was expecting him in the garden. He was shown through the palatial building with its many dark gilt-framed oil paintings. A few needed a good clean, he thought as he walked past. Tina had taught him that.

This was one of those ancient clubs where politicians and the rich met each other in book-lined smoking rooms and sat in leather chairs enjoying their elitism. The Reform was reformed only in that it had represented the Whig party after the Reform Act in 1832 and allowed in women. It was just the kind of place where he would be unmasked as an imposter.

Or would he? Had he now grown into Stephen enough to pass it off in a place like this? He smiled to himself although he could hear his heart beating a little too fast.

Leotakis was sitting at a table reading a small paperback, drinking champagne; Stephen asked for the same from a hovering waiter. He imagined that there was always someone hovering near the Greek, waiting to serve him.

'Paul Klee,' said Leotakis, looking up at his tie. 'I've a couple of very nice Klee paintings in Dorset.'

Stephen had studied Leotakis's home online: Tyneham House was as grand as the club he'd just walked through, though considerably newer as Leotakis had rebuilt it himself on the site of an older, dilapidated building. He imagined it had space for a gallery-worth of paintings.

'Taking a line for a walk,' replied Stephen, recalling Klee's famous description of drawing, 'it's such a good description, though with the Futurists it's more like taking them on a jet.'

'Of course,' replied Leotakis, indicating that Stephen should sit down. 'And when you read Marinetti's manifesto, you understand that.'

'And much besides,' added Stephen, who had skim-read the book. 'I do feel that he tarnished their work, with his fascism.'

'Yes, what was it? Art should be nothing but violence, cruelty, and injustice,' quoted Leotakis.

'What rubbish,' agreed Stephen.

'Indeed,' said Leotakis. 'But enough chit chatter. Who are you?'

'Sorry?' replied Stephen, unbalanced.

'You're not Stephen Mawson; he's a cleverly constructed fake. So, who are you?'

There was a pause Pinter would have appreciated. (Tina had taken him to the theatre). Stephen licked his lips which were suddenly so dry he couldn't speak. He could have lied, tried to argue that his persona was him, but in a split second he decided to do what he had never done before or would do again: he told Leotakis the truth.

'My name is Sam Moss and I come from a council house in Westlea, which is just outside Swindon. My father worked for the railways and my mother at the local supermarket. I got a scholarship to Oxford to read computer science, which was miraculous since I'm deeply dyslexic and had been written off by most of my teachers. I went to Keble and for the first year I hardly put my head out of the door, but of course you have to eat in hall. And in my second year I met a girl there.'

'And everything changed.'

'Yes. Olivia was so old money that she never even had to think about money or class or how different I was from her. She just said I made her laugh. That I listened to her.'

Leotakis smiled.

'Let's put the girlfriend on ice for a moment. I want to know how you got the money to become Stephen. That jacket you're wearing isn't High Street, and you've spent at least six million pounds buying the building for your gallery and at least the same again on the Futurist works to hang there as well as other works which I imagine you have at home.'

'A few. I sold several.'

'And the money?'

Stephen smiled at Leotakis and tried not to let him see that his hands were shaking.

'I stole it.' Leotakis looked at him with bright hooded eyes and said nothing. 'I'm a hacker.'

'I was going to ask who had created your legend. It's very well done; it almost deceived me. And this was your work?'

'It's what I do. I began as a hacker at university. My life was almost all online then. Then I got spotted and to avoid going to prison I went to work for GCHQ.'

'The poacher becomes the gamekeeper.'

'That was the cliché they used. I was there for three years, left in 2011. That's when I began to concentrate on amassing some money. I thought originally I'd go for four million which would keep me comfortably for the rest of my life.'

'Very comfortably,' murmured Leotakis, drily.

You can say that, thought, Stephen. You've got twelve billion which is publicly visible, and almost certainly more that isn't.

'Then I found I wanted to do things. I was still young, and I needed more money.'

'You can't steal millions, surely, without leaving a trace?'

'It depends where you go. I ignored the banks and the big businesses and went for the crime syndicates. In the movies, they always miss every dollar, but in fact most of them don't have a clue how much money they spend and earn as long as they have enough.

'A payment to Mexico or to Bolivia or Belize was usually read by their accountants as a drug purchase and lost along the way. I took between three hundred and five hundred thousand dollars from each one. It didn't take very long to make my target. I created shell companies in the Cayman Islands and elsewhere and routed the money through them until it came to my own bank in Zurich.

'And now,' Stephen paused. Should he tell him? Did he already know? Was this the real reason for the meeting? 'I have a confession to make.'

'I thought you were already doing that.'

'I stole half a million dollars from your son.'

'From my son?'

'Yes. From Antony. I have to say I've never found anyone who was more careless with their money.'

Leotakis put down his glass and began to laugh. It was a huge bellow of a laugh that shook his whole body and caused amused glances from the other diners.

'Oh Stephen…you want me to call you Stephen and not Sam?'

'Sam is dead.'

'Fine, Stephen. That is the funniest thing I've heard in months. My son. The fucking idiot! And you spent my son's money buying art?'

'I did. Do you want the paintings?'

'I have enough paintings.' Leotakis laughed again. 'He would hate that. My son is not only a criminal, but also has no culture. He is the disappointment of my life.' He sat back in his chair and signalled a waiter who arrived as if he'd been watching for this moment.

'Now let us enjoy our lunch.'

Following the lunch, Leotakis had hired him to do a number of jobs including hacking his own son's emails and phone.

'I do have people watching Antony, but I need to know everything,' he said. 'He traffics drugs and sometimes arms. But I need to know what else he does. I need to know in case I have to stop him.'

No, he didn't think Moros was connected to Leotakis. But what if Nikos was the target? If this was the case, he needed to let him know. And to do that he urgently needed to find the identity of Moros. Cox was dead and as Moros continued to scythe down his list, Pam Gregory appeared to be next. But why?

CHAPTER 15

It took just half an hour to get from Chiona to the airport at Sitia; Stavros would probably have done it in twenty, thought Pam, having seen the speed the Greek police officer drove when he'd left the previous evening and remembering their drive a few weeks back. But Stavros had decided to catch a late plane back from Heraklion to Athens the previous evening, and Pam wasn't sure whether she was disappointed or relieved.

'We'll talk soon,' Stavros said, kissing her gently on the lips as he left.

'Yes. And thank you for looking after Zofia and Grace so wonderfully,' she'd replied.

'I like them,' he'd smiled.

'So do I,' she said. 'Most of the time.'

Pam wondered what the three of them had talked about on their trip; she hoped it had been the views, the palm trees and the beach at least some of the time.

'They just wouldn't bloody listen,' she'd stormed at Mike after he got back. 'They think Henry was making it all up and died from stress. Talk about stress! Stavros was so fucking patronising, I nearly slapped him.'

'Just as well he's gone out,' replied Mike. 'But seriously, Pam, if the police won't investigate this, it's not going to be easy.'

'Does that mean…' she began.

'No. No. It's not that I don't want to know how Henry died, but...'

'But what?'

'I'll definitely fly over for the funeral if it's in Cambridge, but to be honest I don't really see how we can investigate this.'

'We could at least begin by finding out whether he was killed,' replied Pam, her anger bubbling up again. 'Or don't you care?'

Mike turned around and began to walk away.

'Sorry, Mike. I didn't mean to shout at you. I didn't mean that. You know I didn't mean that.'

'You did. And I get it. I'm just ... It's everything I've been trying to get away from.'

'I shouldn't have shouted at you.'

'Oh, shout away. You can shout at the gods, too. Henry said he used to shout at the gods every day after Laurent died.'

Pam laughed. 'I can just hear him. Thank goodness you're here and we can share memories.'

'Yes.' She saw a darkness shadow his face; he was thinking of another death.

'I'm going to miss Henry so much and I hardly had time to get to know him,' she knew she was burbling. 'It must be so much worse for you and for his other friends. Do you know them?'

'I think he once mentioned someone called Oliver. He and his wife have a summer house near Agios Nikolaos, but I don't remember ever meeting him.' He looked at her sharply. Perhaps some kind of action was better than the pain. 'So where could we begin? With the notes for the book he was working on?'

'It's all we've got. I think Henry gave his laptop to Stuart. I'll ring him tomorrow and see if he's managed to open it.'

'You'll be back in Cambridge by then.'

'Yes.' She looked out over the bay. There were Sunday visitors throwing and catching a large green ball along the edge of the shore and children running in and out of the sea screaming and laughing. Yet in an hour or so, it would be silent, except for the lap of the waves.

'You don't want to leave,' he said.

'Not at all,' she told him. 'I've been so happy here.'

'Which is why you'll come back.'

'But will it be the same without Henry?'

'No. But he'll always be here. And Stephanie. But now there will be you and maybe others. And Maddalena feeding us all.'

'She's going to be missing Henry as much as we are, if not more. Mike,' she turned to him, a new thought having hit her. 'Could you go and have a chat with her?'

'Now?' he asked. 'Are you hungry?'

'As a matter of fact, I am. But Henry used to go there a lot. He said it was to check his post, but, but I … I don't know… can you ask Maddalena about that. Oh, and yes, let's have some *tiropitas*. I need to think, and I can't do it if I'm hungry.'

'You were right,' he said later, as they munched the cheese pies, 'Henry used to go there to make calls on her landline. He told her he couldn't get a signal on his mobile. I took her number just in case we found ourselves in a position to check the calls.'

'That's really useful. Are Greek phone bills itemised?'

'No idea. I only use my mobile. I'll ask Aunt Sofia.'

She got up and began to move her leg up and down. 'I have to stop it getting stiff,' she told him. 'I'll miss the swimming. Cambridge swimming pools aren't the same as the sea.'

'You really think Henry was killed by this 17 November terrorist?' Mike sighed. 'What if we're wrong? What if he had just had a heart attack?'

'He went to have a check-up just last week,' replied

Pam, 'and his doctor told him he was really fit.' She watched Mike as he began to tidy up the house.

'One of my cousins is getting married next week, next Saturday. I can't let Aunt Sofia down; I have to be there.'

'Of course.' Pam tried not to show how disappointed she was. 'I expect the funeral will be after that.' She paused remembering that Mike had told her it would be dangerous for him in England. Was that the reason for his reticence? Was there really a family wedding? She could hardly ring Aunt Sofia and ask her, especially since this formidable woman hardly spoke any English.

'You're sure that you're still okay coming back to England for the funeral? I don't want anything happening to you.'

'I'm fine. I'll hire a car at the airport,' he said. 'I won't be walking around London. As far as I know, the group I was in didn't have any contacts with Cambridge. There was another group we corresponded with, Stop Huntingdon Animal Cruelty, but I never met any of them. They were active a bit earlier and most of them were arrested and jailed in 2009 and 2010. I didn't go undercover till 2012.'

The rest of the evening, Zofia and Grace stayed in their house; Pam began reading Henry's notebooks and making notes, and Mike sat in the garden reading a book about the 17 November group.

Pam rang Eleni to tell her that she'd also be on the flight with Grace and Sofia.

'Of course,' Eleni said. 'That is not a problem. And indeed it will give us an opportunity to talk. I had to come to Crete this weekend to pick up something for Nikos from the Leotakis house, and I am taking the plane back to England with you all. It will take me back to Dorset after it drops you all in Cambridge. There is one thing,' she added. 'Nikos asked whether you require a doctor to accompany you on the plane.'

'I'll have a doctor with me,' Pam told her. 'My friend Zofia Nowak started as a doctor in A&E before she became a pathologist, and her wife, Grace Montagu had some medical training before becoming a psychotherapist.'

'That is perfect,' said Eleni. Pam could imagine her ticking this off on one of her lists. She was the most efficient administrator Pam had ever encountered. 'Then I will see you all tomorrow morning. I will send a car at nine am.'

'Nice that Nikos is thinking of me,' said Pam, going into the garden and taking Mike some of the fresh lemonade she'd made. I'll miss this, she said to herself as she'd cut and squeezed the fruits Mike had picked only that afternoon. 'I know he has this terrible reputation, being called the Pirate and all that stuff he did when he was making his first millions, but I can't help liking him.'

'I like him a lot,' said Mike. 'I've spent quite a bit of time with him the last year or so, and I think he's a fundamentally good man. Apart from still overseeing his hotel chains, most of his time is spent on his environmental work. He's about to set up a big foundation to fund new schemes.'

'Is he? That's great.'

'Thinking about his legacy, I suppose.'

'As long as his son doesn't stop it all when Nikos dies.' Pam imagined that the old man must have made plans to stop this from happening.

It was strange now being back on the Leotakis jet, though this time without the billionaire or his French bodyguard, Rafael. The stewards were the same as before, Hugh was the senior steward and Frances was the chef. Once again, they offered them champagne and food as soon as they took off.

'Just some nibbles,' Frances said, after going through

the obligatory safety instructions, offering a platter of small Greek *meze*.

'It's now coming up to twelve o'clock in England, so we'll be making you lunch in an hour's time.'

It was the second time Pam, Zofia and Grace had been on this private jet, but they still felt the same excitement at being inside this extraordinary plane with its luxury and its many gadgets. The chairs were twice the width of normal aeroplane seats, and there were sofas and a large cinema screen that dropped down, and a proper shower room and kitchen that had a table where the stewards could sit and eat.

'It's strange how people paint everything blue and white as if they're carrying Greece around with them,' Grace said, looking at the décor with its pictures of indigo seas and white monasteries and the blue cushions and throws on the white sofas.

'Yes,' replied Pam. 'Stephanie's Cambridge house is just the same. All blue and white, I'll feel right at home.'

Zofia and Grace were drinking champagne, but Pam and Eleni chose freshly-made lemonade.

Pam had met Eleni just before and after Stephanie's funeral, when she was still staying with Nikos at his Cretan estate. Eleni had her own suite there with an office and spent most of the day there, working. This, therefore, was the first time that Pam had ever had the chance to talk with her. She'd always been something of a mystery, the woman who made everything happen. Pam wasn't sure how old she was. Henry had said that she and Popi had met during the trials of the torturers in the seventies, so she had to be around seventy. It was amazing she still was working so hard; Pam couldn't imagine herself working at that age.

And Eleni was so thin Pam had wondered whether she ever took time to eat. She certainly wasn't eating now. She wore a simple grey cotton dress that looked as if it had just been ironed that second or maybe it was some kind of expensive fabric that didn't crease, and her brown leather sandals with a low heel looked plain if you overlooked the red and green canvas strip with its gold metal interlocking circles, that even Pam knew meant they were Gucci. Pam had never seen her in anything else but subdued colours; it was almost like a uniform, like the uniform of black trousers and polo shirts she used to wear herself before she came to Greece.

Like Popi, Eleni had thick dark hair with streaks of grey. Her dark eyes had a touch of kohl around them, and her lipstick was bright red. She'd been a beautiful woman once, Pam thought, then caught herself. Eleni was still beautiful, as well as being amazingly efficient.

'How do you manage to do it all?' Pam asked her as they sipped their cooling drinks. 'Do you ever sleep?'

Eleni laughed.

'I don't do it all, Pam,' she replied. 'I'm like the conductor of an orchestra. I have teams working for me in Athens, London, and Paris ... in fact in all the places where Mr Leotakis has his principal homes. He also has a flat in New York, but I let his American PA look after him there. And besides, he rarely goes there these days.'

'So, you don't actually make all the reservations,' replied Pam.

'No,' said Eleni. 'I don't make any of them. I have a team of six people who handle travel and transportation. Then I have two people who liaise with housekeeping. Of course, with the creation of the new Fitzwilliam gallery, I have had to build another team which liaises directly with the architects and the project manager. Though I find it easier if I talk with Anna directly. Nikos is very, as you say, hands on, with his gallery.'

Pam had met Anna Karanaki, the young, volatile architect of the Leotakis Gallery a few weeks previously when Stephanie had been killed in the gallery, and her body impaled on a horn of the huge golden bull. Eleni was almost certainly one of the few people who could stand up to Anna, apart from Leotakis himself.

'So, do you just work for Mr Leotakis?' she asked.

'Not just Mr Leotakis,' she replied. 'I have four principal clients now. I used to have more, but as I took on more and more work for Nikos, I dropped the smaller clients.'

'It must be a lot of work,' said Grace.

'It is very satisfying work,' Eleni smiled at her. 'With Nikos I have the opportunity to make suggestions. He is not an autocrat. And he is now very busy with a major new project.'

'His foundation?' wondered Pam, remembering what Mike had said.

'So, you know. Yes. This has not yet been announced, so you will not discuss it except in private.'

'No,' said Pam quickly. 'Of course not.'

'This will be the Leotakis Foundation and it will lead the way on the environment.' Eleni announced, and they all looked at her and nodded. Zofia smiled. She liked strong women and Eleni was all of that.

'How did you get started?' Pam wondered. 'You seem to have created an amazing business.'

'Yes,' replied Eleni, as if this was stating the obvious. 'It is unique. And how it began? Ah, that was a very long time ago.' Her phone rang and she looked at the number of the caller and switched it off. That reminded Pam that on this private jet you could receive and make calls except during take-off and landing. She felt in her bag and quietly turned on her own phone.

'I married soon after university. I studied law but decided afterwards that I did not want to be a lawyer. My husband, Panos, had a travel agency in Athens and I worked with him. He had a passion for golf, and I suggested he set up specialist golfing trips for rich clients.

This was very successful.'

Pam tried to imagine Eleni playing golf and failed.

'My interests were in the arts. This is why Mr Leotakis and I work so well together, and I would often travel to England where I saw that many companies sponsored arts events. This was, I think, around 1982, and sponsorship of this kind hardly existed in Greece. I approached several arts organisations and using my husband's contacts in business I made the marriages.' She smiled. 'I have since sold that part of my work as a separate consultancy. I found that I preferred working with the business leaders to find events which were the best for them. And, in some cases, to initiate events which I enjoyed because it was more creative. Indeed, Nikos allows me to make suggestions to him.'

Eleni got up. 'And now, if you will excuse me, I must go and work.'

She walked back through the plane into what Pam knew was Nikos's office.

'For-mid-able,' whispered Grace.

'Yes,' said Pam. 'I can't imagine ever saying no to her.'

'Well, tell us all about this Cambridge house you're going to be living in,' said Zofia, and Pam described the small triangular house in Flower Street that Stephanie's husband, Colin, had designed and built for her.

'It has this heavenly private courtyard and huge glass doors leading into it from both the sitting room and the kitchen. I remember thinking when I first saw it that you both would adore it. The kitchen walls are a soft blue and there are turquoise and white tiles, and all the white plates and jars are on open shelves.'

'You're going to have to be tidy, then,' laughed Grace.

'I will,' agreed Pam. Her phone rang and she answered it, frowning.

'Martin,' she said. 'What can I do for you, DCI Hawkswood?' She clicked the phone on to speaker. The voice sounded tetchy and impatient, thought Grace. It reminded her of one of her clients, a senior academic who had been ordered to seek therapy to deal with his anger issues.

'I've just been talking to Mr Ian Coules. He is the solicitor dealing with the affairs of Henry Cox, and he happened to inform me that you are a beneficiary of Mr Cox's estate. So I thought I should ring to say I didn't realise at the time of our last conversation that you were close to the deceased. It explains your strange emotional response. I'm sorry for your loss.'

'That's very kind of you, Martin,' said Pam. A beneficiary? Henry had left her some money?

'Though I imagine you won't be well enough to travel back here for his funeral,' Hawkswood continued.

'You imagine wrong,' replied Pam. 'I'm travelling back as we speak, and we are at this moment somewhere northwest of Greece...'

'Near Venice,' mouthed Zofia.

'Zofia informs me that we're near Venice,' she told the DCI.

'Zofia? Zofia Nowak? She's with you? And why are you using the telephone on a plane? Don't you know it's illegal?'

'Not on private jets,' replied Pam. 'I have permission to use this, and Zofia and her wife have been visiting me in Crete.' She frowned. 'Does this mean you have a date for the funeral?' She turned off the speaker.

'Yes.' He coughed, although it sounded as though it was forced. 'Croyden signed him off after the autopsy this morning and the funeral is on Monday the sixteenth, in just under a week's time.'

'That's very kind of you to let me know. But I'd be even happier if you told me that you were investigating

Henry's death. As I said when we last spoke, I have good reason to believe that it wasn't natural, and I'd very much like to discuss that with you.'

'I thought that after what I said, you would refrain from making these kinds of allegations,' Hawkswood replied. 'Henry Cox died of heart failure. When you return to work, you're going to find that that kind of irresponsible speculation is no longer permitted in my department. If you ever want to make DCI yourself, you're going to have to shape up and do what I tell you. And if your travel on a private jet was a gift of hospitality, I do hope that you cleared it with the JFVU in advance. I'd hate to have to suspend you for gross misconduct.'

CHAPTER 16

Sorry, Martin, what were you saying? I missed it. Were you talking about us working together? Yes, that would have been interesting, but I'm leaving the Force at the end of next month and you can take a running jump.

Pam very nearly said what she was thinking, but this wasn't the moment. Let him suspend me, the bastard, she thought. See how Leotakis reacts to that.

'So, you did manage to find Henry's solicitor?' she asked instead. 'Ian Coules, wasn't it?'

'Mr Coules has been very helpful. He made the formal identification yesterday and will register the death on Monday. Unless you want to do that as Henry's friend. You were clearly close.' There was a prurience in the way he said that that dripped into the words like oil from a leaking sump.

'Martin, are you trying to suggest that my relationship with Henry Cox was something more than a friendship? Henry Cox was in his seventies and most definitely gay.'

She paused. She wasn't going to explain her friendship or why Henry had left her some money. It wasn't even something she could think about right now.

'However, he was a very solid historian,' Pam continued, 'and he did believe his life was in danger. Which is why I would like you to ask the pathologist to have another look. I'm certain he was killed.'

'Out of the question,' replied Hawkswood. 'I have no intention of speaking about this ever again. I'm surprised you would even suggest an investigation based on hearsay and supposition. But I'm beginning to wonder whether this is the kind of way you always conducted yourself.'

'Thank you, Martin,' she replied. 'Goodbye for now.'

Pam closed her eyes and decided to have a small sleep before lunch. Just talking to Hawkswood had been exhausting, and she realised that even if she'd wanted to go back to work, she wasn't well enough yet.

For the remainder of the flight, after she woke up and had lunch, she read one of the books on Greece Henry had lent her. Zofia and Grace seemed to be in a good mood again and had enjoyed the lunch of smoked salmon and fresh tuna which, they both agreed bore no resemblance to any airline food they'd ever eaten before. Pam didn't feel she had enough experience of that to comment, having only once flown abroad apart from this trip to Crete, but was glad they were happier.

The plane arrived at Cambridge City Airport around two-thirty British time, and with a limousine waiting for them virtually on the runway, Pam was deposited outside Stephanie's house in Flower Street within minutes.

'You must come and visit soon,' Pam told Zofia and Grace as the driver carried her bag to the house. 'As you can see, it's nothing from the road, but inside it's beautiful.'

'We'll look forward to that very much,' said Grace. Zofia smiled thinly. She was clearly still angry with Pam. It will all calm down after the funeral, thought Grace. And as soon as Pam stops believing her friend was murdered.

Pam limped upstairs; her leg was still stiff from the

flight, she noticed. She dumped her cases in the larger of the two bedrooms. Roberta had brought over all her clothes from her old home and hung them up. There were none of Jen's clothes here at all, she noticed. She must have come round and packed up. Pam wondered how she was. She'd said very little at Stephanie's funeral, and it was clear she was still in shock. It was probably sensible for her now not to be alone here in her mother's house. And she needed her father.

And who do you need? Pam pushed away the voice in her head and tried not to think about Stavros hurtling away from Chiona the previous evening still angry. It was over, she decided. She didn't need anyone.

Pam opened the door to the other bedroom, the room where Henry had died. The bedding had been stripped, and there was no sign he'd ever been there. His jacket, that Roberta said had been in the house, had also been taken with him, but a beer glass and the plate remained on the drainer, though somebody had washed them up. Perhaps it was just as well Mike wasn't here, it wouldn't be easy to sleep in the bed Henry had just been killed in. She ought to get rid of it, buy Jen a new bed; she still had savings from the salary she'd squirrelled away, but that wasn't going to last for ever.

Nikos had told her he'd put aside a fifty-thousand-pound reward for the person who uncovered Stephanie's killer, but as she'd told him, as a serving police officer she couldn't accept it. But could she take it later, after she'd left? She wasn't sure about the legal niceties of that, and also still felt, just as she'd explained to Henry, that she didn't want to be in debt to someone like Leotakis. And what had he reminded her? That Leotakis had once been in the pay of the Russians, that he, himself might have links with the 17 November group. No, she wouldn't let Mr Leotakis give her a large sum of money.

Pam looked at her watch. It was a quarter to one;

she'd been in the house for fifteen minutes and didn't know what to do next. She walked downstairs and looked around. She wasn't hungry or thirsty; they had been so well fed and watered on the plane she couldn't imagine wanting to eat again for days.

She got up again. If Mike was here, she could have started to talk to him about the case, about Henry. If she was back on duty there would be a case to study, to make notes about and then discuss with colleagues. If she was back in Chiona, she could go for a swim.

She had to do something. She looked around at what had to be the tidiest house in Cambridge. It was also so Greek that it already made her feel homesick for Crete. This must have been the same for Stephanie, thought Pam, sitting on a wicker chair, and gazing at a white sculpture of a dove on a low glass table in front of her. Colin made her this house to stop Stephanie feeling homesick, but it was just a replica. It makes you want the real thing all the more. No wonder Stephanie ran back to Crete.

She got up and removed the dove and put it on one of the bookshelves so that she didn't break it. She pulled a notebook out of her bag and sat down and opened it. Then stared at the blank page.

What on earth was she doing? She was alone with no colleagues to help her. She knew nothing about Greek politics, so how on earth could she discover who was this mysterious terrorist if someone as experienced as Henry hadn't been able to find them? It wasn't surprising that Zofia thought she'd gone mad. Perhaps she should ring her and tell her she was right. She and Grace would come rushing over in a moment if they thought she needed their help.

And what would they suggest? That she rest before returning to work? And if she told them she was about to resign, because she was most certainly going to do that

– there was no way she could work under Hawkswood – then they'd want her to start thinking about getting a new job. Maybe something like the National Crime Agency, Zofia would suggest, the NCA would jump at having someone with her expertise and experience. But is that what she wanted? Pam stared at the empty page of her notebook. She thought about Henry and how he told her she could be a historian or anything she wanted to be.

She decided that she'd take a shower. Not that she needed a shower, but when the tears wouldn't come, she'd always been soothed by the water pouring over her. She walked slowly upstairs again and stood under the strong jet of water until she felt a bit better. Jen had a brilliant power shower, and this really was a wonderful house; in a while she'd begin to enjoy it. Of course, she would.

As she towelled herself dry, she suddenly remembered Popi, that amazing, wise old lady coming up to her just before Stephanie's funeral.

'It's when you are at your weakest that you are at your strongest.' At the time, Pam hadn't understood what she meant. Now, she thought, she was beginning to appreciate the truth of those words.

She walked to the wardrobe and looked at her old uniform of black trousers and polo shirts; she'd hardly ever worn anything else. She found a large black plastic bag and put all the polo shirts and all but one pair of trousers in it. She'd take them to a charity shop in the morning. Old Pam was not about to be resurrected.

She unpacked the turquoise dress she'd first worn when she went to visit Nikos in his Dorset country house and when she'd had dinner with Stavros in Heraklion and put it on. It felt light and floaty, and she smiled as she looked at herself in the mirror; she was slimmer, she didn't know how, after eating all those Greek pastries, and tanned, and her hair was streaked from the sun. Not too bad, she thought, not too bad at all.

Right. Make some lists. She took out a sandal from her bag but couldn't find the second one. She began to go through the trousers in the bin bag – had she scooped it up with those? – when she heard the front door open. She stiffened and looked round for a weapon. Nothing. Whereas in the kitchen there was a wooden block full of sharp knives. Was this the same killer coming back again? Damn it, even her phone was downstairs.

The front door clicked shut again and she heard footsteps coming along the corridor and going towards the kitchen. She could hide, though not for long if they came upstairs, or brazen it out. She took a deep breath.

'Armed police,' she shouted. 'Get down where we can see you!'

'Armed?' asked a familiar voice. 'What with? A sandal?'

'Paul!' she laughed, as she clumped downstairs to find him swinging her lost sandal from its strap. She took it from him, it must have fallen out of her bag when she first came in. 'I was just looking for that,' she told him.

Paul Collins was one of her favourite officers, a bright free-thinking detective, who had only remained a constable because he hadn't wanted promotion.

'My god,' said Paul. 'I'd never thought of you as sexy before. Bloody hell, boss, but being shot seems to suit you. And armed? Have you been smuggling guns back to Cambridge?'

'Inappropriate as ever, DC Collins,' said Pam, laughing, happily. 'What are you doing here?'

'Thought I'd just pop over and make sure everything was ready for you.'

'Yes...' Pam began. 'I noticed that.'

'Oh, and Hawkswood seems to think you're mad and impossible and in breach of any number of regulations, so I decided you must be doing something right. Roberta said you thought Henry might have been murdered, but we've been officially told that this is, in Hawkswood's words, "utter rubbish". Roberta would have come, too, but she's house hunting in Leicestershire.'

Pam couldn't remember feeling quite so happy to see someone.

'It's quite possible I'm mad,' she replied, 'but that would mean that Henry Cox was also crazy which couldn't be further from the truth. And so, yes, I do think he was killed.' She gave Paul a hug. Then remembered that she was officially still his DI, and it wasn't at all correct, but decided she didn't care. Greece had certainly changed her.

'Come into the sitting room, and let's sit down and talk about it. I really need a good mind to bounce ideas off.' She paused. 'If you've got the time.'

'It's Sunday afternoon. I'm not on duty and I'm in no rush,' he replied. He didn't seem to have noticed or minded the hug, she reflected.

'Can I get you anything? I'm not sure what there is. I haven't been into the kitchen yet.'

'Then you won't have seen all the goodies Roberta and I bought for you. But I did happen to see a bottle of wine in the fridge when I was putting away stuff and I wouldn't say no to a glass. Are you allowed to drink?'

'You both brought me stuff? Thank you; you're both such good friends. And I must ring and thank Roberta and you must let me pay you for them. As to your last question, yes, I'm off the antibiotics now so I am allowed to drink, and I'd love a glass.'

She followed Paul into the kitchen where he took a couple of white ceramic goblets off the shelf and found a corkscrew hanging on one of the hooks. He uncorked the wine and poured them both a glass.

'It's incredibly tidy, isn't it?' he said.

'Yes. Terrifyingly.'

She pushed open the large glass doors which led into the private walled garden. 'Actually, why don't we talk out here? I have a feeling that there's a secret cupboard in the passage leading into the house where you'll find some chairs.'

Paul walked back. 'Wow,' he said. 'It's like the Tardis. Come and see, it's as big as a room and there's a bike here and yes, garden stuff and chairs and suitcases and… hey, Pam…there's a rather shabby leather bag, a kind of doctor's bag, but bigger. That doesn't feel like the kind of thing the owner would have. It wouldn't be Henry's, would it?'

'Oh my God, let me see.' Pam peered inside the cupboard which behind its sliding door revealed a space almost as big as a room, lit with two small skylights. She looked at the brown leather bag which she'd last seen in Henry's study. 'Yes, it is Henry's. That's fantastic'.

'I suppose it needs to go to his executors.'

'I'm sure it does. I'll ring his lawyer first thing in the morning.'

'And until then we might as well have a look.'

They took the case into the sitting room and opened it. There was an immediate scent of cloves and lime. It was Henry's aftershave, and it was just like having him there. Pam breathed it in and felt the tears running down her face.

'Oh, Paul, I hardly had time to get to know him, but he was so kind. A bit like having my dad back, or an uncle. Just someone wise and …oh I'm going to miss him.'

Paul came over and patted her shoulder ineffectually.

'In that case, I can understand why you want to find out whether someone killed him and, then if they did, who they were. But when Roberta and I let ourselves in, I have to tell you it really didn't feel as though anyone else had been here apart from Henry.'

Pam sighed. She took a tissue out of her pocket and blew her nose.

'But they could have done,' she argued.

He reached inside the case and took out two shirts and a sweater, a pair of trousers and Henry's neatly-folded pants and put them on to the sofa. There was nothing else in the case except for a large notebook, the kind that she'd brought back with her, and a couple of pens in a leather case. She opened it. There were lists with ticks against them on each page.

'He liked lists,' said Paul, looking over her shoulder. 'Just like you.'

'Yes,' replied Pam, wondering who the names were. This was a good place to start.

'Let's take this and my own notebook and wine into the garden and we can talk,' she said.

'You feel up to it after the journey?' Paul asked her.

'Hardly feel tired at all,' she replied. 'Cars from door to door, and endless food and drink. You've no idea what it's like on private jets. You don't even have to queue for anything.'

'Private jets and smart dresses. My goodness, Pam. Do I still know you?'

Pam laughed again. Paul looked at her and shook his head. This was a woman who laughed and cried and who looked happy. She'd changed a great deal while being in Greece. It was going to be all the harder to tell her how Hawkswood was investigating her and was determined to bring her down.

CHAPTER 17

'Before we start talking about Henry, there are some things you ought to know about what's going on at work,' said Paul taking a hearty swig of wine.

'Really? Do I have to?'

'If you're not well enough…' he began. He stopped and licked his lips, 'I don't know a great deal about wine, but this is delicious.'

'Isn't it?' agreed Pam. 'I wonder whether Henry bought it. In which case we should drink a toast to him.'

'To Henry,' said Paul, and Pam blinked hard to stop herself crying again. Get yourself into gear, woman, she told herself. If you want to honour Henry what you need to do is to find out who killed him.

'Can we talk office politics a bit later? she asked. 'I'd rather tell you about Henry'.

'It's important, Pam. In fact, I probably shouldn't be here.'

'What?' She shouldn't be having a drink in her garden with a colleague? It didn't make sense.

'It's Hawkswood. He hates you.'

'I don't like him much.'

'I mean really hates you.'

'Hates me. Why?'

'Firstly, because he wanted to be the head of EASOU and you got it.'

'I didn't know that. He'd have been useless; he's lazy and he cuts corners.'

'Yes, he does, and he hates the fact you don't. But then he was the one who first picked up the Stephanie Michaels case and rang Murton, and then you got it.'

'He'd never have solved it.'

'No. He wouldn't have followed all those leads, and he certainly wouldn't have gone to Crete. But then you didn't just solve it, you came home something of a heroine and now you've inherited a house by the sea.'

'Sorry. What?'

Had she misheard him?

'Hawkswood hasn't told you?'

'Told me what?'

'Henry's left you his house in Crete.'

Pam rushed indoors and just managed to get to the bathroom before she threw up. She damped a towel with hot water and held it to her face. Henry had done that for her? She'd been right, he did want her to have a new life, he wanted to help make it happen.

'But I wanted it to be with you.' She dried her face and went back outside.

'I'm so sorry, boss. I thought Hawkswood had told you.'

'He knows?' Now that sneering phone call made more sense.

'He went to Murton to see if that was illegal since Henry had at one time been a witness.'

'Fucking Ada. The bastard! Henry left me his house. I still can't quite believe it.' She shook her head and then went inside and poured herself a glass of water. 'And what did Murton say?' she called back.

'He said he didn't believe that inheriting money or property from friends was illegal, even though the whole thing seemed highly irregular, and just the kind of thing that made him glad he hadn't made you DCI. But then

Murton said there might be grounds to investigate you under police conduct regulations. He told Hawkswood and Julie managed to hear the whole thing.'

'Good for Julie. You like her, don't you.'

'Actually, a bit more than that now. We're sort of an item.'

'About bloody time I'd say,' she smiled. 'She's lovely, Paul. That's great news.'

'Unlike what I'm about to tell you.'

'Which is?' Pam steeled herself for more bad news.

'Murton told Hawkswood that your travel to Greece and your stay with Leotakis was signed off up to the time of Stephanie's funeral, but after that you should have returned home once you'd been discharged from hospital. But it appeared that you'd stayed on accepting the hospitality of Leotakis and then allowed him to pay for your medical expenses.'

'Oh shit. And now Hawkswood's going to know that Leotakis flew Zofia and Grace out to Crete and we all came home together on his jet.'

'And you didn't clear that in advance I guess.'

'There's something called Cretan hospitality and it's the opposite of the police regs. Not something you can refuse.'

'You'd better start filling in those forms.'

'So, what's it going to be? Misconduct or disciplinary proceedings? Oh, let the fuckers go ahead. I'm almost past caring.'

'Hawkswood wants to take it further. He rang a friend at the CPS to see whether he could mount a criminal case against you for corruption.'

'Hawkswood has friends?'

'He's really looking to nail you for something.'

'Just as well I want to resign then.'

'You want... are you sure?'

'If I was having doubts before, I don't now. God,

this stinks.'

Paul got up and began to walk round the garden. He saw a newly-dug rose bush and remembered that Roberta and Josh, who was Pam's sergeant had planted it along with the remains of the cat which had been stabbed by Stephanie's killer. This might look like a pretty garden, but it still had a chill about it, not surprising that Jen's daughter didn't want to live here again at the moment. If it was him, he'd sell the place and get away from the memories. First the cat, then her mother and then her godfather. He was surprised that Pam was staying here, especially if she believed that it was a murder scene. Though he felt that was in her head. But he'd listen to her if it helped. She'd been the best boss he'd ever had; he was going to miss her.

'Have you told Murton you're resigning?'

'Not yet. Waiting for the right moment.'

'Well, he'll be pleased. He was furious about your taping Dave. You know they go to the football together every week? And Dave's sister is a close friend of Murton's wife. They grew up in the same place somewhere up north.'

'I didn't know that. I taped the conversation in my office because he was being so aggressive, I thought he might hit me.'

'You... he... what....? But that's something entirely different from the story Murton's telling. Have you talked to the union yet?'

'No. I've only been back in England five minutes, and it's a Sunday afternoon.'

'You could have rung them from Greece. And you should.'

Pam sighed. 'I'm not sure.'

'Pam. This isn't just about you, it's what they think they can get away with. I can do it for you if you like; I'm the local rep. You don't still have the tape by any chance, do you?'

'I suppose so. I haven't deleted it.'

'May I?'

'Why not?' Pam shrugged. 'It's on my phone which is on the glass table in the sitting room. I just don't want to hear it again myself.'

Paul nodded and walked indoors. This was such a pristine and elegant house, it didn't feel like the small, converted garden shed with a minute mezzanine sleeping area, where Pam had lived before, and which had no ornaments and few books. Perhaps living in this space would change her; she seemed different already. Stronger, too, he thought, though it was clear she was deeply shaken by her friend's death.

He picked up the phone thinking how typical of Pam to trust him with it. He couldn't imagine any other of his colleagues doing that, even Roberta. It underlined how open she was. He scrolled through the apps until he came to the voice memo and found the recording.

It started off with Pam offering Dave the opportunity to apologise and save himself from something that he'd previously done, which hadn't been recorded. She was underlining his long service and why he shouldn't destroy his record, but he hadn't accepted that offer. What a tosser, thought Paul, listening to him lash out at the DI, yelling about political correctness and liberals. And the racism was vile, he should have been dismissed. And yes, he thought, it was a verbal assault. The union would back her.

He walked back into the garden. 'May I copy the tape and take it to the union?' he asked.

Pam nodded and sighed.

'Why not? I've been hoping to forget it, but I don't see why I should pay for his behaviour.'

'Nor do I,' he replied.

'It was because of this I didn't get the DCI promotion

I was expecting, but you saw Murton's letter, didn't you?'

'I did. Leave it with me,' Paul smiled at her. 'They really are going to have to pay you for this,' he said. 'Imagine what your new friend Mr Leotakis would say.'

Pam smiled. Leotakis would be livid. 'He'd probably ring the Prime Minister,' she said. 'But I'd never tell him. I don't want to be in his debt.'

'You may have to if they take you to court, but they know that, which is probably what's holding them back. Murton saw the pictures in the press of Leotakis praising you and saying how brave you are.'

'There were pictures in the papers? Leotakis said that?' Pam was even more relieved she'd been away. She shook her head and went back to her notes as Paul went inside to copy the conversation on to his own phone. He came back and poured himself another glass of wine; he needed another drink to take away the taste of Butcher's language. He'd worked with Dave all those five years and knew he was something of a dinosaur, but he'd never known he was quite so racist. He'd kept that very quiet while working for EASOU, presumably guessing his feelings weren't shared by any other members of the team. Though Paul felt that Hawkswood might not have objected. Wouldn't be at all surprised if he wasn't a racist as well as a bastard. He sighed. Time for him to get a transfer. He and Julie could move to London, perhaps. He might enjoy the Met.

'Right. Let's get back to something nicer. Tell me about Henry Cox and why you think he was killed.'

Pam smiled sadly. 'It seems to be all about a terrorist group called 17 November. I don't know a lot about them.' She took a book from her bag. 'I've been reading this which is a history of them, but I've only got halfway through it so far. Mike could help, but he won't be here for a few days, he's got a family wedding.'

'Mike, as in the "black sergeant" Butcher was shouting about?'

'Yup, Mike Petersen, the DS who's on permanent medical leave after what I believe was a horribly botched undercover operation the Met don't want anyone to know about. These days he works as a local builder in Crete, though he's thinking of doing other things, which he should. He's incredibly bright. He was a close friend of Henry's.'

Paul remembered how the women in the unit had reacted to seeing the very good-looking officer when he'd been called in to help on Stephanie's case, and they'd had a Skype meeting. Had he and the DI got close while she was in Greece?

'Actually Paul,' Pam continued, 'it's very sad. He's sort of stuck in limbo. He doesn't have a real job and doesn't feel it's safe for him to come back and live in England. Which means he can't have a relationship even though Jen, Stephanie's daughter is or, at least, was really keen on him and I think he feels much the same.'

'He was deep undercover? Four years. That's a lot.'

'Yup. Not something he talks about. Well, not to me. I think he talked to Popi, she's a therapist, was a close friend of Stephanie and Henry.'

'Would this Popi know what Henry was writing? Could she help?'

'Possibly, but Jen told me this week that she doesn't want to talk to anyone at the moment. It was one of her lost souls, as Henry called them, who killed Stephanie, and Popi brought him to the Leotakis house where he was able to get hold of Jen. We were so lucky Jen didn't die, too. A few minutes later…'

'Talking of therapy, guv, but shouldn't you be getting some after being involved with all that?'

'When I've solved this case, I'll think about it,' Pam replied. 'Right now, the one thing that will help me mentally is to concentrate on Henry. But you don't think it was murder. I know you don't.'

'No. I'm sorry but... Henry was wearing his pyjamas and... if he'd been poisoned, it would be in the tox report. Oh, Pam, he looked so bloody peaceful. Like, really happy, like the best dream ever. Roberta and I couldn't stop talking about it, how it was the way we'd want to go. And if someone did come in the night, they had a key. How many people have the key to this house?'

'Except it wasn't his time if he was killed. Nobody has the right to choose when someone can die. And keys... you can buy lockpicks on Amazon.' She sighed. 'Jen changed the locks after her cat was killed. I have a key and there was also one in my office set and Jen and Henry. But she might have made more.' She put down her notebook. 'I need to read the autopsy report, but Zofia won't give it to me.' She paused for a second. 'You could.'

Paul sat down beside her. 'Yeah, I could, but I won't. No, Pam hear me out,' he continued, as she was about to interrupt him. 'If I get the report and see something that wasn't investigated and show it to Hawkswood. What happens? Hawkswood isn't going to do anything about it except get me dismissed. But even if you got Henry's solicitor to ask for a further investigation, would that be a good thing?'

'Well, yes. If we can prove that he had been injected with drugs, it will prove that he was killed. Which is what I want.'

'But do you? Because then it would be Hawkswood's case and not yours. He could seize your computer and stop you doing any investigations because it would be a live case. And Hawkswood would sit on it until it went away. At the moment, nobody is interested in stopping you because nobody knows what you're doing. If you just assume he was killed, then you can run the case.'

'But Henry's death will be wrongly registered.'

'Is that the worst that can happen? Isn't you having your hands free to investigate more important?'

Pam rubbed her leg. She needed to get up and do some stretches. She'd do it after Paul left. But he had a point. More than a point. What he said made a lot of sense.

'But on my own what can I do? Henry spent ages researching it, and he never discovered their name.'

'OK,' Paul continued 'So you think CID here will do any better than him or you? They won't even go down that route. They'll do what you would do if you were back in your old job: ask who benefitted from his death. The old *cui bono.*'

'I suppose...' she began.

'How much is Henry's house worth?'

'I've no idea. And I didn't even know about it till you told me a few minutes ago.'

'That's what you say, Hawkswood would say. If there was an investigation, he'd make you his number one suspect. If he can't get you for corruption, he'd love to get you on a murder charge.'

CHAPTER 18

It's dark, why's it dark? Why hasn't she put the light on? No. She's not at home, she's in the barn, it's the smell… mould and dust. She's come here to die. She knows that now, and there's someone behind her laughing. It's Stavros, and she wants to ask him why they've come here but he's gone, and now it's Nikos and he's holding a gun.

'You were told I was a murderer,' he's telling her, 'but you didn't believe it.'

'But that was decades ago,' she tells him. 'It's quite alright now. The Prime Minister told me you didn't kill people anymore.'

And Henry is smiling at her and she realises there's something she's forgotten to ask him, and the words won't come out. And the man laughing isn't Stavros, it's Dave Butcher and he's holding the gun and she knows he's going to fire it.

'It's all your fault,' he tells her. 'You deserve this, you know it.'

And she does. She does know it. And he fires the gun.

Pam woke up with a start. The pain in her chest was terrible, but she was awake, though she couldn't breathe and she couldn't move.

Take a deep breath through your nose, she told herself, remembering a first aid course she'd done, and then slowly breathe out through your mouth. Do it ten times while you count the alphabet backwards.

Pam got as far as the letter s but couldn't remember what came before it. I have to start again, she thought. Z y x w, she paused, v u t, then s and r and ... she tried to imagine the letters on the keyboard but that didn't help because e came before r, and that wasn't right. What was it? Go forwards first, o p q and then r. So, r q p and then o. She realised she was breathing. But she did the exercise twice more just to make sure.

The pain in her chest had gone, but she still felt dizzy. She picked up her phone and called Grace.

'Pam, are you okay?' asked Grace with the kind of understanding she always had. Then Pam looked at her phone and realised it was five in the morning, so the question wasn't so strange.

'I couldn't breathe,' she said, 'and I woke up with this pain in my chest'.

'I'm coming straight over,' said Grace.

'I'll go down and let you in,' said Pam, reaching for her dressing gown. She found that moving around made her feel a bit better, and by the time Grace had arrived which was only four minutes later, she began to think she'd imagined it all.

Grace made her sit down and rest while she made her some green tea.

'Now tell me exactly what happened,' she said, curling up on the sofa opposite Pam. This was a comfortable house if you forgot that someone had just died in it. It probably wasn't the best place for Pam to recuperate.

Pam told her about the pain and then the dream. She found she could still walk through it.

'I think Murton might have been there as well,' she said.

'Why do you think Dave shot you?' asked Grace.

'He came here two days ago, on Wednesday,' Pam told her friend. 'He sort of threatened me.'

It had been late, but she'd still been up, reading one of the books on the 17 November terrorists that she'd brought with her and making notes. If nobody else was going to investigate Henry's death, she'd do it on her own.

The knock on the door had set her heart pounding.

'Who is it?' she asked cautiously. Perhaps it was Hawkswood about to arrest her. That knock was either police or pizza delivery and she wasn't expecting the latter.

'Open the door. I know you're in there.'

'Dave?'

Dave had been her sergeant for years, and she wasn't going to be frightened of him. He'd had her back more than once. She opened the door.

Then she smelled the beer.

'Christ, you smell like a brewery,' she said.

'Listen, you bloody bitch!' he'd shouted. 'If you think you can come back here and fuck my pension which I've bloody earned these years, you've got another fucking…I'm not going to let you do it.'

'I don't want your pension…' she began. He lurched towards her.

'If you get beaten up it's only what you deserve.'

'He said that?' asked Grace. It was what Richard had told her many times. Grace had helped her get past the horror of her marriage and listened to her reliving it. 'Have you reported him?'

'No. I don't want to make things worse … I don't think he'll come back. It's sad,' she added. 'He was such a good cop. I told him so. But the racism and the … well, he seems to hate women, especially women in authority.' She could still hear his voice.

'And Henry died here, too. I'm not surprised you're

having nightmares.'

'I was hoping to try and bring some good vibes to the house, but I don't think I'm doing very well so far. It's all a bit shit.'

'Mike's coming here in a couple of days. For Henry's funeral.'

'And after that?'

'I don't know,' she replied hopelessly.

'How did Dave know you were living here?'

'I suppose Murton told him. He and Hawkswood want me to be prosecuted for failing to seek permission for the hospitality Leotakis gave me. Including your flights.'

'This is appalling, Pam. Maybe it is time to find a new job.'

'You didn't think so last week.'

'That was last week. Now let's talk about PTSD. The pains in your chest and the dizziness are almost certainly symptoms of that, as is being shot in your dream. The thing is that you're not just recovering from being shot, but you've lost your unit, which I always thought was your life up to now.'

'I'm going to resign.'

'I'm not surprised you'd decide that, but don't rush. This is all a huge emotional weight, and your subconscious is almost certainly dealing with it. I rather think your conscious mind has pushed it all aside, perhaps using a distraction like finding out who killed your friend.'

'Maybe,' murmured Pam. 'But it is also possible Henry was killed.'

Grace looked at Pam. She wasn't going to dissuade her from this path right now, it could be that the distraction was helpful.

'What did you do when you couldn't breathe?' she asked.

Pam told her about going through the alphabet backwards and Grace gave her another exercise and praised her for remembering her breathing exercise.

'Just remember that it's completely normal for you to have PTSD after what you've been through. And quite honestly, if you are dealing with a union rep, you should tell them that you're suffering from it. You deserve to get paid while you get better. You were injured while on duty which your boss seems to have forgotten. And get a chain on your door.'

Pam hugged Grace warmly as she left. She made herself another cup of tea and slid the garden doors open. It was going to be another hot day. But she had things to do. First, she needed to make the house safe. This person was dangerous. And clever. Somehow, they'd got into this house without leaving any trace behind. She was sure that there weren't any keys unaccounted for after Jen had changed the locks. She could ring Jen but didn't want to alarm her. No, she'd have to assume that the killer entered without a key. It was a standard Yale lock and certainly pickable she knew from past experience of local thefts.

So, who were they? And were they part of this terrorist group?

She'd hoped to find clues in Henry's notebook, but that had been something completely different, just about his will and the money he would give to his friends. She was trying not to think about that, or that he'd left her the house. It should have made her happy, but Henry wasn't there for her to thank. It was all too much. The notebook also contained jottings about future books and notes about the funeral music he wanted. She could just imagine him, perhaps in this very room, thinking ahead, full of ideas, while at the same time preparing for the possibility that he could die at any moment.

'Oh Henry,' she whispered, 'I wish you were here.'

He wasn't, and the burden of trying to find his killer felt frighteningly heavy. She drank her tea and tried to plan ahead. On Sunday Mike was arriving, in time for the funeral and, before that, the World Cup Final. She hadn't told Mike about the house yet, she'd rather do that face to face. She'd met the solicitor, Ian Coules, on Monday, the day after she got back. He'd been charming and recounted how happy Henry had been at the idea of Pam having a little house in Chiona.

'He thought of you as a new honorary goddaughter,' he said, smiling. 'I did wonder about his heart because making the arrangements for his death and his funeral had been so important and urgent.'

'You don't feel that it could have been something else?' she enquired tentatively.

'Well, we'll never know whether it was a stroke or heart, but at least he was at peace. The police officers were very reassuring on that account.'

'Yes. It helps,' Pam lied.

Coules had been willing to show her the will and she had been amazed to realise how rich Henry had been. In his shabby trousers and ancient linen jacket, its pockets bulging with books, papers, and collected oddments, he had never looked wealthy in any way.

She pulled out her notebook and looked at her latest list and added to it. Number one: get a door chain. Number two: chase Stuart about Henry's computer. But Stuart was away on holiday until the following week, so that would have to wait. Cameras in Norfolk Street was number three.

If the killer had come by car, they almost certainly would have had to have come from Norfolk Street, probably from East Road, rather than from Gwydir Street. Hadn't they looked for cameras in Norfolk Street when they were investigating the stabbing of Stephanie Michaels's cat before her murder? Josh, her former sergeant would know. She rang his mobile number. It was early, but if he was still following his old routines, he'd be out running.

'Boss?' he said out of habit. She could hear him panting as he spoke. She'd been right. He was a man who didn't change. 'You alright?'

'Hi, Josh. Thanks. Yes. I'm back.'

'Roberta rang to tell me.'

'I've actually got more news. I'm going to resign, though you're the first to hear this.'

'What? But you're the best DI ever. The job was your life,' he replied.

'Was being the operative word,' she told him. 'That was before protecting a racist was more important than supporting me. And before they disbanded the unit.'

'The worst decision ever,' he agreed.

'But you're doing fine in Norfolk?'

'Great, actually,' he told her. 'The kids love their new schools and Barbara's gone back to nursing. We're renting a little house in a town just north of Norwich and it's only five miles to the sea. We go there every weekend and lots of evenings, too. The kids say they feel it's like being on holiday. And when the school holidays do begin, it will be brilliant for them.'

'That's so good to hear.' Pam smiled. Josh was a good cop, but it was always family first for him, unlike her. 'I've rather fallen in love with the sea, myself.'

'Roberta said something about that; that you sounded different.'

'I think I am different. It feels as though I was sleep walking through life, sorry about the cliché but I don't know how else to put it and now I've woken up. And anything is possible.'

'Wow, Pam. That is different.'

'But some things never change,' she added. 'Like murder.'

'You're back at work? But I thought...'

'No,' she interrupted. 'I'm not going back, but Henry Cox... you remember Henry Cox?'

'The historian. Pompous. You thought he was lying and might be the killer.'

'I did, and he and I laughed about it. We became very close, and he wasn't at all pompous, just had a different way of talking. And he never lied. But he was working on a book about Greek terrorism and thought he was in danger.'

'Was...?'

'He came back here to Stephanie's house, it's where I'm actually living at the moment...'

'In Stephanie's place?' Josh sounded incredulous.

'Jen didn't want to come back here, and she needed someone to water the plants.'

Josh tried to imagine Pam gardening and failed. He also couldn't see her in that immaculate blue and white house.

'Just for the time being. But Henry always stayed here.'

'Yes. He told us that.'

'And he died here a few days ago. In this house.'

'And you're still staying there?'

'I don't believe in ghosts, Josh. But I also don't believe in healthy men who think they're in danger suddenly dying. But I'm bolting the door at night and changing the locks again this morning.'

'It could have been a heart attack. Stress can do that, can't it?'

'It can. And it might have been that, or a stroke, but as Hawkswood won't allow me to see the autopsy report, I don't know.'

'But you think it was murder. You've always had good instincts for that kind of thing.'

'Thanks, Josh. But don't tell any of the old team

that I'm working on it. They'd try to stop me.'

'Don't really talk to many of them anymore, though I've heard there's some really strange things being said about you. You need to be careful. And I'm not going to say anything. You can trust me.'

'I always have, Josh. I always have.'

'You're ringing about that.'

'Yes. Remember when we found out that Jen and Stephanie's cat had been killed?'

'Yes. Skimble. We planted a rose bush when we reburied him.'

'I'm looking at the rose right now,' she told him. 'It's still healthy.'

'Good.'

'So. Didn't you check whether there were any buildings along Norfolk Street that had cameras facing the road?'

'I did, and there was one. We never got round to getting the tape from it because by that time you'd gone to Crete. And then it was all over.'

'Yes. It wrapped up rather faster than most cases I've worked on. But then it escalated into Jen's abduction.'

'How is your leg now? Shouldn't you still be resting?'

'I'm rested and healed. And I promise you I'm not doing any running.'

'Talking of which, Pam I'd better get home, or I'll be late.'

'And the camera?'

'Oh yes, Anglia Ruskin had one. On the corner of Broad Street.'

So, there was a camera. Now she needed a date. She hadn't originally been certain whether Henry had died on Thursday or Friday, but when they opened Henry's notebook, they'd found a receipt in it for the beer and the wine dated the fifth of July. It seemed likely that with the wine still in the fridge and the beer glass just washed up, that Henry had died the night of the fifth. She'd decided to use that as a starting point.

She pulled out her laptop and put in an application to the University. Now it was all waiting. Waiting for the tape, waiting for Stuart to get into Henry's computer, waiting for Mike to arrive, waiting for a miracle. And waiting to see what Hawkswood would do next.

CHAPTER 19

She let the phone ring seven times before she picked it up and, even then, she did it reluctantly. It was a number she knew well.

'I can't believe you're back in England after what we said. What did the monster want this time?'

'Good morning, Popi,' the deep growl of the man she'd come to know very well the past twenty years: 'This is Leotakis'

'Nikos,' Popi didn't sound either embarrassed or upset by her mistake. 'I thought you were Eleni.'

'Eleni is on holiday,' replied Leotakis.

'Holiday?' said Popi incredulously. 'You think she's on holiday.'

'I think it because that is what she told me.'

'She didn't tell you about being in hospital?'

'What! Eleni is in hospital? Where? Why didn't she tell me?'

'She's out now. There's nothing more a hospital can do.'

'What do you mean? I didn't know she was ill.'

'The cancer is terminal. She merely went in while they found the necessary palliative dose. I said she should come here for a while.'

'Cancer?'

'Secondary liver cancer.'

'How long?'

'A few weeks? A few months? She's been ill for about a year but didn't get it checked until it was too late.'

'Why didn't she tell me?'

'She didn't want anyone to know. Except for me. She's keeping herself alive so she can come to the opening of your new Cambridge gallery and the Chiona exhibition.'

I could never have created it without her. She's been extraordinary.'

'She is extraordinary.'

'I know that. It's why I value her so highly. And I thought I knew her.' Leotakis paused for a moment and Popi said nothing to fill the empty air.

'I didn't even know that you and she were close friends,' he said, thoughtfully.

'Since 1973,' Popi told him. 'We were in the Polytechnic together.'

'She was there? That's another thing she never told me, even after Stephanie's murder. This is unbelievable.'

'Yet true.' Popi began to sound irritated. 'But when did you ever sit down with Eleni and listen to her.'

'I listen to her all the time... but she never talks about herself. I should have known she was ill, Popi, but she hid it from me. Look, you were staying with me a couple of weeks ago, and I never saw her talking with you.'

Popi sighed. 'I suppose that's true, too. Eleni keeps her world in sealed boxes, I'm in one, you're in another.'

'Unlike Stephanie. I wonder whether that's why she disliked Steph.'

'One reason perhaps. Stephanie was incontinent, both emotionally and professionally, she never recognised any normal boundaries. But Eleni thought she was weak because of her drinking. She can be quite censorious, Eleni, she doesn't accept failure.'

'That must make it hard for her to accept her illness.'

'I've tried to make her see that it's not a failure, that illness cannot be controlled. You can't will cancer away.'

'No. That must be hard for her. Are you alright, yourself?'

'I'm not going to answer that, Nikos, it's possibly the most stupid question you've ever asked me. And it's not relevant. In fact, I'm getting tired of this conversation. Why did you call me?'

'I wondered whether you'd like to use my plane to take you to Cambridge for Henry's funeral. I heard it was on Monday. Rafael told me. He liked Henry.'

'Which you never did.'

'I never spent time with him. He was obstructive when we needed to create the new village in Chiona, but I indulged him for Stephanie's sake. Though she was equally annoyed at the time.'

'They had monumental rows, those two.'

'Steph had monumental rows with everyone.'

'Yes. She did. And I miss them.'

'You have no idea how much I miss them. Miss her.' He paused again. 'And the plane?'

'I'm not going, Nikos. I can't be in England now while Alexandros is still so ill?'

'Is he still in hospital?'

'Yes, he's in a clinic in Heraklion'

'Is that the best place for him? If I could help?'

'It means I can see him every day,' Popi lied. She hadn't seen him since she got back from Stephanie's funeral. She couldn't bear seeing him there anymore, unresponsive, unable to talk. She wanted her own husband back, not this imposter. He was an incubus who had stolen her Alexandros.

'You can't make people well just by throwing money at them,' she added.

'I'm just trying to help.'

'Yes. You do that. sometimes I wonder why. What past sins are you trying to repent? Killing all those men back in Guatatmala?'

'That was over years ago, Popi, as well you know, and they were as evil as they come... the kind you'd find working for Pablo Escobar and men like him. If I've become a philanthropist, it's because I can afford it and because Alison made me into that kind of man.'

'She was a good woman. I never understood why she married you.'

'Love, Popi? Love. I miss her very much, she died so early. Why are you putting my balls in a punchbag today? What have I done to you?'

'To me, nothing. Perhaps it is only now I am truly angry. I should have been angry a long time ago.'

'I admire you because you never allowed anger to eat you up.'

Popi sighed. 'Perhaps I should have done. I had enough reasons.'

'You're not the only one they tortured.'

'That's meant to make me feel better? You couldn't understand. You've never been in that position.'

Leotakis sighed. 'I've never told anyone, but I was. Once. After I seized those boats and shot the men who were smuggling arms and drugs, I was caught. And tortured. They threw me into the sea for the sharks. Being so close to dying does change you. I learned that.'

'Did it make you a better person or just hungrier for wealth?'

'If you don't need the plane, I don't think we need to continue this conversation. Will you please tell Eleni that I am very concerned about her illness and that if there is anything I can do, she only has to ask. I thought she was my friend as well as my employee.'

'Goodbye Nikos.'

Popi put down the phone slowly. She looked around the room as if it would provide answers, but she felt cut off from its message; Alexandros had designed it for them as a place of refuge and relaxation; it was where they came every year to unwind, before they retired and moved from Athens to Crete. The house, itself, was almost hidden in a circle of cypress trees, and the garden had several small pools with different fountains. Water on pebbles, water flowing into troughs and water bubbling above millstones.

Inside, the theme of greenery and zen calm continued. It was almost as if it denied her her rage. And she wanted to let her rage out, she had kept it in for too long.

'I never told you how angry I was, Alexi,' she said to her absent husband. 'I put all my energy into others, and you never knew.'

There was so much he had never known. He had never known just how much Jen had meant to her, the goddaughter taking the place of the child she could never have, the children denied by the man whose name she even now couldn't say aloud. And then just a few weeks ago, she had nearly lost Jen. If Manolis hadn't killed himself, she would have killed him. She had to admit that, to herself if not to anyone else, though who could she tell? Stephanie and Henry were both dead and Alexander hardly conscious.

It had all begun in that Athens cell when she had been destroyed by that man on a chipped metal table in a dirty cell. And yet she had visited him. Back in the nineties when everyone was preaching reconciliation. She had allowed a Canadian film crew to take her into the Peloponnese and meet him after he had been released from prison.

It was one of those documentaries that pretended to be a serious study of how men became torturers and the effect on their victims. Confrontation with the devil, a chance to take back control. That was worse than the pain, she had written, the fact that they control you, that you have no rights, no power. The director told her how brave she was. So brave: Look at Phoenix Popi, the post-Polytechnic version, the politician, the public persona, the woman who fights for the survivors, who confronts her personal devil.

All that stuff she wrote then: survivors not victims. It was what she told them at her Centre when they came with their stories. 'It was morning...' 'It was night...' 'They came for me...' 'They came for me...' That's how it always started. Just variations on the theme. 'They dragged me out of my cell...' 'They came into my house.' Every survivor with her own tale of horror, each one trying to find their own way back to something Popi called humanity because she couldn't find a different word. But she had taught a lie. She was a victim. She remained a victim.

She can remember every moment of that visit. The pale sun of early March, the small mountain village with its church, its *cafeneion*. There was nothing different about it. His house had been like any other village house: small, just one storey with a flat roof, one window onto the street, and grey shutters that needed painting.

The Canadians bustled about with equipment and loomed over her like protective storks, talking quietly as if they were at a funeral. The director had round glasses and an expression that was so mournful it almost made her want to laugh. Every time she said something he nodded, like one of those sad dogs people hung in cars.

There was only the one room, she remembered; the kitchen table covered in oilcloth with pink roses on it, the bed at the back. There were lots of cardboard boxes and plastic lace mats on every surface. Black and white images of an afternoon quiz programme flickered on a large old television in the corner. Even from the outside, Popi could feel its stale air and its smells of old soup and polish. This was the kind of Greek house she had seen a million times. Not the house of an ogre, not His house.

And when He came out he looked reduced. Maybe it was because the Canadians were towering over him with their boom microphones, and he looked terrified. Him! Small and scared.

He said good afternoon and his voice was much smaller than she remembered. Where was the bravado? He looked up at the Canadians as if they were going to hit him, flinching from every question. Yes, he had been in prison for five years. Yes, generally he'd been treated very well. He had no complaints.

Her voice seemed harsh compared to his. 'I want you to think back.' she'd said. 'It's very hard to think back,' he replied. 'But how could you treat me like that?' she asked him, 'I could have been your sister.'

'No,' he answered very quickly. 'No, please don't say that. I could never hurt my sister. I had to believe you weren't Greek, that you were a Communist.' 'I wasn't,' she had interrupted, but he didn't stop. 'They were dangerous.' 'They?' she told him. 'There never was a "they", there were just people, young people, students, Greeks.'

'He'd looked at her without seeing her. 'Back then to me you weren't a Greek. We were trained, you see…' And then followed the usual horror of how the military police had been trained. Photographs of his girlfriend trampled in excrement, stamping on everything that he held dear, fear of upsetting the peer group, pride when he did something to gain their respect – and the worse it was, the more glory. He'd done what he was trained to do.

Then… then came that moment. She was about to ask him if he had any idea of what he did to her, how sticking that broom handle up inside her caused her to spend months in hospital and prevented her from ever having children. But she heard it, the sound of a baby inside the house. He had a child. She couldn't have children, but he could. His wife had come out then, a faded, tired-looking woman, a baby on her hip and a not very clean blanket around it.

The woman was very unhappy that Popi was there, and she had glared at the Canadians, who ignored her.

Then he said, 'Thank you for coming. Thank you, Madame,' and went back inside. It was the 'Madame' that hurt. Before, she wasn't a person, but now she was 'Madame', now she was a woman, a Greek. Popi had stepped away feeling nauseated, but just as she turned away, the wife grabbed her arm.

'He dreams of you, you know,' she'd said. 'Ever since he saw your picture on television. You're real now. He can't pretend it didn't happen. He cries in his sleep – just like this one.' She looked down at the baby.

'You want me to apologise to you?' Popi had asked, feeling the anger for the first time. The woman had sighed and Popi could see the bruised ridges under her eyes. She was painfully thin.

'Who can say who's to blame? she replied. 'I only know that we're at the bottom of everything in this life. There's no future for us. No one here will speak to us now. There's nowhere we can go. But we have to go on for his sake.' She looked down at the baby on her hip. 'But what will they say to him at school? That's what frightens me. And when this film is shown, what will they say then? Is it his fault what his father did?'

And then...and then. She had had no answers, but the woman hadn't finished.

'You'd give him a good home, wouldn't you?' she'd asked. But at that moment he'd come back out of the house, and his wife turned away again. 'It would be better for the child,' she'd muttered, 'but he'd never allow it. He adores the boy. It's all he has.'

They'd driven back to Athens without speaking. And she had never spoken of it. She had never told Alexandros, she had never told anyone.

'And you wanted children so much, Alexi,' Popi says now, clenching her fists. 'It wasn't fair on you. Somebody should pay for this.'

CHAPTER 20

Nothing made sense. Stephen had never had a job which was so bloody frustrating. Normally, it was a matter of firewalls and passwords and other barriers that people erected to keep the likes of him away from their precious documents and cash. But this whole Moros business was doing his head in.

Since he'd received the information from Salvador in the British Virgin Islands Bank, he'd known that the account had been opened by Alexandros Yotopoulos, the head of the 17N terrorist outfit, along with a second signatory, the one who now controlled the account. She had written the name, Anna Kritikos, which was an invented name if ever there was one. Anna of Crete. I don't think so, he said to himself. But a woman? That was possible. Yes, a woman could have done the killings the way they'd been done. A woman who'd been close to Yotopoulos? A woman close enough to have gone to the Virgin Islands with him to set up an account for the future? Someone he could trust. This made a lot of sense, yes, that was it. Since then, he'd thought of Moros as a woman, as Anna.

The street name was called Tsami Karatasou, but that wasn't a great deal of help. There didn't seem to be anything as advanced as a street directory, and certainly not one that dated back to 1975 or earlier. And while there were references to people living in the street on a couple of websites, these were in Greek and none seemed useful. After a few online passes, he found the number of the house itself, and then on Google maps he went up and down until he found it. It was a honey-coloured two storey neoclassical house with a huge purple flowering plant covering the whole of one side. He looked it up just out of habit. Bougainvillea. It had been there more than a few years, he thought. That was going to make it easier to recognise a photo if he found one.

Two days later, he did. In the Harvard Magazine. The article, dated 1998, was about an honorary degree Harvard was giving to a woman called Popi Filotaki. There was a photograph of her outside her house, and, yes, it was the bougainvillea house, and the caption said it had been her home for many years.

Popi Filotaki.

Stephen now had a name. A few hours later he had a biography and enough information to fill a book. The only problem was that this Popi seemed to be some kind of humanitarian saint. Her background as a student was in left wing politics, but for the past forty-odd years she seemed to be happy supporting the centre left and even the centre right at times. And there was absolutely nothing in her life history that suggested she'd be the kind of person to steal chemical weapons or kill historians. What made the whole thing even more complicated was that he'd realised he'd come across her name before.

It was somewhere in an email sent by Gregory to the other cop, Mike, while he was in Crete and she was in Cambridge.

Lots of stuff about buying him a new bed so he wasn't sleeping in the one Henry died in and telling him about parking in Cambridge.

Jen does have permits but one of her best friends is away for the month, and they've got off-street parking in front of their house on St Barnabas Road, so you can park there. I didn't tell her our worries about Henry's death or that we were investigating it, she said she couldn't bear it if it was violent like her Mum's.

I hope she never does find out then, Mike had replied. *And not really sure we can investigate it. We don't have resources.*

So this Mike wasn't committed. Had some sense, thought Stephen. He read on:

Not sure how much you want to hear, but I've been reading the books about 17 November.

So have I, Mike responded. *Found nothing about this last terrorist as Henry called him. Did find a reference in one book to the testimony of one of the terrorists called Pavlos Seferis and he told the police that Richard Welch was killed by Yotopoulos as well as a woman called Anna and someone else. Didn't Henry mention that someone might be Yiannis Serifis? But he was acquitted, and in any case that killing is way outside the statute of limitations.*

Anna is interesting, wrote Gregory. *Should we be thinking of a woman?*

Maybe, Pam, but even opening it out into an equal opportunities terrorist, doesn't take us any closer.

Stephen stopped reading. She wasn't stupid, this Gregory. What she was thinking certainly made sense in terms of the bank account in the Virgin Islands. Anna. The mysterious Anna/Moros. Who the hell was she, and who was Popi Filotaki?

There was also the money; where did that come from? Did this Popi have money? Stephen read on…he was sure he'd read something about Popi Filotaki. Ah yes, here it was:

Have you heard anything from Popi? Henry's death must really have devastated her so soon after Stephanie's. I keep thinking about her. When I met her first at Leotakis's place in Crete I thought she was so strong, but when she came to visit me at the hospital she seemed ten years older. She was totally unnerved by the fact that Manolis nearly killed her goddaughter, and now with Henry dying so suddenly and her husband having had a stroke, I do worry about her. Just hope she's got her own support just as I've got Grace.

Stephen stopped reading. It was interesting that Popi was the Michaels' daughter's godmother, plus she was at the Leotakis house in Greece along with Gregory. Could be relevant. Might not be. Back to Popi Filotaki, he said to himself.

Born in Athens as Calliope (so that's what Popi is short for) in 1947. Father ran a printing business, mother was a dentist. Studied psychology at Athens University for one year but moved to Paris in 1967. That's when the Junta came in, thought Stephen, making mental footnotes as he read. Finished her degree in psychology and returned to Athens in 1973, was involved with the Polytechnic student thing, and got herself arrested. And here's where all the magazines and websites went to town. Clearly revelling in the description of how Popi was tortured.

This wasn't comfortable reading, even for him, but it was part of the legend of Popi who then set up her centre for victims of torture in Athens. The centre had grown and grown and was still helping refugees from around the world. More interestingly, Popi was also an advisor to successive governments, particularly the current one.

But nothing there which linked her with 17N. Popi Filotaki was a most unlikely terrorist, unless it was her husband, who seemed to be a successful architect and had nothing to do with politics.

He looked at the pictures of her. She had thick dark hair which had been long when she was younger but was now short and grey. Her deep dark eyes hadn't changed. Most of the photographs were at foreign conferences and lectures, but also with groups of refugees she was fundraising for. One included Leotakis who commented that he could never resist her requests.

Until one day he did? Stephen wondered. Had this set her against him? He needed to dig further but, in the meantime, he still had to appease Moros/Anna, whether she was Popi or someone else.

Her latest demand was for more information on Gregory. Stephen opened the file that linked to Pam's emails again. There was one to a colleague called Collins, about the union taking on her case. She was happy for it to go ahead, she wrote, but didn't want to get involved herself. And she didn't want to get caught up in the whole Dave Butcher thing.

Dave Butcher? Stephen needed to find out what this was about before Moros asked. Staying ahead of the game was what made him so useful. He tracked back into the emails of the detective who was writing to Pam. His name was DC Paul Collins, and he'd conveniently written a summary of the case to the police union. It concerned a recording of a racist and verbal attack on Gregory just before she left for Greece. Pam had reported it and Butcher, who was sixty-two, had retired on full pay. Pam, however, had been reprimanded for making the tape without Butcher's knowledge. But Collins pointed out Butcher's aggression, and that she'd turned on her phone recorder because she was afraid he'd attack her physically.

Collins had also emailed someone called Julie. Seemed to be a girlfriend. He read it and laughed out loud. Despite finding the killer of Stephanie Michaels, a case that had received a great deal of exposure and brought nothing but good publicity to the Force, her boss hadn't even congratulated her. She not only hadn't received the promotion to DCI she'd been promised, but the new DCI wanted to prosecute her.

'Well then,' said Stephen aloud. 'I'll give him a reason.'

Stephen had read the emails from the personnel office telling her about the procedure she needed to undergo before she'd be allowed back. Assessments, shrinks, loads of crap. He walked into his grey-tiled bathroom where three neat lines of coke were laid out above several smudged lines. He had a stack of work to do, and some Colombian marching powder would keep his head clear. Moros wanted him to set up the Gregory woman and though it wasn't his usual line of work, it wouldn't be difficult, and it would keep his client off his back.

He took a deep snort through a tightly wound fifty-pound note and rubbed the residue on his gums.

He was ready. He wasn't hungry, but he should eat something or down a power shake. He looked at his laptop. It was four in the morning, he must've been working all evening, but no reason to stop now. He ordered a pizza with extra anchovies from his usual twenty-four-hour takeaway, then sat back down to begin the task of messing with Pam Gregory's life.

It had never been easier for criminals to get guns, thought Stephen; they flowed in from Europe every week in lorries, cars and yachts. He could get one in an instant if he so wanted, which he didn't. Equally a bent cop could get hold of one, from a villain or from raiding an evidence cupboard. But how could he make it look as though Pam Gregory was buying a gun? She was just too fucking clean, everything by the bloody book. She probably had never used the dark web and certainly wouldn't know her way round it.

But if she knew a bent cop, one she'd worked with before? As far as he could see, the only cop in her former unit who might wander into the dark side was Dave Butcher. But he was the one cop Stephen couldn't use, he was going to be Gregory's target.

This was going to take hours. Maybe he'd come back to it tomorrow. In the meantime, he could put out an invite, see who was offering small firearms. Unless she'd use that other cop, Mike, get him to bring one over from Greece. From what he'd read, Crete was full of guns, and even though they might date back half a century or more, they still worked. Or she could have brought it back; she'd travelled on Leotakis's private jet which meant no customs. Yes, it could even be the one that had shot her. A trophy.

That would be just the thing. Save all that dodgy dealing which didn't feel one bit like the DI's way of doing things.

He was brilliant!

The bell to his flat rang and he jumped up, suddenly anxious as if he'd been putting these thoughts on to his laptop and someone had sussed him.

'Yes,' he barked.

'Pizza for 22, extra anchovies,' said a bored voice.

Fucking powder, it always made him so paranoid.

He had to get the email right, make it sound like her. He tried a few drafts.

Next was the delivery of the email: he needed to put it all on her phone but delete it immediately before she could see it. Nobody ever read their deleted files, he was relying on that. But in case they checked the message had to come from Cambridge when he sent it.

Cox's funeral, that would be perfect. And he could go himself and get to see her, just before he sent the email. There was also the possibility that Moros would be there, too. Didn't the police say that killers often went to the funerals, or was that just in fiction?

It might be interesting.

CHAPTER 21

It had been strange coming back to England after so long. For one thing Mike was expecting rain, and it was hot and dry. Been baking for weeks, they told him when he went to collect his rental car at the airport.

Mike had got a morning flight from Heraklion to Gatwick, after his cousin Yiannis's wedding had been danced into the early hours. For once, he was glad that he no longer drank, his head was clear despite a lack of sleep. Another time, he'd have taken Pam, she'd have enjoyed it as he had, especially the time he spent with a very sweet girl called Ioanna, who had a good job in Kalamata as a vet and was therefore not someone who might expect a relationship to follow a one-night fling. They'd danced and then she'd come back to Chiona, and they'd swum in the dawn and spent a few hours together before he drove them both to Heraklion.

But maybe Pam wouldn't have enjoyed it, and it would have been tricky to spend so much time with Ioanna if Pam had been there.

'How are you doing?' he asked, as she let him into the elegant triangular house which narrowed to a single doorway on the street.

'Fine,' she murmured. 'Local doctor said I'm all healed up. Well, leg, anyway. But as for... yes... bit strange being here what with...' Her shrug included the house, Henry's death, and her own loss of her job.

Mike looked around the sitting roomwith its pristine white sofas and chairs. The house was beautiful, but almost like a museum.

'I've put away the more breakable objects,' Pam told him. 'There's a giant store cupboard behind a sliding door in the hall. But...'

'It still feels too clean and perfect,' he finished.

'Not just me then,' she smiled.

Was this house the real Jen? he wondered. And if so, could he live in a place like this? He thought, on balance, he couldn't, which made it just as well that their relationship hadn't developed. What had happened in Crete had smashed up any idea of their getting together. There were too many associations.

'Glass of wine?' asked Pam going into the kitchen. She brought out a bottle of Chablis from the fridge and began to open it.

'God, it's all so tidy,' he said.

Pam laughed. 'She doesn't even have labels on her jars. She must always put them back in the same place.' Mike began to laugh, and Pam started to giggle, a giggle that became uncontrollable.

'My word,' she wheezed, 'I can't remember the last time I laughed like that. Since I've been back...'

She didn't finish. She didn't want to burden Mike with her problems.

'Yeah. When you don't let the emotions out, you get pretty blocked. Got that from Popi,' Mike added. 'She got me laughing at silly things when I hadn't laughed for a long time.'

'Grace was very impressed that we'd met her. One of her heroes.'

'Do you think she'll come to Henry's funeral?' she asked.

'I don't think she's very well.'

'No. Jen said something about that. And she doesn't like leaving her husband for long.'

'Must be so hard when your partner has a stroke and you can't share things anymore. Especially after a whole life together.'

Pam poured out the wine and Mike took a sip and looked at the bottle. It had had the words Premier Cru on the label, along with the information that it had been bottled at its Burgundy vineyard.

'Have you been splashing out?' he asked her.

'Under orders from Jen to empty her wine racks, so I thought this would help soften the blow of having to come back here.'

'Not so much a blow as…' Mike tried to find words for how confused he was being back in England. 'Not sure how I feel about it, to be honest,' he concluded. 'Jen's asked me to say a few words at the funeral. I'm dreading it.'

'I'm not surprised,' Pam replied. 'I'd find that so hard. Trying to balance what you feel and what you know. Oh, talking of feeling stuff,' she continued, 'I worried about your sleeping in the bed where Henry died even though you said you didn't mind. But anyway, I got on to John Lewis in Cambridge. Actually, I rang customer services and pulled strings, channelled a bit of Eleni. Said I was preparing the house for the return of Stephanie's daughter and needed new things immediately and couldn't get to the store because of being shot.

'People do like the vicarious thing of being associated with a murder, it's something we always face. But this time it helped. They'd all read about the case or seen it on the news and were brilliant. They delivered a new mattress and new pillows and took away the old one. I got some plain green sheets and duvet cover. I also got lots of fake palms and an olive tree. I've promised Jen to water her garden, but I certainly don't think I'd risk my plant-caring skills further than that. Indoor plants die the moment they see me. Anyhow, it makes the room upstairs look less bare and more welcoming while you're here. How long are you here for?' she added.

'Don't know, really,' he admitted. 'Depends on what comes up I suppose.'

Pam gave a tight smile. She hoped he'd stay but couldn't force him. This was her city, not his.

'Do you think there'll be many people at Henry's funeral?' she wondered as they took their drinks and a bowl of spiced nuts into the garden. 'I can't imagine he still had many friends in England.'

'No,' Mike agreed. He hated funerals, and this one would be even worse than the others. It had begun with his father and then his mother, and even the Cretan funerals of distant aunts and cousins he'd attended subsequently hadn't removed those memories. And it was less than a month since that strange bleak funeral for Stephanie, with Jen and Pam in wheelchairs and the guilt of having allowed Jen to go off with Manolis weighing on him. He was only here because it was Henry. Henry deserved that. He'd go back to Crete as soon as he could get away, there was nothing he could do here. Moreover, now he was here in Jen's house, he saw clearly that if there had been a killer, they'd let themselves in and left no trace. Which meant they'd had to have had a key, which seemed unlikely. Jen had told him she'd changed the locks and guarded her new keys carefully, having realised, rather too late, that her mother had given copies of the old key to half the world.

Perhaps it had been a natural death, though he wasn't about to start arguing about this with Pam. It was clear that she'd made up her mind. He couldn't lead her life for her. But he could try to support her while he was here.

Pam had bought a selection of meze and they ate it

in the garden talking houses. Neither of them wanted to talk about the funeral or Henry's death. Mike hoped he could postpone discussing that until after the funeral. If there had been another member of 17 November, Henry had never managed to discover who they were, so there was very little likelihood of him and Pam finding out. Like the other members of the terrorist group, they'd stayed hidden for decades. Perhaps Pam would change her mind about it being a murder after the funeral. In the meantime, he could get her to think about life in Chiona. He was delighted Henry had left her his house; it felt right, somehow.

'So,' he began. 'I designed the house for Henry based on his massive library which you don't have. How can I adapt it for you?'

'I can't really believe it's mine,' Pam admitted. 'It will take time, though it is amazing.' She bit her lip. 'To have my own little house by the sea, it feels like a dream.'

'I think you could remove half the bookcase and turn some of the rest into cupboards for your stuff.'

'I don't actually have much stuff. It's currently sitting in three small boxes in Jen's giant cupboard.'

'A gypsy, like me?'

'It would appear so. Though, up to now, a static gypsy if such a thing is possible.'

'If you did begin to collect something, what would it be?

The combination of possible collections took them through lunch and up to the World Cup Final which itself took them through to supper. Pam quickly became a fan of the teenage French player, Kylian Mbappe, and found herself leaping to her feet when he scored the team's fourth goal enabling France to beat Croatia 4-2.

'What a great match,' said Pam as Mike inspected the cupboards and the fridge.

'How about spaghetti carbonara?' he asked.

'Perfect,' she replied. Talking about favourite pastas and pizzas saw them through to a time they felt it wasn't bad manners to say they were having an early night what with the funeral tomorrow. It was odd, thought Mike, they'd been so relaxed and easy with each other in Crete, and here they were moving around each other like strangers. Neither of them wanting an argument, or least hoping to shelve it for the moment.

'By the way, one of my colleagues has warned that Hawkswood, the new DCI is coming to the funeral.'

'Warned.' Mike frowned. 'What haven't you told me?'

Pam explained about the whole hospitality thing, and how Hawkswood hated her and wanted to get her on some kind of charge.

'God, what a bastard. Nikos would be apoplectic if he heard that.' No wonder she was having panic attacks.

'My old staff are being incredibly loyal,' she told him.' They tell me what's going on.'

'I bet you were popular,' Mike smiled at her. 'Did you have a nickname?' Silly question, really.

'Yes, Tips, as in PG,' she added. 'Better than the Chief Constable's which is Wreck, his name being Seaworthy. Hawkswood is Plank'.

'As in thick as a…?' he asked.

'Yup. And he is. Did you have one?' she asked him. 'Such a police thing, isn't it?'

'Yes, Cherry after the boot polish. Before I escaped to go undercover, the level of racism I had to face every day was pretty vile.'

Pam filled him in on how she'd reported her sergeant for using the word 'coon'.

'I've had that word whispered at me by colleagues in the Met, even from other DIs, and I've been called a monkey and the N word to my face,' Mike told her. 'Sorry the bastard stopped you getting promotion. That's vile.'

'My old colleague Paul is taking up the case with the union.'

'Do you want that?'

'Let's put it that I don't not want it. I don't think that the old chums network should let Butcher off the hook. Trouble is I liked Dave. He could drink too much and was something of a dinosaur, but he was an honest cop. And worked hard. Stupid bugger. And now he's drinking. Actually, he came round here and threatened me last week.'

'Jesus, Pam. Are you all right? Did you report it?' he asked.

'No. I dealt with it. It'll blow over. I'm not going to think about it.'

Mike frowned but decided not to argue.

The funeral was scheduled for eleven in the morning to allow mourners to arrive from London. The East Chapel attached to the crematorium was small, only three rows deep, either side of the huge wooden door that felt as though it belonged to a much larger building. There was also an alcove under which was the plain wooden coffin and above it was a Middle Eastern-style wooden canopy with a curtain which, Mike imagined would close before the coffin was taken to the fire.

He shivered. But was burial any better?

It was the smaller of the two chapels at the site, and surprisingly full. Mike counted around thirty people there including a woman in a grey suit who said she was the humanist celebrant. There were also three musicians already sitting at the back with their instruments including a lyra and a bouzouki, so there would also be live Greek music. This wasn't like any funeral he'd been to before. Someone had put a lot of thought into this. Mike imagined how shocked the village would be that Henry hadn't had a priest to say prayers for him, but perhaps the local priest in Palaikastro would arrange a service for the villagers. He'd talk to Aunt Sofia when he got back. They'd also be shocked that the celebrant was a woman; Henry would have loved that, he enjoyed subverting people's ideas of who he was. Perhaps he'd chosen her specially.

The first person Mike recognised was Jen, looking beautiful in a purple dress with a pale grey scarf around her shoulders. She'd cut her hair shorter and it suited her. She smiled at him and came over.

'Henry always said he didn't want black at his funeral, so I did the next best thing,' she told him. 'And thank you for agreeing to speak for Mum. I just couldn't do it.'

'You look lovely,' he said, and she did. 'And it's not a problem.' She smiled at him, wistfully, and then stepped back as Colin, her father, came forward, followed by a pale thin woman and a tall younger man, who looked just like her. Colin hugged Mike and then Pam.

'This is my wife, Caroline and my son Oliver. Luca couldn't make it but sent a donation. We were so fond…'

'Isn't it good to see all these people,' interrupted Jen. 'Henry would have been so touched. He…' she stopped. This was going to be a day of unfinished sentences.

'Well, someone didn't know about his no black wishes,' Mike whispered to Jen, seeing a bald, chubby man, enter wearing a black velvet suit with a white carnation pinned to the jacket. He was sweating already and wiped his head with a large white handkerchief.

'OTT or what!' whispered Jen back, and Mike immediately remembered how they always made each other laugh. He smiled at her and squeezed her shoulder.

'Great moustache,' he noted, as another man came in and started to chat with Velvet Suit. 'Looks as if it belongs in an earlier era.'

'Theodore Roosevelt, perhaps or Trotsky,' she replied.

Mike watched as another man came in, almost arrogantly and sat at the back. Was he the police officer? He didn't look like one in a designer black jacket and a very gym-honed body. He looked to be in his early thirties. Perhaps he had come to Chiona on holiday and got to know Henry. Mike nodded at him and smiled, but he didn't smile back. MI6? he wondered.

Jen and her family sat in the front row, and Pam and Mike sat behind them and beside a young man wearing a purple waistcoat and no jacket, who said he was from the Cambridge office of the Terrence Higgins Trust. 'Henry supported us for years,' he said. 'He'd drop in when he was in town. And all the donations today are coming to us.'

Yet another side of Henry, thought Mike. Along with him being so much richer than we knew. Then he let himself listen to the glorious soaring notes of Allegri's *Miserere* the volume of which had been turned up as everyone took their seats. Perhaps the funeral wouldn't be so bad after all, he thought. And once it was over he could go home to Crete.

CHAPTER 22

If the service lacked religious ceremony, it made up for it in the emotional depth of the music and readings.

Jen spoke first, briefly, saying that Henry had been the most caring of godfathers, and the next person to read was the man with the splendid grey moustache. He stepped up to the lectern with the relaxed grace of someone used to giving readings, almost certainly an academic. He read an extract of a poem by Elytis, both in Greek and English, and he was followed by another man who also had the confidence of someone accustomed to addressing an audience. Not an academic, thought Pam. He had more of the bearing of a soldier, and his deep grey eyes looked as though they missed nothing.

'I've known Henry for most of my life,' he began, 'and, like all those of you who were lucky enough to have him as a friend, I have a very large collection of letters from him.'

The congregation gave a warm murmur of recognition, and Pam remembered the letters that would regularly arrive in Maddalena's bakery. They must have been replies to Henry's own letters.

'Sifting through them,' the man continued, 'trying to find one that embodied Henry, I have chosen this one which he sent me some thirty years ago. As we all know, Henry wrote with a lifetime of knowledge and never used one word where he could throw in two.' Again there was a low murmur of shared pleasure.

He began to read. He had a quiet, melodious voice, but one that easily filled the chapel.

'I write about history, but not about my real fascination in historical quirks, these odd and unpredictable events that change history, which interest me so much more. It amuses me to think that when the Roman army acclaimed the future Emperor Jovian, it was very likely a mistake. They were almost certainly shouting the name of the Emperor Julianus, thinking that he had recovered and was not dead, after all. History as a mistake, as a series of Chinese whispers. It happens more often than you think.

'Memories themselves create fabrications for they are the illusion of a past reality. They are the currency of the old, the fragments of a life refracted through individual observation and experience. Images in a glass. But the images we construct are not necessarily the same as those that others believe they saw.

'We see as through a glass darkly... When I was a boy in chapel at school the vicar would often read that passage from Paul. I never understood the imagery of the glass. If it was glass, I worried, why wasn't it clear? How could you see through a glass if it was dark? Was it like the smoked glass that we were given to watch the eclipse with? I wanted to ask our science master, but I didn't. I was afraid of his ridicule, of the laughter of my classmates. So, I kept quiet and copied the diagrams he wrote on the board. They were, of course, completely mystifying. I much preferred the neat lists of history. Battles, dates, accessions, names, empires, kings. An orderly history of the world for middle class English children. With England still at the centre. England radiating power and benevolence and railways and trade. Like the picture of Britannia in the stained-glass

window of the chapel. Radiating light. Through clear glass.

'And Henry radiated laughter and knowledge and light throughout his life. We shall miss him.'

Pam knew Mike was next and she gave his hand an encouraging squeeze. 'Hope I don't let him down,' he whispered to her.

Mike had written a speech, but she saw he wasn't reading it.

'Good morning,' he began. 'I feel something of a fraud being here when so many of you have known Henry for so long, and I've only known him for two years, but sitting silently together watching the sun rise, as we often did, does create a special bond of friendship.

'But I'm not only remembering Henry on my own behalf. Jen, Henry's goddaughter has asked me to speak on behalf of her mother, Stephanie Michaels, whose own death we are still mourning. So, I will try to do my best.

'Stephanie wrote a great deal about Henry, and they had monumental rows and warm reconciliations. The very last thing she wrote was written for him.'

Mike looked now at his notes. 'She wrote "We were all young in those days, we share that." But they shared so much more. They shared a life, lived separately and together. And I know that Stephanie felt her life was enriched by his wisdom and his kindness as I do. I will miss him arriving on my doorstep with pastries from the wonderful Maddalena, who, I must tell you says that he was the best man she ever knew. And that includes her own husband.

'Henry was a man like no other. There is nobody else who, when you comment on how windy it is will tell you...' Mike glanced down at his notes again, 'that if it hadn't been for contrary winds delaying the British ships, the royalists might have won a crucial battle at Noirmoutier in 1795.'

A small murmur of amusement and recognition again filled the chapel.

'And thinking of St Paul, and following that last letter, Henry would note that he'd had problems with Aegean storms, too. Storms change lives, Henry used to say. Storms change history. Think of the storm that destroyed the Spanish Armada. Weather changes history. I will never forget that he told me how the Americans had three potential targets for their atomic bomb, but two were hidden in the mist. Only Hiroshima was visible that day.

'Henry was particularly conscious of weather since it was a rainstorm which changed his own life and killed Laurent, the young archaeologist both he and Stephanie loved so dearly, and which remained another bond between them.

'I'd like to end with something Henry once said to me. "Rainstorms and rainbows are the unpredictable nature of the world in which we live. We do our best somewhere in the middle of the two." Henry did his best every day of his life. I am so much richer for having had him as a friend.'

Mike returned to his seat and noticed Pam was wiping tears from her cheeks. A man behind him patted him on the shoulder and whispered, 'Well done.'

The celebrant thanked the speakers and said how Henry had touched the lives of so many and would be remembered in so many ways. Then she indicated for the musicians to step forward.

'Good morning,' said the one holding a bouzouki, 'We are the London Greek Collective, and it is a great honour to be able to play here at the funeral of a man who loved our nation.'

They began to play and immediately the congregation realised the music Henry had chosen was the heart-breaking Theodorakis song, *sto perigali.*

Later, Mike explained that the song was all the more powerful because it had been banned by the Junta. Almost everyone in the room was silently crying. As the music faded away, the coffin slid backwards, and the curtain closed. Some of the sobs were louder now. Pam was crying openly, and Mike gave her a hug. Colin was comforting Jen, and his wife Caroline hugging her son.

Then it was over, and everyone began to move outside and examine the many wreaths.

Henry's solicitor had told him that he would organise any messages and wreaths that Henry's friends in Greece might want to send and that they'd be covered by the funeral expenses Henry had put aside. Mike had passed this on to Aunt Sofia and Maddalena and the archaeologist, Irini, and they had clearly told many others as there were a dozen or more wreaths with their names. Mike took pictures of them so he could send them back to Crete. Or show them when he returned, which he hoped would be soon.

Pam was also taking pictures of the wreaths, stepping carefully between them. There was a large one with white lilies from Nikos Leotakis, she saw. It must have been Eleni who organised that, Nikos and Henry were never friends. She took pictures of the labels for future reference. You never knew, she thought, whether the killer couldn't resist that final act. But these appeared to be from friends and universities. She straightened up as she saw one of the readers approach her. It was the elderly man who had read the letter from Henry. He smiled at her as she turned towards him.

'Oliver Timberly,' he said, putting out his hand. 'I have a feeling you may be DI Pam Gregory.'

'I am,' she said, shaking his hand, 'and this is Mike Petersen.'

Mike shook the man's hand, too. It was a firm grip, strong, but not bruising.

'There isn't a wake as such,' he told them, 'though I believe that some of Henry's London friends are heading to The Free Press for a drink, but I wondered whether I might come to your house and have a few words?'

'Well, yes...' began Pam.

'Say in an hour or so. And...' he dropped his voice, '...the man over there with the red hair, in the dark grey suit who is fidgeting with his tie is called Christopher Grey. I think it would be wise not to talk to him.'

He moved a step back.

'Henry would have most certainly appreciated your courtesy in coming here today,' he said, loud enough to be heard by those nearby and moved back towards a slim woman wearing a grey cotton dress. Probably his wife, Pam thought. She smiled at them, and then she and Oliver joined the man with the splendid moustache and began to chat.

After Oliver moved away, Ian Coules himself came up to them.

'Glad to see Oliver has had a word,' he said. 'Such a good friend of Henry's.'

'Do you know who all these people are?' asked Pam.

'Well, the man with Oliver and Petra who read the Elytis is Roderick Beaton, from King's College London, and that's Jules, who was Henry's publisher.' He pointed to the Velvet Suit. 'I think there are a few people from his old college, Emmanuel. Altogether a very moving service I thought. I very much appreciated what you said, Mike.'

'Thank you,' said Mike.

'Never easy these things,' added Ian, picking up Mike's thoughts.

'It all really felt like Henry,' said Pam.

'Yes,' agreed Ian. 'But then he did choose the music and some of the readings. Not the letter. Excellent choice by Oliver. But then Oliver has known him a very long time.'

Mike saw the man Oliver said was Christopher Grey coming in their direction.

'I think this is the moment for us to leave,' he whispered to Pam.

'I don't really want to speak to that man,' Pam told Ian. 'I wonder whether...'

'Of course, my dear,' said Ian, and immediately walked over to Christopher Grey and began to talk.

Mike saw that Jen and her family were chatting with the musicians and he gave her a goodbye wave. She nodded and waved back. They turned away from the wreaths and found a smart elderly woman standing in front of them. She wore a black linen dress with a matching jacket and her round burnished earrings matched the simple circular gold collar which hung around her neck like part of a scimitar.

She was effortlessly elegant, thought Pam, knowing she could never look like that in a hundred years. Somehow, this woman had travelled to the funeral and sat through the service without her dress showing a single crease whereas Pam felt her own linen dress looked as though she'd crumpled it up and sat on it. And, unlike Pam, she also seemed comfortable navigating the gaps between the paving stones in the slimmest of stiletto heels. She reminded Pam of Eleni, perhaps it was her clothes or the single slash of vivid scarlet lipstick or just the sense of confidence and determination.

'Excuse, me, but I believe you are Mike?' The accent was French, Pam heard, Mike's name becoming 'Meek'.

'Madame,' he replied, giving her a quick smile. 'And you are?'

'My name is Deirdre Girard. You may call me Didi...'

'You are Patrice's widow?' interrupted Pam, 'I'm

sorry, I couldn't help hearing...'

'Ah,' continued the woman. 'Then you must be the Detective. I need to talk with you now. My husband was killed two weeks ago, and you will prove who was the assassin.'

CHAPTER 23

'There is a garden over there. We will walk there? Yes?'

Pam nodded. Madame Didi Girard was not a woman you could say no to easily, she thought. Again, rather like Eleni.

Mike shrugged helplessly, and they followed Didi towards a memorial garden with lawns and trees and a couple of benches. They'd tried hard to make it attractive with a small pond, its edges filled with small yellow flowers, while roses cascaded from a wall behind them, but the urns reminded them that this wasn't merely a garden.

There was also a small lawn, dotted with daisies, and Pam had a flash of memory of making a daisy-chain crown and her father placing it on her head. All her happy memories were of the years before he died. Death. It was this place that made you start thinking of other deaths. 'Pull yourself together, Pam' she said to herself. She needed to find out why Patrice's widow was here and what she wanted, not that it was likely that either she or Mike could do anything.

'Before you say anything, Madame Girard,' Pam began, 'I have to warn you that I am on medical leave and not able to conduct any inquiries at this moment and I have no means to work with the French police.'

And wouldn't want to, anyway, she didn't add.

'*Naturellement*,' replied the widow of the assassinated lawyer as if she expected no other response. 'Because this is not, what do you say, an official investigation. That is what the French police pretend to do. Maybe they will arrest a man, but he will not be the man who killed Patrice.'

'Why's that?' asked Mike.

'Because the man who killed my husband is a member of the Intelligence Service. Ours, not yours, the DGSE,' she added. 'His name is Rafael Albin, and he now works with the Greek billionaire, who, I believe you know.'

'Nikos Leotakis?' asked Pam, incredulously. This was becoming a very strange conversation. The woman was clearly unhinged, grief can do that, she knew, but she hadn't expected it here. She needed to extricate them gently.

'Rafael?' asked Mike, and Pam called up her recent memories of Leotakis's French bodyguard. He shimmered, she remembered. He seemed to have a variety of duties, working as Leotakis's personal waiter as well as being his bodyguard. When Pam had dinner with Leotakis in his Dorset manor house, he was there, with a cashmere wrap or a drink or anything you needed just as you realised that this was what you did want. She'd thought of him as a kind of magician; the steward on Nikos's jet had told her he'd previously been maître d' at one of the best restaurants in Paris and he'd learned that shimmer there.

'Rafael works for French intelligence?' she asked. Was this true? In any case, it was hardly relevant. She was certain that Henry's death had nothing at all to do with Leotakis or his French bodyguard.

'This is the truth,' Didi gave a shrug that included both her shoulders and arms and Pam couldn't help admitting how expressive it was. 'And I can tell you that ten years ago they began to watch my husband.' She smiled. 'Patrice was very good at knowing this. He always realised when somebody watched him. It was not so unusual. Or surprising,' she added.

It sounded most unlikely to Pam. She saw Mike frowning, too.

'Of course, when your client is accused of espionage for the Stasi then *naturellement*, people want to know to whom you speak and who you meet. There was one case,' Didi smiled again at the memory. 'Patrice has a client East Germany wants back and, of course this is a very political case, and they watch Patrice. So, every day Patrice has breakfast with Georges Kiejman, who of course then was the lawyer of Jacques Chirac, who was our President. Ah George! He was the most seductive man I ever met, still is perhaps but I have not seen him so many years… he is still married to his little Princesse…'

Mike glanced at Pam whose eyebrows said everything.

'You were talking about Mr Leotakis's bodyguard, Rafael,' she interrupted.

'Bodyguard? No, he does not guard his body, he is executer…'

'Executor?' asked Pam thinking of the tall man, Oliver whose card she could feel in her pocket. And the lawyer, Ian Coules, Henry's executors.

'I think in French it can also mean enforcer,' explained Mike. 'Someone who does jobs for people.'

'*Précisément*,' replied Didi. 'And the job was to kill my husband. But of course the police they will never accept this.'

'And you think he also killed Henry?' asked Pam. 'That is why you're here?'

'Henri was killed? I did not know. I came here because Patrice loved him. It is what he would have wanted.'

'But you didn't?' asked Mike hearing an edge in her words.

'I did not know Henri so much,' she said. 'I thought he was a weak man. What did he do with his life? Nothing. But Patrice, he did not agree. But he knew Henri so many years.'

'Henry was a brilliant historian,' said Pam, furious. How dare this woman turn up at his funeral and attack him. 'And you could hear today how much people loved him.'

'It surprised me how sentimental the English are. I did not expect it. And Henri, too. A sentimental man.'

'Who was possibly killed by the same man who killed your husband,' Mike said quietly, before Pam could start arguing about the funeral service.

'So you will get the proof of this. It was ordered by Nikos Leotakis.'

'Why on earth should Nikos Leotakis kill your husband?' asked Mike, beginning to wish they'd never agreed to talk with this dreadful woman.

'My husband was writing a book on his life. He had many secrets. And yes, perhaps he told Henri some things when he came to see him just two weeks ago. They talked during many hours and Patrice was worried afterwards. Perhaps Henri began to investigate these things. It is one thing he did. Henri in the library. I would laugh at him. But he verified the facts always.'

'But Henry thought that Patrice was killed because of his friendship with Alexandros Yotopoulos,' said Pam. 'Nothing to do with Leotakis.'

'But that is absurd. Of course, Patrice was also writing about Alexandros. They were friends so many years. But now Alexandros is in prison all his life and that chapter is closed. There is no reason to kill. There are no secrets.'

'But...' Pam began, and then felt Mike's hand on

her shoulder. He was right. This wasn't a woman they could trust.

'But how do you know it was Rafael?' she asked instead.

'Because it was his car.'

'The police know that?' she asked.

This changed everything. Ever since Henry had told them about Patrice's death, she had been guessing about his death as she was about Henry's, something far removed from the way she normally approached a case. But if the car of the shooter belonged to Rafael, that was something else entirely. That was evidence. Had Henry been wrong about it all? Had his own death actually been stress?

'It was very early in the morning. It was Sunday morning, and most people were asleep, but Patrice he does not sleep in the morning. He goes to the market for the bread, and sometimes to the café Buci. It opens early and he has the *café crème* and *croissant aux amandes* I do not allow. His liver. And also the cigarette I do not allow. As if that matters now,' she added bitterly.

'He was shot from a car?' asked Mike

'The police tell me this. There was a car and Patrice, they think, walked towards the car. Perhaps, he knew the driver, say the police, because he was very close to the car when they shoot him. Then they drive away. Nobody sees anything.'

'CCTV?' asked Pam.

'Not in our street, rue Mazarine. This is a street away from Boulevard Saint-Germain and which has how do you say a unique direction.'

'A one-way street,' Mike translated.

'*Bien*, and this street goes down towards the Buci and there you can turn left and also an acute left. Of course, when there are cars you cannot make this acute left, but it was early and there was a car which made this turn at seven in the morning. It was a grey Citroen, a very common car, but it turned very fast out of Mazarine and went back up rue Dauphine and towards the Quais.'

'And the police have the number plate of that car?' Pam was now thinking along the lines she'd have followed herself.

'I am certain they do, but they do not tell me. But the camera is on a jewellery shop, and he is my friend, and he shows me the film.'

'And you asked the police about it.'

'Of course not. I do not trust the police. In France the police it is political. It is not the same here?'

'Not often,' said Pam.

'Patrice had friends who can discover these things. They looked at the number and the car belonged to Rafael Albin.'

'But he doesn't live in France. He's in Crete or Dorset with Mr Leotakis.'

'Perhaps. But you have the Channel Tunnel. It is one day to drive from England and return.'

'Could you let me have the details of the number plate?' If the CCTV from Norfolk Street showed the same car, that would change everything.

'I send to your phone,' said Didi.

Pam gave her the number.

'I know you think it's not relevant,' said Mike, 'but can you tell us how Patrice became friends with Henry.'

'Oh, that is simple. Popi introduced them.'

'Popi Filotaki?' asked Mike. Popi seemed to know everyone.

'Yes, she is my good friend. I know her since I am a student. She studied psychology at the Sorbonne and we were friends. Then she went back to Athens for the Polytechnic. You know about this?'

'We do,' said Pam. 'Henry told us about it. His – and Popi's – friend was killed.'

'Ah yes, Stephanie. I met her once. She dressed like a gypsy. And she drank. Not an interesting woman.'

Depends on what you think is interesting, thought Mike. His dislike of Madame Girard intensified.

'After the tragedy I do not see her for many years, then Patrice and I have a house on Crete. I was then an archaeologist and I worked near Palaikastro. And I thought of Popi. I knew the telephone of her parents and we meet. And we become friends again. And Henry comes to stay with us with Laurent. And yes, Henry was kind to Popi. After that, we are always friends.'

'Popi was very upset about Jen.'

'Yes, her goddaughter; she loves her. Popi cannot have children you know because of what they do to her in that prison after she is arrested. Jen is like her daughter.'

'Jen loves her, too,' said Pam.

'Good. So she should.' Didi paused and looked around her as if surprised to find herself in this garden. So provincial. In Paris, it would be more formal.

'Popi should never go to stay with Leotakis. That is the big mistake. I tell her.'

Pam's mind was racing. Could Rafael be responsible for Henry's death? He could certainly have driven from Dorset overnight, and thinking back to their time at the Leotakis estate in Crete, this was the one time when Henry's killer could have stolen the keys to Stephanie's house.

If evidence was beginning to mount up against Rafael, she thought, that led straight to Leotakis with the possible motive being the book Patrice was writing. She hoped it wasn't the case, she'd really warmed to Leotakis. Besides, if it was him, it was never going to go to court, he had far too many powerful friends.

'But Manolis was caught, thanks to Pam,' said Mike. 'And Leotakis,' he added. His voice was icy.

But this woman had known Yotopoulos and that could be helpful.

'Did you know Alexandros Yotopoulos in those days?' he asked, changing his tone to something friendlier.

'Yes. Why do you ask that? Patrice knew him in 1968 and 1969. They marched together and they made plans together. He was writing it in his book.'

'Did the police take that?' This could be crucial.

'They took Patrice's computer and all his files, which I will never see again of course.'

'That's a pity,' said Pam, wondering how she could get hold of them.

'And you will investigate? she asked Pam.

'I will,' said Pam, though she wasn't sure how. 'And now we should leave,' she added, looking around and seeing a new funeral party arrive. She'd seen Hawkswood lurking behind the wreaths, but he'd gone now. She shook hands with Madame Girard and she and Mike began to walk back to their car.

'One good thing about meeting Didi is that we haven't had to talk to Hawkswood or Christopher Grey,' said Pam as they walked into the carpark noticing that all of Henry's mourners had left.

'How do you think you can investigate Patrice's death?' asked Mike.

'I don't. I just didn't want to tell her that.'

'Don't you think she was lying?'

They drove back to St Barnabas Road where Mike had parked and began to walk down Mill Road and through the cemetery to Norfolk Street. A day of cemeteries thought Pam as they stepped between the trees down the dark leafy path.

The old cemetery was a haven for the local druggies, not that they'd be any concern of hers anymore. She turned to Mike. 'Answering your earlier question, I don't know. Why should Didi lie?'

'Possibly because she wants to protect the real killer?'

'You think she's a friend of the killer? Who killed her husband? I can't buy that. She'd have to be an extraordinary actress.'

'Maybe she is.'

'And maybe she isn't. Maybe Rafael is involved in some way.' She sighed. 'What I'm trying to do is separate what I feel as Henry's friend and what I think as a detective. If this was a case I was investigating I'd be looking for evidence.'

'And motive.'

'Yes. Oh yes, motive. As my former colleague, Paul, pointed out, if Hawkswood was investigating this – and I'm glad now he isn't, as all this would infuriate him – he'd ask who benefitted from Henry's death. And that would lead him straight to me.'

'*Cui bono*,' said Mike. 'But you didn't.'

'Well, no. I was in Crete when he died. Anyhow, that's not the point. A dodgy cop could create a case.'

'Is Hawkswood dodgy?'

'Something about him has never smelled quite right. Nothing anyone could prove. But now… He really hates me.' she concluded. 'And Paul says I should take that seriously.'

'Maybe you should.'

'I don't know.' She sighed. 'What I really want to know is whether the Norfolk Street CCTV picked up a car the night Henry died. And if, by any chance the car belongs to Rafael, which might suggest that Rafael killed Patrice.'

'Unless someone stole Rafael's car. Maybe he left it behind in France.'

'That's also possible. And if there is a link with Leotakis, there's nothing we can do. When Stephanie died, the first witness I interviewed was Anna, the architect who designed his new museum here in Cambridge. She said laws didn't apply to Leotakis.'

'I don't think anyone's above murder.'

'If you're as powerful as Nikos, maybe you can get away with anything.'

'Yes. With friends at the very top.'

'From the PM down... yes.'

'But it could be someone wanting to frame Leotakis.' Mike frowned.

'That's always an option. He must have enemies. It's something we thought about when we were investigating Stephanie's death.'

'What are you going to do?' You, Pam thought, not we.

'I'm going to listen to Henry. He thought he was in danger because of a terrorist. So, I'm going to go on exploring that, and no bloody DCI is going to stop me.'

CHAPTER 24

Are terrorist acts crimes?

We say: no. The acts of 17 November are symbolic and necessary. We chose targets which symbolise power, and we attack the imperialist domination of capitalism and the exploitation of the people.

CHAPTER 25

'I don't know about you,' said Pam, letting them into the house, 'but I could use a drink. Oh my God, I'm so sorry. I said that without thinking.'

'I've never felt more like a drink,' replied Mike, 'but I really don't dare. I wasn't ever really an alcoholic in the sense of enjoying drinking; I drank to kill myself, but the amount I drank then was terrifying and I don't know if I started again whether I'd go back to that. It's better not to try it. I'm getting used to being sober.'

'Did you drink a lot when you were undercover?'

'Not much, but we did smoke quite a bit of weed. And that's something I don't miss. I like having a clear head.'

'Coffee then?' she asked. 'We do need clear heads. And let's eat these *pide* before they get cold.'

They'd stopped off at the Box Café when they both realised how hungry they were and had bought the café's famous Turkish flat breads stuffed with Mediterranean vegetables and feta cheese.

'Yes,' replied Mike. 'Definitely coffee, but don't let me stop you having a drink.'

'Perhaps I shouldn't,' she reflected. 'I was drinking a bit too much before I got involved with Stephanie's murder. Actually, seeing Stephanie's liver was something of a wake-up call. Not that I was an alkie, but when

I was working, there weren't many days when I didn't have a drink. And more than one when I was with Richard. Just needed it then to survive. I do need to cut down. Will help me lose weight, too.'

'You look fine,' replied Mike. 'And this is Henry's wake. We should raise a glass or a cup to him.'

'A glass then. Maybe a small whisky. I did notice a bottle. It seems the right thing for a wake.'

Pam smiled at him. There weren't that many straight men she knew who could give you a compliment without flirting but Mike could. And she was glad he'd brought the conversation back to Henry.

'And there's this man ...what was his name? Henry's old friend...coming round in a bit.'

Mike pulled the card out of his pocket. 'Oliver. Oliver Timberly.'

'Why do you think he wants to talk to us?' she asked.

'Could be something to do with the will,' he replied. 'But I don't think...You know, there was something about him.'

'I know what you mean. Quiet authority.'

'I thought he might have been military,' said Mike.

'Yes, he did have that way of walking,' she agreed. 'Henry said he was one of his oldest friends. I wonder how they met.'

'Could have been school or university.'

Of course, thought Pam. That's how most people have old friends. She'd had one or two friends at school, but her mother had never wanted them to come to her house, and the few who had stayed in touch after school were kept away from her by Richard. Then there was only Zofia and Grace and her work colleagues. And now Mike. But there had also been Henry. And Stavros, if she could think of him as a friend.

She put the filled *pide* onto plates. She didn't want

Oliver to arrive and find her stuffing herself.

'Look,' she began as she bit into the *pide* which immediately squirted tomato sauce onto her dress. She went to the kitchen to get some damp kitchen towel and began to dab it.

'I bet Didi doesn't cover her clothes with food,' she complained.

'She probably cuts it into minute portions which she eats with a knife and fork,' agreed Mike, checking his phone.

'Ah. You miss half the pleasure.' She ate a few mouthfuls then put the stuffed bread down.

'So, tell me about Oliver Timberly,' she said.

'How did you…?'

'Because it's what I was about to do, and you and I do think alike on a lot of things.'

'Not army,' Mike said. 'And absolutely not a person to promote themselves. His wife pops up a bit, too. She's a specialist in permaculture, though I have no idea what that means.'

'I don't either.'

'But there is this. It's part of an academic paper on the aftermath of the Yugoslav wars. Seems that Oliver worked for the International Criminal Court gathering evidence against Milosovic and his generals.'

'Wow. Scary stuff. I mean, brave. You'd have to be really brave.'

'There's also a link to some bio. Wow. Interesting. Worked for Amnesty for a few years, and then for the Hague. Director of the Project for International Disarmament. Retired. Spends some of the year at his home at Agios Nikolaos in Crete.'

'Not a soldier then. And a good guy.' Pam sat back and thought for a moment. Why was he coming? Surely not to talk about the will?

'Do you really think he's coming here because I

inherited Henry's house?' she asked.

Mike shook his head.

'Then why?'

'Why don't we ask him when he gets here? How should we play this?'

'We listen and commit ourselves to nothing,' Pam suggested thoughtfully. 'But after what he said in the chapel this morning, I'm totally certain he cared about Henry.'

'Is caring enough? Perhaps he's heard that we think Henry was killed and wants to tell us to move on.' He paused for a moment. 'Perhaps we should.'

'And let Henry's killer get away with murder?'

'If there was a killer. I'm beginning to think maybe Henry was stressed and had heart failure.'

She was about to start arguing but was stopped by a brisk knock at the door. Oliver seemed taller in this small house, and he almost ducked as he walked in through the door.

'It's been rather a day,' she said, escorting him down the passage and into the sitting room. 'I was thinking of a whisky, but there's coffee if you prefer.'

'A whisky would be perfect,' said Oliver. 'Luckily, Petra, that's my wife, is driving me home later. She's meeting an old friend in the Botanic Gardens to talk about plums, I think.'

What was there to say about plums? thought Pam, showing him into the main room.

'Have you ever been here before?' she asked. 'I know Henry used to stay here sometimes.'

'No,' he said, looking around, admiringly. 'Isn't this a wonderful house? Henry always said it was unique. No. I tended to meet him in Heraklion; Petra and I have a house in Agios Nikolaos. It's about halfway between Heraklion and Sitia, but we always seemed to meet in Heraklion.'

'Mike,' Pam called. 'Can you bring us two whiskies, if you don't mind.'

'Will do,' Mike replied from the kitchen. A few moments later, he came in with a bottle of Balvenie under his arm and two tumblers and a small jug of water in his hands. He put them down on the table.

Oliver looked at the bottle. 'Balvenie Doublewood. That's rather splendid.'

'Is it special?' Pam asked. 'It's Jen's. Perhaps we shouldn't...'

'I'll buy her another bottle,' Oliver replied. 'I think it's just what one needs after a funeral.'

Pam watched him pour a small amount of whisky into the glass and then add a teaspoon-full of water. She copied him and then sipped the spirit expecting the usual hit at the back of her throat. Except there wasn't one; this was smooth and warming.

'That's good,' she said, appreciatively. There was so much she was learning every day being with people like Jen and Oliver. It was a world she could get used to, like this whisky.

Mike came back into the room with his coffee, and they all sat down.

Oliver looked around. It was time for him to put his cards on the table. He'd heard from Ian Coules who had heard it from the police, that Pam had questioned the death certificate, and, if that was so, he wondered what she might be thinking. Henry had told him in their last telephone call that he had confided in Mike and Pam, but that didn't mean they'd feel they should begin an investigation. They didn't have any resources for a start.

'Right,' he said, smiling at the two police officers, who for different reasons were not currently working as such. 'If you don't mind, could you tell me everything that has happened over the past few weeks?'

Pam gave him a short resumé about the death of

Patrice, and how Henry felt it had been related to his work.

'Henry was worried,' continued Mike. 'He'd sent a report of what was worrying him to his old handler at MI6.'

'Christopher Grey,' said Pam. 'The man you said we shouldn't talk to. Not a very nice man.'

'No,' Oliver agreed. 'He got Henry's report and did nothing.'

'Henry told us he hadn't responded to the report. But you actually know he did nothing?'

'I do. I have one or two old contacts at the Firm, and nothing has been flagged which should have been flagged if his warning had been taken seriously. I also have a copy of the report which Henry sent to me. Have you read it?'

Pam shook her head.

'He starts by summarising his recent work and how he's been investigating the formation of the 17N terrorist group and then goes on to say why he's worried. You could start here at "What Struck me." because the earlier bit isn't so relevant.'

He handed them his tablet and they began to read it, Mike reading it over Pam's shoulder.

What has struck me from the start, has been certain anomalies regarding the earlier murders. The first assassination of the CIA Greek station chief, Richard Welch, took place in December 1975, and the murder of the former intelligence Chief of the Greek security police, Evangelos Mallios the following year. Because of a twenty-year statute of limitations in Greece, the man who admitted his involvement with the killing of Welch, Pavlos Serifis, could do so with impunity, knowing that he could not be charged with these early felonies. However, it is worth noting that in court he rejected his previous confession and claimed that he was innocent. He was sentenced to ten years in prison for his subsequent involvement in later 17 November bombings. Serifis's original confession was that the shooting of Welch was carried out by Yotopoulos, whom he refers to by his codename Lambros. The others, he states, who were involved in the incident, apart from himself, were: Pavlos's cousin Yiannis Serifis, and a blonde woman known as 'Anna'.

This may appear callous on my part, but it is my contention that there was an agreement (perhaps decided by Yotopoulos) that the earlier murders be ascribed to Yotopoulos and Serifis and his cousin Yiannis, who is a well-known figure of the left and former trade unionist. Yiannis and Pavlos went along with this knowing that not only would it be outside the statute of limitations, but because of the illness of Pavlos. (I'm attaching the judgement of the European Court of Human Rights in relation to this and Pavlos's worsening multiple sclerosis.) This meant he would not be incarcerated for long and, indeed, he was released in 2004. No evidence was given regarding Yannis and he was released after the trial.

What I find problematic here is that Yotopoulos, while he is known to have organised the attacks and murders carried out by 17 November, never took part in them. He was always in the background. I believe there was another person. As for the mysterious 'Anna', I believe this may be an early associate of Yotopoulos and someone who has never appeared on the police radar.

All this would be merely historical, Christopher, and not worthy of your consideration were it not that an old friend of mine, who knew Yotopoulos well in Paris, is now keen to talk. It was he who informed me that it was this associate of Yotopoulos who carried out the Welch killing with two others. The reason for him breaking his silence was that this member of 17

November was preparing a significant attack that might be on British soil and which could endanger the lives of British civilians. According to my source, they call themselves the Last Terrorist, though in the world we live in no nomenclature could be less accurate.

Nomenclature, thought Pam. She could just hear Henry saying it. Dear Henry. She was going to miss his voice. And a woman? That had been her thinking, too.

'Ian Coules showed me Henry's will,' said Pam. 'He sent a message to Christopher.'

'He did,' agreed Oliver. 'The message said: "I assume you will now know what to do", the subtext, being I would suggest: I've been killed by this terrorist, so please now take my earlier report seriously.'

'But Christopher hasn't done that, has he?' Mike asked.

'No. It's more than not taking it seriously,' replied Oliver. 'He came up to me at the funeral and said the death was sad, but it was hardly surprising since it was clear that the old man had, in his words, lost it in recent years. But that was nothing to worry about now.'

'The old man! Lost it!' said Pam furious.

'Why?' asked Mike.

'Maybe he's lazy and didn't want to be bothered,' added Oliver. 'Unless he's working against British interests, which does seem far-fetched, though not impossible.'

'The fucker!' exploded Pam. I was right to dislike Christopher, she thought. Instincts working again.

'Perhaps I should start again,' Oliver continued, 'and say that I believed Henry. He was an extremely thorough and careful historian. If his research led him to believe there was another terrorist, then we should probably go down that path. Similarly, if he thought his life was in danger, then we have to admit that he may have been killed.'

The relief. Somebody, who might have influence, who wanted to listen and not tell her she was fantasising. And someone who had links with MI6, somebody who might be able to give them the resources they needed.

'I haven't been thinking about Henry's death as much as his work, and I've been doing a lot of reading about 17N from Henry's books and the Greek trial transcripts and the news coverage,' said Mike.

'That's very helpful,' said Oliver. 'Have you come to any conclusions?'

'Well, what Henry told us was that he was looking at the beginning of 17 November's actions. So, if we stick to 1975, their first assassination, that rules out most of the members who were on trial.'

Pam nodded. 'I thought the same,' she said. She picked up her notebook and read out her own notes. 'There were three Xiros brothers, they all joined later; I don't think the youngest became a terrorist till 1995.'

Mike nodded. 'Virtually all the terrorists joined November 17 after 1980, apart from the potter, Nikos Papanastasiou.'

'A potter?' asked Oliver.

'Yes. These terrorists did seem to have particularly peaceful jobs,' Mike replied. 'Koufoudinas was a beekeeper, Savvas Xiros painted icons, his brother, Christodoulos, made musical instruments. One of the others was an estate agent and another worked in a children's hospital.'

'But they still killed twenty-three people and carried out dozens of bombings and other attacks,' said Pam.

'Which takes us to the Serifis family,' Mike continued. 'Pavlos Serifis said he was involved in the killing of Welch in 1975, as well as his cousin Yiannis and the mysterious Anna. I remember circling that. Then later he retracted the statement and said he'd been injected with a truth drug.'

'I didn't think there was such a thing,' commented Pam.

'They used to use sodium pentothal, didn't they?' replied Mike. 'In the States, anyway. But then they dropped it, as courts stopped believing in it. Think the general argument was, if I remember my university notes, the drug didn't just make people feel like talking, but made them extremely suggestible, so they'd repeat what the questioners said as if it was fact.'

'You studied criminology?' asked Oliver.

'Yup. Did my MA before becoming a cop.'

'So Pavlos was there at the beginning,' said Pam thoughtfully.

Yes,' agreed Mike. 'He'd have been twenty in 1975, so he could have been involved in the Welch killing, but not around in the sixties, when Yotopoulos first started to talk about revolution.'

'This is all so different from the kind of criminals I'm used to,' Pam said, wishing she had her old team to discuss it with. She missed Josh and Roberta; what would they be saying? 'This lot aren't like the usual scumbags who've never done anything decent in their lives.'

'Which is why they think of themselves as political prisoners and freedom fighters not criminals: "The cause not the laws", as they see it,' said Mike.

'Is that a slogan you wrote when you were working for your animal rights group undercover?' Pam asked him, wondering for the first time how much he'd begun to belong to the group and its ideologies.

'Might have been,' Mike laughed. 'I wrote a few. Which is why I understand their mentality. They were committed Marxists, they really believed in the possibility of a revolution creating a fairer world for the working class. Or at least some of them did.'

'Sounds almost as though you approve of them.

They gunned down Richard Welch in the street in front of his wife. They were murderers.'

'But take Welch. To them, he was the enemy. He was the head of the CIA, and to many on the left in the 1970s, it was the CIA who'd helped the Colonels stay in power and torture and kill. Remember what Henry said about the disappointment in the period after Karamanlis came back? The students wanted retribution, they wanted a revolution.'

'Actually, I don't give a damn about their politics, Mike. Welch was a man doing his job and they shot him. And not just him. They killed at least six police officers, who were also just doing their job, the same job you and I have done, hopefully without being gunned down. Not to mention a public prosecutor, some businessmen …' she glanced down at the list she'd made '… a publisher and a neurosurgeon they kneecapped. They were criminals.'

'But if you want to get close to 17N, Pam, you have to understand how they think. A great many war criminals would say they were just doing their job.'

'I don't need to think like them,' she retorted. 'I need to think like a detective. And so do you.'

'I'm not a detective anymore, and I thought you were about to resign. But in any case, I don't see how we're in a position to find Henry's killer, assuming he didn't die from natural causes.'

'One way we can find out, is by seeing what Stuart finds on Henry's computer,' Pam responded. 'And surely this is the least his friends can do.'

'Stuart?' asked Oliver, slightly worried at the friction between the two.

'Stuart Weir, he joined my unit a few weeks ago, he's ex-Met and GCHQ. Henry gave him his computer, but he's been away since then. He's due back today.' She explained how Henry's laptop had been suddenly hit by a virus.

'This changes everything,' said Oliver. 'You've now got a possible killer with access to cybercrime.' He frowned and shook his head. 'This is different. I think you both have to accept the worrying likelihood that you two might also be targets for the latter, and the first thing to do is ensure your safety.'

Mike sighed. 'Isn't this a bit paranoid?' he asked.

'It could be,' said Pam. 'But there's no harm in taking precautions, is there? I don't want to find that my phone's been hacked.'

Mike shrugged. He hated the thought of someone reading his phone, though there was very little on it and most of that was in Greek. Unless, of course, the hacker was Greek.

'Do you want me to go and get some burner phones then? Probably not too hard. We used to use them in the group.'

'Good idea,' said Oliver. 'Let me give you some money. I do have access to funds for this kind of thing.' He took out his wallet and peeled off three twenty-pound notes.

'That will more than cover it,' said Mike. 'See you later,' he said as he turned and went out, banging the door behind him.

'Actually,' said Pam, ignoring Mike's behaviour and thinking furiously, 'Mike's just given me an idea.'

'That Henry wasn't killed?'

'No. That we have to think differently. I've been trying to think like Henry, when I should have been thinking like me, as if this was one of my cases.'

'And you haven't been doing that?' asked Oliver, interested.

'If I was briefing my team, the first thing I'd do is look for CCTV, which I've already been trying to do for the night Henry died, but, but not for the time Yotopoulos was in Paris. And before you say it, I know there wasn't any CCTV around back then. But there were photographs, weren't there?'

'Just about every photojournalist in the world was in Paris in 1968,' he told her.

'Henry was a historian and a writer. He looked for words and read books. He didn't think about images. But there could be pictures of Yotopoulos in the archives, couldn't there?'

'There is certainly one I've seen,' agreed Oliver. 'I can't remember where I found it, but he looked like this.' He ran through the files on his phone. 'Here it is. Since Henry talked to me, I've made a file of his pictures and this one is when he was young.'

Pam looked at the young man with an oval-shaped head and curly, wispy hair. He had dark eyes, arched eyebrows and full lips that would have been sensuous if they hadn't looked petulant.

'I'd recognise him again,' said Pam. 'Now all we have to do is see whether he was photographed with his accomplice who may turn out to be the mysterious Anna.'

'Then we should begin our search with the archives,' said Oliver. 'This could be the breakthrough Henry hoped for.'

CHAPTER 26

Chris Brook took off his cycle helmet and hung it on the handlebar of his Brompton folding bike.

'Is there anywhere I can park this safely? I don't feel as though I can bring it inside,' he added, looking cautiously down the narrow corridor.

'Actually, there is.' Pam slid open the door on the left of the corridor, which revealed the cavernous cupboard. There was another bike in there already, a large sit-up-and-beg with an old-fashioned wicker basket.

'This yours?'

'No, it's Jen's. You remember Jen? We met a few weeks ago at her father's house; this is her house. I'm house-sitting.'

A few weeks. Pam had to pinch herself constantly to believe that. Back then she was a DI, with a cross-county special crimes unit which had just tied up an important case of County Lines drug trafficking and had begun the Michaels' investigation. She hadn't met Nikos Leotakis or Stavros for that matter, and only knew Mike as someone on the other end of a Skype call. Another life. A time when she hadn't got to know Henry or rescue Jen or been shot. And she hadn't lost her unit and her job.

For this journalist it must be just the other day.

Chris stowed his bike…there was even a special bike hook to hang a portable bike and others for helmets, Jen was clearly a very organised person … And he followed Pam down the corridor into a large kitchen.

There was a shelf with identical white jars with sellotaped labels.

'I couldn't cope with the "guess what's in the jar" routine,' she told him.

Chris laughed. 'Don't think I could either. Tidy house, eh?'

'Spotless.'

The Guardian journalist looked carefully at the police officer. It was less than a month since they'd last met, but she'd changed. He wondered whether she knew it. He'd seen colleagues come back from war zones with the same look. Sometimes it went away, sometimes it didn't. Sometimes they went straight to another war, unable to cope with the everyday until they burned out.

'I'm so glad you called,' he said. 'I'd been hoping you would. If you don't mind going over it all I'd love to hear about what happened in Crete, and of course Leotakis's part in it.'

Pam nodded as she made them both the green tea he'd asked for…not surprising, she thought, that he didn't drink coffee. A health nut, lives on kale smoothies and air. He was wearing jeans today, rather than the cycling shorts he'd worn at their last meeting, and a pale green shirt, sleeves rolled up above the elbow. He looked smarter and less sporty than before.

She'd rung him because of the nagging thought that she'd had that Leotakis was somewhere in this story. If there was to be an attack, she suggested to Mike before he flew back to Crete, then the opening of his gallery in August was where it would happen. Mike had said it was a big 'if'. He'd decided to continue Henry's work and explore the idea of a last terrorist but didn't want to be part of an investigation into Henry's death. Pam hadn't said anything; it might work out, she thought.

They could be looking for the same person.

'Afterwards,' Chris continued, 'I thought we might talk over lunch, as you're not clocking in at the moment. The Oak Bistro isn't bad, and you can eat outside in the courtyard. If you're well enough.'

'Yes, I'm fine, and that would be lovely,' Pam replied, feeling that the day was beginning to look up.

Pam sipped the tea and told Chris what had happened in those few days at the end of June, how Leotakis had offered them all hospitality and any resources they needed. She carefully omitted that this included a room in a splendid hotel in Heraklion where she'd spent a passionate evening with Stavros. Come to think of it, that hadn't gone on to her police gift form either. But she doubted that the police accountants would discover that or that Leotakis had even thought about it as a gift.

'And then, when I realised that it was Manoulis, and Mike discovered that Jen had gone, Nikos burst into action. He smoothed the way with the local headman in the village so we didn't upset the locals and then organised two helicopters. The local police would have done the same, but they wanted to wait for professional hostage negotiators.'

'And you didn't?'

'I thought that it was, to use a cliché, a race against time.'

'And it was?'

'Very much so. A few minutes later, he'd have killed Jen.'

Instead, he nearly killed you, thought Chris. He'd never been shot, but knew a few journalists who had been, and had seen what it did to them to have been in the line of fire.

They walked over to the restaurant which was one of Zofia and Grace's favourites.

Are you allowed alcohol?' he asked as they were

shown to their seats in a leafy courtyard. It seemed he'd booked ahead.

The courtyard was protected from the sun with two giant red umbrellas and while the walls were decorated with images of oaks, the area was lined with bamboos. But the garden setting was the only informal touch, the rest was all white linen tablecloths and napkins and lots of polished wine glasses.

'This is nice,' said Pam, looking around and thinking how different it was from a sandwich at her desk or something grabbed from the police canteen. Don't get too comfortable, she told herself, it's a softening exercise. He thinks I know something, and hopes I'll let it slip out after a few glasses. Interesting. And here am I hoping for the opposite. It all depends how much he actually knows.

'I'm going to let you into my confidence,' she began, intending the opposite. 'A lot has happened since Stephanie died.'

She told him about how she'd become friends with Henry and how he'd been researching the *metapolitefsi*, a term she was delighted to see he didn't know, and she was able to explain.

'The seventies isn't my particular area,' Chris confessed, 'especially in Greece, though colleagues like Helen Smith and Ed Vuillamy know it well.'

'According to Henry, there was a lot of unrest, both from the extreme right and the far left. I've also been reading and found out that the men who were the torturers under the Junta did face trial but got very lenient sentences.'

'Often the way. They're all part of the same judicial system.'

'What was Leotakis doing around then?' she inquired, idly, as though it was just a passing thought.

'Nikos was back in Greece making money. He'd

refused to work with the Junta, did I tell you?'

'Think you may have done.'

'But once Karamanlis was back in power, he was back, buying hotels, the Palace chain in particular and buying infrastructure. He bought huge tracts of land near the coast on the mainland and several islands. They'd only just been made available for purchase, and they weren't expensive back then. And Nikos had very good relations with the new government.'

'He didn't stay in shipping or oil?'

'No. He left that behind him. He didn't want to go into direct conflict with other Greek shipowners on their own territory, and he could see that the hotel and real estate market was wide open and beginning to flourish.'

The waiter arrived with their food… they'd both ordered scallops and sea trout, and Chris had chosen a bottle of *Pouilly Fumé*. Chris said he was paying for lunch, and Pam realised that if he hadn't been, she could have afforded it. In fact, it was something she could now do. She could bring Zofia and Grace here and treat them. She'd had the money before, but not the confidence. It was a liberating feeling. The Cretan effect hadn't worn off.

The scallops were sweet and perfectly cooked and came with a purée of peas and quarters of lemon. So much for Chris living on air, thought Pam. She forced her mind back to Leotakis. She still had a nagging feeling that he was part of this story, though not in the way Madame Girard had suggested. But how, she didn't know.

'I'm not sure whether Nikos is remotely involved in any of this…' she began…

'This being?'

'Stephanie's best friend was a historian called Henry Cox, and two weeks ago he died in Jen's house, the house I'm currently living in.' Pam briefly gave him the resumé of what Henry had been writing and his association with Patrice Girard, and how Patrice had been gunned down.

'You think Henry was murdered?'

'There was an autopsy here. It found nothing untoward, and the police reported that he looked very peaceful.'

'But *you're* not convinced…I can feel your detective antennae from across the table.'

Pam laughed. 'Well, they're not trained on you.'

'And MI6 didn't respond?'

'I feel their attitude was that it was the fantasy of an old man.'

'But that's not how you saw Henry?'

'No. Not at all. But I didn't know him for very long.'

'How intriguing. And where does Nikos fit in?'

'Well, if there was something being planned with a Greek connection, I just wondered whether Nikos was being set up in some way. And I thought you'd be able to tell me if he has any enemies.' Pam wasn't going to mention Didi's belief that it was Leotakis's bodyguard, Rafael. She had her doubts about Didi as an impartial witness, even though she had lost her husband. Mike had been annoyed at her for saying she'd investigate, but it didn't have to be along the lines Madame Girard wanted. As she later told him.

'You don't get to be as rich and powerful as Nikos without getting a slew of enemies,' Chris sipped his wine and smiled, thinking of the list he had of those who hated the billionaire.

'So could you fill me in on any who might be relevant?'

'Okay.' Chris grinned. 'Naturally the number one is his son.'

'Nikos told me about him.'

'An extremely nasty piece of work. I'd love to interview him, but don't think I'd walk out alive.

Associates with a few cartels, plus he's into all kinds of trafficking.'

'It's awful. Just so different from his father,' said Pam. 'Not surprising that Nikos would like him dead.'

'He told you that?'

'Don't quote me, please don't quote me!'

'I won't. And it's not new. He's said the same to me.'

The scallop plates had been scraped clean, and she and Chris were now eating a very fresh-tasting trout which had come with a buttery sauce with capers and finely-chopped fennel. She'd never bought fennel, but then she'd never cooked much. She thought it was time to start.

'So, let's put Antony Leotakis to one side,' Pam suggested. 'Nikos must have other enemies.'

'Obviously. There are business rivals, but I can't see them gunning down a French lawyer and killing an English historian.'

'When you put the two deaths side by side like that, it does sound unlikely.'

'Yes. More the hallmark of a terrorist, or a hostile nation. There were a group of Ukrainian businessmen who he had a big battle with, but that was a while ago.' Chris paused. 'Give me the name of the lawyer again...'

'Patrice Girard.'

Chris took out his phone and began to tap. Then he stopped, looked up and smiled.

'Interesting.'

'Something you can tell me or is it a secret?'

'No, not secret at all. Wikipedia. Girard, as I'm sure you now know, was a very prominent left-wing lawyer who acted on behalf of several communist countries and agencies including the Stasi and the KGB. And defended their agents when they were caught. Plus any number of extreme left-wing French criminals.'

Pam nodded. She'd looked him up but hadn't found

anything that linked him with the Greek terrorist group. Or Leotakis.

'Yes,' she said. 'I read his obituary. And Mike translated one from the *Libération* newspaper. Rather different. They saw him as a hero.'

'They would. We weren't that critical in *The Guardian* either.'

'Nobody mentioned that he'd been an associate of Yotopoulos.'

'That's because it's not something that anyone's aware of. Your Henry was possibly one of the few people to know that.'

'Yes. They were old friends.'

'Girard certainly didn't defend any of the N17 lot, though they had a huge number of lawyers. I wasn't at the trial, but I have a close friend who was, and he's told me about it since. He's writing a book about it. If something new emerges about 17N, he'll be thrilled.'

'Well, there's nothing yet that's worth writing about, just a lot of speculation.'

'But while Girard didn't help Yotopoulos, he might have advised him privately; he was involved in an earlier case that could be relevant.'

'Yes?' asked Pam. She put down her fork and sat back, looking at the journalist, thoughtfully. 'So far this whole thing … I can't really call it a case because I don't know if it is … has been like swimming in mud. I can't see anything clearly.' And mud was putting it mildly. More like quick-drying cement.

'Well, I've no idea whether this will help, but look at this. It's in French…'

'Can you translate it?'

'Sure. It seems there was this Greek who lived in Berlin. He was arrested in Strasbourg, so that's why it was a French case, and charged with plotting to bomb the European Parliament. Girard defended him, but he was found guilty and got twenty years. This was in the eighties, so he's been out now for a while. He accused Girard of being a stooge of the capitalist state after he was convicted. Threatened to kill him.'

'Charming bloke. What was his name?'

'Yiannis Papoutsakis.'

Pam took out a small notebook and began to write it down.

'Pen and paper!' Chris laughed, 'Cuts in the department?'

'Paper doesn't get hacked, and, as you know, I'm on sick leave at the moment.'

'So this isn't official.'

'No...' she hesitated...then decided to trust him with some of the facts.

'The Cambridge police believe Henry's death was from natural causes. They're not investigating it at all.'

'You're working solo?'

'Don't tell anyone, but yes.'

'Tough.' He dipped his last potato into the sauce and chewed it thoughtfully.

'Why did you mention hacking? Have you been hacked?'

He doesn't miss a thing, thought Pam. Not surprising he's a good journalist.

'Not actually hacked, as far as I know, but Henry's computer was targeted with a virus just before he died.'

'Cybercrime. Hate it.'

'I've never had to investigate it. Way out of my league.'

'And mine. Very specialist. The Russian mafia are very big in that area at the moment. And Vlad himself.'

'You're not suggesting...?'

'No. Can't see them involved in this kind of thing. Ditto the Ukrainians. They might shoot Girard, but your friend Henry doesn't feel like them at all.

They'd just mow him down if they wanted him dead.'

'Well, I'll take them off my list then. Just as well. I wouldn't want to come up against any of that lot from what I've read about them.'

Chris put down his knife and fork and took one of her hands.

'Pam, if this killer has shot Girard and killed Henry Cox and also has the resources to attack a computer, then they are dangerous. Really dangerous.'

CHAPTER 27

Pam looked at Chris, who was watching her, frowning. He's a nice man, she thought, this isn't an act.

'I know they're dangerous,' she said. 'I do take precautions.' But did she? she asked herself. Was a small chain on the door a serious deterrent to a professional criminal? 'I can't live looking over my shoulder all the time.'

'I'm not sure I like the idea of you investigating this on your own.'

'I'm not totally alone. Henry's oldest friend has offered to help. But we've gone off subject,' she added hurriedly. 'You were telling me about Nikos's enemies, or was that it?'

'Not quite. There is one more and she certainly has the funds to buy a few criminals and she loathes Nikos.'

'She?'

'Her name is Dimi Forgeron, or it was when I last looked. She changes husbands the way you and I change underwear. There've been six to my knowledge as well as a long-time partner she had when she was young and never married. Or never admitted to having married.

She lives in Lyon with current husband, but spends her summers in Mykonos, where the really rich hang out, or so our travel editor, Jane, says.'

'Jane would love Chiona then. It's part of a big local

euro park, sustainable tourism, that kind of thing.'

'I know. Leotakis helped fund it, and it's going to be a central feature in his new foundation. But we're off again! And while we're off subject, do you want a sweet?'

'Better not,' Pam said reluctantly. They had sounded delicious.

'How about we share a sticky toffee pudding with ice cream?'

Pam grinned. 'Can anyone ever turn down toffee pudding?'

'I can't. Just as well I bike everywhere.'

'Need to take it up myself. Once my leg is fully healed.'

'Better than dieting, but thinking of dieting takes me back to Dimi, who's probably never eaten a toffee pudding in her life. She's one of these women who were stunning at twenty and spend the rest of their lives and all their husbands' money trying to preserve the look. The hair is dyed and curled, and they spend so much time with plastic surgeons they look like waxworks.'

'Horrendous.'

'They still photograph well. But in real life…' He sat back reflecting on his meeting with Dimi. It had been three years ago when she was living part of the year in Nice, in the Hotel Negresco. He'd cycled down from the flat he'd rented in the Cimiez district of the town and was hot and sweaty when he arrived. Dimi was holding court on the turfed terrace on a large sofa with an open bottle of champagne in front of her.

She'd shooed away the others as he arrived and turned to him as though he was the richest, most exciting man she'd ever met.

'She was intense,' Chris told Pam, 'and astonishingly rude. Actually, more than rude. She motioned me to a chair beside her and grabbed my bum as I turned round.'

Pam laughed.

'I think I gave a kind of English cough, you know, that sort of interrogative one...'

Pam laughed again; she was enjoying this lunch.

'Then she gave me a look, and said "You're not *poustis*, are you?" That's a negative Greek word, like fag. "Actually, I am," I told her, "not that it's any of your fucking business." "If you're *poustis*, then it's certainly not my *fucking* business," she replied. That's Dimi.'

'My goodness,' said Pam, trying to picture the encounter.

'It didn't get much better after that. I've had to do a lot of fancy footwork to get the full story of Dimi and Leotakis for the book, because she simply invents everything and tells a different story every time. But she certainly hates Nikos.'

'So who exactly is she?' Pam asked him.

'Yes of course. Sorry. I was about to say and got carried away. Well she was born Demetria Saint-Jacques, in Lille. Father was French, mother Greek. Father died when she was fifteen, leaving them with very little money and the mother's own family had disowned her when she ran off with the Frenchman. But she had something she could sell: her daughter.

'She sold Dimi?'

'To the highest bidder. On a regular basis. Until Dimi had had enough and caught a train to Paris. There, it seems she met a student and fell in love. There are various different versions of the story of what she did when she first got to Paris. But it's clear she met a boy called Michel because there are many accounts of him with her, and also many photographs. I have to admit she was beautiful then, as well as a passionate member of the new revolution. We're talking about 1968, which means Dimi was born around 1948, though she claims it was 1958.'

'Interesting. That's the year when Yotopoulos and Girard were also around.'

'And so many others, yes. And having been exploited herself, she was all about ending workers' exploitation. I won't go into the details here, but there is a biography of her if you want to read more. Seems she and Michel were together until 1970, and then he left her and married a girl he'd known from university. Which indicates that he and Dimi weren't married, though she says they were.'

'Next, Dimi travels to Greece, and soon meets and then marries a wealthy businessman, Spiros Christopoulos, who was thirty years older than her. He had two hotels at the time and was beginning to expand.'

'That's when Greece was under the Junta?'

'Yes. And those who supported the Junta found a way to circumvent all kinds of planning laws. Actually, it was more than that. When you go to Greece today you still see relics of that time.' Chris smiled. 'It's something I've got a bit of a thing about, I keep looking for them now, half-built hotels which have become ruins, and which would cost so much to demolish that they've just been left to rot. But that's now. Back then, the Government gave permits to those close to them, and those who supported them. And not just permits, they helped them to get huge loans to build hotels on virgin sites, loans that were a bit larger than the building costs. But that wasn't enough. The developers discovered they could begin to build the hotels and then stop. And guess what? Nobody ever asked for the loans back. Some of the ruins have walls, some even have bits of plumbing.'

'You should write about them.'

'Funny you should say that. I'm thinking of doing that. Maybe as a basis for a novel.'

'Sounds good. I'd read it.' Pam smiled. 'But that's when Nikos was abroad.'

'Yes. He was in France and England and also in the

US during that period.'

'But that's what he did when he came back?'

'Yes. First under Karamanlis, and then with PASOK, the socialist party, when they came to power in 1981.'

'What the first developers, like Dimi's husband, Christopoulos, did was get permits for electricity and water before he began building. Then he got the Government to build new roads to open up beaches. And you have a resort. What Nikos did was the same, but he also bought up massive tracts of land around the new hotels, and then he waited. Once his hotels became popular, he sold the land with building permission. He made hundreds of millions of pounds on those deals. And you can see the result all over Crete and the mainland. His first billions came from land ownership. Because a new resort needs not only hotels, but also supermarkets and everything else. If there was a decent beach and a road could get there, Nikos bought the land.'

'I wondered where the money came from.'

'From that and other investments. He had a knack for anticipating what would work and what wouldn't. Still has.'

'That's a gift.' Pam dived into the pudding which was as sweet and delicious as she'd hoped. She had to stop eating these things or she wouldn't be able to get into her new dresses. But this was a special occasion. And she was learning a lot.

'Going back to Dimi,' Chris continued. 'She was in her early twenties and her husband was in his late fifties. One day, he went out with his harpoon gun to catch octopus and drowned, though nobody ever knew how, and now there she is, suddenly very rich. And since Christopoulos had been keener on chasing young girls than running his business, she had already placed herself inside the business. So nothing much changed after his death except that she got into bed with a few rabid right wingers.

'If she'd just run her hotels, she'd have been fine, but she stupidly funded a group of thugs who tried to get rid of Karamanlis. One of them was an undercover cop who, unlike many of the cops at that time, was actually against the Junta. In any case he was against assassination and the thugs were arrested. Dimi was offered a choice: jail or sell her hotel chain at a loss and leave the country. And that was the end of Dimi's reign in Greece.'

'And let me guess, Leotakis bought her hotels.'

'At rock bottom prices. She's never forgiven him. She goes to Mykonos because he's never owned any property on that island.'

'But would she go as far as murder?'

'I think so. She certainly tried to destroy his hotels' reputation and I think she still would. Not so long ago, she paid a number of people to write very damaging reviews on Tripadvisor, but again, there was a man who blew the whistle. He was a journalist for the Washington Post and investigating the manipulation of such reviews. Tripadvisor wiped all the negative reviews immediately. But it could have done Nikos a lot of damage.'

Chris pulled out his phone. 'This is what Dimi looked like in her prime. She was famous for her Kolonaki parties in the seventies.'

Pam looked at the picture. It reminded her of pictures she'd seen of Hollywood stars of that time: men very formal in dark suits and ties and the women with sprayed bouffant hair like vast wigs. Dimi stood at the centre of a small group in a very low-cut white dress that was tight at the waist and then loose over her hips. It showed off her figure perfectly and the very large diamond on a chain which nestled just above her breasts. There was no doubt who was at the heart of this gathering. But there was also no doubt of the identity of the woman beside her with long dark hair, in a black shift dress. Dimi had her arm around her, and they were both laughing.

'I know that woman,' said Pam.

'Really? I've never been able to find out who she was.'

'Her name is Didi,' Pam told him. 'And she was the wife of Patrice Girard.'

'Interesting. So we do have a tangential link now between Leotakis and Girard. I've been wondering why you think Nikos is involved in your investigation, which you clearly do. You didn't ask me to come to Cambridge so you could tell me about his involvement with the Michaels' case, although I am very grateful for that information. And it's not just that Henry lived in Crete. There are a great number of people living on that island.'

'No. You're right. But there isn't anything … how can I put it? I don't have any reason to think that Leotakis is involved but I keep having a feeling.'

'A niggle.'

'Exactly.'

'As an investigative journalist I have great respect for the niggle.'

'And as a detective.'

Pam had decided she wasn't going to mention having met Didi at the funeral, or that she'd accused Leotakis, but now she wondered whether she should. But it was just an unsubstantiated accusation. And if Didi was a close friend of this Dimi, it could be part of a plot to attack Nikos. She decided to give Chris a different way of looking at the Leotakis connection.

'Before he died, Henry wrote a report on his research into 17 November and what he thought he'd unearthed. He sent it to this old friend Oliver Timberly.' And I'm certainly not going to give Chris the MI6 connection, she thought. Not yet, anyway.

Chris nodded. The Timberly name rang a bell. He'd look it up later.

'Oliver showed me the report after Henry's funeral. It said very much what I told you earlier, that there was a last terrorist, a member of 17N who had never been caught, and that they'd been one of the founding members. But it also said that they were planning a final act of terrorism, possibly in Britain.'

'An attack here? Have you sent this to the authorities?'

'Oliver has links there,' she prevaricated. 'But of course they may not take it seriously. There's absolutely no evidence. Henry said Patrice was going to give him their name; he thought that was why Patrice was shot. Which, understandably, alarmed Henry. And then, almost immediately, he died. As you can see, it's all supposition. I met Patrice's widow at Henry's funeral, which is how I recognised her, and she told me Patrice was writing a book about his life.'

'Which could upset any number of people.'

'Exactly. The French police have taken all Patrice's papers and his computer, so I imagine they are looking into that.'

'I know what you're thinking,' Chris nodded. 'If there is going to be an attack, the one time they'd choose is the opening of the Leotakis Gallery here in Cambridge. Which is now next month.'

'Yes. The twenty-eighth, August the twenty-eighth.'

'This would be the most effective way to destroy Nikos. The Gallery is huge in his life. Apart from his new foundation, it's everything he's ever worked towards.'

'I know. And there will be massive security. Prince Charles will be there. Which means RaSP.'

'RaSP?'

'The royal protection unit. They're very thorough. And Oliver says he's also going to brief his contacts at MI5 in advance if we don't discover anything before that date. I certainly can't get the local police here involved.

They think I'm imagining it all anyway.'

'Why?'

Pam sighed. She gave Chris an outline of some of her problems with Hawkswood, particularly emphasising the bureaucracy around Leotakis's hospitality.

'But I don't want this to get into the paper. It's totally off the record.'

'It's horrible, though.'

'It is.' She sipped her wine, and Chris quietly filled her glass again. I don't have to drink that, she thought. I'm going to have to watch what I say very carefully here.

'So, going back to the gallery opening, this does seem to be the big event of the summer.'

'And a natural target, I agree with you. Have you told Nikos?'

'No. And I don't want to, not just yet. Of course, I'll call him the moment I have any evidence, however flimsy. But at the moment, there's only an old man's thoughts. And Leotakis and Henry never got along, Mike told me.'

'That's the Mike who helped you with the Michaels' case.'

'Yes.' And I'm not giving you his background, she said to herself. That would be a story he wouldn't want to ignore.

'I can hardly ring Nikos and say there *might* be a terrorist who *might* attack something in England that *might* be his new gallery. And I have to ask you not to worry Nikos about it yet. Nor about my own problems.'

'I won't. He'd be on it like a dog with a bone and it wouldn't be good for his heart.'

'He has heart problems?'

'Mostly in the past. He has a Pacemaker now, and a defibrillator, but he's meant to watch his blood pressure.'

'Well, that would send it sky high,' Pam agreed.

Chris nodded and smiled at her. 'It's been a real pleasure to spend time with you, Pam. When this is all over, will you come down to London to have supper with my partner and me?'

Pam sipped the last of her wine and smiled back. She'd only met him twice now, but she liked him.

'I'd love to,' she said.

'Jake makes an astonishing chocolate cheesecake,' he added.

Pam laughed.

'You know, before I went to Crete, if you'd asked me that, I'd have said no. I'd have thought, my God he writes for *The Guardian*, he's going to find me so stupid, and I won't know what anyone is talking about.'

'We've all been there.'

'You?'

'Massive imposter feelings when I first joined the paper. You'd be surprised how many people still feel that. It's one of the things we face when we come through the door.'

'Actually, it began with a door. A poem about a door rather.'

'There you are. Cultural reference. You're one of us.'

'I think being shot changes things, too.'

Chris grew serious. 'It does. It always does. And now we're friends, please don't get shot again. I don't want to lose you.'

CHAPTER 28

The three-storey greyish-white concrete police station advertised its trade with a small sign on the front, a larger one on the first-floor balcony and a Greek flag, which flapped hotly in the afternoon air. A passer-by might also guess what it was from the nine police cars and trucks parked outside.

Opposite it was a pet shop which boasted a square of Astroturf with plastic rattan armchairs and a table underneath a vast umbrella. Mike had never quite worked out the reason for these since this wasn't exactly a particularly pleasant place to sit on a busy road, and there were cafés only a short stroll away. And why would people buying things for their pets need to sit down? One day he'd go in and ask.

Inside the station, it felt much like any cop shop, printed notices which had faded over the years and a few missing person posters, reminding everyone of cases which had never been solved.

Manos met Mike in the front and led him back outside.

'Let's go and get a coffee,' he said. 'You really don't want to drink ours,' he added, smoothing his crisp shirt into his dark uniform trousers.

'I've drunk Met coffee,' replied Mike. 'Maybe it's some ancient rule that says police canteens aren't allowed to serve decent coffee.'

Manos laughed. There'd been a time when Michaelis first arrived in Sitia and was living in what was basically a shack, only coming into town to buy whisky from the Kritikos supermarket and living purely on the pizzas he had delivered. Manos had had more than a few reports about this dishevelled black man living in a place which hardly much more than a pigsty. He'd sent an officer out who reported back that the man's name was Michaelis, he was half Cretan, Kyria Sofia was his aunt, and he was also a policeman.

'Getting over a bad case,' the officer said; 'four years undercover.' He hadn't asked any more, it was clear something had gone down, and the officer had observed that though the man, Michaelis was drunk, he had food and water and wasn't dirty. The fact he was police made Manos quietly decide to keep an eye out for him in case any trouble brewed up. Plus the fact of his being related to the much-loved and respected Kyria Sofia. The number of ethnic minorities in the town was still very small, though Manos could easily remember when you never saw a black face. Sitia wasn't like Rhodes, which was only three hundred miles away but with a growing refugee problem.

Then Michaelis stopped drinking, and began working on the new village in Chiona, and since then he'd become popular. Even more so now since his involvement with the abduction of the Stefania Michaels' daughter. There would have been many tears if the boy had killed her. Michaelis had also dropped by Manos's office to debrief him on what had happened, and how Leotakis had taken over. He hadn't had to do that, thought the police captain, it hadn't happened on his patch, but he'd appreciated the gesture. Michaelis was a solid man.

And now Enris Cox, the friend of Stefania, had

died and Michaelis wanted to talk to him. The death had surprised him; Enris had always looked so strong. Perhaps that was what Michaelis wanted to talk about.

Thrasivoulis, the owner of Café Corner, started to prepare Manos's coffee as soon as he walked in, and Mike signalled he'd have the same. It turned out to be a cappuccino made with double espresso, and the coffee was excellent.

'Best coffee in Sitia', said Manos. 'They also have good coffee in Edesma, but you don't ever want to go there.'

'Why?' Mike asked.

'It's full of former police officers, and all they do is grumble all day.' He sat back on one of the beige fake leather sofas, leaving Mike to perch on a similarly upholstered round stool.

'Useful knowledge', said Mike, thinking that he might find more information about 17N from some of them. They would have been around during the days the terrorist group was active.

'Alright, so what's on your mind? Is this about Enris?... may you live long and healthily to mourn him,' he added in the traditional way.

'Yes. Pam Gregory, the English police detective thinks it was murder.'

'Murder? Again? So soon after poor Stefania.' Mike nodded. 'But you don't?'

'I don't know, Manos. There was an autopsy in Cambridge, and they found nothing unusual. He was found in bed in his pyjamas, looking happy and peaceful.'

The policeman crossed himself. 'So may we all go. How old was he?'

'Only seventy-six. No age.'

'Not these days. My father is eighty and still walks into town every day and swims until Christmas. Long may he continue.'

'The thing is he'd lost his closest friend and nearly lost his goddaughter, Jennifer, Stefania's daughter.' Mike automatically called Stephanie, Stefania, the name she was called by the locals, the same way they called Henry, Enris, and he was Michaelis.

'That's a lot of stress.'

'And not only that,' Mike told the officer. He explained how Henry had been researching the *metapolitefsi* and the origins of 17N, and how his friend and possible source in Paris had been gunned down.

'He was scared he'd be next,' said Mike. 'That's what he said to Pam and me. And then he died. And while I know that all of that could have added to the stress, it feels like a coincidence. Oh, and the day before he left, his computer was targeted with a virus and wiped.'

'Another coincidence.'

'And as police detectives we don't like coincidences.'

'I can see why your friend has doubts about the death being natural causes.'

'Yes. But I think it's just going to be one of those unanswered questions. What I want to do is to try and finish Henry's work which was about 17 November. I'd really like to know more about the early days of the group, but I imagine most of the police who were around then are long gone.'

'The word I hear is that every member of the group was arrested.'

'Yes. That's what Major Papadakis said. He was visiting Pam when she heard the news.' Manos's eyebrows rose and he gave an amused smile.

'Yes, they are. Not that it's any of your business.'

'Of course not. And he is married?'

'No. Neither of them is married.' Mike laughed. Police gossip. Same everywhere. 'Just a romance.' But possibly not anymore, Mike thought.

'That means she will return to us, wonderful,' said

Manos.

'She will, anyway. Henry gave her his house when he died. He didn't have family. Anyhow, according to Pam, Major Papadakis was insistent that there were no outstanding terrorists. He said he'd heard it directly from one of the officers involved in the arrest.'

'They're GADA,' muttered Manos, referring to the police HQ in Athens, or the Attica General Police Directorate as it called itself. Stavros was based there as part of the International Police Cooperation Division along with other specialist units of the Greek police force including the anti-terrorism unit and the cybercrime division. 'GADA think they know it all.' Manos sipped his coffee. 'Some of 17N are out now. Not that they'd tell you much.'

'I wouldn't want to ask them. Besides, they were very much a group of hermetic cells. Doubt whether the new members knew anything much about those who'd founded the group. Apart from Dimitris Koufoudinas,' he added.

'Yes. He took the role of spokesperson for the whole group at the trial I seem to remember. But he did introduce Yotopoulos to Teslenis, so unless he was lying, he knew the back history.'

'Teslenis was the one who got disillusioned and testified against the others wasn't he?'

'Seem to remember something along those lines.'

'I read some of the trial transcripts last week.'

'You probably know more than me, then. I read the account in the press at the time, and it was wall to wall on the television.'

'Not all of the transcripts, of course, the trial went on for ever.'

'Longest trial in Greek history, cost a bloody fortune.' Manos finished his coffee and wiped the foam moustache from his upper lip with the back of his hand.

'And Yotopoulos got the longest sentence in our history: twenty-one life sentences plus twenty-five years.'

'He won't stay in that long. Don't know why they're releasing them all so early. Seems mad. I'd keep them all locked up. Only five still in jail out of the twenty arrested. Just go to the Edesma café and start that as a conversation and you'll be there all day.'

'Some of them would have got the death penalty in other countries.'

'Thankfully, we don't have that here, and it's not something I'd be comfortable with, though I've put away a few scum who probably deserved it. But all those early releases, it does make you wonder.'

'Yes. Pavlos Serifis, for example.'

'Which one was he?'

'The one who first said he'd been part of the Richard Welch killing.'

'Outside the statute of limitations then. Weren't his other relatives involved? Seem to remember one of our captains talking about that family. He'd been in Athens at the time.'

'They rounded up all the Serifis family at the time. Known left wing sympathisers, the usual suspects.'

'Except these ones plant bombs and kill police officers,' commented Manos, grimly. He had no sympathy for any group which murdered serving officers and 17N had killed at least six, as far as he could remember.

'Some of them do,' said Mike. 'But some are convenient targets. The Serifis cousin Yiannis is one of those. Old union man and definitely worked against the Junta.'

'That's where it started, and that's why the left refused to arrest them later.' Manos shook his head. 'A lot of pressure got put on the police from above.'

'That's what Henry said. Yiannis was certainly a political activist, so he might have been involved with

17 November at the start. What I read from the trial transcripts was that he left 17N before 1983 because he disagreed with its tactics. Anyhow, he did have a history with the police. He was accused of taking part in a terrorist attack on a German company way back. The attack had ended in a shoot-out with police and the death of another terrorist, Christos Kassimis. What I found strange was that Yiannis was then charged with murdering Kassimis, which they said was to prevent him from falling into the hands of the police.'

'Don't remember that. Seems far-fetched.'

'I've read a lot about Yiannis,' said Mike. 'He was acquitted of the Kassimis murder, of course, which he clearly had nothing to do with. He got a huge amount of local support, including from members of PASOK which was about to win the election. So, yes, I can see why politicians would support him. Yiannis was a union activist first and foremost, but he was constantly named as a possible suspect in various assassination attempts. Even when he was miles away.'

'Lazy policing.'

'When Yiannis was arrested in the 17N sweep, he issued a statement to the press saying he was being set up and didn't know Yotopoulos or the woman Anna who was the third person his cousin Pavlos had alleged killed Welch. It's the only time we hear of this mysterious Anna, by the way.'

'I get the feeling it's her you're interested in.'

'Yes, I am.'

'I guess to find that out you'd need find out more about Yotopoulos.'

'Difficult. Yotopoulos said virtually nothing at the trial, he left all the talking to Koufoudinas.'

'As if he was above all that. Arrogant I'd say. Above it all, except they found his fingerprints on papers in their safe house in Ano Patissia. Did you see those photos?'

Mike nodded. He remembered the staged picture with the group's flag, the typewriter and computer they'd used to write their communiqués.

'Strange to think of criminals designing themselves a flag.'

'What made me laugh when I saw the pictures was how ancient the arms were. Apart from the anti-tank rockets and handguns.'

'They stole them from a museum, didn't they?' asked Mike.

'If you say so,' Manos clearly had had enough of the talk. 'Yotopoulos was the mastermind. And if you're asking me if he deserved the life sentences he got, the answer's yes. He was the engine that powered the group.' He picked up the spoon and stirred the empty cup. 'An old colleague of mine met him. He was working on Lipsi at the time, where Yotopoulos had a summer villa.'

'What did he say?'

'Not a lot. Yotopoulos and his French wife didn't associate a great deal with the locals. Though they shopped and went to cafés and restaurants like any other Athenian with a summer home on the islands. Had a row about painting his house pink, said it was the tradition. But he knew a few of the old politicians, they used to visit. He was a man living in the past, my friend said, still believing in the Marxist crap that was all the rage in the seventies.'

'A cult.'

'They certainly believed in what they did. Yotopoulos was charismatic from what I've heard. Like other cults, it was all about belief.'

'So, if there was another member...' began Mike.

'They'd probably be equally obsessive and equally dangerous. Capable of killing Enris if they thought he was a threat. And certainly capable of killing anyone who might unmask them. So, if I were you, I wouldn't go around asking these questions too loudly.'

'I'll be careful,' Mike assured him.

'If you really want to go back to the Richard Welch case there is someone who can help you. Retired here a few years back, but was CIA, though he keeps that to himself. Name's Douglas Stanton. I'll give you his phone number, though I can't guarantee he'll talk to you. He doesn't talk to anyone very much. Just as well, since Greece doesn't have a brilliant record when it comes to CIA agents. The last thing I want on my patch is another death. Be discreet.'

'I will. Thanks, Manos.'

'And try to stay alive, yourself. There's that nice young Jen...'

'I don't know where you hear these things.'

Manos laughed. 'Police gossip, as you said earlier. And your cousin does work in the force here. He thought you were more than keen on a certain girl from Kalamata at Yiannis' wedding this month.'

'She was sweet.'

'And safe. Back in the Peloponnese a few days later. What happens in Sitia stays...'

'You watch too much American television.' Mike grinned. 'But she was nice.'

'Find yourself a good woman and settle down, that's my advice. That way you're less likely to get killed.'

CHAPTER 29

'You have to know I don't like talking about the past. One of the pleasures of being ancient is you get to choose: you can either go over everything you've done in your life, or not done, and drive yourself crazy. Or you can live in the present and enjoy the time you have left. Personally, I prefer the latter.'

'It's what I'm trying to do myself, sir,' replied Mike.

'Sir, I like sir. Manners. Counts for something.'

'I wouldn't bother you if it wasn't important. No, that's not quite it…it could be important. Right now, I simply don't know. It could be a series of coincidences.'

Douglas Stanton sighed and poured the remains of his beer into a long glass. He looked at Mike and shook his head.

'And now, of course, you've got me interested. Sounds like a story, and stories still intrigue me.'

He had unusually bright blue eyes, thought Mike, maybe there were Scandinavian roots in his family. His wispy beard was white, but his head was bald beneath the baseball cap, a faded khaki, the same as his T-shirt. He could be a warden at a game park, though there was a watchfulness that hinted at something else.

It was six in the evening, and they were sitting on the deep veranda of Douglas's home, a gleaming white villa, built like a round fort on three levels and perched at the edge of the small, scattered village of Agia Fotia, about four miles outside Sitia. The veranda was filled with large terracotta pots packed with honeysuckle, bougainvillea and plumbago which all vied with each other to see which could reach the furthest. In the middle of the foliage and greenery was a large pine table with assorted director chairs around it and a couple of bright pink wooden slatted sofas filled with white cushions.

Douglas saw Mike looking at the sofas and smiled. 'That's my wife, Antigone. She's an artist. Pink's not really my thing.'

'Did she do the mosaic on the wall as you come in?'

'She did. It's Philophrosyne, the goddess of welcome.'

'It's beautiful.'

'I'll tell her. She's in town this morning with our grandkids, taking them swimming.'

Douglas walked indoors and came back with another beer. 'Are you sure you don't want one?' he asked. 'It's Notos, excellent. Local microbrewery.'

'I'm fine, thank you.'

'Fine. Good English word. We say good. But I like fine.'

Mike smiled. 'Fine.'

'Ah. The English humour. Like that, too. Spent a year once in Reading, pretty countryside, Antigone practically lived in the local antique shops. Still got a few pieces we bought there.'

'Greenham Common?' asked Mike, trying to think of political activity that would interest the CIA around Reading. The protests at the American airbase would be one.

Douglas gave a lizard-like smile. This was clearly not something he would discuss.

'I was undercover four years,' Mike told him. 'Met a few women who used to stay at the airbase and protest.'

'Four years. That's quite a stint.'

'Messy ending,' said Mike. 'That's what brought me to Crete.'

'But you've got family here I've heard. That's why I agreed to see you. My wife knows your aunt.'

'Yes, she's on my mother's side. My family are half Cretan from Sitia, and half Barbadian. My father was from Barbados.'

'And which do you prefer, Crete or Barbados? Beautiful island.'

'I've never been there.'

'Really? You don't have family there?'

'I don't know. My father died when I was seven, and my mother never talked about him. I rather cut myself away from that.'

And that's all I'm going to say about my family, he thought. I'm not letting him do a Grace on me. He'd bumped into Grace outside the Amnesty bookshop on his way back from buying the burner phones, and over coffee in Sahara, he'd ended up telling her a lot more than he'd intended. And she'd pestered him about Barbados and why he'd never been.

'And you?' he asked Douglas instead. 'How did you find yourself here?'

'That's my wife. She has family in Zakros. We used to come here whenever we could, and after I retired, she wanted to come back. Think all Cretans feel that pull. Zakros was a bit remote, so we found this place, not too far from the airport. Least I could do for her. She'd followed me to some of the more insalubrious parts of the world and never complained. And this suits us.'

'And what a view,' added Mike looking down at the triangle of indigo sea between the greenery.

'Never tire of it. Changes colour every moment.'

'That's what my friend Henry used to say.'

'Henry Cox?

'Yes'.

'Heard about his death. Sorry about that.'

'That's really why I'm here.'

'Thought it might be. Henry came to see me a couple of times.'

'You know he was writing about 17 November?'

'I do. Henry thought it was putting him in danger. And then he died. So maybe he was right. Is that what you think?'

'Possibly. Do you?'

'Seems unlikely. Old history. People don't get killed over old

history. Or not that often.'

'Sometimes they do,' Mike replied.

'Ah yes, the Stephanie Michaels killing. Of course, you were involved with that.'

'It was my friend Pam who worked out it was all about the Polytechnic and what Manolis thought Stephanie had done. Which she hadn't.'

'Crazy,' agreed Douglas, sipping his beer. 'Just as crazy as the bunch of pseudo-Stalinist misfits who thought that blowing up some banks and offices and mowing down a Yank would bring about the revolution. I was in court for the trial. The rubbish they spouted. Would be funny if it hadn't brought about the death of some good men and destroyed their families.'

'I can see why Henry wanted to talk to you,' said Mike, smiling at the old CIA agent. And how many deaths were you responsible for? he thought to himself. He'd read up what he could find on Douglas Stanton and knew he'd been in El Salvador in the eighties and Belgrade a decade later.

'And your friend Pam thinks Henry's death could be associated with 17 November?'

Mike repeated the answer he'd given to Manos the previous day.

'You know that whatever the police say, there are

others who agree with your detective friend?'

'Yes?'

'Yes.'

'Actually, would you mind if I recorded this conversation for Pam?'

'Sure. Nothing new, nothing that isn't on public record. Go ahead.'

Mike turned on the recorder on his phone and put it on the table.

'Sorry to interrupt you. You were saying that there are others who think there is one of 17N who was never arrested.'

'Yes. An academic. She's convinced that at least one of the founder members of 17N is still at large, and that they were responsible for the intelligence for the group, telling them who to target and where to find them. They sent her a bomb, too,' he added.

'Members of 17N did? After the trials?'

'Their friends, the ones who've come after. Same bunch of losers, different names.'

'It took the police a long time to arrest them,' Mike offered, hoping to draw the old man out.

'Didn't it just!' This was clearly a bugbear. 'You know the FBI warned them about Yotopoulos back in the nineties?'

'I didn't,' Mike lied, though he'd read about it in the newspaper *Kathimerini*.

'It's in the records; they knew he was a fanatic. He was the motor that kept the group active. But then his father was a fucking Commie. Worked for Trotsky himself if that wasn't a big enough clue. Bloody miracle anyone was arrested. Total breakdown of communication.'

'Or pressure from above.'

Douglas nodded. 'That's what we thought. Look, I don't want this to sound like I'm criticising this country...'

But you're about to, thought Mike.

'But you have to realise that Greece only got its independence in 1830, 1947 if you want to include Rhodes and that group of islands. I mean you Brits say that America is a new country, but we got free of the British in 1776.'

'Not sure you could call me a Brit,' protested Mike.

'Born and educated there, though, weren't you? Your accent's British. You're more Brit than Barbadian, let's face it...'

Mike shrugged and smiled. It was true, he supposed. He was.

'There are people still alive whose grandparents were alive under Ottoman rule,' Douglas continued, 'so it's not so surprising that the heroes to the Greeks are the revolutionaries, people like Karaiskakis and that woman, Bouboulina.'

'And Daliakis here in Crete.'

'Exactly and so it's gone on, commies like Aris Velouchiotis who fought the British in the Civil War become the next lot of heroes. And Manolis Glezos.'

'He was the one who tore down the Nazi flag from the Acropolis, wasn't he?'

'That's the one. A real fighter all his life. I wouldn't be surprised if he'd known Yotopoulos and some of the others. Yeah, when 17N attacked us, they could rely on support from the left.'

'Welch wasn't the only American they killed.'

'No.' Douglas looked grim. 'They also murdered Sergeant Robert Judd, Norden, Tsantes, and two navy captains. Judd was just a fucking postman, took the mail from our embassy to the base. Why kill him? He was only thirty-six.'

'And nobody was suspected back then?'

'Who knows, Mike? It was only when the Brits got involved after 17N shot Brigadier Saunders, that and the

Athens Olympics with a lot of international pressure, that the police and the politicians got their act together. There was a Minister who got involved, forget his name but he went to Paris with a small group of police. Good ones, and they did what the police should have done twenty-five years previously. They looked for the people who were there at the beginning, the real hell raisers. And they hardly had a long way to go. In 1971, Yotopoulos had been sentenced to five years' imprisonment for trying to recruit members to his anti-Junta group the May 29th Movement.'

'I'd have thought your organisation would have been aware of him then. You were supporting the Junta.'

'If we were aware, I never heard about it. Always possible we gave his name to the Greeks. But Yotopoulos was in Paris then. He didn't return until after the Junta collapsed over Cyprus. And back then, being anti-Junta was to be a hero as I've just said. It was the men who'd worked for the Colonels who were on trial. Our people weren't going to do anything that might make the new Government close the US bases or decide we weren't wanted. Lots of pussyfooting around during those years. Which is why we couldn't make a big thing about Dick Welch's death.'

Unlike previous American pressure, thought Mike, remembering reading an encounter a Greek ambassador had had with President Lyndon Johnson over Cyprus. And three years later, the Americans had supported the Junta. Yes, Mike could see why some Greeks who'd been around then might not support the CIA. He turned his attention back to Douglas who was getting into his stride.

'So, before the Olympics in Athens, this Greek Minister starts to talk with French Intelligence and various former left wingers who'd been around in 1968 and 1969. And guess what? Yotopoulos's name comes up. He was at the original meeting of the May 29 Group, shouting revolution and pissing off anyone who wasn't as extreme as he was. Arrogant was the word they all used. Thought he was the next Che Guevara.'

'I heard he went to Cuba around then.'

'Sounds par for the course. The British were involved with that Paris investigation, too, and they were pushing hard, and I have to say the Greek police did then begin to get their act together. There was one officer in particular, Lieutenant General, Fotis Nasiakos...'

Mike shook his head, 'Lieutenant General!'

'Yeah, these names,' agreed Douglas. 'Goes back to when Karamanlis disbanded the military police to keep the left happy.'

Since they were the most hated having tortured a lot of young people like Popi, Mike didn't say.

'But he let them keep the titles as a concession. But, yeah, sounds odd to us. What's your title?'

'I'm not a working officer anymore,' Mike replied. 'But it was Detective Sergeant.'

Douglas nodded. 'I can make sense of that. But yes. A lieutenant general: is that a lieutenant or a kind of general? Or is it the same as one of our captains?'

'Or one of our superintendents?'

'Well, whatever his title, Nasiakos kept on at his job for the next two years and trailed Yotopoulos, trying to build up enough evidence to arrest him.'

'Which they did in June 2002.'

'Yes. Interesting that. They only just got him. He and his French partner or wife, whatever...who knows if they ever married? ... were getting on to a hovercraft on their way to Turkey just as the police turned up. Half an hour later...'

'You think they were tipped off?'

'What do you think? Neighbours in Lipsi said they were burning boxes of papers for days before they were arrested.'

This tied in with what Manos had told him the previous day, and Mike agreed it looked dodgy.

'Dodgy. That's another good English word.'

'Dead dodgy we say, too.'

'I'll remember that.' He smiled. 'The police hunting Yotopoulos knew they were looking for a white-haired man, possibly an intellectual in his late fifties, but it took them a while to discover that it was him, the man who'd been teaching mathematics in Athens university, known as Michel or Michalis Economou.'

A very long time thought Mike. There had been an eyewitness to the shooting of an arms manufacturer in the eighties who'd said the killer sitting pillion on the motorbike was a white-haired man in his fifties. Had that been Yotopoulos? He'd have been in his forties, but had he gone grey prematurely? 'Yotopoulos studied economics, didn't he?' he asked.

'Yeah. Kind of arrogant that: Economou, economics. But then he was. Probably still is.'

'I certainly hear he was arrogant when he was in Paris at the beginning. That's the period that interested Henry, the first years of 17N.'

Douglas sighed. 'I need another beer. How about you?'

'Some water, please.'

'You don't drink?'

'Not anymore.'

'Enough said. Water it is.'

He went back into the house and returned with another beer and a bottle of water.

'The beginning of 17N. Which is the first murder, that of my former colleague, Dick Welch. You want me to tell you about that night? I wasn't there, but I got most of the details from Ron Estes, Dick's number two.'

He didn't wait for an answer to his question but poured the beer and took a deep gulp and started to talk.

'Well. This is what we heard from Estes. Dick's death really got to him. Got to all of us to tell the truth, especially when the Greek police got the insane idea that it was an internal CIA job. I never believed they investigated it fully. Didn't want to. Certainly true about 17N's later jobs when the Greek Government was trying to keep the far right and the far left happy. Can't be done, of course. Bunch of useless fuckers, excuse my language. But I'm jumping ahead of myself.

'There had been a Christmas party at the Embassy. Usual thing, hosted by the Ambassador, didn't end late. Dick Welch and his wife drove home, a nice villa in Old Psychiko, one of the posher parts of the City, far enough out of the centre to avoid the smog we used to get, and cooler. Lots of trees and gardens. You know the kind of thing. Houses there now sell for millions of euros. Thing was, some Commie journal had printed the names and addresses of key CIA agents abroad, and it had been picked up by the Athens News and published there the month previously. Endangered everyone. And Dick's house had also been the house of the last agent. Which is fucking stupid.

'Richard was urged to move to somewhere safer near the Embassy, but he had a new wife, Kika, and Kika didn't want to move from Psychiko. She liked the big house (and it was huge) and being able to entertain people there. It was all very exciting for her, and Dick enjoyed indulging her. They really hadn't been married that long.

'The house had two entrances, a little gate where you could walk straight up to the front door and a drive at the side. And they had this routine, the chauffeur, his name was Vangelis, still remember that. Funny what you remember over the years and what you forget.'

Mike had the feeling that this was something that Douglas could still recall as if it happened yesterday.

Like one or two memories of his own. He said nothing, not wanting to interrupt the old man and stop the flow.

'Vangelis, the chauffeur, would stop in front of the gate, open the doors for Dick and his wife, then he'd drive the car round the corner up the drive and park it in the garage. So, just like usual, he stops the car, it was a black Ford LTD, lovely car, and another car drives up behind. Someone gets out and walks up to Dick's car and calls his name. "Courteous," Vangelis said.

'Wife later said that Dick thought it was a friend. So he gets out of the car to speak to them, and the very same moment it all goes off. Two other men rush up and point their guns at Kika and Vangelis, then the first one shoots Dick. Right there in front of his house, in front of his wife. Then the three terrorists take off in their stolen car. Car is found, burnt out so no prints. All went off in a few seconds. The men were wearing black, I think, but between you and me, I don't think either the wife or the chauffeur really looked at them.' He paused. 'Have you ever had a gun pointed at you?'

'A few times including just a couple of weeks ago.'

'Of course, in that Stephanie Michaels shooting. And this young man pointed his gun at you?'

'He did, but unfortunately it was my friend Pam who got shot.'

'And what were you looking at when he's doing that? Pointing that pistol at you?'

Mike thought back. He'd been looking at Manolis when he spoke to him, but the moment he'd swivelled the gun towards him, all he'd seen was the gun. He said so.

'It's like facing a cobra. All you see is the head: guns mesmerise you, you can't take in anything else.'

Mike felt sure that Douglas was talking from experience.

'Yes,' he agreed. 'You wouldn't be looking around

at anything else. And that's why neither of them really saw the shooter.'

'Precisely.'

'Then it could have been a woman?'

'First I've heard of that, but yes, it could have been, one with a deep voice. And makes more sense of Dick getting out of the car and going to greet them. As I said, his wife thought it was a friend.'

Mike was glad this was all being recorded. This was a lot more detailed than anything he'd read before.

'So Kika collapses,' continued Douglas, 'and Vangelis gets her into the house and then he runs to a house a few blocks away where Estes is having dinner with his fiancée. Ron comes back with him, takes in the scene and swings into action. Same time, a policeman arrives having heard Vangelis shouting, and calls for an ambulance. But it doesn't come, not so unusual in Athens. Estes and Vangelis put Welch into his own car and go to the hospital where Dick is pronounced dead.

'Next morning, Ron tells the news to Dick's father, who'd been asleep upstairs. Then he came into the office and told all of us. No social media in those days.

'Jeez. Still remember how Estes told us the news as if it was yesterday. There were strong men in tears. One of the team headed for the weapons room shouting he was going to kill the local KGB agent. Had to be subdued. Lots of strong feelings rampaging round the room that day. Devastated Ron. Don't think he ever got over it.

'At least the President... Ford it was... agreed to give Dick a full military funeral. Said yes in a heartbeat. That helped his family. Father was a veteran, died shortly afterwards.'

'I'm sorry.'

'Yeah. Not something I like to remember. This group was the worst, Mike, the very worst.'

'But they're old now. A bunch of ancient commies.'

'Don't underestimate them. They still believe that working people will rise up and claim their revolution, and there's nothing they won't do to bring that about.'

CHAPTER 30

It was another hot morning and with Jen's plants beginning to wilt, Pam actually longed for some rain to freshen up the dusty garden. Only the rosemary and the lavender seemed happy. She was letting Jen down, should she be watering them differently? She really was useless when it came to gardening. She was sure Oliver's wife would know, but as she hadn't yet met her, she could hardly ask.

She went inside and made herself a coffee in Jen's splendid Porsche machine. She'd been up late going through the CCTV footage she'd been sent and now had the list of all the cars which had gone down Norfolk Street the night Henry was killed. She'd discounted local vans. The street wasn't one of the busiest at night, but the list still ran to several pages. It was going to be a slow job.

But at least she had a job to do. She'd got nowhere with the London picture agencies who all just seemed to want to sell her pictures. She'd found a few from the period, but they were all students marching in the streets and setting fires. No sign of Yotopoulos.

Oliver might be having more success in Paris since he had contacts there. And now, Mike, although he still said he wasn't investigating Henry's death, had emailed the recording of his interview with Douglas Stanton along with a brief summary of his meeting with the Greek police detective, Manos.

Pam thought she was getting a better picture about the early days of 17N now. Plus the news about the Greek academic who also believed there was another member of 17N who'd never been caught was a real breakthrough.

Stops making me feel stupid for a start, she'd emailed back to Mike the previous evening. They were using their new burner phones and that, too made her feel safer. Though she also now put clear tape across the bottom of her front door when she went out, and placed Jen's bike across it at night.

You're never stupid, Mike replied.

It wasn't just the idea that there was another member of 17N, but that they'd provided the intelligence. Made sense. Yotopoulos was the driving force, the political one who wrote all the proclamations and kept on about the revolution. He was the energy behind 17N, but there had to be someone with good political and corporate knowledge who chose the victims and where to place the bombs. It meant they weren't looking for another beekeeper or someone outside Athens.

It was seven o'clock, which meant it was nine in Greece; Mike would be back from his morning swim. She rang him.

'Go on, tell me where you are right now, make me jealous.'

Mike laughed.'I'm at home and it's unbelievably hot, not a breath of air today and really humid, even the cicadas are having a rest, and I'm sitting with a damp towel on my neck. Stephanie never got round to putting in air conditioning, something I'm going to have to rectify. It seems to get hotter earlier every year.'

'Does Henry's house have aircon?'

'In his bedrooms. He felt that you could deal with

the heat during the day but had to have a cool room to sleep in.'

'That's good. So maybe not so jealous.'

'Until I tell you about my swim this morning. The sea was like a lake, first thing, just shimmering in the sun with the occasional underwater surge as if some giant sea creatures was turning over.'

'Or a sea god.'

'Yes, we're never far from the old gods here. Did Henry tell you that Jason landed here at Chiona with the Argonauts.'

'He did. Gods and warriors and a giant bull.'

'That's our village,' Mike laughed.

'By the way, thank you so much for all the info. Douglas is an interesting chap, isn't he? I'm still digesting all the information.'

'Yes,' replied Mike. 'He clearly still feels angry that nobody was ever made accountable for Welch's death.'

'That's that statute of limitations thing again. Listening to him really brought home that these are real people with family and friends. I feel that some of Henry's books just deal with 17N from a political perspective, they don't deal with the pain that the families feel.'

'No. They're not about that,' he replied distractedly. Should he tell her he'd finally resigned from the Met? No. Wait till they next saw each other. Strangely, talking with Manos had been the final trigger he needed. And now it was done. He'd be free in a few weeks.

'Interesting that Chris also thought about the opening of the Leotakis Gallery,' she said, changing the subject.

'Yes. It's been in front of us all along.'

'I keep wondering whether I should ring Nikos. I told Chris not to, but now...but what could we say?'

'Just that we have concerns? Actually, I may be able to tell him in person.'

'That would be better. Is Nikos coming to Crete?'

'I'm not sure. But he's asked me, actually being Nikos it's a bit more imperious than ask – he's told me to meet him in Athens on Friday. Hope the fires haven't spread then.'

'Fires? Athens?'

'Terrible wildfires. It's all over our news. Actually, all this heat sort of ties in. You know I told you a while back about his new foundation and how Nikos wants to develop it to bring together all the environmental projects in Greece and help them and fund some new ones, well he's asked me if I'd like to work for it.'

'That's brilliant.'

'Isn't it? It really is exactly what I'd like to do. He'd said he was going to house the centre at his estate, but maybe he now thinks it would be better to build a centre in Athens. I guess I'll know on Friday.'

For the next hour Pam worked on her list checking against police DVLA records. At least she still had her police identification and could access this remotely. Soon, that would be gone. She'd decided to ignore every vehicle whose owner lived within a fifty-mile radius of Cambridge and thus might have a reason to be there. After half an hour every car had been filtered out. 'I only need one rogue car,' she told herself and then looked up startled as someone knocked on the front door.

She walked down the long corridor and put the chain across the door, she really didn't want Dave barging in and shouting at her again. Or worse. There was something about him now that scared her. She opened it carefully.

'Sorry to interrupt you, boss,' said Paul. He looked grim, she thought. She undid the chain and let him in.

'Oh, why change the habit of a lifetime?' she replied, smiling at him.

'It's the emails you sent to Dave,' he said as he walked

down the corridor into the sitting room. 'Hawkswood's taking it very seriously, he's getting a warrant to search this house for a weapon. He thinks you brought the gun back from Crete on the Leotakis jet. Any moment, he'll be here to arrest you.'

'What?' It was as if Paul was talking in a strange language. It didn't make sense.

'The emails you sent to Dave,' he explained. 'They read like a threat to kill. This is really serious, boss. If anyone found out I was here, I'd be in deep trouble.'

'But I haven't emailed Dave for weeks,' said Pam. 'There has to be a mistake. A threat to kill? I'd never kill anyone.'

'Pam I've seen the emails. They came from your phone. Perhaps you were drunk or something...but you need to...'

'Paul, you know me. I don't threaten to kill people, even scum, like that Pell we nicked a few weeks ago.'

'On remand with new charges pending,' replied Paul, 'as well as attempted murder. With those he's not getting off whatever his flash lawyer thinks. The emails clinched it.'

'Is that what Hawkswood's going to say about me? And for your information, I haven't got drunk since I got back.'

'May I see your phone?' Pam automatically reached into her bag and took it out. Paul looked at it.

'This isn't the same one you showed me last week.'

'Oh, for a second I forgot. I've got a new one.'

'Why?'

'In case my phone had been hacked just like Henry's laptop. Oh god... you don't think ... but...I wish Stuart had had time to examine it.'

'Do you still have your old phone? You didn't throw it out?'

'No, it's on the shelf over there. Go and see.'

Paul walked over to the bookshelf and picked up the phone. 'Nothing in Send,' he said scrolling through the few emails. She was right. She hardly used it.

'Nothing in Deleted. In fact, nothing at all in Deleted.'

'I don't bother that much,' said Pam, wishing she could look at the phone herself, not that she didn't trust Paul.

'But if we go to Recall Deleted.'

'Is there such a thing?' Pam asked. She really should have gone to more IT seminars.

'Ah…' Paul came over to the sofa where she'd sat down in shock and showed her the emails.

'The first email was sent last Monday, the sixteenth. I think you should read it.'

Pam took back her phone. 'That was the day of Henry's funeral. I wasn't thinking about anything else.' She looked down at the message and read it out.

'*How dare you come round here and invade my home…*' She stopped. 'Invade my home, I'd never say anything like that. Who wrote this? It's not me.' She began to read again. '*You've gone too far this time and you're going to pay for it. Don't think your friends can protect you.*'

'And Dave emailed you back,' said Paul reading it out loud over her shoulder.

'*Is this a threat,* he asked. And you replied: *A threat is simply a suggestion of action. This is a guarantee.*'

'I don't write like that. I don't even talk like that.'

'Seems Dave ignored it all,' Paul told her. 'He says he thought you were probably drunk. But then there was another one which came on Friday evening, the 20th. Look.'

Pam looked. It read:

Remember my promise. I came back from Crete with a souvenir and I know how to use it…

'You see. All sent from this phone.'

'This is insane,' said Pam gasping for air. 'This can't be happening.'

'Boss, you okay?'

'Can you get me some water?'

Paul went into the kitchen and came back with a glass. Pam's face was white and she looked as though she was about to faint.

'Remember to breathe,' she said quietly.

'What?'

'It's what Grace told me. Seems I've got a bit of PTSD.'

'Didn't think there was such a thing as a bit of PTSD. You need to be careful. This is the kind of thing which could trigger it.'

'Too late for that.' She took another sip of water and stood up. The dizziness had gone, and she could almost feel the adrenaline pumping through her. The good old flee or fight mechanism; she knew which one she was going to use.

'I'm bloody not sitting here waiting for that prick to come and arrest me. He could have talked to me first. What's Murton saying?'

'He always had doubts about you.'

'The utter bastard.' She took a deep breath; the panic attack had passed. 'I'm going to talk to Hawkswood.'

'Is that wise?'

'Bugger wise. I'm not sitting here until he sends in his attack dogs. And I'm not having him disturb Jen's things here. Shit!'

'You're sure?' Paul looked worried. Were these emails a possible side effect of her PTSD? Had she had a memory lapse?

'Let's go,' she replied, picking up her warrant card and putting it into her bag. She hadn't used that for a while. 'Take my phone straight to Stuart. Tell him it's been hacked and ask him to look into it.'

Paul nodded. 'I might even ask Stuart to do it away from the station, so Hawkswood can't grab it away from him.'

Pam locked her door and began to walk, still limping slightly, to Parkside Police Station, where her unit used to have the fifth floor which Hawkswood had now taken over. Paul walked alongside, hoping he didn't get seen by a colleague. If the DI's phone had been hacked, Stuart would find out. He prayed that this was what had happened. He still couldn't imagine Pam threatening to kill Dave, however he'd behaved. She was right: it wasn't like her, and it didn't sound like her. They said nothing more on the ten minutes it took to walk to the station. It was clear her leg was still hurting her, and she still looked worryingly pale.

'I'm going up,' she said as they arrived. 'Take my phone to Stuart and say you met me on the steps outside.'

'Don't you want me...' he began.

'I can still remember where my old office is, Paul. And I can't see Hawkswood throwing me into a cell just like that.'

Paul wasn't so sure, but she was right about the phone. The sooner Stuart got to see it the better.

It felt utterly bizarre going up in the lift to her old office without being on a case or about to brief her team. That's the past she told herself. Now let's sort out the present.

Hawkswood wasn't a particularly tall man, but he had a considerable girth, and filled her old office leaving little room for anyone else; it had always been too small, although she'd liked it. And to be honest, she missed it. She opened the door without knocking.

'I hear you want to talk to me,' she told the new DCI.

'DI Gregory…' he started. 'I didn't hear you knock.'

'Don't you DI Gregory me! What the fuck is this, Martin? You're applying for a warrant to search my house, a house I should not need to remind you, belongs to the daughter of Stephanie Michaels, the woman whose death I have just successfully investigated, the goddaughter of the man whose death there you should be investigating.'

Hawkswood flushed a dark purple red. He stood up behind his desk...my desk she kept thinking... that was my desk.

'I'd hoped to do this in a more private setting, but since you've barged into my office without an invitation, I have no option but to do it here...'

'To your fucking office,' she interrupted, 'which until very recently was my office in case you have forgotten. Where I didn't start arresting people without evidence and without due cause. I've never been so angry in all...'

'Pamela Gregory...' Hawkswood intoned.

The bastard is enjoying this, thought Pam.

'...I am arresting you under the Offences against the Person Act for threats to kill. You do not have to say anything...'

'I think I know the words to that one,' Pam cut in again.

'But it may harm your defence if you do not mention...' he droned on.

'You haven't listened to a word I've said, have you? It's what makes you such a lousy cop. No wonder they call you the Plank, thick as ....'.

'Anything you do say may be given in evidence.'

He'd cautioned her. The bastard had actually cautioned her.

'Finished?' she asked, sarcastically, when he stopped delivering the familiar words. 'If you'd take your head out of your arse for one moment, Martin, you'd realise that my phone was hacked. One of your officers has taken it to Stuart Weir, who you know was previously at GCHQ, and is a specialist in this area, and he's examining it to see how it was hacked.'

'He's no right to do that. It's evidence. It should have been brought to me.'

'Where you could lose it?' she asked, getting more furious by the minute. 'You have to believe me. It was hacked. And you know that Stuart is your best IT person.'

'Hacked? That old excuse!' Hawkswood laughed. 'Thought you might try something a bit more imaginative.'

'It was. Just as Henry Cox's laptop was hacked before he was murdered. Which you refused to investigate. And when Stuart finds out that this was the case, you're going to look even more stupid than you do now. And now I'm out of here. This is insane. Ow...' She'd turned on her heel, a bad move since her injured leg still complained at any sudden movement.

'And don't even think of searching Dr Jennifer Nichol's house for a non-existent weapon' she added. 'As I leave, I'll give the front desk the number of Major Papadakis of the Hellenic Police. He speaks perfect English, and he'll be glad to tell you the gun used to threaten Dr Nichols and to shoot me, was handed in to the Greek police while I was taken to hospital.' She had no idea if this was true but guessed it must have been. She certainly hadn't got it.

'You're a lazy cop, Martin. You want quick results, and you don't bother to check your facts.'

'The trouble with you, Gregory is that you think you're better than the rest of us. Maybe your association with your Greek billionaire gave you a taste for luxury or maybe it was always there. Who knows? You certainly must have got your Mr Cox wound round your finger fast to get his house. Quite an achievement. Or maybe it's more than that. All these accusations of murder. Only person I see benefitting from his death is standing here in my office.'

'You know how absurd that is? I wasn't even in this country.'

'Doesn't mean you couldn't have organised it, as you well know. Or maybe I'm wrong.'

Pam looked at him, surprised. Was he about to admit his mistakes? That would be a first.

'Maybe you haven't turned into a criminal overnight. Which, yes, would be a surprise. Perhaps this is a mental health situation. In which case you should discuss that with your lawyer after we charge you. In fact, I think it might be for the best to see about getting you sectioned under the mental health act.'

'I'm not the one here who's gone mental, Martin,' Pam was so angry she could hardly speak. She was also cold with fear. Could he do it? Get her locked up? Sectioned? Someone had set her up, but who and why? And what if they'd planted a gun near the house? After all, they knew where it was, they'd probably gone there to kill Henry.

If Stuart didn't manage to find the evidence of hacking, was she actually going to end up in jail or in a mental hospital? And if she didn't, would they now kill her? For the first time in her life, Pam felt really frightened. How could this be happening, she thought. How do I stop it? The first thing was to get away before Hawkswood threw her into a cell. And he would. She could see it on his face. He was dying to arrest her.

She turned and walked out of his office and stabbed her finger on the lift button. As usual, it didn't respond.

Bugger, she thought. I'll have to take the stairs. She took the first steps slowly, aware that her leg was throbbing when Hawkswood caught up with her.

'Just because you're a police officer, don't think for

one moment I'm going to treat you any differently from any other bloody criminal,' he shouted. 'I'm going to take you downstairs and put you in a cell right now.'

'You're bloody not,' she shouted. 'Haven't you listened, you stupid man? I've been set up.'

Suddenly, Pam found that she couldn't breathe, and everything was going white around her. Hawkswood moved to grab her shoulder as she began to fall, but her injured leg suddenly gave way and the pressure on her shoulder sent her crashing down the stairs. This is it, she thought, and in the same moment wondered why someone was screaming.

CHAPTER 31

I'm fine,' Pam told the paramedic who was taking her blood pressure, 'I was shot a few weeks ago,' she added as if that was the only reason for her lying on the ground. Four weeks. It can't have been, it was a lifetime ago.

'It's Pam, isn't it? We met a few weeks back, that kid out at Oakington, suspected heroin poisoning. I'm Teresa.'

'Winston,' replied Pam, remembering the boy in the case she'd solved just before Stephanie's murder changed everything. 'The heroin capsule hadn't broken as it happened, but he'd been forced to swallow more capsules than his body could cope with. He made a full recovery, thank goodness.'

'Terrible,' Teresa replied. 'Boy like that should be at school. He looked young enough still to be in primary, like my two.'

'He was twelve,' said Pam. Talking about that case seemed to help, she found she was breathing normally again. She must have fainted, that was it. But why was she at the police station? She couldn't remember walking there.

'But you have been busy since,' continued Teresa. 'They did such a nice piece on you on Look East, they even got your mother...'

My mother, Pam's heart sank. What sarcastic thing

did she say? She hadn't spoken to her mother for some years and had no wish to do so.

'She said she was so proud of you. Always knew you were a heroine, just like your father.'

'She said that?' asked Pam incredulous. Tears welled up. 'My father was a fire fighter. I'd always ...' She stopped. What on earth were they talking about? A television programme? Was she going crazy? She felt strangely muzzy, was she going to faint?'

'I need to find out what's going on,' she said trying to get up off the stretcher. Why was she on a stretcher? Why couldn't she remember what had happened?

'Lie still, lovey,' said Teresa. 'You've had a bit of a tumble down the stairs.'

The stairs? Yes, she'd come to the station to see Hawkswood. She struggled to get up again. He'd cautioned her. It all came back.

'I need to sort some things out,' she told the paramedic.

'Right now, all you need to do is lie down quietly and breathe,' said Teresa. 'I don't like the look of your blood pressure, and you need to have an X-ray. You fell down the stairs.'

'Yes. My back does hurt, come to think of it.' She tried to feel where the pain was.

'Don't try to touch it. Just lie still for me and we'll get you into the ambulance.'

Pam shut her eyes. Perhaps lying still was exactly what she needed to do. Everything else was going to have to wait. What she wanted to do was go home, but it seemed they didn't want her to do that. They wanted her to go to the hospital, and when she got to the hospital, they wanted her to have X-rays and answer questions and respond to their tests.

Now what? She thought as she lay in the cubicle on the A&E ward. She hadn't yet been charged, and the young police officer assigned to watch over her looked more than reluctant to be there. Right now, she imagined Murton and Hawkswood would be putting their heads together and working out how they would avoid a PR disaster. She didn't imagine either would come to the hospital to charge her in front of witnesses.

But once she was out … She thought desperately for someone who could help her. She couldn't ask Paul again; he'd already risked his job and the same went for her other colleagues. Grace would be sympathetic, but wouldn't act and Zofia? She didn't know about Zofia. Leotakis? No, he might make things worse.

Oliver Timberly. He was the only person who knew about the hacking and believed it. It was now just after ten thirty and France was an hour ahead, it could be a good time. And maybe she could join him in Paris.

Paris. If she could get there, she'd be safe; she couldn't imagine Hawkswood applying for a European arrest warrant, and that would take time, anyhow. No, he'd wanted to arrest her so badly, he'd rushed it, and she hadn't been charged or even released on bail pending further enquiries. She hadn't gone through the system.

Someone had put her bag on the bottom of the bed, and she opened it and took out her new phone. It was still there along with her passport. Thank God, Hawkswood hadn't checked her bag when she went in. Thank got she hadn't dropped it when she fell.

Oliver answered on the second ring.

'Oliver,' she said. 'I have a problem. The police think I've threatened to kill one of my colleagues. It looks as though my phone's been hacked and I'm in Addenbrooke's, though not injured, they're just checking me out. I need to get away, and not sure where I can go.'

'If I was in England,' he began, and her heart dropped. 'I'd come right away,' he continued. 'But I'm not, so you'd better come here.'

'I've got a young officer standing the other side of this cubicle which makes it a bit tricky.'

'Ah,' he replied. 'I think we can deal with that. Give me five minutes.'

Pam lay back feeling slightly less desperate. She wondered what he'd do. What could he do? Four minutes later, Oliver rang back.

'I've sorted it out. You're going to get the first train tomorrow to Paris. A friend is coming to take you to London in the meantime. We'll talk tomorrow. Be careful.' He ended the call before she could start asking him questions. Who would this friend be? Somebody he'd worked with, at Amnesty or abroad? There was so much she didn't know about Oliver.

She lay back and shut her eyes. At least she could rest for a moment. They'd decided they wanted to keep her for a few hours and monitor her blood pressure and whether she had concussion.

A little later the blue curtain was pulled back and a woman in a doctor's white coat came in. She had short grey hair cut in a severe bob, but her eyes looked very amused.

'Not a doc,' she whispered. 'Just borrowed the coat. Friend of Oliver. Now let's get you out of here.'

'I need all my stuff from my house,' said Pam.'

'Is it being watched?' The woman seemed utterly unfazed by what she was hearing. She's retired Intelligence, thought Pam. She's enjoying this.

'No. I haven't been charged yet, and they'll assume I'm safe while I'm in hospital. But I do have someone watching me.'

'Saw him. Looks as though he'd rather be anywhere else. Poor child.'

'Yes, I don't think most people in the nick are going to be happy about this,' said Pam. 'Not that I'm perfect or anything, but I do have a few friends.'

'Right. Tell me what you need. Something to cover you more than the hospital gown you're wearing I imagine.'

'My dress and bra are in that yellow plastic bag there,' Pam pointed to the chair beside her. 'I've still got my knickers on.'

The woman laughed. 'One should always keep one's knickers on in an emergency. 'OK,' she continued. 'Where's home? Oh, and what's your name apart from Pam?'

'It's Gregory. Pam Gregory. Actually, DI Pam Gregory.'

The woman's eyebrows raised half an inch. 'Ah. Beginning to make sense,' she said. She took down the details of Pam's address and what she wanted from the house.

'Basically summer clothes and the usual wash things then. Period?'

'Finished two days ago,' said Pam.

'One less thing to think about then,' smiled the woman. Pam nodded. It was the kind of thing no man would ever think of, she thought. And the timing of her period, for once, had been ideal, coming after the funeral and finishing before all this. She gave the woman her house keys and lay back on the starched white sheet and smiled.

'So kind of you,' said Pam, but it was more than kind.

'Okey doke,' the woman said, briskly. She hadn't given Pam her name and it didn't seem the moment to ask. 'Give me an hour. Twenty minutes to Flower Street, depending on traffic, and a few minutes to gather your stuff together and pack them up. Don't move.'

While she waited, Pam hoped that the hospital wouldn't choose this moment to move her to a ward or discharge her, but they seemed content to keep in the cubicle, coming in at regular intervals to check her blood pressure. She lay back and tried to relax.

She must have dozed off because it seemed that no time had passed before Oliver's friend returned, pushing a wheelchair.

'I got your nice PC to unearth this, told him you needed another X-ray. He seemed delighted to have something to do.'

She helped Pam out of bed and into the wheelchair. Pam held on to her handbag and picked up the yellow carrier bag with her clothes, which the woman covered with a folded sheet.

She wheeled Pam out of the emergency ward and down a corridor towards outpatients and nobody stopped them. Once in the outpatients' waiting room, she wheeled Pam into a disabled toilet where Pam got out of the chair and dressed herself. Her back hurt, but she could walk. The woman nodded as Pam did a couple of tentative stretches, then she wheeled the chair down a corridor and left it.

'OK?' asked the woman. Pam nodded.

They walked slowly out of the outpatients' entrance and towards the car park.

'One useful thing to know, if you're ever doing something illegal, do as much as you can legally. So don't park where you'll be noticed as they do in the films. They always get this wrong. Pay for parking and move slowly.'

The car was a large comfortable Volvo and Pam tried to breathe normally as they drove down the Babraham road past fields with neat rows of small green plants, past the Park and Ride and out towards the A11 and the M11 beyond it.

'There's nobody following us,' the woman told Pam after a while. 'You might as well sleep.'

'I'm okay, I think,' said Pam. 'Just practicing my breathing.'

'Always good to breathe,' the other said, drily. 'Mind if I play some music?'

'No, that's fine.'

The woman pressed a knob on an mp3 player, and the car filled with the quiet reflective sound of a piano.

'Satie's *Gymnopédie*,' the woman told her. 'Thought it appropriate for a trip to Paris.'

It was a piece of music that seemed to hover as if in thought between notes and Pam found herself breathing more easily as she listened. The next piece was Debussy and she found herself enjoying the impromptu concert. The woman drove carefully within the speed limit and turned off the M11 onto the M25 London's orbital motorway, famous for its tailbacks and crashes. This time, however, it was clear and very soon, at junction twenty-four, they turned off the road on to a suburban road towards London.

'This is where I leave you,' said the woman, smiling. 'In a few minutes we'll be at Cockfosters Underground station. It's the Piccadilly line and you should take it to South Kensington. Do you have an Oyster?'

'No,' said Pam.

'No problem, you'll find a charged one in the glove compartment in front of you.'

Pam opened it and took it out. It was in a plastic leather case that looked much used.

'Don't worry, I owe Oliver a lot more than this,' she said cheerfully. 'As I expect my daughter Margaret will tell you. She's going to meet you at South Ken and she's as indiscreet as they come. You'll enjoy her company.'

'So, she'll take me to a hotel?' Pam asked.

'Heavens no, she'll put you up overnight. She's used to her mother making odd requests. And now she's retired ... God, that always makes me feel old...she'll be glad of the company. Right, here we are,' she added, turning into a large car park.

Pam took her case which the woman had found back at the house and stowed in the boot and began thanking her again.

'No need,' she said, happily. 'Delighted to be able to help.' She hummed a tune from the last piece of music they listened to and got back inside the car.

An hour later, Pam was in a very comfortable Chelsea flat which had belonged to Margaret's mother, whose name, Pam discovered was Sheila and who had indeed worked for MI6.

Discovering that Pam hadn't eaten all day, Margaret went out and came back with one of the best pizzas Pam had ever tasted, followed by almond cake.

'Polpo,' said Margaret. 'I find myself there at least once a week, so they let me have take-out. Is it true that Mum's just sprung you from a hospital?' she added.

'Yep,' said Pam, licking tomato sauce from her fingers and thinking how unlikely this all was. 'I fell downstairs.'

'You all right?' Margaret asked, frowning.

Pam nodded but confessed she would like to rest for a bit. Margaret showed her into a room that must have belonged to one of Margaret's sons. It turned out she had two and they had families of their own but had still never quite cleared out their own rooms. Margaret, herself, had been a primary teacher and her husband was a civil servant and semi-retired.

'Which means he's on endless committees, works almost as many hours, but just doesn't get the same pay. But we're lucky that Mum gave us this apartment which she'd inherited herself. We'd never be able to afford to live round here otherwise.'

Mid-afternoon, Pam woke up feeling a lot better and after a cup of tea found herself agreeing with Margaret that if Oliver was going to take her to all kinds of smart places in Paris – 'and Oliver does like to do that' – she should probably buy some new clothes.

'We've got Peter Jones virtually opposite,' she said, 'which is the local John Lewis, so why not?'

Strangely enough, unlike the last time she went shopping with Roberta, Pam didn't object to the idea, but kept thinking how Stavros might like her in the dresses she tried on. Only a month ago, all she wore was her personal uniform of black trousers and assorted polo shirts. What a change.Knowing that her new phone was safe, she rang Mike and told him what had happened and gave him permission to ring Stavros. It was easier than ringing him herself. She wanted to, but at the same time didn't want to fight. Perhaps their relationship was doomed not to happen; she wasn't sure she had the energy for it.

CHAPTER 32

The only idea Pam had of Paris was from old films and television programmes. Plus a film Grace and Zofia had taken her to at the Arts Cinema which was about the suburbs where, it seemed, there was virtual war between the gangs and the police. The film had been all hate and despair. 'Makes the Arbury look benign,' she'd said. Zofia had loved it. Pam didn't understand why.

She presumed not all Paris was like that, otherwise millions of visitors wouldn't keep visiting. On the Wednesday morning, Margaret took Pam to St Pancras where she had a coffee in the first-class waiting lounge (Oliver having bought her a first-class ticket) before getting on to the train. There was nobody here to arrest her nor at the border. As soon as they were safely in France, she felt her whole body begin to relax, and in no time at all, the train slid into the Gard du Nord. Here, Oliver met her, taking her bag, and looking at her with obvious concern. He took her to a waiting taxi, round the corner from the station.

'I've told him it's your first time in Paris, so he's going to give you a bit of a scenic journey,' he said, smiling.

And it really was just like the films. They drove past a palace and down the Champs- Élysée, which seemed to contain every major fashion brand she'd ever heard of, and up to the Arc de Triomphe, which Oliver told her was the French equivalent of the Cenotaph, but more triumphalist. Finally, they turned left and ended up in a narrow street with honey-coloured high buildings on either side.

'Some of these houses are embassies, but a few people live round here including an old friend who has a summer house near ours in Agios Nikolaos. They've gone there already and have very kindly lent me their somewhat lavish apartment.'

He pulled open the door onto the street and Pam found it led into a courtyard. There was a square of grass in the centre with a low tree, and the surrounding buildings had a trellis, attached to the wall diagonally covered with ivy and some other climbing plants. There were also many pots of flowers and a few folding chairs and tables.

'This is us,' said Oliver leading her to a flat on the right. 'We're on the ground floor. Just as well…you don't want to be bothering with stairs right now.'

Pam didn't know what to expect but found herself in a flat that looked like a museum.

'Not my taste all this gilded stuff,' laughed Oliver, 'but Georges loves it. He's a banker, by the way, though retired mostly now.'

Pam laughed, too. 'If I've ever imagined how a banker would live, it would be like this.'

'Then you're going to enjoy your room.'

She did. She'd photograph it for Zofia if they were still on speaking terms, she'd have hooted at the sight of it all. It was large, with a cream carpet and a cream oriental rug. The walls had been painted a pale green with gilded actual and painted panelling with a great many curlicues. The four-poster bed itself was also painted and gilded with muslin curtains caught up with gold silk ropes as were the green silk curtains although here the ropes had giant tassels.

'Blimey,' said Pam.

'Yes,' agreed Oliver. 'And this isn't all. I have a treat for you. Thought you deserved one after the nightmare you've been through. I've booked us lunch at a rather special rooftop garden terrace, just round the corner.'

Thank goodness for Margaret and my new dress, thought Pam. It was a fine transparent cotton with a lilac and white floral pattern over white cotton with a scalloped hem. She'd also allowed herself to buy matching lilac sandals. She didn't trust herself in heels until her leg was completely better.

'You look lovely,' Oliver told her, and she felt good as she walked down the elegant road, her dress swishing slightly as she moved.

The restaurant was in a hotel called the Raphael which made Pam think about Leotakis's bodyguard. Was he involved all this? As the killer, or part of a plot to implicate Leotakis?

The rooftop with its view over Paris and the Eiffel Tower took her mind off terrorism; it was everything she'd ever dreamed except she'd never allowed herself such extravagant dreams.

'It's one of the best views in Paris,' Oliver told her. 'I pulled some strings to get us a table at the side so we can view the Tower. It looks so much better from here than it does close up.'

They ate their way through the meal that was memorable for being dishes Pam thought she knew, but clearly didn't because they'd never tasted like this. There was a piece of salmon with a tiny dish of salmon mousse and little blobs of intense green that exploded on her tongue with a blend of basil and mint.

She'd told Oliver to order for her and was slightly disappointed that he'd chosen strawberries and cream. I can get that at home, she thought. But again, she was wrong. These were strawberries which tasted more deeply of strawberries than any she'd ever had before. And they came with a strawberry macaron, strawberry sorbet and a few rose petals dusted in sugar.

'Would it be crass to take a picture?' she asked.

'I rather think the chef expects it,' he replied. 'They create these culinary pictures for you to enjoy.'

'Just think, yesterday I was in hospital and worried about being charged and put in jail.' Or worse, she thought, but didn't say. But Oliver was ahead of her.

'One of the reasons I'm glad you called me was that I'd been feeling that Cambridge wasn't safe for you. Not until the killer is arrested.'

If, she wanted to add. You can never take that for granted. Not every case gets solved. Though was this a case? It didn't feel like a case. There was nobody to interview, no press conference or press interest, and no pressure from brass for a quick solve. It felt more like doing a crossword puzzle, albeit one done in a wonky cage with circling sharks.

She told Oliver the whole story of the past two days and he filled her in on his fruitless searches of the last week. So many photographs, but no sighting of Yotopoulos. But he told her, he had news.

'I think we may have a breakthrough.'

'A breakthrough? Tell me.'

'One of the photographers I met this week mentioned an old friend who'd mixed with some of the extremists back in '68. He was only involved for a few months as he got a job with an orchestra in Lille. I rang him, and he remembers it all clearly. He also speaks excellent English, played in the Philharmonic for nine years.'

'That could be really helpful. And, who knows, a picture might still turn up.'

'It could be it's out there in some undeveloped negative, and we'll never know,' Oliver said. 'It would take years to go through all the pictures taken here at that time.'

'Well let's pray this new contact gives us a useful lead,' she replied.

'Actually, he's just postponed the meeting till tomorrow morning as he's on grandchild duty; his daughter has got stuck in Munich filling in for a sick orchestra member.'

'That's a bit irritating. Hope he doesn't postpone again. After all, he may have actually met our mystery terrorist.'

'Well, that does give us the rest of today for enjoyment. You certainly deserve that. I thought we'd go to the Orangerie. And I'll let that be a surprise.'

The Orangerie turned out to be a small building like a temple with huge windows and inside were the Monet waterlilies in a circle.

'I had to bring you here,' Oliver laughed. 'They match your dress.'

'You see reproductions all the time, but they don't prepare you for the real thing.' Pam just wanted to lose herself in these paintings.

'No, they don't.'

'And now we're going back to the flat so you can rest for a bit. It's only yesterday you fell down those stairs. Or was pushed.'

Pam smiled.

'I was pushed, yes. But that's just between the two of us. I don't want to make a thing about it and get involved with a disciplinary row.'

'Very sensible,' said Oliver.

She was more than grateful for his quiet support as well as his way of knowing exactly what she needed before she did. She was surprisingly tired again, and the four-poster proved to be more comfortable than it looked. Pam lay down thinking she'd just relax for a few minutes, but when she woke, found that it was seven in the evening.

She went into the en-suite bathroom, which was decorated with painted tiles looking like a trellis covered in flowers and had a quick shower, then put on her other new dress, a simple shirt-waister in grey and white.

Oliver was in the kitchen, the only room not invaded by gold leaf, sitting at a black marble table making notes.

'When you feel up to it, I thought we could put together all our thinking and research so far.'

'Now would be fine, if there something as basic as water in that fridge, which I think is larger than my previous kitchen.'

Oliver opened the giant fridge. 'There is an assortment of waters,' he told her. There was. Evian, she recognised, and Perrier, but Badoit was new.

'Meant to be very good for you,' said Oliver. 'Tastes like it.' There were also some very expensive-looking glass bottles, covered in crystals.

'Designer water?'

'They'd pay for designer air if it cost enough,' Oliver shook his head at the mad behaviour of the rich. 'For some people it's just about showing off how rich they are.'

'There must be people who eat like we did today every day and then there's no such thing as treats. I'd hate that. People like Nikos. Though Mike said he seemed happiest in Mike's tiny caique, drinking beer and fishing. And we're talking about a boat that's hardly bigger than the average rowing boat, made out of odd bits of timber and scrap.'

'I think Nikos Leotakis is a highly unusual man.'

'Yes. I'm worried that all this is in some way targeting him, but I can't see how.'

'Let's draw some arrows. I find that does sometimes clarify one's thinking.'

They sat down at the table and Oliver pulled out some large sheets of paper.

He wrote Alexandros Yotopoulos on one side and Nikos Leotakis on the other and circled the names.

'Let's see if there are any connections.'

Pam took the pen and wrote the name Patrice under Yotopoulos and circled it and then linked it to Didi, which she then linked to Dimi which sent an arrow straight to Leotakis.

'One link already,' she said. Oliver nodded. He wrote Moscow in the centre and sent links from that to both Yotopoulos and Leotakis.

'We know that Leotakis was funded by Moscow in the fifties...'

'And by the Americans,' added Pam. 'From what his biographer told me, he took money from everyone back then, when he was operating in Central America. And we know that Patrice acted for Russian clients,' said Pam adding another arrow. 'And possibly Didi was involved. I feel that she might have been a communist, too. Perhaps still is.'

She told Oliver about their encounter with Patrice's widow.

'She was very keen to blame Leotakis, which made Mike and I wonder whether she was deflecting it away from herself.'

'That is a possibility. Patrice also worked for Cuban clients. And Yotopoulos went to Cuba for training.'

'And Leotakis was very active in Cuba when he was gun running back in his past,' she added, recalling what Chris had told her on their first meeting. 'He was called the Pirate back then.'

'But it seems unlikely that Leotakis still has links with Cuba.'

'Who knows? He seems so approachable and nice and open, but actually I know virtually nothing about him except what Chris Brook has told me. And I know Chris has some large chunks missing, particularly in relation to how his millions became billions and where his money is all invested. He's a man with secrets.'

'Who has the ear of the Government in at least two countries.'

'So now let's add Henry.' She wrote his name in the middle and put a dotted arrow to Leotakis.

'He lived near Nikos and Stephanie was his best friend and close to Leotakis.' She then drew another dotted arrow towards Yotopoulos. 'Henry, as you know, was writing a book that included a chapter on 17 November, but his life wasn't connected to them.'

'After what you've told me and I've observed, I want to add Christopher Grey to this. He has links to Henry and is MI6.' He added that. 'And MI6 were peripherally involved in the capture of 17N.'

'And to Leotakis?' asked Pam.

'I don't know.'

'According to Chris, he was working for the CIA in Central America I think some forty years back. But after they supported the Junta in Greece, he didn't want anything more to do with them.'

'Interesting.'

They both stepped back and looked at the arrows.

'Anything we've forgotten? asked Oliver.

'Patrice was writing his autobiography according to Didi, and we have no idea whether his death was to stop that ever being published.'

'Good point.'

'Chris Brook also mentioned that Leotakis had come up against some Ukrainians at one point but thought that was a purely business deal.'

'Ukrainian mafia. Well, we must certainly hope that they aren't behind this. Indeed, if they were, I think we'd have to quietly slip away. There are more arms floating around in that country than anywhere else, and they've got into the hands of some very ruthless men. However, this feels more Greek than Ukrainian. And Henry's death and the way your phone was targeted feels much too subtle for them. But whoever has hired the hacker who got into your phone clearly has deep pockets.'

'Which wasn't the case with 17 November. They stole ancient weapons from a museum and didn't seem to have much money at all.'

'No. They worked on a shoestring budget from what I've read.'

'There was one more name. Yiannis Papoutsakis.' She wrote his name under Patrice. 'He was jailed for trying to bomb the European Parliament in Strasbourg and blamed Patrice, his lawyer, for not getting him off.'

'But he doesn't link with anyone else here?'

'Not as far as I can see.'

'Then I think that's as far as we can go this evening.'

'I'd like to visit Patrice's flat while we're here.'

'Good idea.'

'Didi said the police took his papers, but you never know what might still be there. Is it too late to ring her?'

'No, I don't think so.'

Pam took out her phone and clicked on the Didi's name. She listened to the long ring of the European telephone system and remembered how it had infuriated her during Stephanie's investigation when she'd heard it, because it meant that her witnesses had left the UK. First George, the project manager of the gallery, and then Henry. And Henry had gone to visit Patrice. Where this all started.

'Allo?' Didi sounded irritated.

Pam explained to her that she was following her advice, but it would help them enormously if they could come over to see their apartment. 'I'm with a friend who is helping with this investigation,' Pam added. 'His name is Oliver Timberly. He speaks French,' she added.

Pam ended the call and turned to Oliver.

'Didi is away but is happy for us to go to the apartment tomorrow. She's going to leave our names with the concierge who has the key.'

'Excellent,' said Oliver.

'And guess where she is...' Pam smiled and bit her lip. 'She's on Mykonos with Dimi Forgeron.'

CHAPTER 33

Stephen Mawson glared at the screen.

'Who the hell are you, you bitch?' he muttered for the nth time. Was Moros a Greek or an agent for another country, Turkey perhaps? No love between those two nations. Or the unknown member of 17N as Henry Cox had thought?

If the possibility of a chemical weapons attack was real, he ought to contact MI6, but what could he tell them? A researcher in a Greek lab had died. It might have been suicide. His father had been in debt and then he wasn't in debt.

There was no evidence of a theft and, indeed the only actual evidence he could offer was that he believed he had been involved in a murder. You could be tried for aiding and abetting and, if it was as serious a crime in Greece as it was in England, he'd be looking at a very long jail sentence.

He'd been through this argument too often now. That was not going to happen and, besides, there was no proof of his involvement. The only person who knew what he'd done was Moros, and she wasn't going to start talking. At least he knew that he was dealing with a woman.

He was also pretty sure it wasn't Popi Filotaki, though she fitted into the story somewhere. He'd done more research into her and all he found was more of the same: she was a saint. She had plenty of reasons for hating the police, of attacking the establishment, but that simply did not emerge in any of her articles. Or from the way she'd lived her life, working with politicians, advising, helping.

He read one of the last pieces he'd downloaded from one of her lectures on using doors to close off the past.

It may sound strange to use something as specific as a door as one of the tools in therapy. Doors, after all, can symbolise the doors of a prison, and memories of those doors can continue in the nightmares that victims of torture often have. Sometimes for many years after their release or escape. Indeed, nightmares and flashbacks are common to all of us who have suffered torture. And it is often the most banal incidents that can set off a memory and bring on a panic attack. I myself, have had attacks walking through a supermarket and seeing a selection of household brooms, because it was one such object that was employed by the torturer.

No, Stephen decided. Popi was not Moros. But she had lived in Athens and now lived in Crete. Crete. It began there.

Crete also meant Nikos Leotakis, and now Leotakis wanted to meet him, not in Crete or London, but in Athens. The message came out of the blue, but it was on Nikos' personal phone, and it didn't surprise Stephen too much. He remembered the way Leotakis had researched him before that lunch. He was probably still keeping tabs on what Stephen did, so he'd know that he'd recently bought a couple of Greek artworks and had talked to both Sotheby's and Christie's about the contemporary Greek art scene.

Possible new gallery and new venture. Meet me Friday 27th at 11am at Garittou 187, Halandri, Athens. Please keep this confidential.

Athens. That was ideal, he thought. He could also visit the street where Popi lived. He'd been up and down it a few times and then explored the neighbouring streets. They smelled wealthy: a lot of Mercedes along with new, small run-arounds.

This was exactly like the kind of district where you might find a politician living, but was it the home of a terrorist? All the 17 November terrorists had had jobs, and most of them were working class except for Yotopoulos himself. He'd taught maths at a university and was more middle class than the others. He had a small summer house on the island of Lipsi and a flat, where was it? Ah yes, a district called Pangrati. Damareos Street.

Stephen looked at it. Leafy, like the other, but much less attractive. All apartment blocks and a few shops. No local cafés with seats outside, unlike the first street. Going up and down and around, it seemed there was a kind of invisible boundary along a wide street called Imittou. And Damareos was on the wrong side. But it was a good place to hide; this wasn't a district where neighbours talked to each other. Not surprising that Yotopoulos managed to hide there for so many years.

But did Moros still live in Tsami Karatasou? Was she the wife of a politician? That would enable her to keep hidden, but it was clear she hadn't lived with Yotopoulos for many years. He'd had this French wife, but that didn't mean he and Moros weren't still close.

Walking down the street in person was hardly going to help any more than walking down the street on Google. Except he'd get hot. He'd learned about the heat from Tina whom he'd called the previous evening.

'What do you think about Athens?' he asked.

'Old city, capital of Greece. Has a famous Parthenon. Birthplace of democracy...'

'Yeah,' replied Stephen trying not to sound annoyed.

He couldn't see the point in this kind of humour but knew that people like Tina thought it was amusing. And people like Tina knew the right people and enabled Stephen Mawson to have a legitimacy.

'Thinking about opening a gallery there, and maybe find somewhere with enough space to house installations.'

'Sounds like the kind of thing Peggy Guggenheim did and that didn't work out badly. Plus, you have the eye. That's the most important thing.'

'And the purse,' he laughed, playing her game.

'Yes. You need that, too. But Athens is the perfect choice right now. Gets a lot of visiting Arabs, crossroads with Middle East and Africa and packed with rich Russians.'

'Including the Russian mafia,' added Stephen who'd come across a few online and knew enough about them to want to steer clear. 'I wouldn't want them involved. They have a way of demanding protection money.'

'Really? In Europe?'

Part of Russia is European, you spoilt Daddy's brat, he thought.

'They're even in London, Tina. If you move in the wrong circles.'

'Well, they'd better not come into mine,' she answered, and he could see her pouting.

'You thinking of going there?'

'Flying visit tomorrow,' he replied. 'Bit of land has come up. Going for a look see.'

'Talk to Antigone at the Fonisos Gallery and go and see her. Her gallery's in Kolonaki and I expect you'll be staying near there, won't you?'

'Not far,' Stephen agreed, having no idea yet where he was going to stay.

'I'll ring her now and tell her you're coming. She knows all the good new Greek artists.'

'You're so lovely,' Stephen said. 'And not just because you're beautiful.'

'That's what you say to all your women,' Tina replied, pleased. She could never be sure about Stephen, whether he was serious or not. He had the money and took her to the right places, but it felt as though he'd learned them from a how-to-be-rich manual. There was something about him that didn't feel true. He also was a man without any background, which added to her doubts about him. Not that she'd ever voiced them. But she knew she'd never live with him.

Instead, she told him the name of her favourite bar in Athens and reminded him how hot it was there.

'And I mean really hot. It's why there have been all those terrible fires.'

'Fires?'

'Look it up, Stephen, It's all over the news.'

Stephen sighed. He rarely followed the news. He had other things on his mind.

Gregory for one. He'd found out that she wanted to know whether CCTV footage had caught the car carrying Henry's killer. He wanted to know that too but wasn't about to do the boring checking of every car. So why not get this DI to do it for him? It hadn't been too difficult to get into the CCTV system used by the university, it was owned by a company he'd hacked previously. He copied the film of the hours she'd requested and emailed it to her from a fictional assistant external administration officer.

It all worked perfectly and now there Gregory was, checking every car for him.

But as for the Butcher emails. That hadn't been so successful. He'd sent the first to Butcher the day of the funeral, but he'd done nothing, so he sent another on the Friday and waited and yes, she had been arrested. He read that via Collins, learning that she'd then been rushed to hospital from where she'd disappeared.

Bugger. Moros was not going to like that. But then his day got very much worse. He discovered, again via Paul Collins's emails, that someone called Stuart was looking into the hacking.

It couldn't be Stuart Weir, could it? He was still at GCHQ, wasn't he? It seemed he wasn't. He was in Cambridge.

How the fuck did that happen? thought Stephen. What is Weir doing working for the Cambridge cops? He reluctantly told Moros the bad news, excluding the bit about Weir. That would make him unemployable.

Most unsatisfactory, she replied. *Get rid of Gregory.*

Not what I do, he answered. *I'm a hacker, not a killer, and I don't hire killers. Anyway, nobody knows where she is. Do your own job. This end is watertight.*

But was it? Stuart had been the one person at GCHQ who was as good as he was, possibly even better. He might be able to trace Stephen's actions, but good luck finding out who he was. At GCHQ they'd known him as Sam Moss. Stuart wasn't going to find Stephen Mawson.

He spent all day Wednesday and half Wednesday night cleaning his system and locking away anything that could lead to Stuart finding his identity. Maybe this was the moment to give up hacking and just deal in art. Or even open this art gallery abroad. He didn't have to stay in England. People did reinvent themselves. Maybe Leotakis would help him make this happen.

He decided to fly to Athens on the Thursday and visit a few galleries, see what kind of art sold in the Greek capital. He'd then arrive at his meeting with Leotakis prepared. It could be a new beginning.

Kolonaki, Tina had said. He looked it up. It seemed to be precisely the kind of upmarket district which would appeal to her and her friends. It had expensive boutiques, cafés, and, more importantly, galleries. It was a kind of Mediterranean blend of Bond Street and Chelsea. It also abutted the Parliament, and the square there, called Syntagma and its Metro station.

And that mattered because the blue Metro line went directly from the airport to Syntagma. And along the way it stopped at somewhere called Halandri. And that was near where Nikos Leotakis had askd him to meet him on Friday.

The plane landed at Athens airport on Thursday morning and the heat began the moment the aircrew opened the door outside. It wasn't like a hot day in England: this was a furnace. Not surprising there were wildfires.

He had looked that up, too. According to the BBC News, at least seventy-four people had died in the region around Athens. It was being called Greece's worst fire disaster in more than a decade, and the winds had destroyed a whole village. And two days ago, the Prime Minister had declared three days of national mourning. The pictures showed thick black smoke billowing over an Athens suburb. Not a good day to choose to visit the capital, but hopefully the fires weren't near where they were meeting. The airport, at least, had remained open.

Stephen had booked a suite at the Grande Bretagne and asked for a limo to meet him. At least that would be airconditioned.

It was. And the driver spoke English, which was a bonus.

'Could we go via Halandri?' Stephen asked.

'Of course, he replied.

'The street I want to go down is called Garritou and I want to go along it,' he checked the notes he'd made, 'from Halandriou to the ring road.'

'Not a problem, sir,' said the driver. He was in his early forties, could probably afford to lose some weight, though that was hidden under his suit jacket. He wore dark glasses, not to be cool, Stephen realised, but because of the glare of the road. He was glad not to be driving, and after experiencing Athens traffic for a few minutes, decided he would never drive in this capital.

He wasn't at all sure he wanted to come and work here. He hated the heat. Couldn't he find a place for his new gallery somewhere cooler, like Amsterdam or Oslo? Maybe Toronto?

'We can come in from the ring road and go down to Halandriou if you're happy doing it in that order.'

'Fine,' said Stephen.

Doing it in that order meant that Stephen saw the worst first. The place where Leotakis had chosen was a large empty lot, more like a field, in an area that seemed totally run down. There was nothing there yet except a large derelict building that looked like a small aircraft hangar. Further down, there were other empty lots, a wood yard and some small houses and businesses and areas full of parked cars. They probably used these lots to park and use the Metro, he thought. A free park and ride. This was clearly an area that needed development, but as far as he could see, this wouldn't be for some time.

The car purred on, and in a very short time the road changed completely. There was an expensive-looking office block and then large attractive apartments, some set back from the road, which was now lined with trees. The development had started, but it needed a way to go. This was useful knowledge.

After stepping out of the limo at the hotel, the heat hit him again and once he entered the historic building, he decided he wasn't going to budge until the following morning. He'd chosen it, not just because it was one of the few places that did have a room – he always forgot about people having summer holidays – but because it might very well be where Leotakis himself was staying. He also enjoyed the fact that it had been both the British and the Gestapo HQ. Though that was invisible since its last face lift.

He'd thought of having a swim in the rooftop pool, but that meant going outside again and his pale skin wasn't designed for extreme heat. It was going to be room service and the bar. This wasn't his city; the moment he'd finished his meeting, he was heading straight for the airport and the first plane back to the UK. To Paris, if necessary, he could always get the Eurostar home.

The following morning, he got up early, worked out in the gym and had a leisurely breakfast. He was ready. He'd only brought a couple of shirts and underpants in his briefcase, and it wouldn't be a problem walking with that. He decided to brave the Metro, giving himself adequate time. He wanted to be on top of this meeting, not keep Leotakis waiting for him.

It was only a ten-minute walk from the Metro station at Halandri and although hot and dusty, this wasn't a problem. There was a large tree beside the building and a discarded bucket nearby which he used as a seat as he waited. He had water and it wasn't unbearable in the shade, merely uncomfortable. It was also noisy; the traffic roar from the nearby ring road drowning out the cicadas in the tree. This was going to be a very short meeting. He never wanted to come back here again.

At ten forty-five, he heard footsteps, and got up to greet Leotakis, but it wasn't him. Along the road came the black cop who'd been a friend of Henry Cox, Mike Petersen. What the holy fuck was he doing here? Was this a set up? And it was clear that Petersen recognised him from the funeral, too. He looked equally confused.

Petersen stopped and started to talk to someone on his phone. Then made another call after which he started to run towards him. Stephen had had enough.

Was Leotakis staging this? He was going to have it out with him. He turned back towards the building. There was a lock on the door, but someone had already opened it, the door was slightly ajar.

Mike was still running towards him, though was a good way away, by the trees. 'Stop!' he yelled.

'Fuck off!' shouted Stephen, and pushed the door open, furiously. The supersonic shock wave from the detonated dynamite ruptured his lungs and his bowels, perforated his ear drum, and caused an instant massive cardiac bleed. His body flew into the air, and Sam Moss, also known as Stephen Mawson, was dead even before he hit the ground.

CHAPTER 34

On Thursday morning, Oliver told Pam they were going to the Boulevard St Germain for breakfast.

'That sounds fun.'

'Both fun and a bit of following in the tracks,' Oliver replied. 'We're going to *Les Deux Magots* which along with the *Café de Flore*, was one of two cafes where Sartre and Simone de Beauvoir hung out as well as Picasso and Hemingway, and just about everyone else.'

'And that was where our terrorist gave Sartre the first communiqué?

'Yes.'

Pam had asked Mike about Sartre after Henry first mentioned his name because she had a feeling she'd need to know about him later, and she didn't want to feel stupid. One of the great things about Mike was that he never let her feel that.

'Sartre was one of the people who created a philosophy called existentialism,' Mike had told her. 'Basically, it was a philosophy based on the concept of being a student. I read that somewhere and it's bang on the money.'

'Really?'

'Yup. Wear black? Tick. Sit up arguing all night? Tick. Have as much drink and sex as you want? Tick. Create a movable philosophy that works with whatever happens to be going on at the moment? Tick. Oh, and don't just talk, act on your beliefs. Officially it's a philosophy centred around the individual and what they're thinking and feeling, but I personally like the student definition.'

'Sartre founded the newspaper *Libération*,' Oliver was telling her now, 'which was on the extreme left back then, but has gradually softened its stance.'

'So, a logical place for 17N to bring their communiqué. Pity that moment wasn't picked up by a wandering photographer. That would save us a lot of time.' She tried to imagine Paris back then. Today *Les Deux Magots* seemed mostly filled with tourists.

'My god, they even do a breakfast Jean Paul Sartre!' exclaimed Oliver reading the menu. He laughed. 'It includes yoghurt but doesn't have any alcohol which seems most unlikely.'

Pam laughed with him. Yes, this was touristy, but she loved it. She loved the formal waiters in their black waistcoats and long crisp white aprons and there were even a couple of Frenchmen in their fifties drinking black coffee and talking animatedly with a lot of expressive hand movements.

Having only had some fruit for supper, Pam realised she was starving again, so ordered both a croissant and a *tartine* which was the best bread, butter and jam she'd ever tasted.

'This is delicious,' she said. 'I get it. These are the cafés that all the other cafés try to look like.'

'Precisely.'

'Great place to watch the world go by.'

'When you have time. Which, unfortunately, we don't have today.'

'No, we have a possible terrorist to find.' She paused. 'Being in Paris makes all the various bits and pieces come together: Patrice and 1968 and Yotopoulos and Sartre. And Didi, too.'

'It will be interesting to see Patrice's flat.'

'Yes, it's just down the road from here, isn't it? I checked the map.'

'Yes. First, we have our appointment with Pierre Veilleux. It's just a few stops to Raspail which is in Montparnasse, where a lot of artists used to live, too. There are some delightful small museums around there, but that will be for another visit.'

Pam smiled. The Metro was much more user-friendly than London. She could imagine coming back here. Could she come with Stavros? Would he enjoy it? So much about him she didn't know, and now didn't know if she ever would. But she couldn't think about him now, she had to make full use of this time in Paris.

'Tell me about the man we're meeting.'

'He's a flautist. I think he's played in various orchestras including the Philharmonic. His connection with Yotopoulos goes way back. As far as I can gather, he flirted with the far left during the sixties, but it was something he shed when he started working.'

'So, he's how old?'

'About seventy.'

'Ever since I started investigating Stephanie's death, I've found myself meeting so many interesting older people.'

'I like the older, Pam.' Oliver laughed. 'You can call me old. My wife does, and she's only two years younger than me.'

'In the past, nearly all my contacts with *old* people were very different. I don't know whether you know that the police force does a lot of the things social services used to do before they were cut to the bone. So, we had a lot of cases dealing with people with forms of dementia. The only lively old people tended to be University lecturers and professors who'd been burgled.

This is a very different world.'

'As is this,' she added as they ascended into another wide boulevard, lined with trees and long terraces of tall buildings with similar black iron balconies. 'It all looks very similar, doesn't it?'

'Yes. That's because it was designed. A man called Haussmann was hired to knock down most of old Paris and create a new one. They said the old narrow streets helped diseases to grow, but it was also the fact that the revolutionaries used to use the cobblestones as weapons and to block the narrow streets.'

'Like the students in 1968.'

'The French have a phrase for that: *plus ça change*. But Haussman didn't just divide Paris into street and squares, he also made it a ruling that all the facades had to be built the same colour. And the city planners who followed him and kept that rule going for decades.'

'It's lovely, but I suppose a lot of history got lost along the way. I rather like our remaining cobbled twisty streets.'

'Like Elm Hill in Norwich. Though my own bugbear is what contemporary architects and planners are doing to the London skyline.'

They arrived at Pierre Veilleux's apartment, which was in a courtyard, just off Boulevard Raspail. Pam was both thrilled and slightly scared by the caged lift that shakily took them up to the top floor, but it was worth it for the view.

Pierre was a slim, short man with thick white hair and a wide smile. 'Isn't it a great view? That's the Montparnasse cemetery. Just about everyone is there from Baudelaire to Beckett, not to forget Sartre and de Beauvoir.'

'They're buried there?' asked Pam.

'Yes, in the same grave. Rather romantic. Sorry about the delay. The oboist got the flu and couldn't breathe, so my daughter had to fill in for a whole concert series. Mostly Mahler, but a couple of new commissions and some basic Beethoven.'

Pam wondered what basic Beethoven was but didn't ask.

'And you want to talk to me about Alex Yotopoulos? Yes?'

'You met him?'

'I'd hardly call it meet. I was in his presence and with those around him, but I don't think he deigned to notice me. Mind you, I was very young at the time. I only hung out with the extremists because my girlfriend was mad about them, and I was mad about her. I was twenty and she was twenty-three and so much more sophisticated than me. When she realised that all I really cared about was music, she dumped me pretty quickly and I never went back to any of their meetings. I don't know if she did. I rather think Yotopoulos fancied her, but not seriously. He was totally in love at the time or so it seemed.'

'He had a partner?'

'Oh yes. She was incredible. It's why the memory is so clear.' He paused. 'I'm so sorry, I haven't offered you any coffee.'

'We've just had one, thank you,' replied Pam.

'We've been retracing the 17 November steps,' said Oliver, 'which included a young woman giving Sartre their first communiqué around Christmas 1975.'

'Which most certainly could have been her.' Pierre paused. 'No, I just can't remember her name, but I can remember what she looked like. She had this curtain of dark hair and huge eyes which were all smudgy with kohl, which made them look even bigger.'

'If we found a picture of her, do you think you'd recognise her?'

'Oh yes. I mean I did have a girlfriend, but

Yotopoulos's friend was like one of the film stars who were around back then. I'd never have had the nerve to speak to her. Though she did once say "bravo" after I made a little speech.' He laughed. 'So stupid, I've never forgotten that.'

'And she was working with Yotopoulos?'

'They were like a real couple, ideologically as well as physically – and he couldn't keep his hands off her. She was a real fanatic.'

'And she was French?'

'No, no. Sorry. She was Greek. She was studying here in Paris. I don't know what, though. It might have been economics.'

'Which Yotopoulos was also studying,' said Oliver. 'So that makes sense.'

'But she'd quote all these slogans: America is the tyrant. The future belongs to the revolution. And: terror is the only weapon that works. That was the one that she and Yotopoulos kept on repeating. They'd quote Saint-Just and the others behind the French revolution, which was why a lot of the Greeks who'd followed Yotopoulos at the beginning left his group. That's what I heard, anyhow. The meetings I went to were international. Cohn-Bendit was there sometimes or Dany le Rouge as he called himself then, Alain Krivine and some Italians and a couple of English. I think Tariq Ali might have been there once. Yotopoulos called himself the leader of the May 29 Group and it was all about the need to use terror as a weapon. In all honesty, I was glad to be away from that. I got a job in Lille, playing in a small orchestra and never looked back.'

Before they left, Pam turned to Pierre to thank him. She felt she had a much clearer picture of how 17 November started.

'Would it be terribly rude of me,' she added. 'But could I hear you play something?'

'Not rude at all,' said Pierre, delighted. 'We musicians live for our audiences.'

He took his flute out of its case and took a deep breath then began to play. The music only lasted for three minutes, but for Pam it could have lasted an hour. She was transfixed. Pierre smiled at her.

'I've been playing that for over fifty years and it's still magical. It's called Syrinx, by Debussy.'

After they left Pierre, Pam asked Oliver if they had time to visit the Montparnasse cemetery.

'Absolutely, then we can walk back through the Luxembourg Gardens; there are some very nice small restaurants around there and we'll be hungry again by then, I'm sure.'

Pam was sure, too. And the cemetery fascinated her. It was like opening a book into French culture, all the painters and writers. There was a sculpture of hands, of birds, angels, and a surreal half-man half-horse, plus a couple lying as if in bed and as if the man was about to get up at any moment.

'If you're not too tired or stiff,' Oliver said, 'we can walk to the apartment.'

'No, my back is still bruised, but it's good to get my muscles working. It's sitting too long which is bad for me, I stiffen up. Leg, too.'

'Well, Paris is all about walking.'

'I love it,' she said. They came to the north gate and saw the plain white gravestone marking the tomb of Jean-Paul Sartre and Simone de Beauvoir. People had placed pieces of folded paper on the grave, and flowers which had dried in the sun.

'You've been part of this,' Pam told them silently. 'So, help me find her.'

After a memorable lunch in a tiny restaurant where there was just the menu of the day and everything on it was perfect, they walked to rue Mazarine. and Pam found herself looking for CCTV cameras. She couldn't see any, but there were lots of little galleries and a second-hand bookshop. The street was full of people, and she found it hard to imagine anyone being gunned down. But they had, though no trace remained.

Oliver got the key from the concierge who he said was as fierce as they come, but he'd managed to win her over.

Not surprising, thought Pam, Oliver was charm incarnate.

Patrice and Didi's apartment was hot and airless. It was smaller than Pam had expected with a lot more heavy dark wood furniture which made it look even tinier. There was a living room with a small television in the corner and two old couches with tartan and striped throws covering them. One old leather armchair looked very comfortable, and Pam thought it had almost certainly been Patrice's favourite. There were a lot more signs of Patrice in his study which had one wall of bookcases, half of which were empty. But there were still a great many books remaining, including some, Pam noticed, by Sartre and de Beauvoir.

'The gaps are where his papers were, I expect,' she said. 'Henry said the police took them all.'

Patrice's desk drawers had also been emptied.

'Thorough,' commented Oliver. 'Which leaves us only his books, unless he also kept papers in the bedroom which feels unlikely.'

The bedroom was clearly Didi's domain and had plain white walls with one huge painting. It was abstract, but at the same time it wasn't. There were dozens of blocks of subdued colour, some rounded and some straight, and there was an image within that you could almost see if you looked hard enough.

'My god,' said Oliver looking closely. 'That looks like a Malevich.'

'Is that something special?'

'If it's a genuine one, yes. He's a famous Russian artist. I've only seen his paintings in galleries.'

'Well, Patrice had clients who were linked to the Kremlin.'

'Who just might have given him this painting, which he's hung in the bedroom as if it's not valuable! Good god!'

'So, it would be valuable if it was genuine?'

Oliver laughed. 'Oh yes. His works sell for tens of millions.'

'Ah.' Pam caught her breath. 'Oliver, thank you. I think our Patrice had a sense of humour.'

'And?'

'We've been working blind because I didn't know a thing about his personality. Which is something you need to find in an investigation. And you've given me an idea.'

She ran out of the room, forgetting her leg in the excitement and limped back with a book.

'It's by Simone de Beauvoir. *Adieux* means goodbyes, doesn't it?'

'Yes. Farewells or goodbyes. I see ... you think this is where he might have…?'

Pam opened it. Inside the back cover was written: *Richard Durand. 1968 The May 29 Group, all of us together.*

Oliver took out his phone and called the number. Pam tried to follow what he was saying, but his French accent was too good, and he spoke too fast. He ended the call and smiled.

'Richard Durand died a year ago, but his granddaughter, Jeanne, is living in his house and has recently been digitising his work. She's got most of it sorted into years and is happy for us to come and look at the contact sheets,' Oliver told her.

'In Paris?'

'In Melun. We can go there tomorrow morning.'

'Is it far?'

'I asked that. Thirty minutes by train.'

They arrived at the photographer's house the following day, just after ten in the morning. The house was set back from the road behind blue railings and was painted white with large pale green shutters with a small garden in front with a space to park two cars. Pam could smell the roses as they walked through the front courtyard where Jeanne Durand came to greet them. She was in her early twenties and wore loose blue jeans with a green T-shirt bearing the slogan "I shoot people" with the image of an old-fashioned camera.

'My *grandpère* gave this to me,' she explained.

Oliver began by thanking her for giving them permission to go through the photographs.

'Is no problems. Now I show you the photos. I have sort them by year,' she replied. 'After you telephone, I find *soixante-huit et soixante-neuf*.'

'That's 1968 and 1969, I got that,' nodded Pam. 'That's really helpful.'

Oliver said something to her in French, presumably along the same lines and she smiled warmly. 'I have water because it is a hot day, but you want coffee, beer?'

'Water is perfect for me,' said Pam, and Oliver said the same.

They began at a table but, after an hour, Pam had to sit down as her back was aching badly. She continued to pour over the contact sheets with an eye glass, but then found a pile of contacts where the image was large enough to see without magnifying it. She began to go through them one sheet at a time. They were mostly the marches, but there were also pictures of students prising up flagstones and building fires in the roads.

The next pile was of meetings at a factory. Lots of

men in jackets. They looked very formal and even some of the students wore jackets and ties. This is never going to lead anywhere, Pam thought, but then cheered up as she saw that the next pile of contacts were students in meetings. This could be more useful.

She began to sift through them, page by page. And then she stopped. It wasn't, was it?

'Oliver?'

'Have you...?'

'Take a look at this.'

He picked up the sheet and started to look at the images.

'This young man, yes, with the wavy hair, looking as though he's arguing. I agree. And the next one, with his arm round a girl with long dark hair.'

Pam almost snatched it back out of his hands. 'Yes. That sounds just like the girl Pierre talked about. But I can't see her face.'

'Are there any more of her?'

Pam's hand was shaking as she picked up the next contact sheet, excitedly.

'There are. And...' Pam found she was suddenly ice cold. 'Oh, my god. I know who she is. I know exactly who she is. That's Eleni Apostoli. She's Leotakis's administrator.'

'The link we were looking for?'

'It makes perfect sense. She's a perfect organiser, is close to Nikos, and, yes, I can imagine her being ruthless enough to kill. Oh god, I was on a plane chatting with her just three weeks ago. And all along...'

'Do you think she's working with Leotakis?'

'No. She couldn't be, could she?' She stopped as her phone rang. 'Oh, who's that? I hope it isn't Eleni,' she joked. She looked at the number. Stavros. Bad timing, she thought.

'Stavros,' she began. 'I'm sorry I... but right now...'

'Pam, I don't want you to worry, but there's been a bomb explosion in Athens.'

'Mike?'

'Yes.'

CHAPTER 35

It was three days since Mike had phoned Stavros and told him Pam had been arrested and then pushed down the stairs.

'And you didn't think of telling me last night,' Stavros shouted at him. 'I should be there. Which hospital is she in? I'll book a flight...'

'That's why I didn't ring. Pam told me she'd escaped to London and was about to go to Paris.'

'Paris, what the hell is she going to Paris for? Don't tell me she's investigating that French lawyer's death.'

'Not exactly, but.... look don't yell at me, but she ... no ... we ... have been investigating Henry's death and to see whether there might be a link with the early days of Yotopoulos in Paris when he was a student.'

'What the hell are you talking about?'

'We do both think there's a final terrorist, who may have killed Henry, but now seems to be hacking phones and computers.' He explained how Pam's phone had been hacked to make it look as though she had threatened a fellow-officer. ' Henry thought the terrorist was around when Yotopoulos got started, and Pam got the idea of looking at photos from 1968. We know Yotopoulos was in Paris then, setting up his first group and we know that there are a lot of pictures. We might learn something from seeing who was with him.'

Stavros was about to tell Mike how utterly insane that was, and then didn't. It would get straight back to Pam, and then she definitely wouldn't want to see him again. But if Pam's phone had been hacked, then there was the possibility of some terrorist group targeting her, though he'd never heard of one in Greece that had that kind of sophistication. The only thing he wanted was for Pam not to be involved, but he knew she wouldn't appreciate him saying that. Researching the photographs wasn't a bad idea. How dangerous was it to wander round a photo archive? In fact, it might be safer than Cambridge.

He took a deep breath and asked Mike to send Pam his love and hung up. That was a better message. Then he waited for her to call back. And waited. Now it was Friday, three days later, and she still hadn't rung.

Mike, however, had rung again. He said he had a meeting in Athens and asked whether they could meet later. Stavros had come to like Mike, having loathed him on their first encounter when he thought Pam fancied him. Then came Jen's abduction and the whole nightmare in the barn which ended with Pam getting shot.

He and Mike had talked a lot sitting in the hospital in Heraklion. And while he still felt that Mike was far too good looking: those large brown eyes, perfect smile and the hint of designer stubble that made him look more like a model than a former cop, he knew he had demons that tortured him. What he needed was a nice woman. And Stavros needed Pam. He knew that, but he was damned if he was going to beg. And now she might be in danger?

The question of who might have targeted Pam and hacked her phone bothered him a great deal. Which was why he was sitting in this café in Psychiko talking about it with his friend Costa, who worked in the same building as he did, but was one of the most brilliant police officers working in their much-admired cybercrime unit.

'That kind of hacking isn't cheap, though it can be bought on the dark web if you know where to go.'

'That doesn't sound remotely like 17 November. They didn't buy stuff or operate abroad. All their operations were here in Greece. And they didn't have money, not that kind of money.'

'Well, if your girlfriend's right, then it sounds as though she's accidentally kicked a very unpleasant ants' nest. What I don't understand is why you don't call her. It's clear you're crazy about her. Ring her.'

'She drives me crazy. One minute I think we're beginning the best relationship of my life, then something happens, and she just hurls herself into it.'

'And doesn't listen to you?'

'No. She always thinks she's right.'

'Always? If we're talking Jen Michaels, my boy, she *was* right. And now she's hunting a terrorist you think doesn't exist, but seems to have hacked her phone and possibly killed this English historian.'

'She wouldn't listen to a word I said after Henry died. Just got this absurd idea it was 17N because that was what he was writing about.'

'And if she's right again? Can your ego take that?'

'It's not a question of my ego.'

Costa threw up his arms in mock despair, then sighed and sipped his coffee. It was good. Worth the drive up here to Attiko Grove Park, except that wasn't the only reason…

'Listen to me, you stubborn idiot,' Costa continued. 'Pam could be right. And she's not the only person who believes there could be others who were involved with the group at the beginning.'

'Isn't she?' Stavros twisted a sugar packet in his fingers until it burst and sprayed the table with sugar. He began to sweep it up, then stopped when the waitress came over with a cloth. She wiped it up and gave Costa a warm smile. He smiled back and then blushed. Stavros laughed.

'So that's why we're here! I didn't believe you'd drag me all the way up here just for the view of Filothei.'

'And the mountains. Coffee's good, too.'

'It's good at The Hood,' Stavros replied, mentioning their usual café, 'and it doesn't take ten minutes to get there. Fifteen if you count traffic jams. Why don't you just ring her and ask her out.'

'I did. We went out last night.'

'And?'

'It was great'.

'And she isn't married? How old is she?'

'No. She broke up with her boyfriend when she moved to Athens from Edessa. And she's twenty-seven.'

'A Macedonian? Powerful women. You'll have to watch yourself. Besides, we were talking about 17N.'

'You were. I wanted to know why you hadn't rung Pam. You've been with her twice and both times you've come back, furious and have talked about her nonstop ever since. I haven't ever seen you like this. And you haven't had a serious girlfriend for how many years? Four?'

'Five. And you *were* talking about 17N. You said there was someone else who thought there could be another member of the group.'

'Yes, a terrorism specialist. She was at the trials. She believes there was another member connected with the first terrorist acts who was responsible for their intelligence. Which when you think of who they targeted does make sense. Someone had to know where these people were. So don't you think Pam might be right?'

'Their first crimes are outside the statute of limitations.'

'You didn't answer my question.'

'Stop breaking my balls. It's not relevant anymore.'

'Just ring her, for fuck's sake.'

'I will. I will. Anyhow she's in Paris. She thinks there could be early photos of Yotopoulos with her mystery terrorist.'

'She could be right. Romantic city Paris. Who's she with?'

'I didn't ask.'

'You're utterly useless. Why didn't you ask Mike? He'd know. Unless you're frightened to ask.'

Stavros told Costa he was a wanker who should fuck off and leave him alone. He glared at the view. It was a good view, and it was also slightly cooler up here. Pam would appreciate it, he thought. He'd love to show her Athens. He could picture her here. He could also picture her in Paris. Who was she with? Why hadn't he asked Mike that?

'When you first suggested coming to Psychiko, I thought you wanted me to go and look at the street where Richard Welch was shot,' he said, changing the subject.

Costa was now exchanging secret smiles with the waitress every time she passed by their table and was miles away.

'What?' he replied. 'No. I don't know where that was. Is it near here?'

'Not really, it was in a tiny street near the Filothei open-air cinema, nearer Halandri; it's almost like a pedestrian street with trees and grass down the centre. The previous head of the CIA had lived in the same house. Not very smart. I come to Psychiko quite a lot because so many embassies are round here.'

'Certainly not for the likes of us. Another world. Not just the trees all along the street but the houses are surrounded by greenery.'

'Wonder how much water they use up.'

'Different laws for those kinds of people. Not a good place to live in summer if there are fires. Some of these parks and gardens would go up like a tinderbox.'

Stavros looked at the park around the café, imagining the black smoke engulfing it like it had in Kineta and Rafina that week. 'Any news on casualty numbers?' he asked.

'They vary between eighty and a hundred and twenty dead. Though hundreds made homeless. One of the fires was started because a fucking idiot in Pendeli decided to burn the wood in his garden.'

'In this heat? Christ, I hope they throw the book at him. I also heard it's total chaos up in Rafina. No communication, and roads blocked the wrong way, sending people trying to escape into the flames and into the sea. Which is accounting for a lot of the deaths.'

'I imagine everyone panicked. Sounds like they're going to try and blame the police. That's our government. Remember when…'

Costa was just about to continue listing the many reasons why he hated the Government and everyone in it, when the sounds of Barbie Girl floated up from Stavros's pocket. He took out his phone and answered it.

'That's your ringtone?'

'Since my niece played with it yesterday. And stop laughing.' Stavros glared at his friend who was cracking up. 'Hi,' he said to the caller. 'Mike? That's early, your meeting didn't last long.'

'Listen, Stavros,' Mike sounded worried. 'I thought I was meeting Nikos Leotakis here about his foundation, but I just rang him, and he doesn't know anything about it.'

'What?'

'I know. Something doesn't smell right. And I've just seen this guy. He's quite tall, honed, could be a spook, and he was at Henry Cox's funeral.'

'Mike, get out of there. This sounds like a set-up.'

'Yeah, I will. I don't feel comfortable out here in the suburbs, it's not like Sitia where they all know me. Athens makes me jumpy. Feel I could be stopped for being in possession of a black skin. Anyhow I'm on Garittou near the Halandri Metro, two blocks before the ring road; it's a big empty plot with an old industrial building in it.'

'Like I said. Get out.'

'Oh, hold on. The guy's going into the building. What if he's being set up, too?'

Stavros heard Mike shouting 'Stop' twice, then there was the sound of something heavy hitting the ground followed, for a split second, by a loud roar. Then the phone went dead, but the sound continued. Stavros realised he was hearing it, not on the phone, but echoing across Athens' northern suburbs.

Costa and Stavros both leapt to their feet and began to run out of the café towards their car. Just as Stavros was about to get in, a delivery driver arrived on his motorcycle. Stavros raced over to him and grabbed the bike before he even had time to turn off the engine.

Police emergency,' he barked, 'I need your bike.' He almost pushed the young man off, as he jumped on it, revving the engine. The delivery driver grabbed his package from the back and looked on in horror.

'Costa,' Stavros shouted at his friend, who was still standing by his car. 'Get a private ambulance, one with a doctor on board, and send them to Garittou now. And find out who's responding in Halandri. No, probably Agia Paraskevi. That's closer. Tell them the tall black guy is British police and not a terrorist. They're not to shoot him.'

He tore off down the twisting path back to the road and headed for the scene of the explosion. The bike was a Suzuki 650, not so unlike the police Honda Transalp he often rode, and, as he'd told Costa, he knew the area well including all the back streets. This was normally a quiet peaceful part of town, and as he sped up Karpenisio and down Mouson, he prayed it would be a morning without too much traffic. Below him was the valley and the suburbs of Halandri and Agia Paraskevi and was that smoke or just the usual pollution? He shot left and on through several side streets, weaving between barriers and along private roads until he came to Ammarillidos. He raced on, ignoring stop signs, his hand permanently on the horn, then cut through a few more small streets until he could cross Kiffisias Avenue and get on to Anistaseon. He flew on, weaving between the cars when they stopped at traffic lights, at times leaping up on to the grassed central reservation, ignoring the furious hooting behind him.

The journey from the café to Garittou would normally take about twenty minutes. Stavros did it in six. He could hardly see what had happened because of the smoke. He heard the crackle of the fire as he approached. The plot was all dried grass which had burned furiously, though the fire crew which had got there before him, had confined the blaze to a distant corner. Smoke filled the road, and he began to cough.

There were also three police cars there, unsurprising since the Agia Paraskevi police station was less than a mile away. One of the officers tried to stop him racing up to the scene, then stopped as he saw Stavros's uniform.

As he got closer, Stavros could see more clearly. Mike was lying face down on the ground a police officer kneeling beside him. He was also covered in blood.

Stavros leapt off the bike and ran towards them.

'Is he alive? This is a senior British police officer. He's a friend of mine.'

'He told us he was British police. He came out

through the fire carrying the other guy like some kind of movie hero, and he started to speak then he collapsed. We've rung for an ambulance.'

Stavros looked around, desperately, as if hoping the ambulance would materialise in the empty street. Luckily there weren't any houses close by. If you had to set off a bomb in Athens, this was certainly one of the safest places to do it. Apart from the fire risk.

'We put him face down because of his back,' said the other officer. Mike's trousers and shirt were in tatters and his back looked as though he'd been sprayed with gravel and stones. There were also a lot of small pieces of metal which looked rusty. 'He needs to get that treated as soon as possible.'

'Nasty, isn't it?' said the first, whose single star indicated he was a second lieutenant. 'Bombs illustrate the law of gravity, don't they? What goes up comes down.'

'Thank you for the physics lesson, lieutenant.'

'My father worked in Lebanon,' said the other. 'Had a friend who was walking down a street that got bombed. Thing about bomb damage is that you can't always see it. It can destroy you from inside.'

'I did tell you that this man is my friend,' said Stavros icily, though the officer was only verbalising his own worst fear. 'I've called for a private ambulance. He needs a doctor.' He turned to the men suddenly remembering there were two men caught in the explosion.

'The other man?'

They shook their heads.

'Looks like he caught the full force.'

'Do we know who he is?'

'We picked up his briefcase. Luckily it fell this way and not where the fire is.' He coughed as the smoke blew again across the road. 'We haven't opened it; we were waiting for the Captain.'

'I'll open it.' He outranked a captain in any case, though very soon there would be senior officers taking over. 'Mike Petersen is a close friend of Nikos Leotakis. I have to ring Mr Leotakis. He may know who the other victim is.'

While Leotakis wasn't as well-known in Athens as he was in Crete, he was famous enough for the officers to step back and look at Stavros, slightly differently. They brought him the case, which was black leather with a designer name embossed on the side, and he opened it. There was a computer inside which sat in a padded compartment and miraculously looked undamaged. And inside one of the flaps a return ticket from Heathrow Airport in the name of Stephen Mawson.

'Looks like he's English,' he said. 'I wonder whether...'

He fished further inside the case and brought out a passport.

'Stephen Mawson,' he read out. 'We're going to have to involve the British police.'

Pam, he thought. I should ring her first. Or Leotakis. Perhaps Leotakis and then Pam. He'd had the billionaire's personal number on his phone since being involved with the Stephanie Michaels' case and rang it.

'Leotakis,' came the familiar growl.'

'Major Papadakis here,' he said. 'I'm afraid I've got bad news. There's been a bombing in Athens.'

'Mike?'

'Unconscious. But was able to walk away from the fire to start with.'

'Make sure he gets the very best treatment there is and goes to the best hospital.'

'On it, sir. But there was another man here. I can send you his passport picture. His name is Stephen Mawson.'

'Except it isn't,' replied Leotakis. 'His real name

is Sam Moss and he's a hacker. What on earth was he doing there?'

'We don't know yet. But it may be something DI Gregory knows about.'

'Pam?'

'Her phone was hacked last week. In any case, it seems his computer isn't damaged, so I'm sending it to our cybercrime office… Oh… hold on one moment. The ambulance is coming. I need to be with Mike.'

'Ring me later. And tell Pam to call me now. I want to know everything.'

CHAPTER 36

Pam was back inside the Leotakis private jet. This was something she hadn't expected, but there was a kind of inevitability about it. Everything had led back to Nikos, and this was where he'd take over.

Pam felt deeply weary. Had it been worth it, all this racing around hunting Henry's killer? She'd lost her job, been arrested, and knocked down the stairs and now Mike was lying in hospital after the bombing that had killed her hacker. And the supremely elegant and meticulous administrator, Eleni Apostoli, was the woman behind it all. She was, after all, the woman who could arrange anything.

Pam had lost her initial euphoria of finding out who was Yotopoulos's partner the moment she'd heard about the bomb.

'Mike?' she asked, fearing the very worst.

'Yes,' he replied. 'He got caught in the blast. I don't know how badly he's injured.'

'He's alive?'

'Sorry, yes, he's alive, but he's unconscious. There was another man who I think might have been your hacker. I talked to Leotakis, and he said his name was Sam Moss.'

'I've never heard of him. But I do now know who's behind it all. Stavros, I have to ring Leotakis right away.'

'I need to know, too.'

'I'll ring you straight back.'

'And I need to talk with you too,' he said. 'I've been so worried...'

'I'm fine,' she told him.

'I was wrong,' he said. 'Again. And ...'

Pam ended the call. There were too many things coming at her from all sides. This wasn't the moment to think about her relationship with Stavros. And what? What was he about to say?

Thank goodness she had Nikos's personal phone number, courtesy of Stephanie who'd had half a dozen numbers for the billionaire which Pam had copied into her new phone.

'Leotakis,' came his gruff voice. Of course, she had a new phone. He wouldn't recognise it.

'It's Pam. You know about the bomb in Athens?'

'Major Papadakis rang me. What's going on, Pam?'

'It's a long story, but I've finally got there. I know who is behind the bombing as well as several other killings, but I don't want to speak over the phone.'

'Where are you?'

'Paris. Well just outside Paris. Listen, Nikos, you mustn't speak about this to anyone who is close to you, however much you think you trust them.'

'We need to meet then. Can you be at Le Bourget Airport in two hours?'

She passed the question to Oliver. 'Tell him to make it two and a half,' he said.

'Who is that with you?' Leotakis asked.

'Oliver Timberly,' she replied. 'He was Henry's oldest friend.'

'Oliver... Pam. What *is* going on?'.

'I've discovered the identity of the last member of 17 November. They killed Henry and hacked my phone. And I'm sure they're behind this bombing.'

'Don't say any more until we meet,' he replied. 'It's now ten past eleven. I'll be at Le Bourget at one forty your time. Come to the Landmark terminal.'

Back in the photographer's house in Melun, Oliver had a few words with Jeanne, who looked shocked and told them to keep all the contacts with Yotopoulos since she had the negatives.

'I think we should get a taxi back to the apartment, and then it can wait and take you on to the airport.'

Pam nodded. At least there was someone who was thinking clearly. While they were waiting for the taxi, Oliver took a photograph of the contact sheet and sent it to Pierre Veilleux. Pierre rang back immediately.

'That's the girl I was talking about,' he said.

'Was her name Eleni?' asked Oliver.

'Yes, that was it. Eleni. And that's Greek for Helen, isn't it? Now I recall. I thought, yes, this is another Helen that men would die for.'

Pam's phone rang again. It wasn't a number Pam recognised.

'Gregory?' she said, trying to sound as tough as Leotakis.

'It's Stuart. Stuart Weir. Paul gave me this number.'

'Oh yes, Stuart. Thank you for calling.'

'You definitely were hacked, and I think I know who the hacker was.'

'Sam Moss,' said Pam. 'AKA Stephen Mawson.'

'But how did you …?'

'He's just been killed in a bomb explosion in Athens.'

'Athens?'

'Look. You need to liaise with a Greek officer called Major Papadakis. He can give you more information – he speaks English. And he's got Sam's computer. It seems it survived. Unlike Sam.'

'Jesus.'

'I can't really talk now, Stuart. I'm on my way to

meet Mr Leotakis and sort this whole thing out. My friend Mike got blown up, too.'

Oliver gave her shoulder a squeeze, but mercifully said nothing. Pam looked out of the window at the streets of Paris whizzing by, trying not to cry. She'd been happy here. As if happiness was something she was only allowed for a moment.

They arrived at the banker's apartment where she swiftly packed her things and got back into the taxi saying a quick goodbye to Oliver, who had already paid the driver. That's what he does, Pam thought fleetingly. He sees what needs to be done and does it. Quietly. She was going to miss his company.

As they drove to the airport, she took out her phone and called Stavros again.

'I'm sorry I took so long to get back to you. How's Mike?'

'He's semi-conscious, but they're giving him oxygen for his lungs. I'm in the ambulance right now taking him to a very good hospital in Psychiko. The doctor says that we won't know for a few hours.'

'Oh god,' Pam murmured. She wished that she actually believed in a deity she could pray to.

'It seems Mike's lucky,' Stavros continued. 'He was talking to me on the phone when the bomb went off, but he was near a tree where someone had dug a ditch, I suppose for irrigation, and he threw himself into it.'

'If he comes round, give him my love.' Pam knew a little about the effects of being caught in a bomb explosion, from terrorism conferences she'd attended. A lot of the injuries caused by the blast were internal.

'We'll be at the hospital in a few minutes, but what I need to tell you is that there was a second man. He died in the bombing, but we managed to get identification from his briefcase. His name was Stephen Mawson, though Nikos says his real name is Sam Moss.'

'I know who Sam Moss is now. He's the man who hacked my phone.'

'Christ. What is all this? Anyhow, Stephen/Sam's computer seems to be okay. I'm sending it to our cyber team.'

'They need to liaise with Stuart Weir in Cambridge. I've given him your number and he's investigating the hacking. I'll send you his number, too.' She paused.

'Nikos knew him. It's just clicked. Shit! Do you think he was working for him?'

'It's way above my pay grade to have thoughts like that.'

'I'm about to meet him at Le Bourget Airport. He's taking me to Crete. You think I ought to get into the plane with him?'

'Oh, Christ, Pam. I don't know. Do you trust him? I think I do, but…'

'There's always that 'but'. Yes. I think I do. But if I don't arrive, at least you'll know who killed me. Not that he'd do anything in front of the crew. Maybe on his yacht…'

'Don't even joke about it.'

'No. I'll be fine. Oliver knows it all, that's Oliver Timberly, he was Henry's oldest friend. He was with me in Paris and he's now going to meet someone he knows at MI6 and brief him about the terrorist.'

'I can't believe I haven't asked you that again. It was the one thing I needed to know. You said you knew who planted the bomb.'

'Yes. Sorry. I've just been so worried about Mike, I forgot I hadn't told you. I found her. Just that very moment you called me, I found the picture of her with Alexandros Yotopoulos. It's Eleni, Eleni Apostoli, Nikos's Eleni. She was a girlfriend of Yotopoulos.'

'Holy shit.' Stavros paused. 'Eleni? What?' Pam could feel him thinking. 'You think Nikos knew?'

'That's something I'm going to find out very soon. Listen, I think we need to keep this information to ourselves for the moment. It might be best if Nikos himself tells the politicians. And if he doesn't, then we tell them.'

'Be careful, Pam.'

'I will. I promise. And I do want to talk after all this. Really talk.'

'Please. Yes. And… Pam. I do love you.'

'Oh.' It was what she'd hoped to hear, but now wasn't the time. 'Yes,' she said. 'Yes. We'll talk later.'

She arrived at the terminal only a few minutes before the Leotakis jet, a Boeing 737, arrived and she was escorted on to it. Her name had already been sent ahead. By Nikos himself? she wondered. How was he coping without Eleni to organise his life?

Nikos was in his private compartment, but the stewards, Hugh and Frances, welcomed her as if they were old friends. She asked whether she could have some water and some very strong espresso, both of which were brought to her along with the usual tiny biscuits, and prepared to meet the billionaire again.

Before they took off, Leotakis came through to greet her. He looked pale and older, she thought. The news was going to be hard for him to take. She hoped she was right, but at the same moment decided she did trust him. She didn't think he knew about Eleni. She gave him a hug

'Tell me the whole story from the start,' he commanded.

Pam began with what Henry had been writing, and then told him about the death of Patrice, followed by Henry's own death. She explained how the Cambridge police refused to believe it was suspicious, but she'd begun to investigate.

'It was the fact his computer had been targeted,

too,' she said, 'that made me certain it wasn't a natural death.'

She told Leotakis how her own phone had been hacked to make it look as though she was threatening to kill Dave Butcher which caused her to be arrested and injured, and briefly explained about Butcher and his racist comments to her in June.

'So that was one side of things. Then Patrice's widow came up to Mike and me at Henry's funeral and said you were the man who had killed Patrice.'

'Me?' Leotakis was astonished. 'Why?'

'Because a car seen on a nearby CCTV at that moment belonged to Rafael. I can tell you that neither Mike nor I believed you knew about it.'

'I didn't,' he said. 'This is all new.' He paused. 'My Rafael?'

'Who, Didi Girard also said, works for French Intelligence.'

'He does. That's true. I know that. But I can't see him shooting an elderly lawyer in the centre of Paris. It's not possible.'

'No, I don't think he did either. I'm pretty certain someone took his car, and that person was the terrorist. And that is Eleni.'

Leotakis looked at her as if she'd gone mad.

'The reason I was in Paris was to see whether there were pictures of someone who had been with Alexandros Yotopoulos at the beginning. There was a mysterious Anna who was there when the CIA agent Richard Welch was killed. You know, the first 17N assassination. I had the idea that with all the photographers around, she might have been pictured with him. And she was. We found her.'

Pam opened her bag and showed him the contact sheet. 'I've got witness testimony on how committed she was to the idea of terrorism back then.'

'Eleni has worked for me for over thirty years.'

'I know. I didn't want to talk to you until I had some evidence. It never occurred to me that it would be Eleni.'

'Why? Can you think of a reason?' Pam felt that Leotakis was talking to himself as well as to her.

'I think she still believes in it all, all the revolutionary stuff. But there's more. The reason Patrice Girard felt he had to tell Henry the name of the terrorist was because they were planning another attack. I think she wants to disrupt the opening of your gallery next month, and I also think she may be planning to kill you. I think all these deaths and the bomb today are because the clock is ticking, and she can't allow anyone to stop her before that date. Mike and I felt that things were escalating in a way that suggested she was desperate.'

'If this is true, this is…' Leotakis couldn't even finish the sentence. He shook his head. 'The clock *is* ticking. Eleni has cancer, she's dying. She didn't tell me herself. It was Popi. But to be a killer…?'

'I'm so sorry.'

'You're sorry, my dear. I'm sorry. I hired Moss to hack the phone of my son. Eleni could have got access to him via my own phone and my own computer. I'm partly to blame here.' He wiped his face. 'Oh god, this is terrible.' He suddenly went rigid and clutched his chest.

'Are you all right? Nikos?'

'It's my heart.' He shut his eyes.

'Help!' Pam called. Hugh rushed up.

'Come along,' he said, gently, as he helped Leotakis into the rear of the plane where he had a bed. The steward came back a few moments later and sat down beside Pam who had started to cry.

'It's all right. Mr Leotakis has a defibrillator in his chest. It kicks in when his heart stops. He just needs to rest for an hour and then he'll be fine.'

'You're sure?'

'He's had a few of these attacks. He probably shouldn't be flying, but you can't stop Mr Leotakis.'

That was certainly true, Pam thought.

'You're looking pale,' Hugh continued. 'Can I give you anything? I'm sure Frances would love to make you something to eat. Have you had any lunch?'

Pam shook her head. 'Actually, could I have something to eat? I'm feeling a bit light-headed.'

'Frances will make you something. And drink some more water,' he added.

Pam sat back and wondered what would happen next. She'd been concentrating so much on discovering Henry's killer that she hadn't even thought about what would happen after that. It wasn't the usual case of passing it to the Crown Prosecution Service for charging. Leotakis made his own rules. That was the very first thing she'd been told about him. And what would he do about Eleni? Would he help her escape or would he …?

Yes, she thought. He might very well kill Eleni. And she couldn't let that happen. Whatever Eleni had done, Pam couldn't allow her to be shot in cold blood.

But what could she do? She had no authority in Greece and Nikos had so much power. What if he was protected by politicians? She didn't like the way her thoughts were leading.

Frances brought her a plate of *Salade Nicoise* made with fresh tuna. It was exactly what she needed as was the glass of peach juice with champagne that followed it. She felt instantly perked up. Whatever was going to happen, she'd just have to do her best.

Her phone rang again. It was Stavros.

'How's Mike?' she asked.

'He's conscious and has had a full MRI scan. There's evidence of something called blast lung. It can get worse over the next few hours although he's been on oxygen since he got into the ambulance, which helps, and he's now been sedated again so he can be ventilated. Once that's under control, they're taking him to surgery to treat his back.'

'His back?' she asked

'It was peppered with shrapnel and it needs deep cleaning which would be too painful to do without anaesthetic. We'll know whether he'll be okay within the next four hours. I thought you'd want to know.'

'Thank you, my love.'

'My love? Isn't Nikos with you?'

'He's had a kind of heart seizure, well, maybe it was a heart attack. But he has a defibrillator inside him and now he's resting. Apparently, this happens to him. It was a bit terrifying at the time.'

'God. Hope he's all right. This is all horrible.'

'Isn't it? I think it was a terrible shock for him. Well, of course it was.'

'As long as the shock wasn't finding out that you knew it was Eleni, and that his plans were exposed.'

'My instincts tell me no.'

'And you have very good instincts.'

'Yes, along with my other very good attributes.'

'Have you been drinking on the job, Gregory?'

'Don't you know? I'm unofficial. Just one glass of peach and fizzy wine.'

'And all I get is hospital coffee which is only slightly better than police coffee. I think your drink is called a Bellini. It was invented in Venice.'

'Shall we go to Venice together?'

'You can get a boat from Patras. Or a sleeper train from Paris. I'd like to share a sleeper with you.'

'Should we be having this conversation right now?'

'I don't know what else we should talk about, though I do need to talk with you soon about it all. Things have been moving. As soon as he heard about the bomb and Sam Moss, Leotakis called the Minister of

Public Order, and he called the Chief of Police. And the Chief informed my boss that I should be the principal liaison for this case.'

'Blimey. Nikos does that kind of thing, doesn't he?'

'It's called power. And I might be feeling a bit power crazed with it all if it wasn't for the fact that I've been utterly humiliated several times this morning … Do you want to laugh?'

Pam couldn't imagine laughing at anything.

'My niece ...'

'You have a niece, you never told me …'

'We've never done much of that kind of talking, have we …?'

'I suppose not.'

'Anyhow, my niece got hold of my phone and changed the ringtone.'

'How old is she?'

'Nine.'

'Oh dear. What was it? *Frozen*?'

'Worse. Much, much worse. Picture me at the scene, trying to sound professional and in control and every time my phone rings I hear … no I can't say it ...'

Pam began to feel a laugh bubbling up.

'Tell me. Crazy frog?'

'No, that would just be irritating.' Pam heard him take a deep breath. 'Barbie Girl.'

Pam began to laugh. 'Now I know exactly what to sing to you,' she told him.

'Don't you dare. And stop laughing.'

'I've stopped. But thank you for that. I needed it. Now tell me what's happening your end and I'll fill you in about Eleni and how we found out it was her.'

'I've told the Chief that Mr Leotakis will be calling him to bring him up to date regarding the bombing and informed our terrorist division that it looks like the work of 17N or their followers, and they're sifting through the wreckage looking for anything with a fingerprint that will tie it into their database of terrorists. And my friend Costa who works for the cybercrime team is coming here to the hospital to get Stephen Mawson's computer. Nothing else I can do.'

'Same here. I have to wait until Nikos is rested enough to decide what he's going to do. Actually, I'm worried.'

'Worried?'

'That he might kill Eleni. Is he above the law?'

'Nobody is above the law in Greece,' said Stavros. 'Well, I hope not.'

CHAPTER 37

Pam began to make notes on her phone, so she'd have everything clear later.

It was wonderfully quiet in the plane, and she was almost dozing off when her phone rang. The ringtone of an old telephone, not music, she reflected, smiling at the idea of Stavros having Barbie Girl blasting from his pocket. It was Stuart. Good. She wanted to hear how he'd been getting on.

'Hi Stuart, have you heard from Stavros?'

'Yes, and thanks to him, I'm now in touch with a Greek policeman, who works for their cyber unit, called Costa. He's superb. Oh, and he's also a close friend of Stavros, and told me to tell you that Stavros never stops talking about you, and if the two of you don't start talking soon, he'll lock you up together in a small room. I've no idea what that's about.'

'It's okay. Stavros and I are talking.'

'Excellent. Well: good news and bad news..

'Good news first.'

'Moss's computer is exactly what we've needed; it's enabling us to unlock everything about this case. And probably a few others. But that's for my old colleagues at GCHQ to enjoy.'

'Brilliant. Bad news?'

'I'm praying it isn't as bad as it seems. But something

deeply worrying has emerged. Costa has just told Stavros, who seems to be co-ordinating things, but if it's true, I need to talk with MI5 and the Serious Crime Division. At the moment, there's no factual evidence of anything, but you may know more. Where are you, by the way?'

'I'm on Mr Leotakis's plane, on our way to Crete.'

'Well, that could help. This is about Crete. It's about something that happened in Heraklion.'

'Stavros knows the police chief there, so I imagine he'll want to talk to him. What's it about? Another death?'

'Yes, but more complicated. I'll try and explain. Thing is Sam, or Stephen as he called himself, wrote some stuff in Word but saved it online to One-Drive. I think by mistake. Seems he spent a lot of money on cocaine, so this was probably one of his coke-fuelled thinking-out-loud bits. He was obsessed with finding out who he was working for. He never knew it was Eleni, that was down to your detective skills. As far as he knew, his client called themselves Moros and had links with 17N and also Leotakis. He tracked down their bank account to the British Virgin Islands, and that's where all the funds came from. The address of that account belonged to a woman called Popi Filotaki.'

Popi, thought, Pam. Popi was involved? But Popi had told Nikos about Eleni's illness, so she must be in touch with her. But it just seemed so improbable.

'Stephen thought Leotakis had recommended him to Moros/ Eleni. Eleni seems to have paid him huge amounts of money which is why he went on working for her. He was in it just for the money.'

'Bastard!' said Pam thinking of how he'd nearly destroyed her life.

'But he did have some small traces of a conscience. He was clearly worried about what Moros was doing. Moros also asked him to kill you and he refused.'

'Be thankful for small mercies,' she said. 'I still don't like him.'

'No. He wasn't likeable. But and I'm summarising this as he meandered for pages... he keeps saying the same thing over and over again. *Nerve agent? Surely not. But if...No I can't...* and it goes on and on.'

'Nerve agent?'

'I rang Costa and we looked at this together. As far as we can make out, it's all about a young medical researcher called Lefteris Zembatakis. Seems that Moss fucked up his father's job, he changed the figures and got him sacked, and Eleni bought his apartment block and raised the rent to put Zembatakis's father in debt. Serious debt. And then offered the son a means to help his parents.'

'This is unbelievable. It sounds like a movie.'

'Yes. But that would make Lefteris the hero with a conscience. Which he may have had, but sadly he was killed very soon after all this. Costa translated an obituary of Zembatakis. The police found his body in the sea and thought it was suicide. But what is scary is where he worked, which was a laboratory of microbiology in Heraklion.'

'Microbiology?'

'We looked them up online and their areas of research include bacterial infections. It could be that post Salisbury, we're all extra paranoid, but it also could be that Lefteris stole something very nasty from his lab for Eleni.'

'You mean like a nerve agent. This *is* really worrying. I need to tell Mr Leotakis as soon as I can.'

'Like now?' suggested Nikos, coming back from his quarters in the rear of the plane and sitting down on the sofa opposite her. 'Did I catch you saying nerve agent?'

'Stuart, send me all this and I'll get back to you,' said Pam, finishing the call. She turned to Leotakis. 'Are you all right, Nikos?'

'I'm fine, I'm fine,' he answered snappily. 'What's this about?'

'That was Stuart Weir. He worked at GCHQ with Moss, as I told you earlier. He's now looking at Moss's computer with an opposite number in Athens and they've stumbled on something Moss wrote which linked with a man who died in Heraklion and worked for a microbiology lab. Maybe post the recent Novichok incident, we're all a bit scared of things like this, but it is possible that Eleni got him to steal a nerve agent.'

'Microbiology', he said. 'I don't like the sound of that. Scared can also mean alert.' He looked suddenly awake and focused. 'Frances,' he called to the stewardess, 'please bring me a cup of green tea and some of those ginger biscuits you make.' He turned to Pam. 'Do you want anything?'

'No, thank you, they've been looking after me very well. I'm forwarding the stuff from Stuart to you right now along with the name of the lab in Heraklion.'

'I'll ring the Minister,' said Leotakis. He picked up his own phone and spoke in Greek, raising his voice and making whatever point he was making in no uncertain terms. She caught the word Salisbury and Novichok at the end. He ended the call, and turned to Pam.

'I've told him that he's to contact the director of the Laboratory and get him to check the contents of every single liquid he has. If there's as much as a fraction of a millilitre missing of anything dangerous, we have to know. I told him we don't want another Salisbury. Glad to say he's in total shock and will almost certainly ensure that every single liquid in that lab is measured. He's also going to organise a total sweep of my estate in Crete. I've told him to get the senior officer who will be in charge of doing that to contact me so I can tell him where to start.'

'You think she kept it in your house?'

'It seems the most likely place. She had a small apartment in Athens, but recently has rarely stayed there. She mostly lives in her villa in Crete on my estate, and in her cottage at Tyneham House. Of course, it may be there. She may have brought it to England already.'

'I've just remembered that when I flew back to Cambridge with her, she said she'd been making a flying visit to Crete to pick something up for you.'

'When was this?'

Pam thought back. So much had happened, all the days were merging into one. 'It was just after Henry died,' she said, thinking back. 'That was on Thursday the fifth, and I found out on the Saturday and flew back on the Sunday which was the eighth.'

'About three weeks ago. No, I never asked her to get anything for me. I wasn't aware she'd gone to Crete that week.' He sighed.

'This feels surreal, Pam. I imagine it does for you, too.'

She nodded.

'I've been involved with some crazy things in my life...' he began.

Like gun running in Central America, she thought, and stealing the boats from the gangsters. She'd heard a few stories from Chris Brook.

'But this...' he continued. 'A nerve agent in my house. And Eleni, my friend, my confidante... I can't begin to think about that. I have to concentrate.'

He picked up his phone again and dialled a number.

'Put me through to the Home Secretary. No, I don't care if he is in the House about to make a speech. Tell him that there's another possible Salisbury, and it could be even worse.'

What on earth did it feel like, Pam wondered to be able to have that amount of confidence, and to make government ministers drop everything to answer your calls? She couldn't begin to imagine it. But it worked. In a few moments his phone rang. He must contribute a lot of money to the Government.

'Home Secretary,' his voice was much less aggressive than when he talked to the Greek minister. 'Thank you so much for getting back to me so swiftly. And congratulations on your new post. I haven't yet had the opportunity to congratulate you in person.' He paused and listened. 'Not at all. Yes, this is a serious situation. It concerns a Greek terrorist who I have learned this afternoon is planning an attack to take place during the official opening of the Leotakis Gallery in Cambridge. Where, of course the Prince of Wales and his wife will be present as well as several ministers. Thanks to the extraordinary dedication of one of your police officers, we now know the name of that terrorist, and I regret to say that she works for me. But within the past few minutes I have also been given information that leads me to believe that she may have brought a dangerous nerve agent from Greece to your country.'

'No, I don't know what it is, but as we speak our police are working with the laboratory in Crete, from which it came, to ascertain what is missing.'

He listened again.

'Sadly, we cannot question the thief, since the young man was killed some months ago, by the terrorist it would seem.'

And he's not giving him Eleni's name, thought Pam. Interesting.

'Yes, it does sound unlikely, but so was Salisbury. I wonder whether you could ensure that your best people from Porton Down go to Tyneham House immediately and search for this substance. I believe that if it is anywhere, it is there. I think that it was brought to England in my own plane. No, I can't do that. I'm in the plane at this very moment and am somewhere above Croatia.'

'No, that doesn't worry me. Knowing the ability of the terrorist I am quite certain that it would have been sealed and packed securely. Thank you, Home Secretary. Yes. I have every faith in your people.'

Leotakis was again on the phone now talking in Greek. He finished the call and turned to her.

'It seems that nobody knows about Eleni's illness, but she did say she was going to stay with a friend. After a very odd conversation with Popi a week or so ago, I think that that is where she is.'

'Popi!'

'Until that call, I didn't know that she and Popi were close.'

'That's odd. I never saw her talking with Popi when Popi stayed with you when I came for Stephanie's funeral,' replied Pam. Should I tell him about the bank account? she wondered. Later, perhaps.

'No. I also said that. It seems I didn't know Eleni at all. Only the part she wished to show me.' He sat back, thinking. 'If she is with Popi, then I think that is where we must go. Hugh,' he called.

The steward came up, looking anxious.

'Can you ask David to get us a slot at Heraklion. I think we need to land there instead of Sitia.'

He turned back to Pam and smiled ruefully.

'Normally, I would ring Eleni to organise a car. When she's not around, I ring her Athens office where her staff work. Her number two, Dimitris, is wonderfully efficient. But since you first rang me today, I did what you asked and did not speak to her or to Rafael. He was very surprised that I asked Patricia, you remember Patricia my housekeeper...' Pam nodded. '... and got her to drive me to Bournemouth Airport. He will be wondering what is happening.'

'Better not to talk to him until we are sure he isn't involved.'

'You're thinking about his car. Yes, you are right.'

'I could ask Major Papadakis to send a police car to the airport, then you'll have a police escort,' Pam suggested.

And someone to back me up if Nikos takes things into his own hands, she thought.

'That is a good idea.'

'I'll ring him. I need to update him, anyway.'

'Stavros, I'm here with Mr Leotakis.'

'Who's listening to you?'

'Yes,' she said. 'I've got a lot to tell you.'

She reported what Stuart had told her, leaving out the bit about the bank account and Popi, and that they were now going to Heraklion.

'I imagine that Mr Leotakis is going to visit his friend Popi to see whether Eleni is there. Of course, Eleni does not yet know that we know about her.'

'She could be armed,' replied Stavros. 'I can't stop Nikos, but I don't want you going in there. Though I cannot imagine that Mrs Filotakis is a threat.'

But you can't stop me either, she thought. I can't let you over-protect me.

'So, if you could ensure there's a car waiting for his plane with back up.'

'Who will be armed, I promise you,' said Stavros.

'That seems ideal,' said Pam. 'Our arrival time will be ...' she looked over at Leotakis.

'Eighteen hundred hours Greek time,' he replied.

Pam told Stavros this and promised to keep him fully informed of everything that was happening.

'Six o'clock your time,' said Pam. She ended the call and turned to Leotakis. 'It's now three thirty in Paris, and that means it's four thirty in Crete. So, we have another hour and a half.'

'Which gives me time for you to tell me everything in detail,' he said. 'And I want to know why you didn't contact me before today.'

'Before today all I had was Henry's ideas. The death of Patrice could have been about the book he was writing. Cambridge CID thought I was insane, and even Mike wondered whether we were imagining it all. And there was nothing to link you to 17 November.'

'There isn't. I never supported them ideologically; they killed two of my friends. And I never supported them financially, either…' he paused, thinking for a moment. 'Unless Eleni did. I suppose she could have stolen money from me, but I do have excellent accountants. I think they would have picked that up.'

'She could have added to the sums you paid her.' Pam suggested. 'Say ten thousand pounds a year over thirty years.'

'Yes. Her company runs all my cultural activities and most of my charitable ones. She could easily have taken that kind of money and it wouldn't have been noticed.' He sighed. 'The level of her betrayal gets worse every moment. I feel utterly…' He stopped. 'Angry, of course. I am livid, but also the pain, the trust I had in her.'

'Betrayal is something that's the hardest to forgive,' said Pam. She thought about her former husband. She'd trusted him once. If Leotakis was now planning to confront Eleni, it was going to be very hard to stop him from taking the revenge he thought he deserved.

It was an hour later that the flood of phone calls began. The first one came from the laboratory in Heraklion. Leotakis answered it and Pam saw him blench as he heard the news as if he was being physically assaulted.

'Bad news?' she asked, after he ended the call.

'They've found the missing chemical. It's something called dimethylmercury, deadly by touch and has no known antidote. And it results in a long and very painful death.'

'God.'

'And Eleni was going to kill me with this? She is utterly insane.'

'And very dangerous,' Pam warned. Leotakis looked at her.

'When cornered yes, but for the present she doesn't know any of this. She doesn't know I have this knowledge.'

'No. That's true.'

'I imagine that you and Major Papadakis will be thinking of sending in armed police.'

'I imagine that Major Papadakis and his colleagues will be thinking along those lines.'

'In which case she will kill herself and I will have too many unanswered questions. I have to talk with her before the police arrive.'

'I think that if I tell you that's a very bad idea, you won't take any notice of me,' replied Pam.

'You begin to know me.' Leotakis smiled at her, sadly, as his phone rang again.

'Leotakis,' he replied with the usual growl he gave before he knew who he was talking to. 'Yes, Good afternoon, Doctor Ferris, thank you for calling me.' He continued to listen, nodding as he heard the news. 'That is extremely efficient. And yes, I can update you on that. The substance that was stolen from the laboratory in Crete was dimethylmercury and the amount stolen was point zero five mils. Does that make sense?... Enough to kill a few people?' He listened. 'That is terrifying. No, I agree with you. I think it highly unlikely that there is any other trace of it elsewhere in the house, but the house should certainly be searched and decontaminated. I'll speak to my housekeeper and tell her to evacuate all the staff.'

Pam looked up the chemical… was it a chemical? she didn't know. Just reading about it was enough to make her shudder. She looked it up. It was something called a neuro toxin, she read, and then learned how it was best known because of how it killed a research chemist called Dr Karen Wetterhahn. The American chemistry professor had accidentally spilt a few drops of the toxin from the tip of a pipette onto her latex-gloved hand. What the chemist hadn't known was that the compound could permeate latex and within fifteen seconds enter the skin. After that, came a slow agonising death. And Eleni had wanted to use that to kill Leotakis? He was right; she was insane.

Leotakis finished the call. 'They found a silver cylinder with a glass cylinder inside it and a liquid inside that. It was in a small jiffy bag locked in her desk. No trace of anything on the bag. It had clearly been sealed before it went into the silver cylinder. They're taking it back to Porton Down for analysis.' He breathed out. 'What a relief they found it.'

'They were incredibly quick.'

'Helicopter from Porton Down. After the Novichok attack, they can swing into action very quickly it seems. And Eleni's desk in her office was the first place they looked.'

'She just assumed nobody would go there.'

'Usually nobody did. We all trusted each other. None of my cleaners would try and break into a locked desk. She knew that.'

'When she finds out that it's over, she's going to be desperate,' said Pam. 'And from what she's done so far, when she's desperate, she kills.'

CHAPTER 38

The house had been designed to create an oasis of calm. A large window with shutters looked out on to a Japanese garden at the back, with trimmed green bushes and carefully-placed stones. Inside the main room, the walls were a pale green and there were plentiful rattan chairs and sofas filled with green and white cushions. A low table held a single sculpture of a tree. It was idyllic apart from the fact that its owner, Popi Filotaki, was standing beside the sculpture pointing a gun at Pam.

If Popi had been surprised to see Leotakis, she was even more surprised to see Pam. Leotakis had wanted to hold off from confronting Eleni until he heard that the scientists from Porton Down could confirm that the cylinder contained the same amount of nerve agent that the lab in Heraklion said was missing. And that no other substances had been stolen.

They waited inside the plane. Nikos slept and Pam worried about Mike. Stavros told her that he was still in surgery. They just had to wait.

Eventually, the call came through from Dorset to confirm that all was well, and Leotakis's housekeeper in Crete told him his whole estate there was clear. So, it was already dark when they set off.

Nikos had also got permission from the police to have a quiet word with Eleni and persuade her to be arrested quietly. She didn't know if they believed him, but they'd given in to his wishes and arrived at Popi's house with a single plain clothes police officer in an unmarked car, with armed units waiting down the hill out of sight. Pam knew Stavros would be furious if he knew she was going in unarmed and without body armour. But having come so far, what she wanted more than anything else was to know the truth. And perhaps to begin to understand it. She knew if she'd been in Cambridge, she'd never allow one of her officers to do what she was doing, and she'd always been meticulous at doing things by the book. How come she'd changed so much these last weeks?

'Hello, Popi,' said Leotakis, quietly, walking inside before she could stop them. 'We've come to have a word with Eleni.'

'Why didn't you call?' Popi asked.

'You'll understand that very soon,' continued Leotakis. 'Is Eleni through there?' he asked opening a side door. Which was the moment that Popi had produced the gun which must have been under one of the cushions.

'She said I was to use this if anyone came. I didn't know she meant you.'

'And that didn't worry you?' he asked.

'She wants to be alone, to gather her strength.' She looked at them as if seeing them for the first time. 'Why are you here?'

'Eleni has been planning something very dangerous,' Pam told Popi. She'd only met the famous therapist a couple of times and had liked her very much and respected her enormously. Was it Mike who'd thought she'd had a breakdown after Jen's abduction? He'd been right; Popi's behaviour was clearly irrational.

Pam didn't look at the gun but walked up to Popi as if it wasn't there and they were just having a conversation. She took the therapist's arm, gently. She tried to remember everything she'd learned about how to defuse a situation. Get them talking, get them to relax and trust you.

'This isn't you, Popi,' she said. 'Guns?'

'You have no idea what is me,' retorted the woman, furious, stepping back. 'You see me... and what do you see? Wonderful Popi, brave Popi? The image, not the woman. You think of me as the woman who was tortured and became a healer.'

'Yes, I see all that,' replied Pam, calmly. How was she staying so calm, was it that this was what she'd been seeing in her dreams and the reality was not as frightening? 'I also know, both from you and from my own life, that it isn't the pain that hurts most, it's the shame. And it makes you very angry with yourself. But I'm not the person you're angry with.'

'You're police. It was the police who injured me.'

'I'm not buying that,' Pam shook her head. 'I have nothing to do with a police force that happened to be in this country before I was born. Besides, I also believe you have values. You wouldn't protect someone who killed an innocent young medical student...'

'What medical student?'

'Why don't you ask Eleni to come in. You can ask her about him?'

'I am here,' said Eleni. 'You talk to me.' She stormed into the room and turned to Leotakis, shouting at him in Greek.

'Shall we speak in English, Eleni?' replied Leotakis. 'Your English is as perfect as mine and I believe DI Gregory has earned this after everything she has done to find you.'

'What is she doing here?' replied Eleni in English. 'I should have killed her. I asked him to kill her, but he was weak.'

'You mean Stephen Mawson,' said Pam, 'the hacker you killed in a bomb this morning when you sent an invitation to him and Mike which sounded as though it came from Mr Leotakis.'

Popi was frowning, trying to make sense of any of this.

'Mike?' she asked. 'Mike's been killed in a bomb explosion?'

'We're waiting to hear from the hospital,' said Pam.

'Enough of this,' snapped Eleni. She stepped forward and before anyone could move, produced a small kitchen knife, and held it at Pam's throat. 'Sit,' she ordered her boss. Leotakis looked at her, shocked, but sank down on one of the chairs. 'Get some string, Popi,' Eleni commanded.

Popi suddenly smiled. She's in another world, thought Pam.

'People are always giving me gifts done up with blue string and I never throw it away,' she said. She put the gun on the table and walked into the adjacent kitchen, returning with a large ball of blue and white plastic string. Pam could see that it was extremely tough. It wouldn't be easy to wriggle out of.

'Now tie their hands to the chairs,' ordered Eleni. 'I don't trust either of them.'

Popi tied Leotakis's hands to the sides of the chair and he winced as the string dug into his wrists. Eleni manoeuvred Pam to another upright chair and pushed her down into it. Popi then efficiently tied her hands. Pam tried to move them but couldn't.

This was it then. Her stupidity and stubbornness had finally led her into this trap where she was going to die. And Mike, was he going to die in hospital? She felt a sense of lethargy creep inside her and tried to fight it off. At least she should get some answers before Eleni killed them both.

'Eleni couldn't have set a bomb, she has been here for several days,' Popi was saying.

'Can we come to that later?' Pam asked, as though she was in charge of an interrogation and not a prisoner. 'So much has happened and it would be so helpful to understand it. Perhaps first, Eleni, you can tell Popi about Lefteris. I'm in the dark about this.'

'Lefteris Zembatakis,' added Leotakis. 'He was a research student in Heraklion, a young man with a great deal of promise. Why did you choose him?' he asked Eleni. 'How did you know him?'

'I did not know him. I chose him because his father was weak.'

Leotakis nodded. 'I suppose you had someone research that for you. How did you do that? You gave the impression I might want to buy the laboratory and needed to know all about its personnel.'

'If you know, why do you ask?' She paused. 'It was a good choice. And then, thanks to you, I came across Stephen. He had the skills and was efficient, I will allow him that. He placed mistakes into the father's work so that he was fired. Then he induced the father to take out a loan and I bought his apartment block and increased the rent. The son was happy to steal the chemical for me to pay off his family debts. I had relied on that, and I was right. I have good judgement.'

'I have always relied on it,' said Leotakis.

She thinks she is always right, Pam realised. She has no self-doubt at all and no sense of guilt. If we are to get out of this, it is going to be only if we can make Popi understand what's going on. She turned to Popi and smiled at her.

'And that's how Eleni put pressure on the young man to steal a deadly nerve agent,' continued Pam, as if recounting a fictional story. She saw Popi frown. Pam had been right thinking this was the best way in. Popi didn't know about the nerve agent.

'And however angry you are, Popi, I am sure you wouldn't want anything to do with nerve agents,' Leotakis added. He gets it, Pam saw, he's going to play the same game.

'Of course not. Nobody in their right mind would want to have anything to do with those terrible things.'

'Then do ask Eleni precisely what she got Lefteris to steal from the laboratory in Heraklion. Before she killed him,' he continued.

Pam also didn't know whether Lefteris had been killed or whether he'd killed himself, though in Pam's eyes, Eleni was guilty either way.

'You have no evidence,' said Eleni.

'What was it,' remarked Leotakis, turning his attention on Eleni, idly, as if it was not really significant, 'honey venom?

'That merely causes anaphylaxis. You cannot rely on it,' said Eleni, scornfully. 'You think I do not research these things? It is stronger.'

'Like dimethylmercury.'

'You know,' Eleni glared at him. 'Why do you play these games, Nikos?' She paused. 'How did you find out?'

'Firstly, from notes in Stephen Mawson's briefcase, which got thrown clear of the explosion. That led us to the laboratory which is meticulous in its records. When we asked it to examine its most deadly toxins, it found that point five of a millilitre of dimethylmercury was missing. Such a tiny drop, but easily enough to kill me.'

'I wasn't going to kill you. I could kill you at any time.'

Pam continued watching Popi during this exchange and saw the confusion on her face. She turned back to Popi.

'My thinking is that you supported Eleni and knew

she was part of 17 November, but you didn't always support what the group did. I can't imagine that you went along with their kneecapping of a neurosurgeon just because the medical insurance companies were late in making their payments.'

'No, I didn't approve of that. Eleni…' she broke into Greek and Pam wasn't able to follow her. Then Popi remembered Pam and turned to her. 'I ask her to tell me that this is all rubbish. You coming here to my house with these terrible accusations.'

'Why don't you tell Popi,' said Leotakis in English. 'If she is protecting you here, she deserves to know the truth.'

'What is truth is that you are an old fool who has never understood anything,' replied Eleni.

'That may be true, but I think Popi wants to know whether you killed Lefteris Zembatakis.'

'His death was unfortunate, but it was necessary. We always worked hard to avoid unnecessary deaths and Popi knows this.'

'You killed a medical researcher?' asked Popi.

'It was necessary. This is going to be the greatest coup for 17 November, my final gift to Alexandros. When you make these decisions, sadly there will be other deaths. But we always tried to minimise collateral damage. Have you read our proclamations? We would cancel an operation if we thought there would be civilian deaths. We targeted precisely.'

Leotakis sighed. 'The question I have to ask, Eleni, is why did you betray me?'

Eleni looked at him with contempt. 'This is not about you. You think only of you. I am going to destroy you by destroying your grand gallery opening. I planned every detail.'

'But then came Henry Cox who was writing about 17 November, and he was an old friend of Patrice

Girard,' continued Pam. She wondered whether Popi knew that he'd been killed by Eleni.

'Patrice was the betrayer. I had always told him everything. He was a man who kept our secrets. But this time. Why? He says he will tell this Henry.'

Leotakis shook his head. 'Perhaps, because, like most of us, he thought the time for such actions had passed. Your group belonged to the twentieth century, Eleni. The world has moved on. There won't be any Marxist revolutions.'

'No, you don't understand, our ideas are yet to come. The next generation will bring the revolution. It is you, with your words about climate change while you jet around the world, that is the hypocrite. Your generation: they should all die. I had to stop Patrice, so I take Rafael's car, I know where it is parked, and I shoot Patrice. It was not difficult. He walked to the same café every morning. It was very simple.'

'But Henry wasn't going to stop digging after that,' said Pam.

'I realise that very swiftly, so it is necessary to dispatch him, too.'

'How did you kill him? The Cambridge police couldn't find any poison in him.'

'I put Valium into a bottle of wine. I wrote a note saying that it came from you to welcome him. I knew he would drink it. It was a very good wine.'

Pam felt sick at the idea of Henry being duped through her own friendship.

'I came during the night. I copy his key from Jen when she is staying in Crete. You see I plan everything. I injected him with air into his vein because it is very hard to trace. It is not always successful that there is an embolism, but I was lucky.'

Pam gritted her teeth. She had to keep her feelings under control if they were to get out of this. Popi was sitting on a sofa now, drinking a glass of water. Her hand was shaking.

'Well, you killed Henry Cox, but that wasn't the end. Pam and Mike began to investigate his death.' Leotakis picked up the thread.

'Yes. I did not expect you to do that. I should have shot you immediately. Or you should have gone to Athens with Mike and died there.'

Popi let out a moan and dropped her glass which rolled away spilling water on to the rug. She began to weep quietly.

'But you didn't, and your plan to have me arrested went wrong because the idiot police inspector was so angry, he pushed me down the stairs. And then in Paris I found the picture of you and Yotopoulos together.'

'There is a picture of me and Alexandros?' Eleni's voice changed. 'I have never seen it. Show it to me.'

'It's on my phone,' said Leotakis, 'inside my jacket.' Pam wondered whether he knew she was recording everything on her phone, which she didn't want Eleni to take. Although after they died, it would hardly matter. Eleni walked over to him and took it out of his pocket. She flicked through the stored photographs and found it. Her expression changed.

'Oh, my dearest.' Her voice became conversational, and she turned to Popi. 'Have you ever seen a more beautiful man? You and I with our two Alexanders.' She sighed. 'We were so young, so full of hope. We were going to change the world.' She shook her head as if puzzled by it all. 'Do you know why Alexandros was condemned? For moral instigation. That's what they called it. Because he believes in a better world than this one, a world where capitalism does not keep the poor in poverty. He has a burning wish to make others believe.'

'He is a fanatic,' said Leotakis.

'That is the term used by those who want to discredit

those who believe. They call us terrorists, fanatics. Because what we believe terrifies them.'

She looked at the photograph once more. 'It's forty years since I saw my beautiful boy, yet just as I think of him every single day, I know he thinks of me. What we had was far greater than any domestic partnership, it has a purity that few could understand. Popi, you understand that. And he will understand what I do. He will read my proclamation and smile.'

'Pity you don't have Sartre around to publish it,' commented Pam, hoping to get Eleni to talk more about what she'd done.

'That one. Hand up my skirt like a snake. And his breath stank. His teeth must have been rotten. Another weak man. They didn't dare publish it for a whole year. We had to act again to get their attention. And we killed a torturer. I would have killed them all.' She turned back to the photograph.

'Alexandros was the bravest. Thank you for bringing me this.'

'My pleasure,' replied Pam, drily. 'It did, after all, bring me here to find you.'

Eleni's voice changed to the authoritative tone Pam knew well. 'You must send me this picture now.'

'I don't think you will have a phone in the future, Eleni,' said Leotakis. 'The police are waiting…'

'But the reason you had to kill all these people,' interrupted Pam, 'was because they might have interfered with your plan,' She wanted Eleni to think of her success, not that she would be arrested or shot.

'My plan is to kill Prince Charles, the descendant of the German fascist who tried to rule Greece. I remember my grandmother talking about the war: the King eats meat every day, and the people starve. It will bring an end to your gallery. But, of course, you will be already dead. Pity I would have enjoyed your shame. I will put the dimethylmercury on to my hand and then I shake hands with the Prince.'

She believes she can still do it, thought Pam.

Leotakis slumped in his chair. He imagined the line-up. Eleni immaculate as ever shaking hands and the Prince of Wales feeling something damp. He takes out a handkerchief and wipes his hand before moving on to shake hands with whoever was next. Who would also have been killed.

'I will then go outside. I have enough morphine to die quickly.'

'But the Prince of Wales would suffer a terrible slow death,' said Pam, trying not to imagine the scene. 'And anyone else who touched any of that liquid that afternoon.'

'Everybody in the world will know about it. People will realise there are those willing to die to bring an end to capitalism and fake democracy. Revolution is an act of faith.'

Popi stepped forward and picked up the gun. Eleni smiled at her like a mother smiles at a clever child. And this is where we die, thought Pam. And what have I done in my life?

'You want the right to kill them, my dear. Of course. You have earned that.'

'No,' said Popi, her voice quivering. 'This is not what I believe. This has to stop.' She aimed the gun at Eleni. 'This has to stop now.'

'You think you will shoot me, Popi, after everything we have been through together? You do not have the courage. Give me the gun.'

Popi took a deep breath and pressed the trigger. Eleni fell backwards on to the marble floor, blood splattering around her. Then Popi collapsed on to the floor.

A few minutes later, after a shocked police officer rushed in and released them, Pam rang Stavros.

'It's all over. Eleni is dead. Popi shot her before she could kill us. We need an ambulance to remove her body. I recorded her full confession. Please let everyone know.' She was so tired she could hardly speak. 'I can't talk any more tonight,' she told him, 'I'll tell you everything tomorrow. The police are all here. It's over.' She began to sway, and one of the officers who had now taken charge of the room, helped her to a chair.

'I want to get away from all this,' she told Leotakis.

'Yes…' he agreed. 'We'll go to my home. I will get medical assistance for Popi, there, too.'

'What I need now is quiet,' said Pam. 'Quiet and the sea.'

CHAPTER 39

The last time she'd been to this gallery, thought Pam, looking around the immaculate white space with the golden bull at its centre, there was a woman impaled on those horns and blood all over the floor. Now she was in a line-up with Mike and Oliver as well as the director of the new gallery, Mark Kitson, still looking as though he should be in school, and the gallery's architect Anna Karanaki, who was wearing an extraordinary white floaty dress that looked as though someone had thrown paint on it from a distance.

'Vintage McQueen,' Anna whispered, when Pam pointed to the dress and gave her a thumbs up. Anna's assistant George wasn't there. Since he'd protected Manolis, and thus allowed Jen to be abducted, he'd stopped working with Anna and had moved to Athens. But Jen, herself, was there, looking elegant and happy and representing her mother, Stephanie, whose discovery had triggered the dig and the extraordinary discovery of the Chiona treasure.

While they waited for Prince Charles, Pam had had time to explore the gallery, designed in the shape of a labyrinth, and which had so very nearly ended once again with death at its heart.

Pam didn't have any worries about that today. The police presence outside was highly visible, and she didn't believe there'd be a retaliatory attack in response to Eleni's death. Nobody outside a very small group knew what she'd planned; it had died with her.

Leotakis had talked with the British, Greek and French governments who all agreed with him that the best thing was to keep it a secret. Eleni's death had been an accident caused when her gun had gone off accidentally, Patrice had been shot by an unknown assailant, Henry had died in his sleep. The explosion in Athens had been put down to a bomb from the Second World War, disturbed by some building work. Anything else was dismissed as baseless rumours.

Pam was relieved. There were no recriminations or enquiries and no press hounding her for a story. Chris Brook had been given some information along with a D-notice advising that it would be against the safety of the state to reveal anything. Pam had promised him the full story for his book after Leotakis died. She knew he wasn't aiming to publish it until then in any case.

Stavros told Pam that there had been fingerprints at the scene of the bombing and the bomber had been one of the newer 17N members. But he was not going to be arrested.

'The Government has decided it doesn't want the public thinking they released the 17N terrorists too early so they can start bombing again. But it does mean that surveillance on them all has been increased.'

She'd done a lot of talking with Stavros over the past month, but also with many others. Outwardly, it was as if the world was the same, but for Pam everything had changed. It had changed since that moment she'd sat trussed up in that chair, waiting to die. It was as if she'd faced all her monsters in that room and they'd crumpled. There were no more anxious dreams or panic attacks.

'I thought I was going to die,' she told Mike.

'So did I,' he replied. 'It changes you, doesn't it?'

She nodded. 'Makes you want to start living. Deal with stuff.'

They both had a lot of stuff.

Following days of sleeping and swimming, Pam began to talk with her friends. First with Leotakis, himself, to stop him going down the blame road, then with Stavros and Mike.

Mike had arrived on the Leotakis yacht with a small team of nurses who clearly already adored him. He'd had an operation to remove the shrapnel from his back and would need the dressings changed regularly until the wounds had all healed.

'He's very lucky to be alive,' Leotakis told her. 'It seems the worst of the blast passed over him. And that was why he was able to lift up Stephen and take him away from the fire. If he'd been standing…' However, Mike had suffered a degree of blast lung combined with smoke inhalation, not a good combination. Although the doctors believed he would make a full recovery.

'My aunt tells me I have to breathe in steam with thyme and dittany, that's a Cretan herb they think has miraculous powers,' he whispered on the first day.

'And are you?'

'Yes. Voula, one of the nurses is Cretan, and thinks it's a good idea. Actually, it feels good. And I have to drink ginger tea with honey.'

His voice had dropped almost an octave from the fire damage and was now very husky.

'It's not enough you look a bit like Al Pacino, only black, now you have to sound like him,' she told him. 'As if you couldn't be any sexier? You're going to have to fight off the women.'

'Don't make me laugh,' he said. 'It hurts.'

But they did find themselves laughing a lot over the next few weeks. They watched the sun rise as Henry had and dropped rose petals into the sea for him. Although his death certificate wasn't going to be altered, he had been awarded a posthumous OBE and an announcement in the Times for services to the Crown.

'He loved this island,' said Mike, hoarsely, watching the petals drift on the calm surface of the deep blue water.

'Jules wants to come to Greece to finish Henry's book,' said Pam, 'but exclude anything about the last terrorist. I've offered him Henry's house. I'm not ready to stay there yet.'

Mike smiled. 'I'm letting Stephanie's house to one of Jen's friends, too.'

'You've got a new home here,' said Pam, thinking of the perfect garden and the infinity pool leading down to the sea, surrounded by small villas.

It had been one of the first things Leotakis had agreed with Mike. He would become the first director of the Leotakis Foundation, a job which came with a small villa like the one Eleni had had. That one was going to be demolished and rebuilt as was her cottage at Tyneham House.

But the job wouldn't start until the beginning of the following year. Mike wanted some time for himself first; he knew that once he began, the job would be all consuming.

'Nikos just wants his apartment in the main villa by the rose garden. He said all he needs is a bed, a chair and a table.'

'And a few villas for visiting friends with plunge pools,' added Pam. 'Mind you, why not?'

'Well, you know you have an open invitation here.'

'I know.' And she did. She had invitations to stay with Oliver in Norfolk, and with Leotakis both in Crete and Dorset. And then there was an apartment on Dimokratias Street, in an Athenian district called Zografou which was where Stavros lived. How strange she'd never asked him about that before.

'Democracy Street. What a wonderful name.'

'It's a very ordinary street. But Zografou does have a lot of very good places for coffee. And a good nearby bakery.'

'And you. It has you.'

'I hope that's in its favour.'

'I'll come and stay. I'd like that.'

He held her close to him, stroking her back gently and then moving his hand around her to cup her breasts as she wriggled herself closer. He'd been sent to Crete to write up the case so that it could be filed away. But much of their time had been spent gradually discovering each other, as friends as well as lovers.

'I'm so sorry,' Pam whispered to him, the first day they were together again. 'Just at the moment when I thought Eleni was going to cut my throat, I thought of you and how cross you'd be.'

'Very cross,' he agreed. 'But you know you don't have to get nearly killed to understand that sometimes I'm right. Or that I love you.'

'No,' she agreed. 'But sometimes I'm right, too.'

'Twice,' he replied. 'You've been right twice. If I was a proper Greek man I'd be insulted by your superior intelligence.'

'Instinct more like.'

'I'm so sorry, Pam.'

'We don't have to talk about it again,' she said.

It had taken four days to slowly go through everything as it had happened and fill in the details she now knew.

'Footnotes,' said Stavros. 'I've always liked footnotes.'

They didn't make love those first days although they exchanged kisses and Stavros gave her gentle shoulder massages. Her back was still yellow from the bruises from when she'd been pushed down the stairs and he wanted very badly to take Hawkswood into a dark alley and pound him into a bloody mess. Pam just wanted to forget him.

The footnotes now included confirmation that neither Didi Girard not Dimi Forgeron had had anything to do with the killings. It noted, too, that Rafael Albin did work for the DGSE, the French Directorate-General for External Security. Pam had also discovered that Leotakis, himself, was consulted by MI6 and shared intelligence through Rafael with the French. This was told to her and Stavros in confidence and did not make the document. Neither did the information about Christopher Grey.

Pam was told about Grey a couple of weeks later when she and Mike had flown to Norfolk to stay with Oliver and his wife, Petra. Both Pam and Mike had been astonished when they first arrived at the Timberly house, which was down a long winding drive hedged with yews and beech and eventually gave way to an open vista of parkland leading down to a lake.

Pam had looked it up on the plane over and read it to Mike, who was being given oxygen while flying.

'*The Old Manor at Warham has been in the Timberly family for over two hundred years and was originally an Elizabethan manor house built by the third son of Edward Coke. It burned down in the late seventeenth century and was replaced by a small manor house designed and built by the new owner, Sir Nathanial Timberly in 1732. The original park was designed by Thomas Baker* ... goes on a bit here... influence of Versailles. Versailles? But that's a palace.' She continued to read.

'*The park and gardens were redesigned in 1774, by Lancelot Capability Brown with an artificial lake, and three follies in the Grecian style. The lake remains, but the follies no longer stand.* Blimey,' she added, 'I mean

Oliver has that sense about him of being self-assured. And rich. He never seems to worry about spending money, but I didn't know he was grand.'

But unlike Leotakis's manor at Tyneham, Oliver's house with its battered leather sofas and faded rugs, was anything but luxurious. It was a home. They'd arrived still exhausted and not wanting to talk very much, and Petra had instantly picked up on this, feeding them homemade shepherd's pie, followed by something light and lemony.

After which they'd moved from the large farmhouse kitchen to a large sitting room which had a vast fireplace, now filled with flowers and enough sofas for everyone and their dog. Pam had always wanted a dog when she was growing up, and the elderly Labrador which came and curled up beside her with his head in her lap was wonderfully comforting.

Mike had been targeted by a tabby cat which leaped on to his lap and began to purr.

'You're honoured,' said Petra. 'Kita normally ignores visitors or scratches them. Even we rarely get a purr.'

Pam saw a flash of real pleasure cross Mike's face. That's the first time I've ever seen him look truly happy for ages, she thought. She seemed to remember there was somewhere called the Houses of Healing in *The Lord of the Rings*, one of her favourite books when she was growing up. This old home certainly qualified for that title.

The weather continued to be summery, and they spent most of their days either walking along the sea path with the dogs or sitting on the lawn at the back of the house where there was an assortment of chairs, many of whose legs had been chewed. Meals took place here around a scrubbed pine table, covered by a faded floral tablecloth, and it was here that Pam sat most days in a, old deck chair while Mike lay on a sofa that had been specially padded with many layers of foam cushions to support his injured back.

Petra Timberly seemed instinctively to understand when people needed to talk and when they wanted to be silent. Pam had discovered that on her first evening when she'd fallen asleep on the sofa with the dog leaning against her.

'Mike's gone up to his room and Oliver's taken the other dogs out for a walk,' Petra had said.

'I'm so sorry, I didn't mean… you must think me so rude,' Pam began.

'I knew it the moment Tan curled up beside you. The dogs always did that with Oliver when he came back from a war zone. He suffered a lot from PTSD, not that it had a name back then.'

Pam had been convinced that night that she wouldn't be able to sleep after everything that had happened to her. She'd slept a lot during the day while at the Leotakis villa but found it hard to sleep at night. Here was different.

People have been very happy in this house, thought Pam as she lay back that first evening and almost instantly fell asleep. She'd slept well ever since and felt calmer day by day, ready to talk to the various people who needed to talk with her. It seemed there were a long list of them.

One at a time, Pam decided. One thing I've gained is the ability to say no. And to say yes. Which she did when Stavros suggested he come to Norfolk and visit.

Other people who came fell roughly into two groups: those who wanted to apologise and those who wanted to offer information and, in some cases, a job.

Various law enforcement agencies offered her work, but she turned them all down. She would take a job somewhere, but not yet, she told them.

'I've always envied students,' she told Mike one afternoon, 'and I'm going to give myself that time. No, don't tell me I don't need a degree, I know that, and I don't know whether I'll even do one, but I want time to do everything else. I want to learn about things, about music and films and I want to learn a language.'

'Greek?'

'Stavros would like that, but if it was Greek, I'd be doing it for him and not for me. I'm going to spend some time in France and learn French.'

'In Paris?'

'No. Paris is too big. I'm not a city girl, I don't like the noise of big cities. I'm going to go walking and find somewhere.'

'On your own?' This was a very different Pam.

'Some of the time. Raffa is going to walk with me, too. And Stavros has said he'll meet up with me when he can.'

'And then?'

'I think Oliver is working on something. He's asked me if I could spare him a year.'

'That would be good. But you're not going to be a spook?'

'No. I don't think I'm very good at obeying orders anymore.'

Pam had met Oliver's friend from MI6 the previous week. He was a tall man called James Fisher with Hugh Grant-like floppy brown hair. He and Oliver had been in Kosovo together, Petra informed her.

'I can tell you we're bloody grateful you went on digging and didn't give up,' James said, after they'd sat down together on the lawn.

'Good clear report, by the way, wish some of my officers were so succinct. And I was very impressed at your idea of hunting photographs from the archives. Don't think we do that enough, rely on our own archives.'

Pam smiled at him. They were drinking one of the bottles of wine which Petra and Oliver brought up from their cellar on a daily basis and which tasted glorious.

'I say, Montrachet, we're being spoiled,' he said when Petra brought it out to them. James was staying for lunch and Pam could already smell glorious scents wafting out of the kitchen.

'The things I'm going to tell you are confidential and you probably should sign the Official Secrets Act,' James told her at their first meeting. 'But I'm not going to bother you with that.'

'Thank you, she replied. 'So, can you tell me why Christopher Grey ignored Henry?' It was one thing she still didn't understand.

'This is where your Eleni was very clever. She had her own emails she used to contact Stephen Mawson…'

'AKA Sam Moss.'

'Yes. Such a waste of a good mind.'

'And thanks to your Stuart Weir and the Greek cyber wizard, Costa, we now have access to all the emails she sent on that account. The Greek counter-terrorism unit is fizzing with delight. She had a lot of contacts with terrorists, although she funded them without their knowing the money came from her. She was very secretive; it really was a miracle you exposed her. Anyhow, she also managed to use Mr Leotakis's computer when he wasn't in his office. She had the run of all his houses, and he had total confidence in her.'

'Yes. It's hit him very hard.'

'Not surprised. That kind of betrayal is always the hardest. And we've had our share of it.'

'Christopher wasn't working for her?'

'Not at all. He thought he was getting intel from Leotakis. Being the central guy on the Greek desk in Vauxhall, he knew about Nikos being a consultant for the Firm. Which is why when he got an email that seemed to be from Leotakis Grey believed it. The email said that he'd met Henry Cox recently and thought he had early dementia. This was why Grey decided to ignore Cox. Grey is devasted that this could have led to the assassination of the Prince of Wales. He's going to retire, and I don't blame him. Hard thing to live with.'

Pam nodded. She then declined James Fisher's offer for her to join the Firm, and instead sat back watching him and Oliver over lunch. Oliver had saved his life, James told her, when he was starting out.

'I can believe that,' said Pam. 'He is inherently a life-saver.'

'As are you,' said James, something she was still struggling to believe. 'I suppose I am,' she said.

Among those who came to apologise were Zofia and Popi. Leotakis had found a specialist hospital for Popi's husband, Alexander, who was working with various therapists on improving his speech and movement. Popi, herself, had been staying in the same hospital where Grace visited her every week.

'I knew you would save me,' Pam told her. 'Well, I hoped you would.'

'I wasn't so sure. I pointed a gun at you.'

'But you didn't shoot me. You are innately good, Popi. That was what I knew, that's what I had to work on.'

'Grace says that. I don't feel like a good person.'

Pam smiled at her. 'You can't come here and tell me you don't deserve to live. Mike has that privilege here.'

Popi shook her head. 'I'm happy to live. So is Alexander. He and Colin want to design you a house. Have you heard?'

Pam laughed. Another place to live, she thought. 'I don't even know what country I want to live in,' she said. 'I'm filling in the growing up bit of my life I missed. I suppose Nikos wants to pay for my new home.'

There seemed to be nothing that he didn't want to give her, but she told him she'd settle for friendship. One of the last people to visit her in the Norfolk garden was Dave Butcher.

'You're sure you want to see him? asked Oliver.

'Yes. He's not going to attack me here, and I can always call the dogs, though they'd probably wag their tails at him.'

'Not if you were being hurt they wouldn't. Anyhow, do you want to see him? If not, I'll tell him to bugger off.'

'No. I rather think I would like to talk to him.'

'Okay.'

To say Dave Butcher looked sheepish would be unfair to sheep, she decided. He wandered round the garden table as if in a dream.

'Dave, sit the fuck down,' she told him.

He nodded and pulled up a chair.

'Boss...' He looked haggard. 'I'm so sorry, boss. The thought that because of me you might have been killed, it right shook me up. That's it. I'm off the drink.'

'Good.'

'I really fucked up, didn't I?'

'Yes. It shocked me, Dave. I didn't know you felt like that. All that hatred.'

'Well, I don't, not deep down, but it's when things go wrong, it seems to bubble up and I'm saying all this crap. It's not helped by hearing it in my local.'

'Perhaps you need a new local.'

'Yeah. Find myself a coffee shop. After all it isn't as if Cambridge doesn't have enough of them. Though I'm not staying there, Cambridge I mean. Decided to go back home to Hull. My sister's there, and I've hardly seen her for years.'

'That sounds like a plan, Dave. I think what upset me most was that I'd always relied on you. You were an excellent sergeant. The team couldn't have functioned so well without you.'

'Thanks, boss, but I think leaving the Force is the best thing for me. My sister has a small business, I'm going to work for her.'

'Sounds good. You do know I didn't send those emails to you.'

'Not your way of writing, boss. If I hadn't been drunk, I'd have seen that straight off. Actually, I did go to Hawkswood and told him, but he didn't want to hear that. Are you bringing charges against him?'

'What for?'

'Pushing you down the stairs. He might have killed you.'

'I don't know if he did push me or whether I slipped,' she lied again. 'And no, I'm not going to bring charges. Last thing I want to do. And the people who set me up are both dead.'

'Really crap thing to do.'

'Better than killing me. Which is what happened to Henry Cox.'

'In the future, boss, be careful, and if you need a bodyguard, you have my number.'

'Thanks, Dave, I'll remember that.'

Dave looked around him. 'It's a bit massive this, isn't it, this place?

'Are you going to tell me I'm a lucky bitch?'

'You nearly got killed, you were arrested and thrown down the stairs. You lost your unit. No, boss you deserve everything you get.'

'And that brought it all to an end,' she told Stavros a few days later.

'And does deserving everything you get include me?'

'Some of the time,' she said. 'I'm not ready to move in with you, but I don't want to lose you.'

'You won't,' he promised her. 'I can live with "some

of the time".'

'I want to go walking,' she told him. 'I don't know why, but I do.'

'We can walk in Crete when it's cooler.'

'I'd like that,' she said. 'And stay in little places up on those mountains.'

'Then we'd better buy some hiking boots,' he told her.

CHAPTER 40

Through the windows, Pam could see a gardener, one of a team of gardeners, she imagined, trimming an already-neat hedge. The huge room she was standing in was about the size of a football pitch, and it was filled with an astonishing quantity of things: table lamps, sculptures, a piano and giant tapestries on the walls. Despite this, all Pam could focus on was the large oak door which was opening to allow in the woman whose son's life she had recently saved.

Pam, forgetting all her republican tendencies, gave a small bob as Queen Elizabeth approached her, smiling warmly.

'I won't keep you long,' she said in the clipped voice Pam knew so well from a lifetime of televised Christmas messages, 'I know that Charles is going to give you tea in the sitting room, but I did want to thank you personally.'

'It was nothing, ma'am.'

She'd looked up the correct way to speak to members of the royal family.

'I am happy to see that we are giving you the Queen's Police Medal for Gallantry, and an OBE, which is the very least we can award you, but...' she paused and looked at Pam thoughtfully. Pam was aware of the sharpness behind those very blue eyes. This was a woman who missed nothing, even in her nineties.

'Medals are symbols,' the Queen continued. 'As you might very well say is the monarchy itself. But beneath the emblems of state and under the crown, I am also a mother, and a mother who cares very much for her children.'

Pam smiled at her and nodded.

'Charles did not give me the details. I did not want to hear the details, but I do know there was a significant threat to the life of my son and that you succeeded in preventing that. And, as a mother, for that I shall always be grateful.'

She took Pam's hand and did not shake it, but rather held it for a moment, then released it and gave a small nod.

'And now,' she said, 'I shall leave you to your tea.'

This is the second Pam Gregory novel.
The first was *A Public Murder.*

Praise for *A Public Murder*:

"An absolutely fantastic book!"

"Pam Gregory joins the ranks of the country's most compelling fictional detectives. This book doesn't let you go until the final page — bring on the next!"

"Totally engaging. Vicarious pleasure in reading about Crete while in the cold wet winter lockdown here. Reflects on the writer's rich life experience, humour, powers of observation and thorough research."

" ... an enthralling journey ... Bring on the next Pam Gregory murder mystery!"

ANTOINETTE MOSES

The author at Chiona in Crete

Antoinette Moses always wanted to be a writer but didn't start writing until she was in her fifties. Since then, she's published over twenty books and written seven plays. She enjoyed a long career running arts festivals, then went back to university, got a creative writing MA and PhD at the University of East Anglia, and taught creative writing there for ten years. She is currently several writing new plays and working as an occasional dramaturg for Norwich Theatre. She lives in Norwich, but also spends time each year in Crete.

Antoinette's bestselling books of short fiction for foreign learners have won three Extensive Reading Awards, and *Jojo's Story* was described by one critic as 'a classic for all time.'

ACKNOWLEDGEMENTS AND THANKS

I could not have written or researched this novel without the help of many people, and I'd like to thank every one of them. First, the excellent writers whose books and articles helped me navigate the history of 17 November. In particular George Kassimeris, who is the real specialist of this subject. I have learned so much from his work, and any facts I have got wrong are mine and not his. For those wanting to learn more about 17 November, I recommend, *Europe's Last Red Terrorists* and *Inside Greek Terrorism*. Other writers consulted include Ioanna K Lekea, and Kostas Kornetis. I'd also like to thank Robert Carson for Zofia's Glaswegian.

Transcription of Greek words and names is always problematic as there are often several versions. I have tried to make them as easy as possible for non-Greek readers and have therefore kept names to one single tense. I hope my Greek readers will forgive me for the errors that thus arise. Alexandros Yotopoulos' name is frequently written as Giotopoulos, but I decided that Yotopoulos was closer to the pronunciation and therefore easier.

Dan Kaszeta was wonderfully patient with my questions on nerve agents and his book *Toxic: A History of Nerve Agents* is a fascinating and terrifying read. For the background history I was indebted to Roderick Beaton and *Greece: Biography of a Modern Nation*. Roderick also kindly allowed me to give him a walk on part in this work as did The London Greek Collective. Sharp-eyed readers will also spot that Jacques Vergès and Jean Paul Sartre are also not the characters of my imagination. Nor are any of the members of 17 November, whose lives I have taken from historical accounts, newspaper archives and transcripts of their trials. I'd also like to thank Dr (Major) Nick Petropoulos who assured me that there are no other members of 17N. I hope he forgives me for this flight of fancy.

It was Antonis Anipsitakis who told me about the legend that Jason and the Argonauts landed in Chiona, and I would like to thank him and all my many friends in Sitia for their help and advice while I was writing this. And love to all at my second home: Portobelis.

Finally, I am deeply indebted to Val Taylor, Edward Gimbrere and Zanna Foley-Davis for their painstaking and sensitive editing of the manuscript.

COMING IN 2022
BOOK 3 OF THE PAM GREGORY CRIME SERIES

NO ENTRY!

DCI Pam Gregory has a new job far away from her previous work as a detective, but a sudden death in Crete means that once again she has a murder to solve.